I0743111

False Promises
Emmanuelle Snow

First edition - June 2023 (V_1) (2025 update)

ISBN eBook: 978-1-990429-86-6

ISBN paperback: 978-1-990429-91-0

Editor: Shalini G.

Cover: SMART Lily publishing inc.

Published by SMART Lily Publishing inc.

———

Emmanuelle Snow
emmanuellesnow.com

FALSE PROMISES

EMMANUELLE

USA TODAY BESTSELLING AUTHOR

SNOW

Smart Lily
Publishing

CARTER HILLS BAND UNIVERSE
(SUGGESTED READING ORDER)

Carter Hills Band series
False Promises

HEART SONG DUET
Blindsided
Forevermore

Whiskey Melody series
Sweet Agony

SECOND TEAR DUET
Cruel Destiny
Beautiful Salvation

BREATHLESS DUET
Wild Encounter
Brittle Scars

Upon A Star series
Last Hope

Midnight Sparks

Love Song For Two series
<u>Lonesome Heart Duet</u>
Fallen Legend
Rising Star

<u>Two of Us Duet</u>
Snowbound

Wicked Love

All titles available at
emmanuellesnow.com

For the best experience, read in the order as shown above

TRIGGER WARNINGS

Disclaimer

My books are realistic and emotional love stories.

I'm an advocate for mental health, and some topics could be sensitive for certain readers since they are portrayed as close to real life as possible.

I've listed the potential trigger warnings for each title on my website.

Be advised that those trigger warnings could potentially be spoiler alerts for the storylines.

Those sensitive topics have been written with the utmost care and respect. Please reach out if you have questions or comments.

All books contain sexuality, mature content, and language not intended for people under 18 years of age.
For other readers' sake, please avoid spoilers in your reviews.

Thank you and have a wonderful day!

Emmanuelle

emmanuellesnow.com

For my kids.
Don't ever settle for less than what you deserve.
Because all of you deserve greatness.
And love.

Mom

BECOME A VIP
TO NEVER MISS A THING

Snow's VIP

Join **Emmanuelle Snow's VIP newsletter** for all the cool stuff, promos, new releases, giveaways, and gifts.

emmanuellesnow.com

Snow's Soulmates

Join Emmanuelle Snow's Facebook VIP group, **Snow's Soulmates**, to chat with her and other readers, get updates, and more bonus content.

facebook.com/groups/snowvip

DON'T ASK ME
THE SONG

No, I won't tell you twice
I'm not here for anyone's enter-
    tainment
I'm not here to indulge in some
    meaningless fun
No more games or tricks
You want me, you'll get the new me,
    the best I can be

[Chorus]

Don't ask me, girl, no, don't ask me
Oh, oh, oh
To be someone I'm not
Don't ask me, girl, no, don't ask me
Oh, oh, oh
To pretend what we're not
Together or strangers, I don't care
    what you tell the world

But don't ask me to lie 'cause this
    time I'm done playing
This time, it's you and me, because
    I'm ready

No, I won't tell you twice
I want to stroll down the street
    holding your hand
I want to kiss you even when people
    are watching
No more games or tricks
You and me in love, and happy is
    the only way it's gonna be

[Chorus]
No, I won't tell you twice
No one else but me will ask for
    your hand
No one else but me will promise you
    forever
No more games or tricks
I want you to believe in me, being
    with you is the only thing
    making me happy

[Chorus]
It took me a long time to realize
    what I wanted
But then you left me, and my world
    crumbled
Now this is me, telling you that I'm
    ready
No more games or tricks
No, no more games or tricks, baby

This is what I want too, now I know
    that I can be
The man you've always pictured me
    to be

The one I had a hard time finding
    in me
The one I thought got lost until you
    showed me
That together we could be

Don't tell me, girl, no, don't tell me
That tonight you're leaving me
This time, I'll run after you
Until I can show you
That it will always be you and me

Music and lyrics by Carter Hills

Chapter 1
Carter

Moving my legs out of the way, I bent forward to grab the pen that had slid from my fingers and landed on the linoleum floor of our class. Mr. Bell, the math teacher, was talking about something I couldn't care less. I was usually a straight A student, but these days, my attention span in class lasted about ten minutes.

My chair squeaked, and Dahlia, my childhood best friend, turned around with a hypnotizing smile, her copper curls floating over her shoulders. She raised a finger to her lips. "Cart, stop squirming." Her eyes widened as she watched me, asking a silent question. *Are you okay?*

I shrugged and stared at her. I knew she would be able to read my wordless reply. *Yeah. Preoccupied. Don't worry.*

Is it the band?

I shook my head once. I didn't want to tell her what it was about. The source of my distraction had long red hair, the color of fire. And moss-green irises I was always willing to get lost in.

Yes, lately, I'd started having feelings for my best friend that couldn't be categorized in the friend zone anymore. Well, it started almost two years ago. Blame it on my hormones, my growth spurt, or my age, but at fifteen, I was having a hard time staying indifferent to her with each passing day.

The other night, she smiled at me in a way she had never done before, and it messed up with my composure. So much so that I had to leave the room and pretend to take a leak to calm the throbbing in my lower body. Yeah, Dahlia Ellis was bothering me in ways I'd never felt before.

Last weekend, when I climbed in through her bedroom window and we spent the night with each other—in a bunking together kind of way, like we'd been doing since we were little kids without our parents knowing—I couldn't sleep. All I did was picture how she'd react if I kissed her. What her lips would taste like. How soft her skin would feel under the pads of my fingers. If she would let me touch her in ways I'd never done before. It was pure torture to have her sleep next to me, our heads pressed together and our hands connected, and not being able to do anything about it when I yearned for so much more. For hours, I just watched her sleep, enjoying the closeness we'd always shared.

That night, just the sound of her steady breathing was enough to send waves of warmth through my body.

Dahlia turned around, switching her focus back on our math teacher while I lost myself in yet another daydream about her.

I fidgeted with my pen, tapped my foot on the floor, twisted strands of my hair between my fingers, scratched my nape. Anything to prevent my thoughts from going to places that would harden parts of my body as her floral scent enveloped me.

The bell rang, and I risked a glance at my notebook. There was nothing there except for some ideas for a new song I was working on. And doodles. Guitars and hearts. I sighed. I was now the guy drawing hearts in his books.

I had to tell Dahlia how I felt—soon—or I would combust. This had become an impossible situation given how much time I was spending around her. Because Dahlia and I, we hung out together. All. The. Time. And we had music practice in our spare hours on top of that. Just the two of us. When we were seven years old, we formed the Ellis and Hills Band, and these days, we were getting attention on the music scene. So far, we'd performed at festivals and events. At weddings. We got interviewed on the radio last year and played our first original song. One day, we would tour the world and become as famous as all our country music idols.

Now on my feet, I picked up my stuff, ready to bolt out of there. One more class and the day would be over. My breathing hitched as a small hand grabbed my elbow.

"Cart, where are you going? You sure you're all right?"

I led Dahlia to a corner of the hallway, and she positioned herself before me, rubbing my scalp with her fingers like she had always done when I was tense. Shivers traveled down the length of my spine. This girl. Everything she was got me addicted. My eyes locked on hers, and her shiny pink lips curled into the most blinding smile. All aimed at me. I blinked, trying to break the spell. If I didn't, I would kiss her here and now.

The only thing preventing me from being honest with her about my growing feelings was my fear it could jeopardize our relationship. Our friendship.

What if she didn't mirror my feelings?

Was I ready to learn the truth the hard way?

"I am. Just a lot on my mind. That's all."

Dahlia nodded, withdrawing her hand from my hair.

I missed the contact but relished the space she put between us.

Love was so confusing. It always appeared simple in songs and movies. Even my parents made it look easy. But the truth was that if I couldn't understand my own feelings, how would I be able to express them the right way?

Phoenix and Addison, the school's only twins and our best friends, joined us, and I thanked them mentally for their timely interruption.

Addison averted her eyes. Since she'd cornered me in the locker room after gym class a few months ago and kissed me, she'd been avoiding me. That day, I freaked out and ran away without a word. I felt bad for doing so, and now it seemed too late to apologize. So, we were stuck with this awkwardness between us whenever we were around each other.

"Hey, you two. We're having a bonfire tomorrow night. Are you coming?" my friend asked.

"I can't. I promised my brother I would help him fix his truck," I said.

Addison addressed Dahlia. "And you? The entire football team will be there, and I need some girl company. Plus, it might be fun to watch them play, especially if it's shirts versus skins." She waggled her eyebrows, and Dahlia snickered behind her hand.

"Addi, you know the rule. I'm not allowed to go unless Cart comes along."

"Dah, your mama loves me. She trusts me with her hair but not to look after you? Why isn't she letting you come to parties with me? I'm not over six feet tall like Cart, but I can throw a mean punch."

Dahlia giggled, the sweetest melody I'd ever heard. "She thinks you're too wild for me." She leaned against me, and I pulled her closer. This was normal for us. Being affectionate with each other. Hugging. We'd always been. "Carter never gets into trouble. And Jeff always comes to pick us up if we wanna leave. I'm sorry. I don't agree with the rule, but even if I plead my case, she won't hear me out." An apologetic grimace stretched her lips.

A fragment of me felt bad that Dahlia couldn't hang out with her other best friend because I had plans. But Mrs. Ellis was right. Addison Wilde, like her name implied, was a bit crazy sometimes. She would never hurt Dahlia, though, or do anything stupid that could harm her. Like her twin brother, she was trustable, honest, and caring. She just loved having a good time. Boys, booze, no rules. She always flirted with the forbidden.

"Saturday night, the four of us. Why don't we make plans?" I proposed. "I can even ask Jeff to drive us somewhere. As a thank you for helping him tonight."

Addison jumped and clapped her hands. "Oh, that would be awesome. Think he could drive us to Nashville? I heard there's an outdoor concert this weekend, and I'm sure if we ask Mark nicely, he could get us tickets. The radio station his daddy owns always does giveaways, and Mark once said they get extra tickets for friends and family."

"That would be amazing," Dahlia exclaimed, watching me and silently asking if I agreed with the idea.

I nodded. "Count me in. I'll deal with my brother. Addi, talk to Mark."

"Consider it done," she said. "I'll keep you updated tomorrow."

"It's a plan," Phoenix said. The bell for the next class rang. "We gotta go. Let's talk later." We fist-bumped, and he led his sister away. "Come on, Addi, don't make us late."

They turned the corner, and Dahlia stepped away.

"I'll see you at dinner?" she asked.

"Sure. Let's meet at my place at five."

Most Tuesday and Wednesday nights, Dahlia ate at my house. Since our rehearsal space also happened to be my garage, it was easier when she was already there, and we could play music before and after dinner on those nights after we attacked our homework. Often, Jeff would sit on the old couch and listen to us, giving us pointers and cheering us on. He was the one always driving us around when we performed. My parents weren't super invested in my passion, so they usually didn't follow us wherever we played. It stung. The idea my talent in music wasn't appealing enough to them. I'd always suspected they preferred my brother to me. Their level of enthusiasm when Jeff did something always surpassed my own achievements and successes.

Dahlia hugged me. "I have arts and a study group right after. I'll see you later."

I hugged her back. A couple of seconds longer than usual.

Since Dahlia and I were experts at understanding each other without a word, I wondered why she couldn't tell I was madly in love with her by now. Was she this clueless, or did the thought that our friendship could evolve into something more, something we both knew nothing about, scare her too?

One day I'd be brave enough to ask her out. On a real date. To her favorite restaurant. And I would write her a song. And kiss her on her front porch.

A hunch told me, no matter what, Dahlia and I would be together forever.

———

"Hey, can I come in?" I asked after I knocked on Jeff's bedroom door. While mine was always a bit messy with clothes thrown on the bed and posters of my favorite music bands hung on the walls along with a couple of my acoustic guitars leaning against the dresser, my brother's room was neat. With bare charcoal walls, white trims, a navy-blue comforter, and matching curtains, it lacked a personal touch. There was a stack of dumbbells right next to his bed, and a computer in the middle of his wall-length desk. Nothing was out of place.

"Sure. How are things going?" he asked.

"Great. Is something wrong? You're never home, and it's like you're avoiding me. Did I do anything to piss you off?"

Since the night he drove the twins, Dahlia, and I to Nashville, Jeff had grown aloof. And I missed my brother. We were inseparable most of the time, always looking out for the other. He once said we were twins born a little over two years apart, and I couldn't agree more. He gestured for me to sit on his bed as he swiveled his chair to face me.

"Got a lot on my mind. I haven't picked a college yet, and Mom is on my back about it. She wants me to get a college education before enlisting or doing whatever else I'm supposed to do."

"What do you want to do?" I asked. The idea of my brother joining the Army awoke a weird feeling in the pit of my stomach. His intentions were noble. But the thought of his fighting in another country scared the shit out of me.

"I don't know. Maybe getting away from here is the right thing to do." He dropped his head on the desk.

"It can't be that hard. Pick a college, get Mom and Dad off your back, then take some time to decide."

"Maybe you're right. I'm sorry I've been distant."

I breathed in some courage and asked, "Are you serious about the Army stuff, though? I'm not sure it suits you."

He lifted his head and shrugged. "Yes. No. I'm not sure either. Maybe I could do some good, you know? Change the world or something. It's not really about the Army, but more about helping people who might need it. Be part of something…"

He didn't give me time to reply before springing up and grabbing me in a headlock. We both started laughing and tumbled off the bed. With my now six-foot-five height, I towered over my brother by three inches. His shoulders were broader than mine and he was stronger, therefore it compensated for his lack of height.

"I'll drive you to the restaurant on Saturday night. Tell Dahlia she can come along if she wants."

Dahlia and I played in a restaurant owned by a coworker of her dad every Saturday night. It was great exposure and good money. Any occasion for Ellis and Hills Band to play in front of a crowd made me happy.

We broke apart. "Thanks, man. I appreciate it. You should apply to be our road manager. I'm sure you'd be good at it. I might even get you a 'Number One Fan' ribbon to wear to every show. Something bright pink with glitter and flashing lights."

"You're so stupid," he said, laughing his heart out. "How about I treat you to burgers instead?"

"With milkshake and Cajun fries?"

"I wouldn't offer anything less."

"Count me in. I'll meet you downstairs in fifteen."

Bryce's Burgers looked like it was straight out of the 1980s California, with colorful surfboards hanging on the walls. The walls were coated in a rich royal blue, while the ceiling shimmered with a soft silver hue. The staff donned vibrant leis and bright red shirts adorned with exotic birds, and everything about this place felt festive. And so out of place here, in Tennessee.

Sitting in a booth, I studied my brother. By the tenseness around his eyes and his serious demeanor, I could tell something was bothering him.

I pushed a handful of fries into my mouth and chewed as I asked, "So, whom are you taking to prom?"

"Man, you're gross."

"Any name?" I asked with a mouthful. "I heard there were at least ten girls who asked you to go with them already. Did you pick one?"

He shook his head. "There's only one girl I want to ask to prom. But I'm not sure she'll agree to be my date."

"Who is she? Anyone I know?"

He shrugged and averted his eyes. "It doesn't matter. I won't ask her."

"Since when do you chicken out?"

He shrugged again.

"C'mon, Jeff. Don't be a chickenshit. Grow some balls. What's the worst that can happen? Being rejected? So what? Girls are lining up to go with you. It's not like you'll end up going alone."

"I'm not even sure I wanna go. So, it doesn't really matter."

"You can't skip all the traditions, man. You've already bailed out on Homecoming and Winter Formal. You know Mom is dying to buy you a suit and take embarrassing pictures of you and your date, right?"

He threw a fry at my chest.

"Anyway, I don't think I'm on this girl's radar."

I fished a quarter out of my pocket and smirked at him. "You asked for it. I'll take the matter into my own hands. Brace yourself, big brother. Destiny will decide.

Heads, you're asking this mystery girl. Tails, you bail out on prom or pick a girl from your fan club. You should've asked for my help sooner. I'm a miracle maker, and I'll fix your prom problems."

I tossed the coin, and it flipped multiple times before I caught it.

Jeff watched me the entire time, mute.

"Heads. The coin has decided," I announced. "You ask her. I'll give you two days to man up and get your head out of your ass. And I'll need a full report in forty-eight hours. Don't let me down, brother."

We stared at each other for a long minute. Something was wrong with my brother. He was usually much more outspoken than this. Perhaps he really liked that girl—as much as I liked Dahlia—and was afraid she wouldn't return his feelings.

"Promise me you'll ask this girl to prom. No matter what."

He nodded. "I will."

Without another word, he moved to his feet. "Let's get out of here."

I clapped his back before we reached his truck. "You'd tell me if something was wrong, right?"

Jeff turned to face me. "Always. You're the one person I trust the most, Carter. Never doubt it. Whatever happens in the future, just know I'll always be there for you. No matter what. Even if I'm deployed on the other side of the world." He swallowed as if overwhelmed with emotions.

"Same, okay? Other than Dah, you're my most favorite person. And if the girl doesn't agree to go to prom with you, she doesn't deserve you. You're the greatest guy I know, and you deserve the best. Always."

"You really think that?"

I bobbed my head before he circled his vehicle, and we both climbed inside.

"Carter, I love you, man," my big brother said after a while. "Never forget it."

"I know. I love you too."

———

Locked in my bedroom, I was putting the finishing touches to the song I'd been writing for Dahlia. After my conversation with Jeff two days ago, I had decided I should grow some balls too and ask my best friend out. I thought it sounded hypocritical to tell Jeff to act on his crush when I was the one who'd been avoiding mine for the last two years.

Earlier, I had made a reservation for us on Friday night at the restaurant we always went to when we had something to celebrate. Dahlia loved their risotto, and it made her smile when we dined there. As long as she kept smiling, my life would forever be fulfilled.

I heard her enter through the kitchen door minutes ago, and now she was talking with Mom downstairs.

Since I came back from school, I had been so busy with my plan and hadn't done the math homework that was due tomorrow. Once I was satisfied with the song, I rushed downstairs with my schoolwork and settled at the kitchen counter. Dahlia and I exchanged a grin as her gaze took me in while I flipped through the textbook. "You aren't done?" she asked.

"Nah. I had something to do first."

My heart galloped wild in my chest at the idea tonight would be *the* night. In the garage, I had put lilacs in a vase and set candles on the table. Purple ones because that was Dahlia's favorite color. I had learned the new song by heart. I would pretend I needed her input on it, and then I would open my heart to her. Tell her what she meant to me. How much I loved her. That she wasn't just my best friend, but my whole world. She would be scared it would change our friendship—I knew her—but I would assure her that it wouldn't change us. Only make us better. Unstoppable. She and I against this world. She would worry about the consequences if we didn't work out, but little did she know I had never been so sure of something. Dahlia and I belonged together. We had fifteen years of unconditional friendship and silent communication to prove it.

She was helping Mom with dinner, and I was finishing my homework when Jeff joined us in the kitchen.

His face was ghostly white and he looked like he was about to faint. I squinted, hoping he would talk to me. I guessed his asking that girl to prom didn't go so well after all. For a moment, I felt bad for encouraging him, but I hadn't known she would turn him down. I'd find a way to cheer him up. Tomorrow. Because tonight, I had plans.

He neared us and cleared his throat. I watched him, wishing he would look at me. "Hey, Dah. I've been wanting to ask you something for a while now." She glanced at him. "Will you go to prom with me?"

Some sort of gasp passed my lips, and my eyes widened. Heat traveled to my face, and I dropped the pencil I was holding.

I blinked. This couldn't be happening. I was dreaming. No, it was a nightmare. How could he? He must have known how I felt. I was pretty sure the entire world could tell I was in love with my best friend.

No doubt she would turn him down. Dahlia would never agree to go to prom with my brother. She was my girl. Always had been. Even when we were running around, the three of us as little kids, she was always drawn to me. From day one. She was *my* best friend. Jeff and she never hung out together. They could hold a conversation, sure, but that was the extent of it. They had never been close. Never been more than friendly acquaintances.

Jeff was wrong, and now things would be awkward between all of us.

His impromptu *promposal* fucked with my own plans to ask Dahlia out tonight. My fists clenched at my sides. This was a disaster.

Mom gasped, and she pivoted on her heels to watch the scene unfold between them.

I would have to comfort my brother *and* find a solution so my best friend wouldn't avoid coming over from now on because Jeff made a fool of himself.

Dahlia lifted her eyes and looked at Jeff. Then her gaze drifted to me and stayed fixed.

Without her lips moving, I could hear all the words she didn't speak out loud.

We fixated on each other for a long beat as time idled while my heart fractured piece by piece, bleeding on the kitchen floor.

Chapter 2

A boulder of emotions forming in my throat clogged my airways, preventing oxygen from reaching my brain. This was a joke. This couldn't be happening. The back of my eyes burned with unshed tears. Dahlia didn't have to utter a word for me to understand what she was about to say.

How could I have been so clueless?

Had my best friend had a crush on my brother all this time?

Was this a nightmare, or was I fully awake and watching my life—and my heart—shatter at a slow speed without being able to prevent the impact?

"So?" Jeff asked, rocking on his heels, waiting for Dahlia to answer.

She inched closer to him and looped her arms around his neck, and he lifted her up in his arms as if it were the most natural thing in the world. As if they had rehearsed this dance a million times before.

My head spun.

My mouth went dry.

Every drop of blood in my veins transformed into ice.

We were all in the same room, but for some reason, I felt like I was watching a movie I wasn't part of. As if my life was unfolding on a screen and I had no right to interfere.

Their chatter sounded miles away, and I blocked everyone out.

My eyes stayed on Dahlia and Jeff, but I couldn't see them.

I averted my gaze, locking it in the distance. No, I couldn't deal with this right now.

Was this how being heartbroken felt like? Because it was the deepest kind of pain. If I could unfreeze, I would hurry away, hiding my humiliation far away from the two people I loved the most in this world. The ones who clearly didn't need me right now.

Many questions swirled in my mind, and their fast pace got me dizzy.

How long had Jeff and Dahlia been infatuated with each other? Were they in love?

Had they been playing me all this time when we were together, the three of us?

Nothing made sense anymore.

My hands got clammy, and the gears in my head turned faster, reaching a vertiginous speed.

My heart lurched in my throat.

I was going to be sick. Or I was going to curl up and bawl my eyes out. I needed to escape but my body refused to move, glued to the spot. Even the air reaching my lungs hurt on its way in.

I clamped my fingers around the countertop, wishing the room would stop spinning too. And that I could breathe on my own.

"Carter, set the table," Mom said, the tone and her words hitting me like she'd slapped me. "Dinner will be ready in five minutes." She turned to look at Jeff and Dahlia, sparks waltzing in her eyes. "You two make me so proud. I can't wait to see you all dressed up." She kissed Jeff's cheek before hugging my best friend. "You'll make my boy happy, Dahlia," she whispered in her ear. "I just know it."

My heart plummeted to my feet, breaking the chains of my rib cavity.

Even my own mother was against me on this one.

Always and forever Jeff.

Whatever he did, he could always get away with it. No matter if it hurt me in the process.

Mom didn't care at all about my feelings. Once again, she acted as if my heartbreak wasn't important. Like I didn't matter.

No *Carter, you'll be okay.* Or *I know it hurts right now, but time will make things better.* Or *I know how you feel, but believe me, your heart will heal. Give it some time.*

Nothing. Just *Carter, set the table.*

I waited, hoping sanity would hit her and she would hug me, trying to make me feel better. To infuse me with the motherly love I longed for at this moment. Instead, she returned to the sauce simmering on the stove.

The two women in my life, the ones I thought loved me, had turned their backs on me tonight.

Moisture pooled in my eyes, and I fought the tear dam about to rupture, plastering the most neutral expression I could muster on my face.

Seconds later, Dahlia stood next to me and placed a

hand on my forearm. As it always did, her touch soothed the earthquake growing inside me.

I breathed out whatever air was left in my lungs and squeezed her hand. Our eyes met, and hers shone with unshed tears. Probably mirroring mine.

In that instant, I could tell she was aware of my feelings for her and that hers weren't reciprocated the way I wished they were.

We both acknowledged in the silent exchange that things would never be the same. Our relationship would change. It already had. It would never be just Carter and Dahlia against the world anymore. That part had dissipated right in front of my eyes in the last few minutes.

The scars of my heart, the ones exposing the wounds of my heartbreak, would never fully heal. Even if I patched them up, there would always be a mark. For the rest of time.

If I thought I was infatuated with my best friend, I was wrong. I wasn't infatuated. I was in love. Dahlia was my entire world. Always had been. The one person I would sacrifice everything for, even my most precious dreams.

Tears flowed down her cheeks, and for once, I had no idea how to fix her sadness because it wasn't even close to the abyss swallowing me from the inside.

"Hey," she murmured.

I nodded, unable to speak all the words I wished I could express.

With a deep intake of air, I faked another smile on my lips. A part of me—the one not about to break into sobs—was happy for her. "I'm glad for you two. I was the one who wanted Jeff to ask the girl he liked to prom. I just didn't know it would be you."

"I'm sorry, Cart. I shouldn't have said yes so quickly. Jeff should've asked me in private, and we should've talked about this. The three of us. I don't want things to be weird between us. You'll always be my best friend. Forever. It changes nothing. It's only prom, okay? We won't make a big deal out of it. I promise."

I avoided the piercing gaze I could feel aimed at me.

"We can talk after dinner."

Gathering all the courage I had left, I said, "No. No need to hear all about that stupid glittery chiffon dress you'll want to wear." I made a gagging sound and winked to ease the tension between us.

She smiled. Maybe we could salvage our friendship.

"Thanks," Dahlia said, pulling me into her arms. The one place I always felt safe and protected. I fastened my arms around her. "And yes, I'll even try on the ugliest dress we find at the store just for your sake. And I might even let you take a picture if you promise not to laugh when you see me in it."

I shook my head and failed at reeling in the smile threatening to break free.

Dahlia fisted my shirt, pulled me in, and kissed my cheek. "You're the best." She lifted the pile of plates and silverware Mom had placed on the kitchen island and took it upon herself to set the table.

———

Spread on my back on my comforter, I threw a football to the ceiling, catching it before sending it back up. Jeff and Dahlia had left for prom about two hours ago. Since the night he asked her to be his date, I had tried to lock my emotions in, but every time my gaze landed on her, my heart twisted with pain.

We both agreed, no matter what, our friendship was our priority. I couldn't imagine a life without Dahlia Ellis in it, and she said I would forever be her best friend. Guess it was better than nothing. In the end, I preferred not dating her to losing her.

With my sleeve, I wiped my teary eyes. Earlier, I had walked her from her house to mine. She looked so beautiful in the steel-blue gown that highlighted the striking color of her hair. Dahlia could light up a room with her presence only, but tonight she glowed. It crushed my heart to see her all dressed up for another guy. I ended up smiling for pictures along with them. Something clicked when I watched my brother and her pose together, though. Jeff was in love with the girl of my dreams. There was no hiding it. It was in the way he looked at her when she wasn't aware.

I also realized something else. Jeff had looked at her like this in the past. Before he asked her to go to prom. My own feelings had blinded me; hence, I didn't notice it sooner.

I tried to swallow, but it ended up in a choked sob when I moved to sit.

The worst thing of all was that my best friend was also in love with my brother. There was no denying it either anymore.

Mom made a big deal of their relationship tonight. She took at least a hundred pictures of them. Mrs. Ellis insisted on including me in her own photo shoot, stating those pictures of the three of us would become the memories we'd cherish later when we got older.

Tears clouded my vision now. No matter what I told myself, I couldn't hold my sadness in. Heart-wrecked, I wondered if the pain would ever subside. Maybe one day.

When I confided in my friend Phoenix last week, he said I should get myself a girlfriend to forget about Dahlia. His reasoning made sense. What he ignored was that I didn't want to hold another girl's hand or kiss someone else.

With both hands, I cupped my heart, as if its pounding could drive it out of my chest, and bending forward, I cried until the lining of my throat felt raw and the back of my eyes burned.

When I heard Jeff's pickup pull into the driveway sometime later, I should have been able to go to him to ask him a thousand questions, feigning interest in his night. Instead, I undressed in a hurry, locked myself in the bathroom, and let the stream of scorching water from the shower flush my sorrows away. Until I had no more tears left and I felt a bit lighter.

Not in the mood to cross paths with him in the hallway or attract his attention, I tiptoed to my room and slipped under the covers, watching the clock on my bedside table tick each second. That night, for the first time, I didn't join Dahlia in her bedroom.

I lay in the dark instead, trying to figure a way out to heal the broken pieces of me and be happy for Dahlia and Jeff, who—I had no doubt—would get together for real sooner than later. I had to toughen myself up—and my heart—before it happened.

———

Sara picked me up, and we joined a group of her friends partying in a vacant lot on the outskirts of town. "I'm so glad you came tonight, Carter."

She kissed me, and I let her. She saw me as a big rock star, even though Carter Hills Band hadn't been signed yet. The other day, Dahlia surprised me with merch and swag carrying our new band name and logo. She had made the decision to rename our band after me. She didn't have to, but I appreciated the gesture. Our relationship was still fragile, but since Jeff left for college, we had started spending more time together. All summer, I kept myself busy by writing songs in the comfort of my bedroom, giving them their space and avoiding any awkward encounters. The one time I walked in on my brother and my best friend kissing, it took me two days to erase those images from my mind. No, thank you. They tried very hard to include me when they went out and to avoid getting too close every time I was around, yet I didn't miss their heated stares and hands touching when they thought I wasn't looking.

After I decided to give Phoenix's idea a go, he'd been setting me up with different girls, hoping I would *click*, like he said, with one. Last week I went on three dates with Tiffany. Now it was Sara. No matter however much I was willing to give it a shot, my heart wasn't into it. It always felt wrong to date them, to hold their hands, to kiss their lips.

I sighed and pushed my reluctance down, and Sara nestled between my arms, showing me off to her friends as if I were a prize she'd won. "This is my boyfriend, Carter. This is Emily. Chloe. And Chelsea."

A chill slithered down my back. Sara and I would never be a long-term couple, but perhaps I could still enjoy her company for the time being. As long as she didn't get clingy, I could do this.

My insides recoiled. I had become a version of myself I didn't recognize.

Not in the mood to play pretend, I left the party early and returned to my room, my sanctuary, to write music. Yeah, this was more like it. My self-therapy.

Tomorrow, we were scheduled to play at Green Mountain Fest, and we had secured a bigger scene this year. The thought of it sent a rush of adrenaline through me. With music as the priority in my life, I could, no pun intended, move mountains.

My phone went off, and I answered after the first ring. The sound of her voice soothed the agitated parts of me. "Ohmygod, Carter, can you believe we're playing at Green Mountain Fest tomorrow? I'm not sure I'll be able to sleep tonight."

"Are you still out with Addi?"

"No, I'm back home. For once, I'm not sad about having a curfew. It will force me to try to catch some sleep. If I can stop pacing the house for more than a minute."

"We'll be fine, Dah. You know I have your back. Always."

"Yeah, I know. I couldn't do this without you. It's way too stressful otherwise. My daddy wanted me to tell you we'll be there at seven in the morning and to be ready." She hesitated for a second. "Is Sara coming?"

I sighed. I had forgotten I invited her. "She's driving with her girlfriends. She'll meet us there. Jeff should arrive after lunch. I'll drive back with him. He's coming home afterward."

Dahlia's voice softened. "Yeah, he told me when we talked earlier. You must miss him."

"I'm not used to him not being around to mess with me."

The truth was that I was dreading how the return of my brother—even for just a few days—would affect the new equilibrium of Dahlia's and my relationship.

We remained silent for a beat. "Cart, do you wanna maybe come over?"

My heart swelled in my chest. Last week, I was feeling down after arguing with my mother about my poor career choice—yeah, I wanted to be a musician and nothing else.

I was good at it. Nah, I was great at it. From the first time I picked up a guitar, I could play a full song. It was instinctive. Something I could do without being taught. That night, I wanted to be with her, but I had no idea if it was still one of *our* things, so I stayed home, not wanting to risk doing something that would complicate our relationship even more.

After I locked myself in my room, I decided tonight would be different. I was ready to sneak out and climb in through Dahlia's window once again. We hadn't had a sleepover in months, but tonight I needed her. No matter what the status of our relationship was, she was the one person who truly understood me. She got me. Without explanation. And for that lone reason, never would I be able to cut Dahlia Ellis out of my life. Even when it hurt me to witness her love for someone else.

A wide smile shaped my lips. "I was hoping you'd say that. And I wrote another song tonight. I can't wait to play it for you."

"Ohmygod, you're on fire, Cart. Maybe you can record it on your phone, and I can listen to it when you get here. I'll never get tired of hearing all the words and melodies you come up with. It's fascinating how your brain works. I'll get us snacks and leave the window open if you get here before I'm back into my room."

"See you soon." And just like that, I recorded the song and ran away from the house which sometimes felt like a suffocating prison. If only my parents could support my dreams, things would be so much easier. All they cared about was college, no matter whether it made Jeff or me happy. There was more to life than being stuck at a job that didn't make your soul vibrate. Regardless of how many times I tried to explain it, Mom always said I was silly for believing I'd be one of the lucky ones to make it big one day and to stop dreaming and come back into the real world.

———

After the success of Green Mountain Fest, Carter Hills Band performed all over Tennessee. We got invited to festivals, town gatherings, special events. Dahlia and I were ecstatic. Every day, we could feel our dream becoming a reality. It was right there, ready to be grabbed.

While in college in Nashville and working part-time in a bar, Jeff got us a meeting with a big-shot manager on the rise. After he came to see us play, we got signed to a major record label.

Dahlia, Jeff, and I were seated in a booth at Bryce's Burgers celebrating.

Stud, the newest member of our band joined us and slid next to me. "We're gonna travel the world and be rich and famous, you motherfuckers," he singsonged, his face fixed into a permanent grin.

He fist-bumped my brother and draped an arm around my shoulders to pull me closer.

One day, we were playing at a festival when Stud Burgess begged to audition for us. Having nothing to lose, Dahlia and I gave him a shot, and impressed with his talent, Riley Burns, our manager, said we'd get a better offer if we brought him into our band permanently.

My best friend and I were incredible together, but the three of us, we were magic.

Carter Hills Band was all of us. Plus, Jeff, our unofficial road-manager. And our biggest supporter.

"I feel like we're gonna wake up from this and it will all have been a dream," Dahlia said, sipping on her soda.

I gripped her hand across the table. "I've told you we

are ready for the big leagues. It's about time you realize it too."

"Still, it sounds too good to be true. Can you imagine us touring Europe and having our songs played on the radio? Because I can't."

Jeff leaned closer and kissed her cheek. "I believe it. You guys are destined for greatness."

From across the table, we exchanged a high five. "I agree with you, big bro."

"We're throwing a party next weekend. With all our friends," my brother announced. "I can be your official party manager too." He nodded. "Yes, that title sounds pretty good."

Dahlia backhanded his chest. "We need to focus, not party too much. This is the chance of a lifetime. No way are we being stupid. No sex, drugs, and rock 'n' roll, guys. Not under my watch."

I laughed. "Dah, it's us you're talking about. Since when are we the wild ones?" I offered her my best smirk and wiggled my brows.

She sighed. "Yeah, but don't let it get to your head, Cart. Promise me, here and now, that you'll never let success change you."

I extended my hand to shake hers. "Never. This is my dream right here. I'm not wasting a minute of it. You have my word."

Stud scratched his temple, confusion marking his face. With a scruffy blond beard and longish hair, he still looked like the roadie we met a while ago. Not the *über*talented and versatile musician we all knew him to be. My friend was destined for greatness. "Dah, we can still party a little, right?"

Her smile reached both ears. "As long as you don't get into trouble and it doesn't mess with the band, I guess you're allowed to party *sometimes*. Anyway, we have a few years to go until we are twenty-one, so we won't get invited to big club openings and stuff."

"Watch out, girl. Eighteen is the legal drinking age in most Canadian provinces. And parts of Europe too."

She flipped her wrist. "I'm not even afraid you two will get in a pretty pickle. You want this too much to mess it up. But pretend to be rock stars if it pleases you."

"That's it, Princess. Keep the boys in line." Jeff kissed her temple.

We all chuckled and clinked our drinks together.

"To you guys," my brother said. "I'm proud of you." He angled himself to face me. "And to you, little bro. I love you. So fucking much. All this time, you were right. I cannot believe this is happening. You deserve it." We exchanged smirks. "You guys will be huge. I can tell."

Chapter 3

Dahlia, Jeff, and I were sitting around the table in my house. I had bought this place, a small bungalow on the outskirts of my hometown with some of the money from our signing bonus almost three years ago. It wasn't huge or expensive, but it was all mine. White siding and navy-blue shutters, dark wooden floors, slate-gray walls, and straight-lined modern furniture, I loved everything about it. Dahlia had helped with the decor, and Jeff had put in some hours to renovate the place. My brother and my best friend lived together a few miles from here. For all of us, White Crest, Tennessee, was still home. For now.

Since we'd gone on our first world tour when we were eighteen, we'd been quite busy, barely ever taking any time off for ourselves. I'd never complain. I loved the thrill and adrenaline rush it provided. It paid off because a little over two years later, we had reached the top so many aspired to.

Two albums and extensive world tours propelled us to stardom. Until we tumbled down. That period of our existence looked like a ghost of a dream while reflecting back. If it weren't for the framed platinum albums on the living room walls and pictures of all of us performing onstage across different continents, gifted by Dahlia, I would think those moments had never happened.

Dahlia and Jeff were talking, I was pretty sure of it, but all I heard was noise. White noise that didn't reach my brain. They came over tonight after I'd been refusing to see them for weeks. The last time we were together, I had a meltdown in my hotel room in Australia after the final show of our second world tour. When my entire world had shattered in a matter of minutes and I had lost everything I'd been working to achieve.

The crowd screamed our names. The energy in the stadium was electric. I could feel it reverberating through my body. Their pulsating enthusiasm echoed in my blood. We made it. Carter Hills Band was at the top. The new sensation in country music worldwide.

Unable to hide the smile splitting my face, I locked my arms around the necks of my bandmates.

Nothing could steal this moment from us. From me.

Until Dahlia met me backstage and her words stabbed me. Straight through the heart. "I'm pregnant, Carter."

For a long beat, I watched her. Not sure I heard her right.

"Wait. What?"

Keeping her gaze cast down, she refused to look at me. She kept going, as if eventually, I would agree with what she was saying. She was throwing all this shit at me, and I had no time to react. To process her words.

"Carter, you and I…" She kept talking, but my brain refused to acknowledge what she was saying. "…It's not right. I'm in love with Jeff."

No. She shouldn't be. Dahlia and I were meant to be together.

What more did she need to finally figure it out? It all sounded so wrong. Once again, I'd be the one left behind. The one with the broken heart.

Every cell in me trembled with soul-crushing pain, anchored so deep I couldn't pinpoint the source. My chest fractured in two. The ache spread all through my being. Like a house of glass, my walls were shattering and the pieces dispersing in every direction. For a quick second, I shut my eyes, hoping to find my bearings—and the control that was slipping away from me.

In an attempt to salvage my bleeding heart, I sucked in a long breath, doing my best to keep my boiling emotions under wraps, and said, "Don't say shit like this, Dah. We were never just friends, and you know it. I love you. I've always loved you. And you told me you love me just as much."

The need to touch her grew inside me, and my hands found her upper arms, keeping her in place as we faced each other. Did the despair in her eyes match what she could read in mine? When I spoke again—my voice rough from the show we just gave and the agony slicing through it—I did a poor job of hiding my true feelings from her. "Never say you don't love me again. It's complete bullshit, and you know it." Why did she have to be so blind to us? To everything we were? She had no right to deny the depth of our connection because she knew better now.

Tears cascaded down Dahlia's cheeks. And her eyes… They didn't light up her face anymore. They had lost their spark.

We were about to drown, and I had no idea how to stop the darkness from engulfing us, its grip too tight around my beating organ.

The next words passing her lips killed the remnants of hope waltzing inside me. "We can't be together, Carter. It'd kill Jeff. You know that," she said in a choked voice between sobs.

"Screw him. I love Jeff; he's my brother. But I'm in love with you. Too fucking much. I want this with you. The family, the life, the future. Please, Dah, don't lose faith in us. Don't turn your back on

me. I've loved you forever. You know it's true. There's no one else out there for me but you."

"I'm sorry, Carter. I've made my choice. Jeff proposed to me last night. We're getting married next month."

As if I'd been gut-punched, I folded in two, unable to breathe on my own. She kept talking, and every word escaping her mouth sounded foreign. A crater of pain and sorrow grew inside me. Burying everything that was good in its cavity.

"Don't be sad, Carter. It's for the best. You'll be part of the baby's life."

None of what she was saying was right. How could she be so wrong? About us? About everything?

"I'm leaving the band."

At that instant, I thought I would die. Right there. After rising to the top, I was falling to my lowest of lows. So fast, I couldn't do anything to stop myself from plunging into the abyss.

The world spun around me, and no matter how hard I tried, I couldn't get a hold of it. To stop its motion. The pounding of my heart deafened me, drowning every one of Dahlia's words. I must have blacked out that night because all my memories from there on were hazy. Like they weren't mine. The next day, I was late for the flight bringing us back home, locked in the hotel room I had trashed, unable to talk or process anything, my entire self frozen in place. And all my dreams, gone.

Since the night Dahlia left the band, I'd become a pro at hiding from my two favorite people and drinking my pain away. Guess they were tired of my avoidance because they both showed up at my house when I was out, acting as if they owned the place, prepping dinner and setting the table for the three of us. Just like old times. I bet they didn't receive the memo I was out of the equation by now. Never again would it be the three of us together. That era was over.

They had their own stuff going on. Things I wasn't

part of. Things I wasn't allowed to envy. Things that didn't concern me anymore.

From my side of the table, I studied them. Even though they tried not to rub their happiness in my face, it poured out from them. It was sickening.

Springing to my feet, I sauntered to the kitchen, grabbed two beers from the fridge, and handed my brother one. At least I could pretend to be a good host even though I wasn't in the mood for fake smiles and pretend play.

Dahlia reached out over the table to grab my hand once I sat back down, but I retracted it. She frowned at the gesture, questions swirling in her eyes. Even in my most wretched phase, she was the one person who always found a way to reach me. To help me heal. This time, though, it felt wrong to share that intimate connection.

Like it was dirty somehow.

I shook my head at her. "Don't."

She brought her hand back to her side of the table. "Okay." Her voice was a whisper.

I could read on her face I'd hurt her feelings, but somehow, I couldn't pretend to care because mine hurt so bad right now, I believed I would explode. Every truth I kept locked inside, every emotion I never expressed before, would burst out all at once. And no doubt the mess it would leave in its trail would ruin us. Forever. Taint us with secrets we weren't ready for. There would be no turning back. No way to fix us if I did. So, I kept my mouth shut.

We ate in silence until my brother decided to speak up. "Carter, I'm aware you're hurting. We're all aware. Alienating everyone who loves you and becoming a drunk aren't the solutions to healing. To get through this funk."

I kept my focus on my plate, playing with my food, my stomach too tight to eat anything.

"Look at me, Cart."

"Nah, I'm fine," I said. How could I let my brother see the truths I kept hidden in my eyes? I would never risk his seeing what was inside me. Instead, I kept avoiding the piercing gaze I could feel aimed at me.

"Come on, man. We gotta talk about this. It concerns all three of us. You can't avoid Dahlia and me forever. We're not the enemies here."

I shrugged.

"Cart, I'm trying. I really am. In the last year, we all went through some serious shit. I fucking hit rock bottom, and without both of you, I'm not sure I would be sitting here right now. Dahlia and you kept me sane through the struggles. Every one of them. And I'll forever be grateful."

His hand found Dahlia's, and they intertwined their fingers. As if it gave him the courage to keep going. I knew because having her next to me did the same to me too.

Running the back of my hand underneath my nose, I did my best to keep my emotions at bay.

"Cart," Dahlia said, her voice broken and raw. "Please. Talk to me." She paused. "Talk to us."

I flung my arms out on either side of me. "Why? Why would I need to open up to any of you? I'm just a third wheel in this"—my hand traveled between us—"relationship or friendship or whatever this is. When you got together, at least I still had the band, the music. Dahlia was still part of my life. Now I'm all alone. You all turned your backs on me. The band is gone. You're having a baby, and you're getting married. I can't be stuck in the middle forever." I spewed the venomous words. The ones burning my tongue as they spilled out from my mouth. "The thing is, I don't have a fucking band anymore. I lost nothing short of everything. E-V-E-R-Y-T-H-I-N-G. All that I'd worked my butt off since I was just a kid." I snapped my fingers. "Like this. All gone. *Poof.* One moment I was at the top of the world, having the best night of my life, and minutes later, it all came crashing down. Sorry if I don't feel like being lectured about my lack of enthusiasm."

For the longest time, we all remained silent, the weight of my words heavy between us.

"Cart," my brother said in a tentative voice. "It doesn't have to be this way. You'll figure it out. You always do."

My chair scraped the floor as I pushed it back and moved to stand, my fork clinking against my plate when I dropped it. "What if I don't want to? What if I have no idea how to process the loss? I feel cheated. It's not just you two. It's Stud too. He left me and moved to fucking Oregon. I'm just tired of always being the one left behind. The reasonable one. Maybe I'm done trying to fix things up. And be the nice guy. Maybe I just wanna be left the fuck alone for a change. Because I chose to." I walked away from the table and grabbed the whiskey bottle on the countertop in the kitchen. The one that was starting to feel too much like a friend lately. Tilting my head back, I gulped a mouthful and wiped my lips with my hand. "You can see yourselves out. No need to clean up here. I might do it later…or not. Who cares, right? I got nothing better to do anyway." With a dozen strides, I reached my bedroom and slammed the door behind me before dropping onto my bed. The tears I'd been holding in for the last hour leaked from my eyes, tiny drops of lava carving their way into my skin.

Sobs rocked my body, and after I threw the whiskey bottle across the room to avoid drinking myself numb, I curled up into a ball and let the sadness finally express itself.

Some time later, a small knock on the door broke the silence of my harsh breathing.

"Cart, can I come in?" Dahlia asked.

I didn't reply.

"Please. It doesn't have to be this way. We said we'd talk about this, but you keep shutting us out. Shutting *me* out. We never talked about what happened between us that night. And we need to address it…to…huh…to move forward."

I remained silent. I had nothing to say. The only thing I wanted to talk about, she didn't wanna hear my thoughts about it. Anyway, I wouldn't be able to break her heart. That I knew for sure.

I heard Jeff's muffled voice on the other side of the door. "Want me to give it a try?" he asked her.

I didn't hear Dahlia's reply, but I knew she would refuse. In the past, when things got rough, I opened up to her first. Always did. Then I let my brother in.

"Okay, I'll run some errands. Call me if you need me. His refrigerator is empty. He can't survive on a booze diet forever. I'll go grocery shopping and be right back." Jeff murmured something I didn't catch, and seconds later, I heard the front door shut.

Dahlia's soft voice broke the silence once again. "Cart, I'm coming in."

I snorted. Whatever. She wouldn't take *No* for an answer anyway.

I opened my burning eyes to my best friend sitting next to me on the bed. "Why did it have to be him, Dah?" I asked after a beat, the lining of my throat sensitive after all the tears I'd cried. "Why couldn't you choose me?"

"Cart, it doesn't have to be one or the other. I have a place in my heart for both of you." I rested my cheek on the side of her leg, and she combed my hair back with her fingers. "Never in my life did I mean to hurt you. I love you too much, and seeing you suffer is my greatest pain."

"Dah, I miss you." I hiccupped.

"I miss you too." Sadness coated her admission.

"I need time. I'm not ready to forget and forgive just yet. The wedding…the baby…the band…that…us… It's a tough pill to swallow. It's too fucking much all at once."

She nodded. "When you're ready, we'll be here, okay? All of us. You're a force to reckon with, Carter Hills. You always get back on your feet. I have faith in you. I always do."

Memories of a night I was trying to put behind me flashed before my eyes. I could still play every second of it in my head if I let myself.

A fragment of my heart would never recover from the feeling of treachery.

Closing my eyes, I drifted to sleep, barely sensing Dahlia when she lay on her back beside me, never letting go of my hand. For an instant, I imagined what life could have been if she had chosen me instead as I meandered into my dreams.

When I woke up later, I searched the darkness for my best friend, patting the mattress beside me. She had left. The realization acted like a sting to my heart.

On wobbly legs, with a dry mouth, I padded to the kitchen for water. Leftovers from dinner had been cleaned up, and the week-long dirty dishes piled up in the sink were gone. On the island was a piece of paper. I turned on the light and read it, the writing I recognized to be Dahlia's.

Cart,

We'll give you your space. Like you asked me.
I'm sorry for everything. I hope one day we'll all be able to move forward.
I already miss you.

Love,
Dah xx

My brother had added his own words below.

Carter,
I'll always be there for you.
As you were for me when I needed you the most.
Just call me and I'll drop everything.
Don't be a stranger.
I love you, little bro xx

New tears filled my eyes. Unable to look at the words they wrote, I crumpled the piece of paper and tossed it in the garbage can. When I returned to bed, I lay on my back, staring at the ceiling above me.

Could I reinvent myself one day, or were all my dreams and aspirations forever gone?

What if I was destined to be on my own always? I had no one to share my life with. Dahlia was slipping away. She was moving on. I was stuck here, in the past, and in a life we would never spend together, with no idea how to turn things around.

In that instant, I felt so alone—and lost—as I'd never felt before when darkness crept in. And the thought I would never recover from this loss scared me senseless.

Chapter 4
Carter

In the semi-darkness, my hands went to my temples, and I massaged them with the heels of my hands. Was the pounding in my skull, or was someone at the door? I tried to open my eyes, but my lids were too heavy. Damn it. I breathed in and cracked one open. The single ray of light piercing the room through the split in the curtains blinded me, and I closed my lid again.

In the last few weeks, I had barely left my bed during the day, too busy recovering from the previous night's hangover. I had also succeeded at pushing everyone away. Whoever stood on my front porch now clearly didn't get the memo. I wanted to be left the fuck alone. No exception.

With both hands over my ears, I tried to block the sound that made my body vibrate like I'd been sleeping next to a jackhammer during Manhattan's rush hour.

The hammering increased. My stomach churned.

"Carter, open up. C'mon, man. I know you're in there."

What the actual fuck. How early was too early for someone to bang at the door?

"Go away," I growled low, my voice too rough to resonate across the room. "Just leave me alone." I coughed, the lining of my throat raspy from my binge drinking and subsequent dehydration.

The thundering in my skull increased.

"Open the door, or I'm breaking it."

"Fine. Fine. Just gimme a—" I got to my feet, my legs collapsing under my weight, the whiskey bottle rolling onto the floor. "Great," I said as I gripped the backrest of the couch to steady myself until I could stand on shaky feet. How long had I been out? I made a detour to the kitchen to place the bottle—one out of many—on the island. How many had I drunk? I shrugged and a loud devilish laugh passed my lips, sending a cold shiver through me. Who cared, right? I had no clue and no intention of counting them all. Still drowsy, I stumbled to the front door.

I met my reflection in the mirror hanging on the slate-gray wall of the hallway and stopped. My hair was a dark mess, and staring at my scruffy jaw, I wondered when I'd last shaved. I blinked as I next took in the black suit I was wearing, the rumpled button-down white shirt with the top three buttons missing, and the black bowtie hanging around my neck. Why was I so dressed up? Where the hell had I been last night…or early this morning?

I dragged a hand over my face, erasing the signs of my drunkenness. Yeah, right. Not happening. My glossy eyes and the dry drool at the corner of my mouth were giving me away. I looked like I'd spent the night on the street and hadn't showered in days.

My brother's voice roared from the other side of the door. "Carter, I'm not kidding. I'll break in."

"Stop screaming, big brother. I'm coming. Jesus. Can't you let a man sleep?"

My hand found the doorknob. I straightened my back and inhaled.

With a smug smirk plastered on my face, I yanked the door open, bracing myself against the doorframe.

"Hey man, what's up?" My eyes traveled from his perfectly coiffed hair to his shiny black dress shoes. "Wow. Looking sharp." A hiccup escaped my lips, and I silenced it with a hand over my mouth.

Jeff's eyes widened, and his nostrils flared. He clenched his hands at his sides, and a dark flush rose on his cheeks.

"What are you so pissed off about? Chill, for fuck's sake. You're the one who just woke me up." I tousled my hair with my hand to prove my point.

"If you're joking, now isn't the time. Why aren't you dressed up and ready to go?"

I waved my hand over the length of my body. "Are you blind? I'm dressed all right. Geez, relax."

Jeff scratched the back of his neck and shook his head. "Okay, Cart. This is worse than I imagined." He closed his eyes for a minute and breathed. Another hiccup left my mouth. "Dahlia and I are getting married in an hour, and you look like shit. Did you forget you're the best man? You…you agreed to this. I gave you a choice, and you said you'd be fine. That you'd show up and act like a decent human being for a few hours. You either forgot, or you… or you don't care. Which one is it? Damn it, Carter. Look at you. You're a mess."

Our eyes met, and the disappointment I could read in his gaze broke something inside my heart.

I swallowed the lump forming in my throat, and as if

the distress in my brother's eyes was some sort of voodoo shit, my level of intoxication dropped a few notches.

The aftertaste of whiskey lingered on my pasty tongue. I scratched my forehead with my thumbnail. "I'm sorry, man. I…huh…I screwed up."

Jeff shook his head and clapped my shoulder. "It's okay, Cart. I knew this day would be hard for you. Let's get you cleaned up." My brother pulled me into a hug. A strong and tight embrace. "There's a lot of history between you two. We'll deal with it. Talk about it. Or whatever. When you're ready."

I nodded, and Jeff pushed me inside, straight into the bathroom. He turned the water on and helped me undress, stripping off my wrinkled suit. Why was I in a suit again? Did I put in on last night to get a head start and be ready for the wedding? Fuck. I had no idea. Whatever. It was stupid.

"I'll make some coffee and secure another suit for you to wear. Just get in the shower, okay?"

I bowed my head and entered the— "For God's sake," I screamed as the cold water rained on my skin. "Fucker," I grumbled as I adjusted the temperature and cursed at my brother.

———

With my hands linked in front of me, I stood beside Jeff, watching the girl of my dreams walk down the aisle. Toward him. A large, pink-painted smile brightening her face, Dahlia's moss-green eyes glinted like stars in an inky sky.

In her strapless dress, her red hair knotted at the back of her head in some girly-fancy shit, she looked everything like a princess. Jeff was right all this time. He'd been calling her *Princess* since we were kids when Dahlia wouldn't jump into mud holes with us because she had a white dress on. Just like the one she was wearing right now.

Each step in our direction—in my brother's direction—killed another chunk of my already-aching heart.

Our eyes met for a flash-second before she brought hers back to her future husband.

I tried to breathe, but the oxygen wouldn't reach my brain. My hands were moist. My head was light, and the room seemed to tilt around me. My stomach had become a pit of fire.

All the muscles in my back and neck tensed. One little push and I would snap at the seams. Shatter like a glass castle hit by a boulder.

I closed my eyes and drifted far away from here. Someplace where I could feel the breeze across my face and the sand between my toes. Where my heart hadn't died a thousand times and all my dreams and hopes hadn't been crushed yet.

And happiness still existed.

An elbow nudged my ribs, and I forced my eyes open, bringing me back to the present.

My brother gave me a pointed look. "Cart, you need to walk Addi back down the aisle."

Oh yeah. Right. My head was still swimming in gallons of whiskey. I might have forgotten what my role as the best man consisted of. Or I might have chosen to.

———

"Now, time for the best man's speech," some guy—I had no clue who he was—announced into a microphone. I cleared my throat and got up. I unfolded the piece of paper found in my trouser pocket. Damn it, I wrote nothing. I had only scribbled words and doodled some stick figures in black ink. I raked my fingers through my hair.

Jeff clamped my forearm so tight I wasn't even sure blood could reach my fingertips anymore. "You sure you want to do this?"

I stared at him, the information processing center of my brain debating. "Sure. Why not?" I offered him a dismissive shrug.

My brother blinked.

I swallowed hard. My eyes found Dahlia's. She gazed at me with a glint in her eye and a soft smile curling her lips. She looked so beautiful. I loosened the bowtie around my neck. The temperature in the room felt twenty degrees warmer. The walls of the ballroom closed in on me. This was a fucking joke. Why did I agree to give a speech at the wedding of my brother and my best friend, whom I'd loved with every little piece of my stupid heart for as long as I could remember?

Dahlia's stare burned my skin.

She nodded in my direction. I didn't need her to say a single word to understand all that she was telling me. *You can do this, Cart. Please don't make a scene. You can be mad later.*

I pinched my lips together and bowed my head. Even if I tried, I could never hurt her.

I shut my eyes, fighting my emotions down. When I reopened them, I inhaled through my mouth. I could do this.

"Today, my big brother has married the most beautiful and selfless girl I've ever known. From our early childhood days, Dahlia has always been my best friend. My other half. My soul mate. Everything I've done so far, it's been with her by my side. She's the most important person in my life. But here's the thing. There's another person I love as much as I love Dah, and it's my brother, Jeff. In all our

Hills brothers' shenanigans, Jeff has always been the smart one. And from the day my parents brought me home from the hospital after my birth, he's made it his mission in life to watch over me. He's also been my biggest fan from the day I held my first guitar. I tried to teach him, but wow, this guy has absolutely no musical talent whatsoever." A soft laugh resonated through the room. "But Jeff is one hell of a person. He's resourceful, generous, and he's always there for those he loves. He always puts his heart into everything he does."

My finger slid between my neck and bowtie, trying to massage the lump lodged in my throat. I breathed in. And out. *C'mon, Cart.*

"Today, my two best friends got married, and I couldn't be more—" My voice cracked. I tried to regain my composure but couldn't finish my speech. Even though I tried, I couldn't say those words out loud.

I pinched the bridge of my nose and blinked my tears away, a storm of emotions raging inside me. All I wanted to do was to steal the bride and run away with her. Hell. I was a mess. My tongue darted out and swept my lips. My heart banged in my chest. I exhaled.

Hanging to the last thread of my self-control, I added, "Congrats, you've got the girl, brother. And Dahlia, I hope Jeff makes you as happy as you deserve to be." I raised my glass. "And also, the baby... I hope he or she will be the perfect mix between you two." Acid filled my throat, and I pushed it down.

I chugged my glass of wine and slammed it onto the white-clothed table before slouching back in my seat. The irony? Of the three of us, only Jeff was of legal drinking age. The rest of the wedding party—my parents included —well, aside from the newlyweds, didn't seem to care at all about my drinking. With my elbows propped on the table, I buried my face in my hands. This was a nightmare. The back of my eyes burned with unshed tears. I sniffled, unable to face the two people sitting next to me.

People congratulated them, but I remained there, frozen in time.

Dinner. Toasts. Kisses. Smiles. More toasts. Pictures. Kisses. Wedding cake. More kisses. Another toast. Music playing. Bride and groom's dance. And people filling the dance floor.

A tap on my shoulder snapped me out of my state.

"Hey, Cart. Wanna dance?" Dahlia looked at me with expectant eyes as she sat in the chair next to mine. The sparks were gone. Instead, they were filled with something resembling pain. Or sadness. Maybe pity… Or whatever shit she felt when she looked at me. Loose strands of her copper hair now fell freely around her face.

I shook my head. "Nah. I'll just sit by the bar."

She squeezed my forearm with her small hand. "Thanks for what you said earlier. It meant the world to me. And…and to Jeff too. I'm sorry for everything. I-I'm sorry I can't love you like you love me. You deserve to be happy, Cart." Dahlia wiped the tears rolling down her cheeks with her fingertips. "When you're ready to talk, I'll be there, okay?"

I nodded, avoiding her heavy stare.

"If you get wasted, please don't get *too* wasted. I'm worried about you."

I nodded again, my throat too tight to speak a word.

"And Carter, one day you'll find the one. I know you will. In the meantime, just hang on. We'll be fine. You and I. We'll get through this, I promise. Just give it some time."

She rose to her feet and leaned in to drop a kiss on my cheek, her lips warm against my skin. I breathed her floral scent in, and it calmed the tidal waves inside me. It always did.

I breathed out. Was she right? Was there someone out there—other than her—made just for me?

I dropped my shoulders and gave the back of my neck a scratch.

If what Dahlia just said was true, I hoped I was lucky enough to find her one day. Because right now, life had never felt so lonely.

———

Sixteen missed calls. All from the same number. Dahlia Ellis. My childhood best friend and the one person I could never hate even after what went down between us.

All night, she'd been calling. Fucking nonstop.

In the last few months, she'd screwed up my existence in more ways than I could count—starting when she left the band. Our band. The one we created when we were seven-year-old kids with dreams of making it big one day.

How ironic. We succeeded. We reached the top. And it all came crashing down. Now only a shadow of myself remained.

I gulped another mouthful of whiskey and discarded the bottle as the room spun faster around me. A weird laugh bubbled out from me. I'd become a pathetic man in a matter of months. Tears burned the back of my eyeballs, and my laughter died down. A mass grew in my chest, the heavy one that always crushed my organs. I leaned forward, trying to catch my breath. Every cell in me hurt with agony. Tremors started in my core, extending to my fingers. A black void opened at my feet, ready to suck me in. I fought with my breathing. Lumps down my throat made it harder than it should have been.

Another bout of heartbreaking sobs pierced the silence of the night and reverberated against the walls of my house. Yeah, I'd been having a lot of those breakdowns, fueled by booze, lately.

Nothing in my life made sense anymore. I had everything and lost it all just as fast. I had no idea who I was anymore and to go back out there and shine. I had barely touched my dream when it vanished in thin air like it had been an illusion all along.

Anger simmered in the pit of my stomach. It replaced my sadness. It always did.

On shaky legs, I stumbled to the bathroom. Drinking my weight in liquor had become my full-time job. Who would have thought months ago, when I was a music superstar topping the charts, this was how my existence would turn out to be ? No one. Not even I could have predicted that. What a joke. At just twenty years old, I was reduced to a drunken mess. The worst part was that booze, lots of it, didn't erase the clusterfuck my life had turned into.

It just numbed some of my thoughts.

Sometimes.

I slid the back of my hand over my mouth after I emptied the content of my stomach in the toilet and moved back to my feet to assess the state I was in.

In the mirror, I cringed at my reflection. The guy standing in front of me looked nothing like the Carter Hills I'd known my entire life.

Surrounded by dark circles, my steel irises stared back at me, looking bluish than they usually did. For a long second, I was transfixed by the sight. Chapped lips, scruffy stubble, disheveled dark locks—longer than usual—I looked like I'd escaped a crack house and hadn't slept in a while.

I burst out into a fit of manic laughter, unable to silence it this time.

With both hands, I splashed cold water over my ghostly-white face that hadn't seen the sunlight in too fucking long, trying to wake myself up. In vain.

Closing my eyes and gripping the edge of the counter, I tried to stop the spinning in my head. Fucking waste of time. As if my will alone could alter my physical and mental state.

With a hand, I lifted the collar of my T-shirt, raised my arm, and took a whiff of my armpit. Geez, I smelled.

Lost in my thoughts, I looked into the distance. When was the last time I showered?

I snorted. No. Clue. I didn't even know what day it was.

My brain swam in the bliss of alcohol, but the grumbling of my stomach hinted I should eat something more consistent than a liquid diet.

In the kitchen, I gathered a slice of bread and peanut butter, trying to make myself a sandwich, without dropping anything.

My phone rang again.

Dahlia.

Couldn't she take a hint? I didn't want to talk.

She had put her mind to calling me all the freaking time to get me to open up. Once a week, she even drove here and begged me to talk about what happened. To clear the air. And move forward from what I now called *The Mistake* with a capital M. *No thanks, I'll pass.*

Since the wedding, I wasn't sure we had a full discussion, she and I. Nope. I was fine drowning my sorrows on my own. Thank you very much.

Tonight, she was persistent, though. I had to give it to her.

With my device in hand, I perused the room, making a list of the options in my head. *A.* Drown it in the kitchen sink. *B.* Throw it outside. *C.* Let it die. The first two options would demand too much energy from me, so I ended up silencing the damn thing and putting it in the junk drawer.

I exhaled.

There. I could breathe easier now.

Silence. I freaking enjoyed the sound of nothing these days.

Gone was the guy who came alive at the resonance of an stadium full of screaming fans.

Poof! Vanished.

With my snack in hand, I returned to my favorite couch. The one that now had the imprint of my butt in it since I spent most of my days in the same exact spot.

I must have fallen asleep at some point because the sound of someone pounding on the door woke me up with a start.

My eyes flickered open, and I scanned the room.

With one hand, I chased the sleep from my face, trying to remember the time of the day. One quick glance through the living room window and I realized it must have been late because the night was a dark pall around my house.

"Carter."

I recognized Dahlia's distinctive tone. Her voice sounded weak. She was angry. Or crying. I couldn't tell through the numbness of my brain and the remnant of alcohol circulating in my bloodstream.

"I'm using my key. I know you're in there. And your truck is parked in the driveway."

Before I could tell her to leave me the fuck alone, her pregnant figure appeared in the doorway.

My face fell.

Dahlia's entire body shook with tremors.

A high-pitched cry escaped her lips, sending chills down my spine.

Her face was a mixture of distress and grief.

I stood up, facing her.

My heart cracked in my chest. I'd never witnessed Dahlia looking so broken before.

Her body swayed, and before she could hit the floor, I rushed to her and held her against me. And just then, most of my own heartache vanished. Oxygen reached my brain. Dizziness left me.

I swallowed hard, my mouth pasty as I tried to speak.

Her grip around me tightened. If Jeff did something to her, he would have to deal with me. Once I was sober. I knew how fucked up he'd gotten not so long ago. His demons had been dark and haunting. Deep down, I doubted he was done with them, no matter what he claimed.

In a tentative gesture, I brushed Dahlia's hair back with my fingers and kissed the crown of her head. It oddly felt like no time had passed since it was us against the world.

"Cart… Wh-where were you?" She hiccupped. "I-I…I tried—" Another hiccup. "To call you for hours—" She exploded into heart-wrenching sobs that iced my blood.

I moistened my lips, my words still locked in. Something was wrong. Dahlia wasn't one to fall apart for nothing. A clamp fastened around my heart. Each gulp of air I sucked in turned into a boulder in my chest. Moisture welled up in my eyes at the sight of her pain. One look at my best friend and I could tell the news she was about to deliver would hurt. Nausea filled my mouth, and I swallowed it down.

I took the biggest inhale I could muster. "Dah. Talk to me. Wh-what happened?"

She leaned back, her eyes locking on mine. From the unsaid words that filled them, I knew it was bad. Uncontrollable tremors shook my body. A burning sensation developed deep inside me. The last beating chunk of my heart burst into bleeding particles. This was it. The moment when I'd wish I was either dead or in another one of my nightmares.

My gut told me this was neither, though. It was real. I wouldn't be able to escape the pain of it. And I would never recover from it.

"Dah," I urged. "What happened?"

"Cart, it's...it's Jeff."

"Did he do something to you?"

"He's...he's... No. Huh...he's dead."

The words I wished she never spoke echoed in my skull. They made no sense. Not at all.

A sour taste filled my mouth. Everything in me tightened as if coils of steel were wrapped around my vital organs.

I blinked. I needed her to repeat that. It was the whiskey. It fucked with my brain cells.

"Carter, listen to me... Jeff is... He-he is never coming back."

"NO," I barked. "Stop lying. Please. It-it can't be tr... It can't be true. No, my brother is NOT dead. He's alive. Dah, I'm sure he's just late. He'll be home soon."

"Cart. Stop. It's—" Her voice cracked. "Cart, he's gone. For...forever."

I folded in two as if a train had just hit me in the stomach at full speed. It stole every molecule of oxygen from my lungs. A loud bellow escaped my mouth. "*Howww?* It's not possible. He called...he called me this morning. I-I didn't pick up. I was still mad at him… For every…for everything that went down between the three of us. For our relationship blowing up. For the…for the wedding. The band. The baby… He can't be gone. We-we…we haven't talked in a while or made peace…hugged each other or forgiven… We…we haven't said I love you in too fucking long."

Dahlia's cries intensified. She held on to me as if I were her lifeline, her fingernails digging into my flesh. As if I could save her from drowning in her own heartache. "He…he died. Suddenly. I think. I-I don't know… I found him in the driveway. He wasn't…huh…breathing. Th-they…they took him. The paramedics. The coroner. He just dropped dead without saying goodbye to me. I…I don't even remember if I told him that I loved him today. It went down too fast. He had bought flowers…for me… They were just…huh…they were just lying beside him. Dead. Too. We were doing great. We-we had found our way back to each other… And he'll never…he'll never be around me, around us, ever again. I'll n-never be able to say goodbye. To hug him one last time. Ever." She sniffed. "The ba-baby. He was so ecstatic about the pregnancy. We…we had just finished the nursery. He'll never hold our… ohmygod, he'll never hold our son. Never watch him take his first steps… Or teach him how to-to swim."

Fresh tears—scorching hot—pooled in my eyes.

This couldn't be true.

A sharp pain pierced my heart. In many ways, I wished it were a sword. Because I'd trade my life for my brother's anytime. Even though we were at odds right now, I never stopped loving him. He was still one of my two favorite people in this world.

Every cell of my body hurt.

"Cart, talk…talk to me," my best friend pleaded. "I-I

know you hate me. But I…huh…I need you. And I miss you. I've been missing you for months."

"Dah, that's the problem. I…I never hated you. I wanted to, though. I really did. But I-I couldn't. Neither one of you. I was mad at the world. At the circumstances. At every-everything I wished would be mine but couldn't have."

"I'm not-not sure how to…how to keep living. I'm not sure I want to…"

I shook my head. "No. *No, no, no*. Dah, don't say that. You hear me? Never say that again. I need you too. I always have. And always will. You are the best part of me… You've always been."

"Don't. I destroyed your relationship with your brother. I got stuck in the middle, and my mess impacted all of us. I…I never meant to hurt any of you, Cart. I swear."

"Dah—"

"Stop. I fucked us up. You two were my entire life. Now we'll never…never be able to mend our relationship. How am I supposed to do this on my own? I need him to come back to me."

"Dah, Jeff can't be gone. I need him too. Please tell me…tell me it's a prank." My eyes begged her to take back what she'd said. To admit she'd lied.

"It's not. He…he's not coming back." She held on to me. "Cart, I'm so sorry. Jeff loved you. And he…he missed you too. I-I swear. He talked about you all the time, trying to figure out how-how to fix what you two once had… He felt responsible for the distance between you two and between you and me. He-he knew in some ways he'd betrayed your trust. Twice. Believe me, he never wanted to hurt you. We…huh…we didn't plan for this all those years ago when we fell in love. Don't shut me out. I'm here, o-okay? We're in this together."

I hugged her a little tighter. "Dah, I never said sorry to him... Oh god, I've been acting so childish. I-I chose to keep him away." My body quivered with sobs. "I'll never get a chance... I'll never get a chance to make things better now. To make amends. It's...too late." My eyes moved toward the ceiling. "I'm fucking sorry, big bro." In that instant, I knew I'd never heal from this heartbreak. "I... love y-you. I'm sorry I didn't tell you lately."

Together, Dahlia and I slid down onto the wooden floor in a tangled mess of limbs as we cried every tear filling our hearts. Later, we moved to the couch and fell asleep in each other's embrace, exhausted. As the first rays of sunshine illuminated our frozen forms, I had the certitude that life as I knew it would never be the same.

Chapter 5
Carter

My heart pounded in my chest. It hesitated between jumping around and freezing as the anxiety of the approaching night tightened every fiber of my being. A mix of angst and excitement swirled inside me. If it was any other time, I would have put on my sneakers and run until oxygen couldn't reach my lungs and my legs quivered with muscle spasms. Intense exercising, or rather hours of grueling workout, helped to rest my mind.

Since my brother's passing a year ago, I'd started having episodes. Panic attacks that paralyzed me and haunted my nights sometimes—or my days.

Gone was the version of me who drowned his sorrows in booze, though. I was back to being Carter Hills, the trustworthy and leveled-headed man I had been most of my life.

I had people counting on me. People I couldn't let down.

The shadows of my existence were parting to cede their place to a fresh start.

Tonight, the professional side of me would make a comeback. It took every bit of convincing from my friends and managing team for me to agree to give my musical career another try.

Usually, the idea of walking onstage and being greeted by enthusiastic fans was enough to shoot me with with bursts of energy and life. Adrenaline would course through my veins, powerful and addictive. But right now, it felt as if I was about to jump off a cliff with no safety net.

Standing upright, I shook my hands, cracked my neck, and stretched my legs, a mix of fervor and nervous restlessness making it hard for me to stay still.

Breathe in. Breathe out.

The psychologist I'd met a dozen times had recommended breathing exercises to refocus. Sometimes, they worked, oftentimes they didn't.

Right now, I wished they would be enough to avoid having a meltdown that could ruin my performance. That they would help me stay focused.

Come on, Cart. You got this. You've done this hundreds of times in the past. It's like riding a bike. It will all come back to you even though right now you feel like your brain is a blank mass.

Riley Burns, my manager and the one who got us signed to a big label and helped us reach stardom when we were eighteen, moved closer and clapped my shoulder. Back then, my brother gave our demo to one of his friends, and Riley came to see us play. He believed in us and our talent from the start and led us to the top. "Fine," he said, raising both hands in surrender. "I'll go. Take the time you need to calm the fuck down. I'll meet you by the stage. Don't doubt yourself, okay? You'll do great, man. I believe in you."

"Yeah. Thanks."

He closed the door behind him, and I found myself alone with my thoughts.

I rubbed my hands together, grounding myself with a surge of energy. Yes, I could do this. I would do this. I was Carter Hills, and I could walk on that stage and rock a crowd.

Tiny doubts lingered deep inside me. Carter Hills Band had been Dahlia and me. From the start. The two of us against the world. The two of us against all odds.

Alone in the dimly lit room, I wondered how to launch this new chapter without her.

Dahlia was done with the business. She had other dreams—and Jack. The baby kept her fully busy. We talked about this, and she had no intention of pursuing a musical career ever again.

"Cart, I loved every minute of it. But it's not my destiny as it is yours. Please don't deny yourself the dreams and living them a thousand times over because I chose to walk away." These words were what she had said the last time we discussed the matter.

I got it. I really did. But it didn't mean the thought didn't sting, though.

After we buried Jeff, Dahlia and I chose to co-parent Jack together. No matter the status of our relationship, her son would never have to suffer from his father's absence. I would make sure of it. After all, that little boy shared part of my DNA. And owned my heart.

It began with babbles and bright-eyed wonder, the tiny smiles lighting up the room. Then came the sleepless nights, the diaper rashes, and the quiet fatigue. I stood beside her, sharing the joys and exhaustion of newborn life whenever I could. And so far, we were doing great, which added an extra layer of stress and guilt to the fact I was about to go back on tour and travel the world while Dahlia would be home by herself, looking after Jack, on her own.

After everything we'd been through, one thing never changed. Dahlia Ellis was still my entire world. I never stopped loving her—and I probably never would—even though she insisted we'd always be just friends.

Circumstances made it wrong for me to still bear feelings for my best friend. Our situation was messy. And unconventional in every way. But also, beautiful in its own complexity.

Breathe in. Breathe out. You can do this, Carter. You'll do great out there. This is your calling.

Before a show, in the past, I would have focused on my mindset, following a specific ritual.

Tonight, I'd chosen to do something else. Instead of sauntering through the city I was playing in and immersing myself in the energy it provided, I had locked myself in the green room. My nerves were raw, and every second before walking on that stage felt like hours.

It's like riding a bike. It will all come back to you.

Would it, though?

A knock on the door stopped my racing thoughts. June, Riley's assistant slash *my* personal assistant, opened the door and poked her head in, her exotic caramel-brown eyes fixed on me. "Hey, Carter. Are you ready? It's time. The whole stadium is chanting your name."

I coughed and swallowed the nervousness tightening my throat. Yes, I was ready. Sixty thousand people were waiting for me. Jitters spread through my stomach. My heart felt as if it could escape my chest. I wasn't a fan of big crowds, usually preferring the smaller, more intimate shows that let me connect with my fans. When we got signed as a band all those years ago, the big stadiums were impressive and were a measure of success in our minds. Back then, entertaining huge crowds shot me with adrenaline. It became addictive. But nowadays, and even more, now that I was about to do this on my own, they had somehow lost their appeal.

Or perhaps it was just the nerves talking.

With a long exhale, I straightened my back. "Yes. Coming." I rose to my feet, relishing the tingles of excitement, the ones I only got whenever I went onstage, that were begging to make a comeback too. I stretched my arms and legs to release the numbness that had taken over me in the last hour.

Breathe in. Breathe out.

Grabbing my Taylor—my favorite and lucky guitar—I adjusted the gray plaid shirt I had on, paired with my usual faded denims, and the leather bracelet around my wrist, ready to follow June through the dark hallways leading to the back of the stage.

The sound of screaming fans jolted my heart back to life.

They're chanting your name.

The realization sent a surge of ecstasy through me. It quieted the screams in my head that had echoed a solo career wasn't in the cards for me.

Carter, Carter, Carter.

A large grin, impossible to tame, stretched my lips. Yep, that was my name they were yelling.

With a firm back and a high chin, I walked toward the stage. Toward my destiny.

I fastened my grip around my guitar, the one thing in my life that had never failed me. The one thing I could always count on, no matter what.

"Carter, you'll do great," June encouraged, slowing down to meet my more relaxed stride. At six feet five inches, I was over a foot taller than her, even when she wore high heels. Yes, June was a tiny, pocket-sized woman, but she had fortitude. More than anyone would ever give her credit for. Through the years, she had become my personal watchdog. Nobody, no matter how big or powerful they were, should ever underestimate Juniper Stewart.

People in the industry feared her whenever she got upset. Angry June was not a pretty sight. Always making sure I got the best of everything, she never took *No* for an answer. Our professional relationship had evolved into friendship, and every day, I was thankful Riley had added her to our team.

"It's weird, you know. The idea of being out there by myself…"

Riley joined us as the words left my mouth. Just like June, our relationship wasn't just professional. Over the years, he had become a brother to me. A role model. And a confidant. We watched each other's backs. All the time. He had witnessed my ups and downs. Highs and lows. My tears and joys. And my fears. We traveled the world together and grew up to be the men we were now by each other's side.

"Carter, listen"—he squeezed my shoulder—"we're all proud of you. I know it's been a rough year, but you are ready. I wouldn't send you out there if you weren't." He pulled me into a hug. "It will be epic. You need to go back on a stage. Trust me."

I hugged him back. "I always do. You know that." I sucked in a shaky breath. "It's just a big step. After everything…you know…this seems like…like a dream. Everyone's deserted me since my last concert—everyone but you two. It's…it's hard to explain."

In the last fourteen months, my life had changed a lot. Stud moved to fucking Oregon, Dahlia to Green Mountain, and following my brother's death, my parents—heartbroken—ditched me too, right after the burial. What was left was me, a lonely life, and a career I was trying to revive.

Jack was the only shining light in my life. And my music. I refused to lose them too.

June rubbed my forearm with her tiny hand. "This seems like a big deal right now, but please enjoy every minute." She looked at the screen of her phone and lifted a finger in my direction. "Gimme a sec, I'll be right back." She left us, and I brought my attention back to Riley.

"It's your night," my manager continued, "and you gotta make the most of it. Your album has been number one for weeks now. Stop worrying. I promise you'll do great. I have faith in you. June has faith in you. The entire planet has faith in you. He—"

"What?"

"Huh… He'd be proud of you too. From wherever he is, I'm sure he's watching over you. Cheering you on. Jeff was always your biggest fan, man. Imagine you're dedicating this show to him. It could be a great way to honor his memory."

I stared at my friend silently, at a loss for words. Emotions I hadn't revisited lately balled inside my chest.

"Jeff would be right here if he could. He would never miss your big return." Riley waved a hand around us. "In many ways, I know he is with you tonight. Making sure the show runs smoothly. That you get your bearings back and shine like you're meant to."

I swept my lower lip with my tongue as I processed his

words. "You know what? You're right. I'm sure he would approve of the solo career."

Memories of my late brother flashed in quick succession before my eyes. He was the reason Dahlia and I met Riley when we were still teenagers. I owed him for a lot of happy moments in my life.

My lips curled into a half-smile at the thought. I cleared my throat before speaking again. "I miss him you know… Her… Them… All of them…"

"Carter, you've seen the numbers. They don't lie. The new album sales are spiking. Your fans have missed you. And if that's any indication, Carter Hills will be even bigger than Carter Hills Band. It's all you, man. You did this."

My happiness returned. "I still can't believe it."

"Well, I can." He looked at something on his phone. "C'mon, let's get this show rolling. The opening band has only a couple of minutes left to their set."

I turned the corner leading to the stage when my eyes took her in. Dahlia Ellis. My family. My best friend in the entire world. My soul mate. The one I had to let go of months ago. The one I should've held on to. Forever.

Our eyes locked.

With the new album and show rehearsals, we hadn't seen each other in over a month. Way too long if you asked me.

"Dah, you came?" I swallowed the emotions blocking my airways and scratched my forehead with a finger, eyeing her as my heart thumped a staccato rhythm in my chest.

She smiled and inched closer, winding her arms around me. Her floral scent filled my nostrils, just like it always had. The jitters in me settled down. Dahlia was my home. Always had been. And forever would be.

All my doubts evaded me. Yes, she had that much power over my being even after all these years and the rough patches that peppered our road.

"Cart, I wouldn't have missed it for the world. You ready?" She leaned back to study my face. I lost myself in the depths of her moss-green eyes, like I'd been doing all my life. She brushed my hair back, her fingertips leaving shivers in their wake as she massaged my scalp. The little gesture was everything to me. Reminding me of what we had been a long time ago. When things were simpler and our feelings hadn't entered the mix yet.

I closed my eyes and relished the sensations washing through me, my tension dissolving.

With a sharp intake of breath, I nodded.

"You'll do great. I believe in you, Cart. Amongst all of us, you're the true star and always have been. Even if you try to deny it, you should be aware it has always been *your* destiny. Now it's time for you to show everyone what you're made of. To prove to yourself there's nothing to be afraid of because you've got this."

My eyes burned with unshed tears, and I blinked them away. I couldn't lose it minutes before walking on that stage.

With her presence, memories of our pasts weighed heavy on my chest.

"Dah, it's supposed to be us up there," I whispered, pointing in the direction of the stage with my chin.

My best friend shook her head. "No. It's not. I'm glad we did it together, but *now* it is your turn to shine. You gotta do this on your own. That's where you belong, Carter Hills. Up there, onstage, with thousands of fans screaming your name. Including me. I *am* your biggest fan now."

The sound of clicking heels, which I recognized to be June's, neared us.

My eyes sprang open when Jack babbled something, chewing on his fist from his stroller, as my assistant pushed him in our direction. My focus returned to his mother. "You brought him?"

Dahlia stepped back and smiled. "Tonight, you need all the support you can get. And your family will always have your back. Forever." That word. Again.

I moved to the side, picked up the chubby baby, and ran a hand through his dark mass of soft baby hair, the same shade as mine.

"Hey you," I said, pressing a kiss to the crown of his head. "Oh Jack, I've missed you so much." I cradled the baby boy closer to my heart and turned my head until I faced his mama. "Thank you for being here. It means the world to me. You're both my rock. I love you guys. Without you, I'd be a mess."

Jack giggled, and I kissed his digits when they rested on my lips.

Clutching Dahlia to me, I hugged the two most important people in my life, unable to wipe the grin off my face. "I gotta go. Will I see you later?"

Dahlia lifted Jack from my arms, her smile never faltering. "We'll be here, waiting for you. In fact, we're not going away. We're spending a few days with you on the road."

My eyes flared.

Tonight was day one of a two-month US tour to launch my new solo career, which would be followed by an on-and-off world tour over the next six months.

Shaking my hands and stretching my legs, I released the last fragments of tension swirling inside me, my eyes rounding. "You are?"

"Yes. June set everything up. I wanted it to be a surprise. We'll be on the road with you for three shows, then we'll go back to Green Mountain."

My breath caught in my lungs, and fresh tears threatened to break my composure. With a long inhale, I wrapped my arms around Dahlia and Jack. "Dah, I think you just gave me the strength to commit fully to this solo career. Wow. I can't believe you're coming on this tour with me. Even if it's only for a few days. And even if you are not onstage with me"—my grin doubled in size—"it'll still feel like you are."

All the weight I'd been carrying around for the longest time dissolved. The fog in my head cleared. A sense of lightness I hadn't felt in months spread through me.

"Wish me luck. I'll see you two after the show. God, I love you so much." I kissed her cheek, ruffled Jack's hair, and stormed to the place where I still belonged, my heart so big that I feared it'd burst out of my chest.

Standing in the middle of the stage, I took a full minute to take every detail in. The screaming crowd. The *I love you, Carter* and *We miss you* handwritten signs some people were holding above their heads. The intoxicating energy emanating from everyone in attendance.

With a palm over my heart, thankful for the chance and overwhelmed by a cocktail of emotions, I swallowed hard, branding the moment into my memory. "How is it going, guys?"

More screams. More cheers. More applauses. My lips stretched so wide I feared I would never be able to erase the smile off my face.

"I know it's been a while. Life happened and for a moment, I got lost." These people who came to see me weren't fools. They had seen the media headlines announcing my retirement after my bandmates quit. And about my brother's passing. I believed being honest and vulnerable was the least I could offer them tonight. I heard a *Will you marry me, Carter?* from my right and people chanting my name from my left. "My brother Jeff was my biggest supporter. Even when I was just a teen, he would drive me and my bandmates to every festival or event so we could play. He never complained. He did it from the selflessness of his heart. He was a good man who got stolen from us, from me, way too early. If he were here with us tonight, he'd be standing on the side of the stage"—I pointed to my left—"not missing a second of my performance. That was the kind of guy he was. Generous, honest, forgiving." I tilted my head back and looked up for a split second and cupped my heart. "He's in here." I pressed my chest. "And in every song I've ever written. Tonight, I wanna dedicate my first show as a solo artist to him. Because I know he would approve."

I blinked and swallowed, trying to keep my emotions under control, even though I was sure anyone standing too close could witness the moisture filling my eyes.

"Guys, it is an honor being here and sharing this night with you. Thank you, all y'all. For believing in me. Are you ready for some great music?"

The enthusiasm of the crowd warmed up my blood. My name on their lips created a furor inside me. An energizing high I would never grow tired of.

With steady fingers, I strummed the first chord cementing the Carter Hills 2.0 version of me.

Exhilaration waltzed through my veins.

Music was my drug of choice. My salvation. And my life.

For an instant, I could picture Jeff standing backstage, like he always did, giving me a thumbs-up. And Dahlia and Stud playing beside me.

I perused the space around me and caught sight of Riley, who nodded his encouragement. June had her hands clasped together under her chin, smiling. Dahlia stood tall by their sides and blew a kiss my way, with Jack, wearing noise-canceling earmuffs, fast asleep in her arms. Regardless of what happened in my life and what would happen in the future, the people who really mattered were still beside me. My tribe. My family. My heart.

They were right when they said I was back where I belonged.

Chapter 6

Carter

High on adrenaline, I couldn't walk offstage. This was my place. Where I should be. Where my heart, body, and soul felt the most at peace. But the memory of the last show I gave a little over a year ago—and the aftermath of it—still made my bones shudder with pain and bitterness.

It had been the trigger for my downward spiral.

The beginning of the end.

After my bandmates and I gave one of our best shows, everything good in my life crumbled.

Tightness grew in my chest at the mere thought of it.

My throat constricted.

The encouragement from the crowd brought me back to the present moment. At the love aimed at me, my heart swelled, jumping in all directions inside my chest cavity.

"Okay, guys. It's been a long time since I've done a concert. Earlier, the idea of being back up here by myself scared me a little, to be honest. But here I am. I couldn't have done any of this without you. You guys tonight are amazing. I think this deserves a little celebration. Some of the next songs"—I coughed to clear the thickness in my throat—"are Carter Hills Band originals I wrote a long time ago, but I've made them my own. They'll be sprinkled between tracks from my new album. So, here goes."

I attacked the first chords of "Heart for Rent."

The crowd sang along.

I lost touch with everything else around me.

Adrenaline coursed through me with an exhilarating intensity as I played my entire set.

Finally, I played "Forever" as an encore. A ballad that had won me the *Songwriter of the Year* award a few years back.

"Thank you, Jacksonville," I screamed, raising my arm over my head to wave at the fans who'd made my night ultra-special. Under cheers and wolf whistles, I exited the stage, as if floating, unable to stop grinning like an idiot.

I did it. I freaking did it.

Pride filled me. After over a year of storms and chaos, I had broken the spell.

I spotted Dahlia still standing on the side of the stage —Jack now in his stroller—and ran straight into her arms, lifting her up and twirling her around.

"Cart, you did it. I knew you had it in you. Can you believe how amazing you were up there? I had goose bumps."

"Dah, I could have stayed on that stage for days. It felt liberating. Like I was reconnecting with that part of me who had gotten lost."

"I'm so proud of you." Her voice broke under the weight of her own emotions. "And you owned that stage. You faced your fears."

I lowered her back to her feet. "No, we did it. You might not have been up there with me, but having Jack and you here, believing in me, was all I needed to go through with this." My eyes darted to the little boy deep asleep, his baby-size noise-canceling earmuffs still on. He snored, sucking on his thumb, unaware of the commotion around him—and the part he played in my everyday life. And tonight. I watched him breathe for a few beats. The peaceful movements of his chest filled me with another wave of pride.

Jack deserved the best. And I'd make it my life's mission to ensure he thrived wherever he was. Whatever he did. This baby was a part of me, and I loved him beyond words. I studied his breathing for a few more seconds before bringing my attention back to his mama.

I draped an arm around her shoulders and drew her close to me. "I'm sorry I smell." I gave her an apologetic smile, cringing as I noticed my sweat-drenched T-shirt clinging to my skin beneath my plaid shirt.

"I've never cared, Carter. I won't start now."

Dahlia and I shared a chuckle. For months, I thought I'd never smile again. Time proved me wrong. Music proved me wrong. Both had healed some of my wounds. And right now, smiling was all I wanted to do.

June and Riley neared us.

"Carter, you were fantastic out there. From day one, I knew you had it in you to entertain an entire stadium. Success runs in your blood." He squeezed me in a warm hug. Like he always did. "Man, I'm proud of you. For the kickass show you gave tonight and also for getting up there after everything you've been through. I know it was hard, but music is the best therapy you'll ever get. You proved it again tonight. Big time."

His words beelined straight to my heart, and my lips shaped into a wide grin.

"Thanks for pushing me to do this, Ry. I needed this. You were right. All along. I'm grateful. Again."

My friend slapped my shoulder. "Glad you're seeing it now. Carter, this is the beginning of a new adventure. And it will be awesome. I can already tell. Now relax. Enjoy time with your family, and we'll talk tomorrow once we board the tour bus."

He sidestepped and pulled Dahlia in for a kiss on the cheek and a hug. "Don't be a stranger. I'll see you two later. I need to spend some time with your little guy. He's growing up so fast. Dahlia, I'm glad you came. It feels like old times. It means a lot to me too. And only you could convince this grump to walk on that stage."

Over the years, Riley had become Nashville's most sought-after music manager, and together, we were quite a pair in the business.

He shifted his attention to me again. "You killed it, man. Again, proud of you. Really."

"Thanks."

Dahlia and I parted ways with my team, except for Taylor, my security detail, who shadowed me almost twenty-four-seven, trailing a few feet behind us.

"Hotel?" Dahlia asked as I pushed the stroller with one hand and squeezed her hand with the other.

"Yeah. We're boarding the bus tomorrow morning. Tonight, I have a suite, so you two will stay with me. Anyway, we have some catching up to do."

My friend chuckled. "I knew you'd say that. June already made sure our luggage was sent to your room. Jack and I, we'll stay by your side for as long as we're around. We wouldn't wish to be anywhere else." Her lips drew into an upward curl, and my pulse picked up.

God, I loved her.

Chapter 7
Carter

I woke up with a start, breathless, with sweat lining my spine. *This was just a nightmare,* I told myself. A mantra I'd been repeating for many nights since the news of Jeff's sudden death. In my dream, I had been standing on the sidewalk and watching my brother as his life left him but couldn't do anything. There was a barrier between him and me. As if I was watching the scene through a glass wall. I could see him taking his final breath. The last rise and abrupt fall of his chest. Every move unfolded in slow motion, each consequence burning through me, ten times sharper than it should have been. My heart was dying, one beat at a time, with each second that passed by. I parted my lips to call for help, but the words got tangled in my vocal cords. I was encased in a soundproof bubble of my own making, separating me from the rest of the world. The dream was surreal, impossible, and yet its echoes clung to me, blurring the line between what was real and what wasn't.

Tiptoeing out of the room, I grabbed a bottle of water from the kitchen area of my hotel suite and chugged it down while staring through the floor-to-ceiling window wall, the night sucking me into its abyss. Other than my deafening heartbeat, all I could hear were Dahlia and Jack's soft breathing coming from the second bedroom.

This was the last night my family would be by my side. Tomorrow, they would go back to their lives, and I would continue this journey, the performances, on my own.

Could the trepidation of their absence trigger my nightmares?

No doubt the void they would leave in their wake would take me a long time to fill. I was grateful they helped me dust myself off, though. These, the moments we spent together, were precious and would forever be memories I'd cherish.

The sound of feet padding behind me caught my attention. "Can't sleep?" I asked Dahlia, not bothering to turn around. Like a well-rehearsed choreography, I knew all her movements from instinct. Soon she would lean against me, and together we would enjoy the silence, offering each other comfort. Then she would offer to share my bed, like we'd been doing since we were kids, because just like me, Dahlia's nights got haunted sometimes. She didn't have to tell me. From the dark circles under her eyes to the glare around her pupils and the trembling of her hands when she thought I wasn't paying attention, I knew the signs. The ones keeping her awake. Or troubling her mind.

No matter how many years had passed, we still connected as we did when we were toddlers in our hometown of White Crest, Tennessee.

It was beautiful and a curse at the same time.

Beautiful because not a lot of people had this kind of relationship.

And a curse, because no matter how much I thought we were destined to be together, my best friend never shared my feelings. Sure, she loved me. But as a friend. A brother. Or a bandmate. Or maybe a little more than all those, but still, she wasn't in love with me and never had been.

With her in my arms, we stayed in front of the window, no words required to interpret our thoughts.

After a while, I turned toward her. "Come on, let's go to bed. You have a long drive ahead of you tomorrow. You need the rest."

"Can I sleep with you?" she asked like I knew she would. "I don't know whether it's the idea of leaving you or the memories of the tours we shared, but there's a mass in my chest that won't melt away. And your screaming and crying in your sleep isn't how a restful night should be." She stopped and studied me. "I thought you were doing better?"

I could read all the worries swimming in her eyes.

"I am. My episodes are mostly triggered by stress nowadays. I still have the urge to exercise to the point where I almost collapse when it gets too intense, but my nightmares, I can't pinpoint the exact source. They come and go, not as often as they used to. My therapist said it's my brain coping with all that happened. Finding closure. Don't make a big deal out of it, okay? I'm learning to work through them. They're getting spaced in time. It's all good."

"You promise?"

"I promise." Dropping a kiss on her forehead, I led her to her bedroom. Hand in hand, we lay next to each other after I made sure Jack was still fast asleep—and breathing —something I always ascertained every time he was around. Like we always did, we both scooted over until our heads pressed together, her small hand resting in my larger one.

"Good night, Cart."

"Night, Dah. Now sleep, okay? I'm watching over you two."

She nodded, and soon sleep claimed her.

For the longest time, I stayed awake, just to hear the steady sound of her breathing. Once I was convinced she was all right, I closed my eyes and surrendered myself to sleep.

———

I took another bite, wishing my disinterest wouldn't show up on my face. I blinked to reboot my brain after I zoned out.

"…and then I called my girlfriend and she drove me to the emergency room. You should have seen the bump on the side of my head. It was impressive."

I swallowed and flushed my food down with a sip of water.

"You wanna get out of here?" I asked my date, discarding the cloth napkin on the table and pushing my chair back.

"Huh, sure." Her eyes traveled back and forth between my face and her still half-full plate. If she had spent less time talking about her college years, she would have had time to eat.

The server met with us, and I handed him my credit card.

"I'll be right back," I told Rosie, pointing to her plate. "Keep eating. I'll just be a minute."

In the men's room, I splashed cold water over my face and stared at my reflection in the mirror. My gray irises, the same shade as Jeff's and Jack's, looked back at me. "What are you doing, Carter? You've been on three dates so far this week, and none of them have held your interest for more than an hour. Get your groove back."

Rosie sounded like a nice girl, if you forgot about the fact she hadn't gotten over her teen years yet. Her smile was enticing, and her eyes shone with sparks. She was my accountant's niece. Last Friday, we ran into each other when she was at his office, filling out her taxes. We chatted while her uncle was on the phone, and I asked her out on a date. Unlike Theresa on Monday, who I met through common friends, at least Rosie wasn't just pretty, she could hold a full conversation, however inane it might be.

With a shake of my head, I exited the confinement of the suffocating restroom.

When I neared the table, Rosie was deep in conversation with the server, who I noticed was slipping a piece of paper into her hand. I bet it was his phone number. Maybe between the two of us, someone would be getting lucky tonight.

The thought helped me feel less like a motherfucker about to ditch a girl I had no interest in.

While I stowed my credit card back into my wallet, Rosie cleared her throat. "Listen, Carter. I had a great time tonight. But I'm not sure we're…like…huh…you know… connecting?" She fidgeted with her napkin. "I'm sorry, but I think we should each go our separate ways." She offered me a timid smile. "Are we okay?"

I sighed. "Yeah, all fine."

She moved to her feet and hugged me. "Thanks for dinner. I still had a lovely time."

I nodded, and before I exited the restaurant, I spotted the server, probably having finished his shift, meeting Rosie by the bar.

Tonight, I had played matchmaker. At least my night wasn't a total loss.

Climbing into my SUV, I drove around for the next few hours, blasting rock music so loud my eardrums were at risk of bursting. It silenced the nagging voices in my head.

Why couldn't I date like a normal guy my age? I wasn't sixty-five, but twenty-one. With baggage. And an unavailable heart. But still, I couldn't be that much of a loser in the relationship department, right?

Dating. For a long minute, I wondered if I, someday, would be able to go through with it. And meet a girl I would fall head over heels for. Someone who wasn't Dahlia, but who would send my heart into overdrive just the same.

Just the thought was enough to send my mind spiraling.

And my breath halting.

Lyla, a woman I had invited as my plus-one to events in the past and who lived in Los Angeles, texted me after I stopped to fuel my vehicle.

LYLA

I'm in town for less than twenty-four hours.
Just got here. Leaving in the morning.
Wanna meet up?

She was the only woman I had regular sex with. She wasn't interested in a serious relationship nor was she moving to Nashville, and our agreement suited me, for now, so I wasn't complaining.

Glad to have given Taylor the night off after my dead-end date, I merged onto the highway and exited fifteen minutes later. Once I got to the hotel Lyla was staying at, I handed over my black SUV to the valet.

"Hey you," I said after she opened the door.

"Ohmygod, Carter. Sorry, but you look like shit. Everything all right?"

I pressed a kiss to her lips and sat on the edge of the bed once I shut the door behind me. "Bad night. I was on a date, and she left with the server instead of me."

Lyla's eyes widened. "For real?"

I let out a sarcastic laugh. "Yep. Said we weren't compatible or some shit like that."

"Wow. You can't accuse this one of being a groupie."

"Well, yeah. Anyway, I had no interest in taking things further with her, so it's fine. Whatever. It wasn't meant to be."

"If you're nice, I can make you forget about your shitty date." She wiggled her eyebrows, and I burst into laughter.

Still standing, Lyla positioned herself between my legs, and I clutched her sides, pulling her closer.

"I was hoping you'd say that. I'm overdue for some action. The last time was months ago, and I prefer it to be with you than anyone else right now."

She splayed both hands across my chest. "Well, in that case, let's not waste any more time."

Her lips descended on mine, soft and familiar, and I forgot all about the last few hours and the sense of panic that had paralyzed me earlier as we both made each other feel better, even if only for a moment.

"Thank you, Amsterdam," I screamed, my guitar held high above my head. "You were the best crowd tonight. How about an encore?"

Droplets of sweat traced my spine. I pushed my wet locks away from my forehead and adjusted the instrument around my neck.

Wolf-whistles and screams filled the stadium. I nodded to a technician on the side of the stage, and he brought me a wooden stool. The lights turned off, and a lone spot shone on me as I performed the acoustic version of "Forever."

I strummed the first few chords. All sounds died down in the stadium. It always impressed me how everyone fell silent the moment I started playing, not wanting to miss a single lyric.

Lights glowed around me like little stars when people lifted their phones and sang along with me.

Warmth flooded my chest. My eyes brimmed with emotions.

I'd been doing this for years, and each time people sang my songs and knew all the lyrics, it hit me. Like a balm of love enveloping every inch of my being.

The show ended, and I was flying—or at least, that's how I felt. Light and content. Nothing could bother me when I was surfing this post-concert bliss.

After I showered and changed, I met up with my musicians.

I had been invited to a club opening tonight, and I promised I would make an appearance.

Bradley, the owner, and a fellow guitarist I had the honor to play with in the past, welcomed me when I reached the VIP section. We chatted for a couple of hours, and after a short night of sleep, I boarded the plane to my next destination.

I had a concert scheduled in Germany tonight. This was the European leg of my tour. Three months across Europe. One month off. Then two months across Asia.

These days, I couldn't get enough of the music. Never in the past had I pictured myself as a solo artist, but so far, I was enjoying the freedom it provided me. Sure, some days felt lonely since I was used to having my bandmates—slash best friends—with me all the time, but there were also perks.

June called as I was about to leave for a sound check. I greeted her in a teasing tone. "Hey you. Miss me already?"

Her clear laughter resonated through the phone. "Hello to you too, Carter. You seem to be in a great mood. Everything going as planned?"

"Yes. Last night's show was perfection. It always puts me in a good mood for days afterward when it happens. What can I do for you?"

"Listen. I was thinking… That wedding you said you would come to with me next month? I'm not sure it's a good idea after all."

"Why not?" At her invitation, I had agreed to accompany June to her cousin's wedding in her hometown. She didn't want to go alone, and I was fine with being her plus-one if it meant great food, music, and a fun night. And June and I always had a good time together.

"I-I heard he might make an appearance… I won't put you in the middle of my clusterfuck. It wouldn't be fair to you."

"At some point, you'll have to talk to him. Explain everything. If I were him, I'd wanna know. Wouldn't you if the roles were reversed?"

She sighed. "Yeah. I would. We had a nasty breakup. I

lied to him. Rather, I hid the truth from him. And when I decided to come clean, he never returned my calls. What was I supposed to do? Pursue him? Harass him until he talked to me?"

"Still, the guy had no idea. I'm sure once you tell him the truth, he'll regret not showing up for you when you needed him the most. And not taking the time to talk to you. And see you."

"Maybe. We really loved each other. I'm not sure I'll ever find someone like him. It felt like a *one chance in a lifetime* kind of love."

"June, don't stress over it."

"It's easy for you to say." She paused. "Sorry, that was a shitty thing to throw at you. You and I…we-we're both stuck in dead-end situations. Anyway, I'll let you know what I choose for the wedding. I'm sorry I'm a mess about it."

Juniper Stewards didn't do emotions. In our professional and personal relationships, I was the one ruled by feelings. She was driven by logic and facts. Except when it concerned her ex. Then she became agitated and could barely think straight.

Of all the people she knew, if someone could understand her, it was me. Not that her story was similar to mine, but in a way, it was too.

"Hey, are you okay?"

Her voice was a low whisper. "I will be. Sorry for the almost-breakdown just about now. My mother called and spewed all this information on me, and I panicked. And you're the only one who knows the whole story. The truth about my…huh…situation. Okay, I'm done complaining. I'm back to being the cutthroat business badass you all know me to be. If you tell anyone about this conversation,

I'll deny it ever happened. Nobody in the industry is allowed to be aware I have a soft side."

"I wouldn't pretend otherwise."

"Enjoy Germany, Carter. Eat a slice of *Schwarzwälder Kirschtorte* thinking of me. You know how Black Forest cake is my favorite."

"I'll get you one for your birthday this year."

"Carter Hills, we have a deal. Call me tomorrow. We have a few things to go over in your schedule for the next two weeks."

"Perfect. Gotta go. The guys won't be happy I'm late for sound check."

"Go. Have fun tonight."

We hung up, and I hurried to the stadium where I'd be playing tonight.

My conversation with June replayed in my head as I sat in the car. *You and I…we-we're both stuck in dead-end situations.* I ran my palm over my face. Every time I thought I was doing better, something—or someone—reopened the wounds of my heart, and reminded me I was alone. And that my heartbreak scars were still fresh and friable.

Discomfort stirred my insides. Guess we all had secrets keeping us up at night.

Stretching my neck, I tried to return to my previous state of bliss. In vain. Agitation spread through me.

Breathe in. Breathe out.

My finger hovered above Dahlia's name on my phone for seconds before I pressed the video chat button.

"Hey. Dah."

"Carter, are you in Frankfurt already?"

"Yeah. Got here early this morning. Is Jack around?"

"Huh, sure. Everything okay?"

"I just need to see his face and talk to him. Won't be long. I'm on my way to sound check right now."

As if on cue, we passed the Frankfurt Cathedral, and my gaze lingered there for a beat. I wasn't a fan of architecture, but I enjoyed its old European charm. There was just something about the traditional timbered German houses I found inviting.

"Let me get him. He just woke up from his nap. Your timing is impeccable."

Dahlia came back with the dark-haired baby. His big eyes locked on me through the screen, his tiny fingers tapping the camera as he babbled, drool covering his chin. Watching him silenced the battle rising inside me.

Chapter 8
Carter

"Dah, if you wanna move, there will be enough place on my land for you to build a home. Or a cabin. Or whatever you like. And the view is stunning. You can see the entire valley below and the mountaintops in the distance. Imagine how beautiful it will be in the wintertime." I had come home from the last leg of my tour and had decided to get a permanent residence in Green Mountain so that I could be around Dahlia and Jack every time I had some time off.

The lot I bought was surrounded by wood areas, and on cloudy days, it appeared as if we could touch the sky if we rose to our tiptoes and stretched our arms above our heads. It offered the most spectacular view of the town and valley. My house would be built on the western mountainside to never miss one of the breathtaking sunsets Green Mountain was famous for.

With Jack in a baby carrier mounted on my back,

Dahlia and I were walking around my newest acquisition where I intended to spend as much time as I could. Living in Nashville had its perks, but if she had decided to raise her son here, then this was where I'd be too. Co-parenting with us living a three-hour drive apart and with me gone on tours and playing events like festivals and fundraisers all through the year wasn't the easiest way to do this.

Moving to Green Mountain sounded like the most logical decision I would ever make. And I loved it here. The mountain air, the green landscape, the silence. They all helped soothe my mind.

I pointed to the parcel of land in front of me. "The cabin will be there. Three-stories. All wood. With large windows to let the sunlight in and make you believe you're outside even when you're not."

"I love it. It's charming." Charming was Dahlia's way of saying beautiful. "I can see it in my mind. This will be amazing, Cart." She spun on herself. "What about the rest of the property? It's huge. Any plans for it?"

"Like I said, if you wanna move here, you get whatever size you want. For the rest, I was thinking of building smaller cabins. Rentals. Until the day I have guests coming over and they can stay in them. What do you think?"

Dahlia reflected on it for a second. "It makes sense."

"My dad always used to say real estate is the best investment. I don't know. It could be fun to start a business on the side. I could get more cabins in the area and have my own little real estate development. It's still just a thought, though."

"Let's talk about it when you have a clear vision. Or if you wanna brainstorm ideas with me." She became quiet, staring into the distance.

"Dah? What's wrong?" I could tell something was weighing heavy on her mind.

"I'm not sure Jack and I moving here is a good thing."

"But—"

She lifted a finger. "Hear me out."

"Okay." My shoulders sagged at the thought that she wasn't excited about my plan.

"I'm doing good on my own. Raising Jack has turned out to be a challenge, but I'm proud of what I've achieved so far. It's not easy, and I would love to have you around more often. But I also think it's best if we each have our own place. Close enough but not next door to each other. If we have friends over, or lovers, or whatever…it would be weird if we see each other's decks. And I love my house. It's not perfect, but it's home. It's where Jack was born. Where he and I had learned to be on our own. I love my independence. It means a lot to me. All my life, you've been taking care of me, making sure I was okay. Always putting my needs before yours. And then Jeff did too. This is the first time I get to do things my way." She squeezed my forearm, studying my reaction. "For now, it's what's good for me. In a year or two, it may change, but right now, I don't wanna move."

I averted my eyes.

"Are we okay? Talk to me."

I swallowed my uneasiness. "Yeah. It's fine. I was just excited and thought you would share my enthusiasm."

"Cart, I am. And you know that even if we live a few minutes' drive from each other, I'll be staying with you every time you're in town, right?"

"You will?"

Dahlia nodded. "Yes. You can't get rid of me that easily. Let's say we were neighbors and then you would leave for months. I would be sad, watching your empty house every day. It will be easier my way."

"You'll have your own room. And Jack will have his too. Don't say no, please."

She shook her head, the contagious sound of her laughter warming my heart. "That's more like it." She moved to her tiptoes, and we hugged for the longest time.

"I have another surprise," I said once we broke apart. I released Jack from the carrier, and Dahlia picked him up.

"What is it?"

"Picnic. I made all your favorites. Gimme a sec. I'll get everything we need from my truck. I found a big rock where the view is jaw-dropping. You'll love it."

Dahlia stopped my retreat with a hand over mine.

"What?" I looked into her eyes.

"Cart, promise me you'll get the place fenced. Security code and all that stuff." She pleaded with her eyes. "Do it for me if you won't do it for yourself."

"Dah, you can't freak out forever because of that guy who harassed me. It was a one-time thing. Taylor is practically in my pants twenty-four-seven for that reason."

"Where is he now?"

"In Nashville. I gave him the week off."

Dahlia's lips twisted. "See? You're too trusting. There are many crazy people out there, Carter. Don't take chances. You never know. And when the press learns you're setting up here, some may try to snap pictures of you. Don't risk your security or your privacy."

"Fine. You convinced me when you said the press. I hate these vultures." I draped my arm over her shoulders and pulled Dahlia against me. "Think Jack would love a guitar-shaped bed? I could ask Stud to make one for him. What do you think?"

Stud, our ex-bandmate, now ran his own wood workshop business in Oregon. He was as talented with manual labor as with music. Anything his fingers touched transformed into gems.

"Cart, Jack is just a baby."

"Sure, but one day he'll run around and won't sleep in a crib anymore. I'm thinking long-term here. If I'm doing this, I'm doing it right."

Dahlia kissed my cheek. "You always do the right thing, even when you're stubborn. In the end, your heart always leads the way."

"Yeah, well, let's see how it turns out this time around." I sighed. "I have a great feeling about this."

For the first time in what seemed like forever, flutters invaded my stomach at the idea I was doing something for myself. Something that I knew would make me proud. And happy.

Sitting on the large rock with Jack positioned on a blanket between us, we ate while discussing anything and everything.

The warm breeze swept Dahlia's hair, and for a minute, I got lost in the sight of her, admiring each of her features. My heart did one of its flips in my chest, followed by a band of tightness that I felt only around her. Even after all this time, my feelings for my best friend hadn't changed. They might have even multiplied. Perhaps it was for the best that we weren't next-door neighbors after all. As she said, if she had a man coming over, it would drive me nuts. Dahlia wasn't even dating, and just the thought of her offering her heart to someone else one day had me gritting my teeth. A wave of jealousy, that I had no right to feel, messed with my breathing. Not wanting her to read my thoughts, I moved to my feet and pretended to make a phone call. "Gimme a few minutes. I'll be right back." I kissed the top of her head and Jack's cheek and scurried away.

The more distance I put between us, the more air returned to my lungs.

Hiding behind my truck, I pressed my forehead against the warm steel frame and exhaled the remnants of angst tightening my stomach.

"She needs you as a friend. Don't screw it up," I said to myself. "Get your heart in check."

Easier said than done.

I paced the ground where Dahlia couldn't see me from that giant rock she was sitting on, tugged at the roots of my hair, and dragged a hand over my face. Right now, I wished I could change into running gear and evade the present for an hour or two.

Breathe in. Breathe out.

For now, I could be Dahlia's best friend. I had to be. There was no place in her life for love. She repeated it every time I tried to bring up the subject.

"I'm perfectly content with my life at the moment. I'm thriving. And Jack, for now, is the love of my life. I've never been on my own, and even though some days it scares me, it's also satisfying to realize I can do this and that I'm enough."

I understood how she felt because it was the same way I felt when I agreed to become Carter Hills the solo artist instead of the band. That I was enough on my own and didn't need other people to make me shine.

With confident steps, I returned to my family's side.

Dahlia's gaze met mine as I took a seat on her right. *Everything all right?* her eyes asked.

Yes, they will be. Thank you for being here. With me, I replied.

For now, our friendship would have to be enough. Together, we lost ourselves in quiet contemplation.

As I took in Dahlia watching the scenery with a relaxed stance and with Jack fast asleep in my arms, I had no doubt I belonged here with them. Even though it was just

part-time for now. Even though the status of our relationship was still hard to define.

———

"I'm done. Finally," I announced as I slumped down into
Dahlia's cream leather couch, exhaustion lacing my words.
"It was the shortest world tour I ever did, but the most
tiring."

Last night, I had come home after intense few months
abroad, touring Europe, Australia, and parts of Asia, in-
between a stretch in Canada and the US. I had released
my second solo album almost a year ago. Time flew.

Dahlia handed me a bottle of water and sat beside me,
resting her head on my shoulder, her copper hair a
contrasting halo around the fair skin of her angelic face.

"Can you imagine it's been almost three years since
that day Jack and I were watching your big return from the
side of the stage in Jacksonville? It feels like a lifetime ago."

"He was so tiny back then. To this day, it's still one of
the best surprises of my life. It was really what I needed to
keep going. Every time I'm about to walk onstage, I always
look at the picture June took of the three of us that night I
keep in my guitar case."

A lot had happened in the last three years. I had
reclaimed my position at the top of the charts, built the
house of my dreams on the piece of land I bought in
Green Mountain, and had learned to consider Dahlia as
just a friend. Well, I was still struggling with this one some
days, but I was doing better. Getting there. My love for her
would forever be there. Strong and unapologetic. But a
part of me now understood she wouldn't be my happily-
ever-after. Even though sometimes, it still stung to think
about it. Seeing her and Nick together wasn't easy, but I

recognized how blissfully happy my best friend was, and the realization healed some of the scars on my heart. One by one. Even after everything we'd shared, she only saw me as her friend. Her best friend. Not her endgame. Not her forever.

A quick glance at the shiny diamond on her ring finger reminded me we would never happen. Not in this lifetime.

I swallowed the uneasiness tightening my vocal cords and mirrored her smile.

As if she sensed I needed a distraction, my best friend raised her glass to clink my bottle. "To you, Cart. You did it. Once again, you proved you're the best there is."

"And to you too. Because you're making the cover of *Wedding Bliss* magazine next month," Nick, her fiancé, said when he joined us after checking on Jack to make sure he was still fast asleep, as we had heard him talk in his sleep through the baby monitor.

I leaned myself away from Dahlia. "Wait. What? You are? Why didn't you tell me?" I tried my best to hide the hurt lacing my voice.

"Listen, I wanted to tell you in person." Dahlia poked her tongue out at Nick. "Thanks for ruining the surprise," she told him, unable to hide the amusement in her voice.

They were nauseatingly in love.

I rolled my eyes at their exchange.

"Sorry, babe, I thought you'd already told him. You two are always telling each other everything. It's kind of disturbing sometimes." Nick let out a heartfelt laugh, reached for his glass, and took the chair before us, raking his hand through his blond locks.

Dahlia squeezed my hand. "Okay, I agree. You may be right. From an outsider's point of view, our relationship can be misunderstood." She shrugged. "But I don't care, though. Carter and I have always been this way. And I love the way we are. It's us."

I dragged a hand over my face and shook my head. "I guess it can be intimidating. Anyway, I can't believe you hadn't told me the big news. You know I'll buy an entire stand of magazines, right?"

Dahlia's eyes widened, and she snickered. "Oh God, you're always overdoing things. Perhaps I should've told you months after it actually came out. Or gifted you a copy on your birthday or something. Saved you a single dedicated copy."

"Dah, you wouldn't have been able to keep it a secret from me that long."

She barked out a laugh. "I guess."

"Are they featuring the shop or you as a bride?"

Dahlia now owned a bridal shop in Green Mountain. A successful business she built from scratch. She even co-designed a line of affordable wedding gowns along with a famous designer. My best friend had turned her life around, and I couldn't be prouder.

"Both. I'll make the front page and have a ten-page article where I try a dozen gowns from the shop and talk about trends and wedding stuff."

I nodded. "I really need an entire stand. Do you want the front page to be framed? I can get it done for you."

Her laughter warmed my heart. "Nah, I don't wanna watch my face on an oversized poster because I know you'll get it resized to gigantic proportions." She shook her head, holding my hand in hers. "I'm glad you're back," she said once her laughter died down, her voice strained. "I missed you while you were away."

"I missed you too. It's good to be home."

Nick sighed. "I think I'll never get the extent of your friendship, guys. It's as amazing as it is disconcerting." He took a sip of the whiskey. "But it's something everyone should aim for because it's quite extraordinary that it survived through everything you two faced. You're both lucky to have each other."

I nodded.

Dahlia wiped the tears now filling her eyes with her fingertips. "I'm not sure I would have made it through everything without Cart by my side." Her voice was low and saturated with emotions. These days, we rarely talked about the obstacles we overcame together. It'd been almost four years since our lives changed forever, and we laid Jeff to rest. So much had happened since then. "From moving here alone to raising Jack and starting the business, and you going solo and touring the world twice while launching two albums and building a house here, it's been quite a ride. Can you believe we accomplished all this before turning twenty five?"

Tightness grew in my chest, and I kissed the side of her head, tugging her closer. "It's like we've grown up twenty years in a short span of time."

But hey, we made it to the other side. Alive. Fairly happy. And when I looked back, I couldn't be prouder of the family we had created.

It had been hard on both of us, but it also sealed our friendship bond forever.

My emotions constricted my throat, making my breathing harsh. Moisture enveloped my eyeballs while I reminisced all the challenges we conquered together.

"Dah, I know I wouldn't have made it without you. And Jack. You are both my anchors and my reason to keep going and be better." I fought a yawn. "Anyway, I'll let you two be. It's getting late."

I unfolded my tall self from the couch and stretched my arms over my head. I was finally in a good place with

Nick. I wouldn't call us best friends yet, but I chose to get along with him. He was a decent enough guy—no, he was awesome—and he loved my favorite people with all his heart. As if they were his too. And they loved him back.

The four of us were an unconventional family, but we made it work. "Thanks for dinner. I'll see you guys later." My lips met Dahlia's cheek as she squeezed my forearm, and I held out my hand to shake Nick's.

"Take care, man," he said.

Dahlia let go of me. "Behave, Cart. And call me if you need anything."

I nodded and blended into the dark night, before hauling myself into my truck.

My heart flipped in my chest, unable to decide if it was happy or sad. Aching or excited. Seeing Dahlia with Nick made my heart flinch, twisting with remnants of pain each time. Would I get there one day? Find my person, just like she had done twice?

Or was I destined to be alone forever?

The idea I wasn't meant for reciprocated long-lasting love scared me.

A fucking lot.

It felt like a thousand needles were piercing the hard armor I had grown around my bruised heart a long time ago. Back when we were teenagers and Dahlia fell for my brother just when I was about to admit my feelings to her.

———

Three months later, I found myself sitting on a white garden chair, with Jack in my arms. With a deep inhale, I inhaled his scent, trying to hold my heart together, though its smoldering ashes had already claimed too much space inside me. Nerves tangled me up. Breathing got harder. And my body quivered.

Chills ran up and down my spine. The not-so-good kind.

The tie around my neck felt too tight.

My skin itched under the fabric of my trousers.

I tried to avert my gaze, but somehow, it stayed glued to the scene playing before me.

Tears stung the back of my eyes. I closed my eyelids, hoping to lock them inside.

Even though I had grown accustomed to the idea of Dahlia moving on and marrying Nick, the sight of them up at the altar under an arch of white roses unleashed a tsunami of emotions inside me.

The last six weeks, since their combined bachelor-bachelorette party, had cemented the truth I knew deep down. This was it. Dahlia and I would never be together, no matter what. The last thread of the relationship we had built after Jeff passed away would be severed forever. Things would never be the same between us from now on.

The realization dredged up feelings I thought were buried for good.

A witness to their love story, all I could think was that I wish it'd been me, standing up there, exchanging those vows, sharing those smiles. Those love promises. And being on the receiving end of the look in Dahlia's sparkling eyes. The ones I'd spent years yearning would be directed at me someday. Something I had for a moment—so brief I still wondered sometimes if that night really happened—and then lost.

My eyes drifted to the woman wiping her tears beside Dahlia. Addison Wilde, her other childhood best friend and the maid of honor. And Tucker, Nick's best man, standing tall next to him, his gaze focused on Addison, never faltering away, his jaw tense, the look in his eyes betraying his own withheld emotions. Guess I wasn't the only one suffering in silence. Last night, the five of us had a pre-wedding dinner together, and I could tell he had feelings for her. When Addison turned him down, he looked crushed. I felt for him—I could relate in more ways than one.

With one arm around his small body, I kept Jack close to my heart because only he had the power to heal the broken fragments scattered in my chest.

"By the power vested in me by the State of Tennessee, I now pronounce you husband and wife. You may now kiss the bride," the officiant, a man with thick white hair and dark-framed glasses, said. My heart fell ten stories down my chest and ended up in the tips of my toes, fighting between life and death.

I sucked in some air. It didn't go through.

My head spun.

Breathe in. Breathe out. Breathe in. Breathe out.

My lungs collapsed. I blinked. The air coming in and out of me burned my throat, as if flames licked its lining.

This was it. The day I had to move on too. The first day of a new chapter of my life. I ventured a look around me. Huge smiles. Happy demeanor. Lively chatter.

Was I the only one stuck in the past?

I coughed and fastened my grip around the boy jiggling in my arms. The older Jack got, the more he looked like me. Unruly dark hair, steel-gray irises, piercing gaze. He laughed at something, and I kissed his cheek. "I love you, buddy, and I always will. You'll forever be my family, mine to love and protect, no matter whom your mama chooses to love. I'm not going away, okay? Never. You'll always be able to count on me. I love you so much.

Whatever happens, you are a son to me. That will never change, I swear."

We exchanged a glance, and when he smiled at me, the first few pieces of my fragile heart, that hung loosely inside my chest cavity, found their way back to one another.

Jack put a finger between my lips, and I kissed the small digit.

"You and me, buddy, we're cut from the same tree. No matter what happens in my life, your mama and you will always be my top priority. That's my promise to you."

I blinked my tears away as I watched Dahlia and Nick kissing at the altar as if they were the only two people in the world. Dahlia wrapped her arms around her husband's neck, and he lifted her up, both of them smiling like fools. Fools in love. Fools now united for life. Something I never seemed to achieve for myself. No matter how hard I tried.

I swallowed the searing rock down my throat, wishing I could have what they had. Wishing I could have the bride. That she'd love me as much as I loved her. Wishing I could love this way, and be loved just as much.

Or wishing I could have *a* bride. One person loving me without any conditions or *what-ifs*. One I could see myself growing old with. Was it Dahlia I still wanted or the idea of an *us*? Right now, I couldn't tell.

The ceremony ended.

This wedding was a *déjà-vu*. It dug up memories I never thought I'd revisit someday. Images of my brother kissing Dahlia and promising her forever a long time ago. Or more like almost four years ago to be exact.

How many times could I go through this? Dahlia getting married? Dahlia promising forever to another man? Dahlia stomping on my fucking heart and me, watching her do it without being able to stop the pain?

The Mistake, the one with the capital M, would annihilate me. Forever.

Why was I still hanging on to it even years later?

There was something wrong with me. If not, nothing could explain why I was being such an idiot.

Could there be a sadomasochistic part of me relishing the pain?

Here I was, thinking I had made progress in the last few months. Maybe this was a relapse. Or the closure I needed to move forward once and for all.

Jack's smile grew wider, and he caught all my attention.

"We can do this, buddy. Hills men against the world. Hills men stick together. Always For better or for worse."

"*Cattter.*"

I nuzzled his neck, and he giggled. Warm, innocent giggles. The ones able to glue back together all the broken pieces of me every time I heard them. The ones telling me I was still alive. That I could pull through the pain.

"Yeah, buddy. I'm right here."

He planted a drooling kiss on my cheek, and we both watched as his mama and Nick walked down the aisle, a halo of light around them, their happiness visible probably even from space.

"Mama is pretty," Jack said against my neck, clapping his hands together.

"Yeah, she is. Always has been."

The clamp around my heart tautened.

Dahlia's eyes locked on mine, and we shared more in our gazes than any word could.

I've always loved you, mine said.

I know. I will always love you too. Thanks for everything, hers replied.

A part of me wished it'd been me.

I'm sorry I'm not in love with you. Don't give up. Your turn will come.

After dinner, and once Jack was in the care of the babysitter the newlyweds had hired for the night, couples paired up on the dance floor while I nursed yet another glass of water with some fancy green paper umbrella and a Maraschino cherry on a pick, doing my best to pull off a nonchalant vibe.

Everything in me was screaming in agony.

I couldn't keep yearning for my childhood best friend. This had to stop.

Time to create a new life for myself.

And to let go of the past.

Chapter 9
Carter

"**A**re you here by yourself?" I asked the woman with long dark hair, falling in soft curls behind her back. She was taller than most women I knew. Five-nine, or maybe even five-ten, without her heels. Who could have predicted this night would turn out to be interesting after all? I didn't. This morning, I flew into New York early, dreading the mandatory smiles, photos, and handshakes being here required. But now? Perhaps this trip could turn around and be exciting. A man could always be hopeful.

Nick and Dahlia had just returned from their month-long honeymoon a few days ago, which meant I had spent the past four weeks alone with Jack in Green Mountain. After the wedding, we talked about it, and they decided to delay their trip until my schedule cleared and I had a full month off with no commitments. Those four weeks were some of the best ones of my existence. That child really possessed a special key to my heart.

Tonight was my first night away from Green Mountain, and for a moment, even though it sounded silly, I preferred being a daddy instead of a grownup. The playful version of me suited me best, and I relished the freedom it provided me.

With a grin, I placed a glass of red wine on the small table before the woman standing in front of me. Not that I'd been studying what she'd been drinking since I got here. Well, I tried not to. And failed.

Her eyes brightened when they met mine, and she offered me a smile that made my heart come alive inside its cage.

I held out my hand, and she met mine for a handshake. "Hey, I'm Carter." I cringed mentally. I was so not good at this. The whole flirting thing. Not that I was rusty. I just hated it. Women usually knew who I was and came on to me. I never had to be the one chasing them. Right now, I felt so out of my element, but that was the point, no? Getting out of my comfort zone if I wanted to give my life a new direction. I breathed in. I could do this. "You looked lonely just now, and I thought you might enjoy some company." Yeah, so bad at this. I sipped my water, trying to moisten my dry mouth.

She raised her fresh glass of wine and nodded. "Thanks for this. I'm Savannah. Savannah Prince."

"Are you here on business?" I asked, trying to keep the momentum going. "Or are you here with the crew?"

The woman cleared her throat. "I might star in Wesley's next movie. I'm here because he asked me to come and mingle with people. I'm not an A-list actress, so it requires more work to get my name out there. I want the role so bad I'd do just about anything. But I've socialized all night, and now I'm done. It's quite intimidating."

She perused the space around us, and when her eyes returned to mine, something shone in her onyx-brown irises.

Under the dim lights of the night, she sparkled amongst the other guests. She nibbled her lower lip, her cheeks flushing as I stared at her. The shy side of her appealed to me. I remembered how it was when I first started in the business and met my own idols. In that instant, some part of me yearned to protect her against the vultures of the industry. Back then, I had Riley watching over me. Having grown up with a famous father, he knew the ropes. He wasn't easily starstruck or impressionable. Tonight, Savannah looked like easy prey in a sea of experienced cutthroat sharks.

"I can empathize. I'm here because I need to be. This isn't my scene either. I'd prefer being home right now than having to smile at all these people and pretend I'm interested in this Hollywood circus."

"Right? I can totally relate." She took a sip, her eyes locked on mine. "I've never seen you around. Are you an actor?"

"No."

"Oh, are you someone else's date?"

I raked my fingers through the mass of my dark hair and sighed.

"I'm Carter Hills. It's nice to meet you." I crossed my fingers behind my back, hoping my name would ring a bell and I wouldn't have to explain myself.

Savannah's cheeks flushed. "Like *the* Carter Hills? The music superstar Carter Hills?"

A weird sound bubbled out of my mouth. "That would be me."

"It's nice to meet you. I know nothing about the music industry, but I've heard your name a lot. I know you're a big shot on the country music scene."

I forced a smile.

I hated fame.

And the recognition.

That had always been awkward.

"So why are you here, Mr. Hills? Why did you agree to suffer through this night?"

"Carter, please. No Mr. Hills. I'm not old enough for that." The flush on Savannah's face darkened. "One of my songs is featured on the soundtrack, so this is a requirement of the job."

Her eyes rounded. I shrugged. It wasn't a big deal for me.

Savannah folded her arms across her chest, pushing her tits up, and I struggled not to look at them. Was she doing this on purpose? I swallowed hard and brought my attention back to her face. My stare lingered a few seconds on her plump red lips, looking too perfect to be real. Right now, I didn't care, though. I'd pay a lot of money to have them wrapped around me.

As if he'd read my mind, my dick twitched in my pants.

Easy, boy.

"I'm out of here. Do you want to grab a bite or something? I ate nothing since I got here, and now I'm starving." Her stomach grumbled as if on cue.

"A midnight snack sounds awesome." I chugged the rest of my water and dropped the now-empty glass on the small table between us.

Savannah Prince and I exchanged a smile, and once again, her lips drew me in. They were like a poison apple. Forbidden, but oh so tempting.

"After you," I said as my hand rested on her lower back. "If you like Mediterranean, I know just the place a few blocks from here that's open round the clock."

"You come to New York City a lot?" she asked, getting in step with me.

"Not as often as I'd like. But from years of traveling the globe, I've made it my mission to find the best spots in every major city to get food at any time of the day. And night. Places where tourists don't go, so I can keep a low profile and eat in peace."

Taylor, my security detail, stayed close to us, but far enough to allow us some privacy.

"It's my first time in New York. I'm from Los Angeles. Born and raised there. I'm a sucker for the California weather. Not sure I'd survive the winter here." Savannah let out a warm chuckle that rippled through me. "What about you?"

"Born and raised in Tennessee. I like my four seasons and enjoy a little snow on occasion. And I prefer the mountains to the city anytime. How's the movie career going so far?"

She snaked her arm around mine, and something vibrated inside me."I've been offered an audition for the leading role in Wesley's next blockbuster, but I'm going up against actresses with years of experience. One of them even won an Oscar two years ago. I guess we'll see. It's scary to be the newcomer. I can sense all of them judging me because I have no credits so far to back up my talent. A couple of people refused to even acknowledge my presence tonight. They acted as if I weren't even there."

"Yeah, you'll meet all kinds of people. The trick is to grow a thick skin. I'm not saying it's an easy process, but it gets better and easier with time." We arrived at the little joint in the basement of a gray-bricked building with a yellow awning over the front door. "We're here," I announced.

"Huh, you're sure it's safe? It looks a bit…well, it looks…"

I grabbed her hand and led her down the few stairs. "C'mon, follow me. I eat here all the time."

We sat in a corner booth and ordered. The conversation flowed easily between us.

I pushed my empty bowl of lentils and chickpeas salad away, my stomach satisfied.

Savannah raised her eyes as she washed her last bite down with water. "That was pretty good."

I arched a brow at her, eyeing the half-eaten shrimp and tomato plate in front of her. "But you ate almost nothing."

"I'm not a big eater, and I never eat at this time of the night. Not sure my stomach will forgive me."

"You'll be just fine. After all, you've been starving all night, no?"

"I guess. Are you in town for a while, or are you going back home soon?"

"I'm leaving in the morning."

Savannah's lips drew into a faint curl. "I was thinking… This is awkward. I'm not ready for the night to be over just yet. It's great, for once, not to have to pretend around someone else. All night, I felt like I was playing a role. Those people expected me to be someone I'm not. To play naïve and insecure so they could feel superior. Anyway, I'm enjoying how normal I feel around you. Would you like to come to my hotel for one last drink?"

"I don't drink," I said, studying her while twirling my glass around, the ice cubes clicking together.

Her lips stretched, and she raised one perfectly shaped brow. "Not a problem. I can feed you other things." She didn't even blink when the words left her mouth.

My entire self pulsed while I pondered the offer. My dick decided on its own, not giving a fuck about my brain's reluctance, when Savannah leaned over the table, giving me a full view of her cleavage as she wrapped her hands around mine.

It'd been a while since I had slept with a random woman—one I'd met just hours before. Faced with a choice, I debated the pros and cons in my head.

Savannah was Hollywood gorgeous, and I would be stupid to refuse her invitation and walk away. Who knew? Maybe this could be the start of something good for me. Something new. Something different. The fresh lease on life I was longing for. Since Dahlia and Nick's wedding, I had time to think, and I promised myself I would take more chances, make myself available for more opportunities. It was about time I tried a new approach to love and relationships because my old ways were clearly not working. What was I risking, other than one wasted night?

"I'd like that," I agreed as I watched Taylor stand to pay the bill.

"Great. Let's go then."

We settled on the backseat of the rental Taylor drove—some luxury sedan with a privacy partition separating the back from the front. When we drove to tonight's events, I sat in the passenger seat—I hated sitting in the backseat when not required. Taylor was my friend, not just an employee. We were equals, and no matter my career choice or his, I would never behave in a way that made me seem superior to him.

Savannah dragged her long ruby fingernails across my chest, and I shivered. My dick thickened in my pants, ready to play.

"I've been dying to do this since you handed me that drink." Her lips landed on mine. Unapologetic. With force. Full of hunger and desire.

At first, I stiffened under her touch, unsure whether I should go for it or not, but when her tongue met mine, I relaxed in my seat. She unfastened the first three buttons of my white dress shirt and licked a line from my collarbones to my chin, her hands exploring my chest over the fabric.

With confidence—a contrast to the shy personality she projected all night—she lapped, kissed, and bit my flesh.

Where was the woman standing alone in her corner earlier? In front of my eyes, Savannah Prince transformed into a siren. A starving animal ready to eat me up alive.

Every inch of me loved the attention she was providing as if she could tell what I craved.

With one swift movement, I lifted her so she straddled me, her dress bunching around her thighs.

Her eyes glimmered in the low light.

This woman was ready to offer me a night of wild passion, and there was no way I'd turn her down right now. My logical thoughts had deserted me. Yeah, I could really use the distraction.

She closed a hand around my stone-hard erection, and a loud growl escaped my lips when she tightened her grip.

She stroked me over the fabric of my pants and swallowed every sound tumbling out of my mouth.

"You like that, don't you?" she teased.

I nodded, my throat working and making it difficult for me to talk.

With expert fingers, she lifted her dress higher around her hips and guided my hand between her legs. I squeezed the soft skin of her thighs, making her yelp as I kissed her, both of us fighting to get the upper hand. It was a battle. One I intended to win.

I moved my fingers north and brushed against the warm, moist flesh ready for me. Savannah wore no underwear. Had she spent her entire night going commando, or had she removed them at the restaurant? Either way, the thought of it got me harder.

I slid one finger inside her tight channel, her warm moisture coating my finger as it dived in and out of her at a fast pace. She tilted her head back and purred, and I almost came undone at the sound of her whimpers.

"God, you're so wet."

She crashed her lips on mine. "No talking, just fucking."

Fine by me.

I entered a second, then a third finger inside her and curved them just at the right angle to make her moan louder.

With my other hand, I pushed the strap of her dress down and exposed her bare chest. I grabbed a handful of one of her breasts. There was nothing natural about them, but they were still a sin, filling my palm to the brim. I leaned forward and circled one hard nipple with the tip of my tongue. Savannah writhed under my touch.

The base of my spinal cord tingled.

Something broke inside me. A restraint I'd been hesitant to let go of. Gone were my rational thoughts. Tonight was nothing like I expected it to be, and for once, I would act instead of battling with my reasons for ways to remove myself from a situation I hadn't planned. From my jacket inner pocket, I fished out my wallet and grabbed one of the condoms I kept in there.

"You want to get fucked? Then shut your mouth and spread your legs."

Savannah's lips stretched into a diabolical tilt.

Something dark shone in her eyes as she released me from the tightness of my pants.

Once I suited my dick up, I rammed into her from beneath, my hold on her hips firm and bruising.

The whole alphabet of sounds escaped her plump red lips. "Harder," she demanded as I plunged in and out of her with punishing strokes.

The car stopped, and we both stared at each other, breathless. Was my face as flushed as hers? For once, I was glad I hadn't shaved my short stubble tonight and hoped it could provide some cover to my blazing cheeks.

I exhaled. "We better finish this upstairs."

Savannah nodded as she pushed her sinful tits back inside her tight dress.

Now that I knew how they looked, tasted, and felt, I craved them all the more.

I couldn't wait to drown myself in her mass of flesh and enjoy her body for the rest of the night.

I removed the condom and stashed it in my pocket. After I promised Taylor to call him later so he could come get me, I got down from the car and followed Savannah inside.

With our hands unable to let go of each other and our tongues entangled in a dirty tango, we made it to the room.

I'd fucked my share of women since Carter Hills Band got signed, released its first single, and soared to stardom when I was eighteen, but I'd never kissed a woman like this before. It was like she could swallow my tongue as she ravaged my mouth.

Would she feel just as good around my cock?

This wasn't love or any other shit we saw in movies. This was pure, wicked lust.

The door to the room wasn't even shut and Savannah

was on her knees, freeing my cock and engulfing its length in her mouth. Every inch of it. The tip pushed against the back of her throat with every thrust of my hips.

I fisted her hair, setting the pace.

She sucked me, moaning and begging for more.

Sex had never felt this bestial before. We were two animals in heat, in search of wild and untamed pleasure.

When I tried to pull out, not wanting to come inside her mouth, she pinched my ass cheeks and drew me in deeper. I wanted to last longer. To fuck her properly. To have her orgasm around my fingers. And my dick.

With both hands on her shoulders, I pushed her backward. "I won't last. God. Shit, if you don't slow down, I won't be able to—" A groan left my mouth as I tilted my head back, closing my eyes, trying to avoid coming down her throat.

When I reopened them, our gazes met, and she winked —*she fucking winked*—and increased the pace.

I was a goner. Nothing I could do would stop me from exploding inside her greedy mouth.

Another groan tumbled out as I came.

I tried to step back, but Savannah tightened her grip on my still-hardened length.

Her tongue swirled around the tip, cleaning every last drop of cum.

I blinked.

And swallowed hard.

Was she for real?

"You better recharge quick because now I want to be fucked in every possible position," she challenged as she rose to her feet. She undressed slowly, in front of me, swaying her hips, her wrinkled dress billowing on the floor and her giant boobs hanging free over her chest.

She turned and leaned over—her ass on display—and fished something out of her suitcase.

When she spun around, mischievous sparks danced in her smoldering stare while she held a blue vibrator in her hand.

Without breaking eye contact, she kneeled on the mattress, spread her legs, and inserted the silicon length inside her, inch by inch, strings of whimpers passing her lips as she did so.

At the push of a button, a soft vibrating sound filled the silence.

She lay on her back, her tongue peeking out of her filthy mouth, her gaze fixed on me, lust flowing from her hooded lids.

Like a fool, I stood there, unable to move.

Bewildered.

My heart raced at the sight she made, legs spread, pleasuring herself.

Was I dreaming? I had to be. With a shake of my head, I tried to rouse myself from my dream, but in vain. This was happening. For real.

Savannah glided the sex toy in and out of her at a slow pace, moaning louder every time she rammed it in.

"Carter, you want to help me out, or you prefer to watch?"

I said nothing because right now, I couldn't decide.

All the blood pooled back between my legs, and my cock sprang wood, hard as a flagpole.

It took me half a second to decide.

"I'll make you come with your little friend, then I'll make you come again with mine. You better not be tired because we'll be at it until I say it's over."

Savannah was dangerous. I saw the greed in her eyes. But I was also drawn to her. Like a moth to the flame.

Her contradictory attitude screamed at me to stay away. The voices in my head told me to run as fast as I could and never look back. That this could be dangerous. Feral. And I would regret it later. She could ruin me.

But I decided to ignore the warning signs. The voices of reason.

To just live, for once, without overthinking everything. To let go of the past and move forward.

Blank slate.

New beginning, Carter. New beginning, I repeated in my head.

All things considered, maybe I needed a little danger in my life. Something new and exciting. Something I had no control over. Something to make me forget about all the things I'd lost over the years. My parents. My unrequited love. My band. My brother.

I had to start living for myself. To chase my own destiny.

And make things happen.

All logical thoughts left my mind when I leaned over her, kissing the shit out of the woman who had the power to ruin me.

Pleasure alone ruled my body.

Savannah brought my hand over hers, and we both maneuvered the vibrator until her body went rigid and her eyes rolled to the back of her head.

She screamed so loud when she came that I knew, without a doubt, the entire floor heard her.

My cock throbbed against my lower belly, ready to play, desperate for attention.

I rolled a condom over, flipped Savannah around, positioning her on all fours. With one push, I entered her from behind and pounded into her with complete abandon. My balls grew sensitive, and a sheen of sweat covered my back.

Tremors shook her body as I fucked her until all the angst polluting my life vanished. Until all my thoughts deserted me and I felt lighter than I'd been in years. She met me thrust for thrust, her fingernails leaving imprints on my thighs. Using her finger, she rubbed the mound between her legs, clenching so hard around me when she came that she milked my cock.

Later, when I left her room, spent but energized at the same time, my lips were permanently bent into a tiny curl lifting their corners.

The next morning, in my own hotel suite, after a two-hour nap, I gathered my stuff, ready to board the private jet flying me back to Tennessee. Taking me back home.

The images of the previous night swam in my head, leaving me with a permanent erection.

I had a show scheduled in Las Vegas next month, and right now, the thought of making a detour to Los Angeles while I was there seemed like the perfect idea.

A cocky, smug grin stretched my lips. Yeah, I needed another night with Savannah Prince.

To fuck the first one out of my system.

Because I wouldn't be able to think about anything else until I got a do-over.

That I knew for sure.

I had played with fire, and now I yearned for the burn.

Chapter 10
Carter

For almost two hours, I rocked the stage of the Pelican, the casino I was playing at tonight. Over forty-thousand people were singing along with me as I strummed the last verse of "Don't Ask Me," the song I wrote for Dahlia when we were twenty and the lines of our relationship got blurry for a moment. One night, when I felt vulnerable, I played it for her, hoping she would understand the extent of my feelings better through music. We had a long talk afterward, but it didn't change the status of our relationship. Just like the one I wrote when we were fifteen and I had planned to lay my heart bare to her. I had no intention of recording the song, but she convinced me it had to be on my first solo album. And that year, it won the *Best Country Song of The Year* award at a prestigious music ceremony.

The crowd was screaming, chanting, on their feet, waving their arms in the air.

With a slow perusal, I tried to burn the sight and feeling into my memory. To anchor it to my heart.

The song ended, and I wiped the sweat pearling on my forehead with the crook of my arm. "You guys want another encore?" I asked, breathless, but unable to tame my grin.

The energy tonight was contagious. Electric.

I pivoted to face my musicians, and they all nodded. This song wasn't planned, but sue me, I couldn't walk offstage right now. I was exhausted—in the best possible way—but no matter what, like a drug shot straight into my veins, I craved more.

I strummed the opening chords of "Forever," and my musicians joined me on the first chorus. And so did the crowd, singing along.

My lips stretched wider. *This.* This was the definition of perfect.

"You guys have been incredible." I waved a hand above my head. "Good night, Las Vegas."

The enthusiastic cheers and applauses filled me with renewed energy. I ran off the stage, clapping hands with Taylor and my musicians.

Once they all dispersed, I focused my attention on my head of security. "Did you find what I requested?"

A single nod. "Yes. And I arranged for you two to meet tomorrow. Anything else?"

I shook my head, a foreign feeling zipping through me. "Nope. That's all. Thanks again. I'll shower and change and meet you in thirty."

He walked me to the green room. "I'll be right outside the door," he said, adjusting his earpiece. I had an entire security detail dedicated to me every time I gave a concert, all under Taylor's orders. "You have that TV appearance tomorrow morning at nine, then we'll drive to California. Unless you prefer I book us a flight."

"Nah. Driving is fine. It will give us more time to catch up. Any news from Ry?"

"No, but June called mid-show. She booked you two engagements for when you are in LA. She'll send the details in the morning. Riley will be in touch around noon to discuss some additional concert dates with you."

"Thanks."

Twenty minutes later, the adrenaline of the night slowly receded as I slipped into a pair of sweatpants and a hoodie. Any other day, I would seize the opportunity to enjoy Las Vegas and its night life—my musicians had plans for the rest of the night and asked me to join them—but I just wanted some time to relax on my own. Big concerts meant tons of people surrounding me. Tons of prep. Zero time for myself. And I found it tiring. Sometimes, I wished I could do smaller venues. I loved the music, the performance, the thrill that came with it. I was addicted to it. But I hated the fame that accompanied it. The press trying to snap pictures of me or my family, the gossip, the unwarranted pressure it added to my existence.

Every time I stopped and thought about it, my insides coiled, and my breaths picked up.

Taylor and I entered my suite. A symbol of the Las Vegas extravaganza. So far from the man I was and the things I cared about. I would have been satisfied with a regular room with two queen-size beds. Instead, this one had a high ceiling—at least ten feet—golden trims, and what appeared to be expensive pieces of art hanging on the walls and spread all over the place on coffee and side tables. A black-and-gold, cheetah-patterned rug covered the dark marble floor. It was exuberant and not even tasteful in my opinion. Like they tried to overdo the decor, thinking it would impress people. Well, it didn't impress me. This cacophony of patterns and colors even increased my uneasiness. As I scanned the area around me, it suddenly hit me. I bet June did this on purpose. She knew I was a simple guy, and I could picture Riley and her making bets and trying to find the worst room for me to sleep in, just to get a rise out of me. With a shake of my head and a tired curl of my lips, I kicked my shoes off and turned to face Taylor still beside me, taking in every detail of this decor the same way I did. A small smile peeked through his otherwise collected composure.

"Don't say it, man," I said, nudging his side. "I'm sure it was meant as a joke. No way would June book this room on purpose unless it was to mess with me."

His unruffled facade broke, and a warm laugh left him. "I was thinking the same thing. Think it was a bet? Or a test?"

I shrugged. "No idea, but it's hideous."

"Well, you're the one spending the night here. And footing the bill."

"Don't speak so fast. Perhaps she's subjecting you to the same treatment."

His humor dissolved.

"Anyway, wanna go for a run with me? I can't stay here unless I'm so exhausted I'll go straight to bed."

My friend looked at me with a quizzical expression that quickly transformed into worry. "You still got energy after that show? You really wanna escape this room, or is it one of your episodes?"

I sighed. "Other than this hideous piece of museum exhibition"—I waved an arm around me—"my mind is restless. Before it turns into a panic attack, I better get the angst out. Will you be able to follow me?" I teased. Taylor was an ex-secret service agent. If someone could outrun me, it was him. "Or is it too late for your old self to keep up?" He was only a few years older than me.

"Better tie your sneakers tight enough, man." His face lit up at the challenge. "We'll see who puts who to bed first tonight."

I extended my arm to shake his proffered hand. "Deal. You should know by now when panic invades my thoughts, I'm unstoppable for hours."

"Well, you just performed for two hours. I might win this time."

He left to get ready while I changed into my running gear and a baseball cap. I pulled the hood of my light-gray sweater over it, praying the disguise would be inconspicuous at this late hour with the partygoers and tourists still filling the busy sidewalks.

———

Taylor parked the car in the back alley and escorted me inside through the rear door. Since we were in Los Angeles and not Nashville, my security had to be reevaluated. Here, there were paparazzi camped in front of every popular venue and famous restaurant on the lookout for the next compromising picture they would be able to sell to make a name for themselves. I had no interest in playing a part in this celebrity scheme. First, I never considered myself to be a person of interest and had no clue why those photographers took pleasure in catching sight of me. Second, all this appeared like a game, and I wasn't in the mood to play. I much preferred my privacy to any unwanted scrutiny.

My bodyguard exchanged a few words with a man, and seconds later, I was led to a table in the far corner at the back, away from most of the patrons. The small Italian eatery had a burgundy carpeted floor, dark wooden walls, and wrought-iron chandeliers over each table. It didn't have the slick straight lines of modern decors or an abundance of frigid stainless steel and white marble surfaces. Instead, it was both warm and welcoming, with its wood-fired oven embedded into an extensive red bricked-wall.

My mouth watered at the scent of garlic and fresh bread filling the air.

Back in my band days, we would have dinner here every time we were in town. The food was chef's kiss, the service top-notch, and the atmosphere convivial.

"How is it going, Mr. Hills?" Roberto, the owner, welcomed me.

"Amazing. Thank you for having me on such short notice."

"It's always my pleasure to have you over. Let me know if you need anything. Have a great night."

We shook hands, and after Taylor sat at the table reserved for him, I walked to Savannah Prince, dressed in red leather pants and a white blouse, waiting for me. Her dark brown hair fell in soft waves over her shoulders, and her onyx eyes were framed by thick mascara-coated lashes.

My memory of our time together didn't fail me. She was still gorgeous, her lips enticing when they shaped into a smile directed at me.

"Carter," she exclaimed, moving to her feet so I could kiss her cheek.

"You look beautiful." I pushed her chair forward when she sat back before sitting across from her. The server filled our glasses of water, promising to come back soon to take our order.

"I must say, when I arrived, I thought I'd gotten the wrong address." She perused the room. "That it was a mistake… I didn't picture a date in such…such a rustic environment. Then I remembered you were from Tennessee and maybe you're used to these outdated decors." She shrugged and brought her glass to her lips.

"You've never been here before?" I asked.

Savannah shook her head. "No. I didn't even know it existed ten minutes ago."

"I'm aware Bellagio doesn't give the trendy Los Angeles vibe, but I swear the menu is exquisite." I searched her eyes. "Do you trust me?"

She bit her lower lip before saying, "Yes."

A warm feeling spread through me. Right now, Savannah resembled the woman I met at the movie premiere in New York more than the temptress she turned into in her hotel room later that night. Studying her folding and unfolding the cloth napkin on the table, looking nervous, I had a hard time believing these two women lived in the same body. Once again, I felt protective of her. She would get eaten up by the big bad wolves of Hollywood in one bite if she didn't improve the confidence she projected.

"How was your show last night?" she asked after I ordered a bottle of red and the server poured her a glass while I stuck to water on the rocks.

"Awesome. The energy was unbelievable. I could have sung all night. It was really something. What about you? Any news from Wesley about that leading role?"

She huffed and dropped her shoulders. "Not yet. My agent talked to him two days ago, but he's still auditioning. All this waiting gives me anxiety. His financing got delayed which means filming won't start anytime soon."

Fragility filled her eyes.

"I'm a pro at dealing with anxiety. You're lucky. I can teach you a few tricks."

She sipped her wine, her eyes rounding at my words. "You can?"

"Yeah. There are a lot of things you can try. Trust me, I've given all of them a shot. One day, you'll find what works best for you. For me, it's controlled breathing and an extreme amount of exercise."

"What do you mean?"

"My brother passed away a few years ago——"

"I'm sorry." She covered my hand with hers, squeezing it in a comforting gesture.

"Thank you. Well, as I was saying, I've been dealing with panic attacks since then. Nights and days. But lately, they only make an appearance during my waking hours. When it gets too much and I feel like I'm losing control, usually, I breathe in and out a few times, and it helps. And when my mind gets restless and breathing is not enough, then I run. For hours. Or lift weights. Until my body gets tired and my mind forfeits the game too. It's not the best coping mechanism, but it's my way. I'm trying to grow out of it. To control myself through breathing exercises only. Next time you feel overwhelmed, give it a try. I'm telling you they work wonders sometimes."

"I will. Thanks. For sharing your struggles with me."

"Anytime. I'm happy if my experience can help other people. Ready to order?"

"Yes, I'm starving."

I nodded to the server waiting for us in a corner, and he neared us, a pad in hand.

Just as it did the night we met, conversation flowed easily between Savannah and me. She told me about her last audition and her first TV interview while I shared news about my upcoming shows.

The sound of her fork hitting the porcelain plate hard had me looking up. Savanna's complexion had become white if she'd seen a ghost, eyes wide and lips trembling, and she looked downward, hiding the side of her face with the napkin.

I leaned forward and touched her hand. "Hey, what's wrong? Did something happen?"

She cocked her face to the side, her eyes unsure as they locked on mine. She swallowed before speaking in a low voice, "I think it's him."

"Who?"

She jerked her head toward a group of middle-aged men in suits, sitting at a table, far enough not to be able to eavesdrop on our conversation.

"Who's *him*?"

"Jerry," she whispered.

"Who's Jerry?"

My gaze ping-ponged between the men and my date. Knots tied my stomach as Savannah blanched a little more. Then my uneasiness transformed into simmering fury. My hands clenched until my knuckles turned white. "Start talking," I urged her. "Who the fuck is Jerry, and what did he ever do to you?"

Keeping the napkin as a wall, blocking everyone in the restaurant from looking at her profile, Savannah whispered, a haunted look taking over her eyes, "My mom's boyfriend."

I risked another glance toward the far table. "Which one is he?"

"I'm not looking. If he sees me… Ohmygod, I prefer not to think about it."

I squeezed her hand. "One look. If it's him, we're leaving, and you won't have to face him if you don't want to. I have security." I pointed in Taylor's direction with my chin. "He won't bother you."

She lowered the napkin and peeked at the four men laughing.

Her shoulders sagged. Color returned to her cheeks.

"It's not him. I-I thought… I'm so sorry. You must think I'm crazy." She buried her face in her hands. "I must look stupid right now. I'm sorry, Carter. This is so embarrassing."

"Savannah, talk to me."

She lowered her hands. Her eyes shimmered with unshed tears.

I grabbed her hand again, drawing circles with my thumb over her flesh. "Don't lock it all in. What did Jerry do to you?"

"He… I can't even say it out loud…without…those memories… I'm-I'm sorry, Carter. I…oh gosh…I can't do this now. It's asking too much from me. For the last four years, I-I've been trying to leave the past behind. I hope you can forgive me. Maybe some other time, okay? When I…huh…don't feel so helpless and scared."

"Sure. I won't ever push you to talk about your past. Over the years, I've been through some hardships myself. I know how difficult it can get to open up. And to heal."

Her lips tilted into a tentative smile. "Thank you. For being so understanding. And I'm…well, I'm sorry you had it rough. One day, we'll share the awful stories of our past. But not today, okay?" She pushed her untouched dinner aside.

With her shoulders slouched forward and a sad expression straining her face, Savannah looked fragile. And vulnerable.

The caring side of me, the one that always made an appearance for the people I loved, kicked in. Right now, all I wanted to do was hold her against me and heal whatever wounds the memories of her step-dad brought up.

"Wanna get out of here?" I asked.

Savannah bobbed her head without another word. She used her fingertips to erase the remaining trace of the tears that had built up in her eyes. "Thank you."

Taylor led us outside through the rear door and back to his rental.

"The evening is still young. Want me to drop you at your place, or do you want to go somewhere else?"

Her words sounded weak as they passed the rim of her red-painted lips. "I'd like to go home. If it's okay with you."

With her hand nestled in mine and her head pressing against my shoulder, we remained silent as Taylor weaved through the ever-present traffic of Los Angeles. A comfortable silence enveloped us.

Taylor parked the rental, and I exited, holding my hand out for Savannah to follow suit. "I'll be right back," I told my bodyguard before shutting the door behind us.

Savannah watched me, with confusion painting her features. "Carter, this is not how I envisioned our evening together." Her lips shook. "I'm usually not easily disturbed. It won't happen again…if you deign to give me another chance. I was so excited when I got the call inviting me to join you tonight."

The part of me that had suffered many forms of abandonment growing up related to her words. I'd been that guy. Lost and confused. A train wreck. And I had people who loved me enough to give me another chance. To help me stand up for myself and who cheered me on no matter how wrong I was.

With the tips of my fingers, I tucked a lock of her hair behind her ear. "Hey, I'm the one person who'll never judge you. As I told you earlier, I've been through a lot, so I get it. Sometimes, little details can trigger past pain. It gets better. With time. I know it sounds cliché, but that's the truth. We can talk and find another day to get together." I scavenged from the depth of me the courage to say these words out loud. They were foreign to me. I had never felt this close to a woman who wasn't Dahlia before. "I'd like for us to get to know each other better. If that's what you desire too."

I stood there, rocking on my heels, waiting for Savannah to agree—or not.

Her lips curled up. "I'd like that too. There's something about you, Carter. Like you can understand me. We barely know each other, but I just… You'll think it's stupid."

"Say it." I watched her lips, waiting for the words about to leave them.

"I feel a connection. I've never felt this comfortable around someone in a long time. Please don't lose hope in me, okay?"

My lips descended on hers, soft and warm. "I won't. You have my number now. Feel free to call or text whenever you want, okay?"

She nodded. "Do you maybe…I mean…do you wanna stay over tonight? I don't wanna be alone."

I closed my eyes for a long second, trying to think about my engagements over the next few days. Savannah watched me with expectation. Even if I tried, I couldn't refuse her. She looked so broken and afraid right now.

I had people to catch me when I tumbled down in my life. For all I knew, she had no one.

I opened my eyes. "Sure. Let me talk to Taylor. I'll be right back."

She intertwined her fingers with mine. "Thank you, Carter. You're a good man. I can already tell."

From the entryway, Savannah watched as I hurried back to the car.

Minutes later, I was climbing the flight of stairs to Savannah's apartment on the fifth floor, her hand nestled in mine.

"I wish I could afford a place with an elevator," she said once we reached the landing. "This is home. It's not big by any means, but it's the first place I could afford by myself." She unlocked the door and stepped aside, making room for me.

The entryway had only a couple of hooks on the wall behind the door and a floating shelf under a white-framed mirror. A corridor on our right led to what I assumed were the bedroom and bathroom. Open floor space with a living room and a kitchen doubling as a dining room, the apartment was small but looked inviting. White walls, stainless steel, and red accents. By now, I could tell red was Savannah Prince's color of choice. From her lipstick to her wardrobe and the pillows on her white couch.

"This is lovely," I said.

Savannah backhanded my chest. "Stop it. I'm sure you're used to the rich and famous lifestyle."

I pushed my hands into my pockets. "Well, contrary to what you might think, I much prefer simple things to over-the-top whatever. Restaurants. Apartments. Hotel suites. Clothing. I'm a small-town guy at heart and will always be. I don't need fancy shit to feel fulfilled or happy."

"It's refreshing to listen to you. Want some tea? I must have a few varieties somewhere."

"Sure. Need any help?"

"Nah." She pointed to the couch on her way to the kitchen, leaving me alone in the living room. "Make yourself comfortable. I'll be with you in a minute."

I studied the picture frames hung on the wall next to the large window offering a view of another building and the busy street below. All the shots of Savannah had been taken over the last couple of years. In a tiny string bikini on a beach. In gorgeous gowns at what looked like movie premieres. Riding a horse. No one else was featured in any of the shots. From what I could tell, I wasn't the only one not close to his parents. In my penthouse in Nashville and my cabin in Green Mountain, I had pictures of the shows I'd given in the past, Dahlia and Jack, Jeff, my friends back in White Crest, Riley and me at one of the fundraisers we went to, Stud and his family. Platinum albums and the tickets to the first concert I ever gave, framed. It was a mix of everyone important in my life. People I cared about. Events and relationships that shaped me into the person I was today.

I felt sad for Savannah as I realized she was all alone in this world, or appeared to be. I wanted to ask about her family, but after her panic episode earlier at dinner, I refused to open that can of worms tonight.

She joined me and wrapped her arms around my middle from behind, her chin resting in the crook of my neck. "See that picture of me there? When I was a teenager, I went to an all-girls private school and used to compete in equestrian competitions. I had a bad fall, dislocated my shoulder, and had to stop. His name was Savane. It means Savannah in French. We were best friends."

I turned until we faced each other and combed her hair back. "I'm sorry you had to give it up."

She shrugged. "Well, it's okay. It's in the past anyway." She detached from me and grabbed the steaming mugs of tea she had set on the coffee table and handed me one. We drank in silence as I pulled her against me and kissed her forehead before we sat side by side on the white leather couch, my arm around her shoulders, holding her close.

"Thanks for dinner," Savannah said, pivoting to stare at me. "I didn't say it earlier, but I had a great time before the incident." She discarded her empty mug on the floor and shifted until she straddled me. I chugged the rest of my beverage, and she placed the mug next to hers on the floor. "I was thinking I could thank you the proper way."

Her eyes lit up. The corners of her lips lifted into a crooked smile.

"You don't have to," I said, my throat bobbing at the sight of the promises flashing in her eyes.

Savannah watched me like I was her next meal. Gone was the shy girl at dinner, the one who shared about her horse. Back was the woman in the hotel room in New York. The sex maniac I'd experienced for a night.

I tried to swallow, but the intensity of her gaze made the simple action harder than it should have been.

She caressed the corner of my mouth with hers, and the scent of her—that expensive fragrance I remembered pretty well—tipped all my senses.

Her voice, husky and filled with untamed lust, made every cell of my body tremble with need when she spoke. "What do you say, Carter? Want me to thank you like you deserve to be thanked?"

When I chose to come to LA tonight, it was with the intent to continue what we started in New York. To fuck Savannah Prince out of my system and move on with my life. But then I discovered a sweeter side of her that reminded me a lot of myself in many ways, and we connected on a deeper level. We shared about our lives. A bit. I told her about my anxiety episodes. And Jeff's passing. Never in the past had I been that upfront about it with a person I barely knew. Usually, I was much more discreet about my personal life. Something about Savannah's vulnerable side appealed to me. My instinct to protect kicked in with the need to shield her from a hurtful past she was trying to leave behind. I'd been that guy. If someone could understand, it was me.

Perhaps Savannah Prince didn't come into my life by accident. Perhaps we were destined to meet. I never believed in that shit before, but life was clearly sending me a signal. We were too much alike to ignore the coincidences.

When I agreed to come inside her apartment, it was because I believed she needed a friend, but now that her fingers toyed with the fly of my denims and her warm breath tickled the shell of my ear, I was starting to overthink everything.

She wrapped her hand around my hard-on, and all rational thoughts left me.

A strangled growl exited my mouth when she worked me in slow, painful strokes. A tease. Just enough to make me see stars, but not enough to get me to completion.

Her movements accelerated.

"What do you say, Carter? Wanna play with me tonight?"

I inhaled a scorching breath and pushed her hand away. "Wait. I'm here to keep you company, not to fuck you."

She pumped me faster now.

"I...I really want to be your friend tonight, Savannah."

"Well, fucking me is the best way to be my friend." She unbuttoned the front of her blouse with the fingers of her other hand, exposing her sinful cleavage covered by a lacy red bra.

My body tensed, all my senses on high alert. I couldn't think clearly anymore. Our definitions of friendship were the opposite. Making the other come wasn't how Dahlia and I had each other's backs when things got tough.

I regrouped my thoughts. "That's what you want?" I

asked, my voice cracking, my vocal cords vibrating with desire.

Savannah nodded.

The last thread of my restraints broke free. Something snapped in me, and soon Savannah was spread underneath me on the couch, the rise and fall of her chest hastening, her red lips parting, and her eyes glossy with lust.

And I lost it.

We were both panting, catching our breaths as we sat on her living room floor, our limbs entangled and our skin marked by our passion. Bites. Scratches. Stubble burns.

"It was… Oh god, it was out of this world." She looked beautiful and wild with her disheveled hair and smeared lipstick.

"Feeling better?" I asked.

She nodded fast.

I inhaled and asked the question I'd never gotten to ask. "Want me to spend the night?"

"Yes."

I scratched my nape, thinking about my next question. "Wanna cuddle?" I blew out a breath. I'd never asked a woman to cuddle before. This was all new to me and part of getting out there and giving my love life a meaning. And a real chance.

Savannah raised a perfectly shaped dark eyebrow, her eyes burrowing into mine. For a second, I believed she'd refuse, but then her mouth stretched into a smile. "I'd like to."

And just like that, I spent an entire night with a woman, but most importantly, I spent the night with a woman I barely knew nestled in my arms.

Somehow, it felt oddly familiar and comforting.

Chapter 11
Carter

"Carter, your relationship with Savannah Prince is big news out there," my new publicist Carla said, flipping her long black hair over her shoulder. Something she did quite often, and that annoyed the shit out of me. My label had hired her to deal with all the PR stuff, a new strategy they came out with to get their artists to sell more albums and increase their presence on social media.

Since the night I spent in Los Angeles over two months ago, pictures of Savannah Prince and I had been starting to pop up every time I flew to California to meet with her.

I sighed. "Well, we're getting to know each other better, and it's nobody's business. It's not a relationship yet, so stop meddling in my personal life. It has nothing to do with my career."

"We should talk about this. We could use it to propel you to stardom."

Beside me, Riley chuckled. Dickhead. He usually would give her a run for her money, but for some reason, he looked amused by the battle of wills taking place in Carla's office.

"Stardom? Are you fucking kidding me? I'm your best-selling artist. My name is a brand in itself. I'm not trying to sound arrogant or anything. If you knew me, you'd know I couldn't care less about any of this. But c'mon, stop trying to sell me something and make promises that make no sense."

Riley jumped in. "Carla, you set this meeting to talk about social media, so get to the point."

Her eyes rounded, but she quickly composed herself and schooled her features. "As I was saying, Carter's relationship could be part of the strategy. We could tip paparazzi so they would follow his whereabouts and take pictures and increase his exposure."

"Please. Stop. I'm not your media clown,'" I said. "Not doing it. Find something else, or I'm out of here. And, by the way, we're not in a relationship. Stop calling it that. We fucked on the side a few times and get along fine. Not my fault if somehow, someone followed us last weekend and snapped a few juicy pictures of us. We're two adults who are having fun. Nothing to stir anyone's attention or go crazy about."

Carla's hands hit the hard surface of her desk with a loud thud. "These weren't *just* pictures of you two, Carter. These were pictures of you two eating each other's faces in that bar."

I pressed both palms to my head, my elbows resting on my knees. Could I get the press off my back for once? My life wasn't even interesting. Why couldn't they gimme a break?

"Who cares?"

Carla fished a pile of magazines out of a drawer and dumped it on the desk before me. She showed me the covers of one, two, four of them. Then she typed something on her tablet and turned the device for me to look at the screen. One by one, she swiped images of Savannah and me. Hand in hand in a hotel lobby, smiling on the sidewalk, kissing in the shadow of a building, having coffee at the shop around the corner from her apartment. There were dozens of them.

Each one projected the image of a couple in love.

Smiles. Hand on the lower back. Kisses. More smiles. Thumb grazing cheek. Stares.

My throat worked with some uneasy feeling.

I darted my tongue out to moisten my lips.

"See what I'm telling you, Carter? You guys look perfect together. You have a chemistry people envy. I don't care if you despise each other or if she drives you nuts or can't spell her own name. The fact is the camera loves you two together. I watched your reaction. You saw it too. Don't pretend you didn't."

Why couldn't she get the memo I was not interested in her stupid idea?

"I'm not looking for attention," I said, lifting my eyes to hers. "Case closed." If needed, would I be able to stop seeing Savannah? I still had to figure out if we could be an item.

Every time we hooked up, I felt the withdrawal once we parted ways.

Like the most powerful drug, she controlled my will power with her charming mannerisms and wicked mouth. And then she'd get vulnerable, and I would drop everything to give her a tight hug and promise her everything would turn out just fine.

I was a new version of myself when I was with

Savannah Prince. One I'd never been before. One I had no idea even existed before we met.

One that let his body rule the game without analyzing anything.

Birds. Grasshoppers. Rotten tomatoes. Carla.

Fuck, I needed to think about something else, or I'd spend this meeting with a boner.

My publicist's voice acted like a cold shower, dissolving the naughty images swirling in my head. And murdered my erection.

"Are you even listening to me?" she asked, doing nothing to hide her condescending tone. She brought her attention to Riley. "How can you deal with him? He doesn't take anything I say seriously."

My manager rose to his feet. "This meeting is over. Please do yourself a favor and stop insulting my artist. I understand you're new to this job, and the label put you up to this, but you better research your subjects before throwing a bunch of insanities at us and thinking we'll agree to your gossip rag scheme. It's the first and last time you make me waste my hours, lady. Be prepared if you ever want us to meet again, or I'm charging you. By the way, Carter does come with an hourly fee I'm sure exceeds your weekly pay. He's not a pawn in your game, and neither am I. Thank you for your brilliant ideas, but we'll pass."

I forced my lips into an upward curl as I stood. "Like Ry said, we won't do business together. Find yourself another guinea pig for your social experiment."

Carla jumped to her feet. "Sit. Both of you. I'm not done with you. This meeting is only over when I say it is."

I blinked. Was she kidding?

Riley and I exchanged a glance. He was as clueless as I was about the most ridiculous proposition I'd ever heard.

We both stood our ground, not motioning to sit.

Carla's face turned bright red. "Ohmygod, why am I even bothering with you two?" She paced the room, flipping her hair again. "Why is your label paying me big money to work with you if you don't even listen to anything I suggest?"

I straightened my position and crossed my arms.

Riley said, "Carter, if you wanna stay, your call, but I'm out of here. Don't agree to anything without consulting me first." He shook his head. "This is getting more ridiculous by the minute."

I took a seat. "Let's hear what you have to say, lady." The last thing I needed was to have my label on my back. I flipped my phone over. "You have thirteen minutes to convince me your ideas are actually decent. And smart. Go on, impress me." Resting my ankle on my bent knee, I joined my hands and slouched back in my seat.

Carla went on and on about social media stats and how to reach new segments of the population with her *infallible tactics* as she called them. On her tablet screen, she displayed graphs and other data I couldn't care less about. It was a snooze fest.

Before I could hold it in, a loud yawn escaped my mouth.

"Are you for real? Carter, you allow me thirteen minutes, and you're not even paying attention." She balled her hands and murdered me with her gaze.

"Sorry, I was just distracted…by things."

"Things?"

"Yes. Things. You know, thoughts that most people process with their brains. Anyway, I'm listening now." I straightened my back and looked at my phone. "Six minutes left. Either you talk about what matters or I'm leaving. Stop showing me data, and tell me what other PR plans you have for me that don't involve tipping vultures or my dating life."

The publicist huffed an upset breath, looking defeated. "What I was saying is that"—she exhaled again and swallowed—"if you would agree to show up to a few planned dates with Savannah Prince, we could use that little stunt to our advantage."

I arched a brow as a warning she was treading a dangerous path—one I'd already refused to take.

Carla returned to full-business mode. "Carter, listen. Fundraisers, movie premieres, and other formalities. Nothing extreme. Just to create a buzz. It'll give you free publicity when your new album comes out. You don't need me to remind you how exposure is good for you. Good or bad, it gets people talking. The more they talk, the more they wanna know all about you, and the more albums and tickets to your next tour they buy. It's marketing 101, a win-win situation for all parties involved." She nodded, looking satisfied by the little speech she'd just delivered.

I blinked, not sure I heard her right. "Let's recap. You want me to be seen out and about with Savannah to sell more albums and concert tickets?" I offered her a dubious stare. "How is my love life a stepping stone to my career? Anyway, you know how much I hate having those damn paparazzi following me. Or my face plastered on every gossip trash out there. I really don't see the appeal. And I already told you I'm not doing it." I sighed. This was such a bad idea. Carla spoke nonsense. Nothing she said added up. Why would I agree to this drivel?

As if she could read my mind, she broke my train of thought once again.

"Exposure, Carter. They do it all the time in Lala land. Maybe it's about time, we Nashville people, do the same."

"Nah, Nashville is nothing like LA. We don't have

picture hunters waiting for us outside our homes or following us every time we're running errands. It's a different reality. Here, people can be."

"Still, it wouldn't hurt to take some of their ways of doing things. They're the best at this game."

I sighed. "No. Sorry, but this is not the way I roll. No games. Maybe you should call Riley back to get a reality check. I'm a regular guy and don't need the attention. I'm not a fame seeker. Truth? I despise it most of the time."

"Carter, you were the one who said you needed to step out of your comfort zone, remember?"

"So? Doesn't mean I want the press following my ass."

Carla moved to her feet, rounded her desk, and sat on the edge facing me. "Your label convinced you to trust me because they want to increase your street notoriety… project you differently. A grown-up version of the boy you were when you first started in the business. It's time to try something new. Like you mentioned, Carter, your name is a brand. And we need to surf on it. Pairing you with an actress on the rise is a great way to do so. She'll attract younger fans. People love celebrities in steady relationships."

"I'm no celebrity."

"Yeah, yeah, keep feeding yourself that bullshit." She paused and stared at me for a long moment.

I grabbed my phone. "Our time is up." I stood up, ready to get out of there.

Carla watched me with a frown. "Think about everything I said. We can schedule another meeting if you change your mind. Trust me, I have your best interests at heart."

"Carla, you're wasting your time." With three strides, I reached the door.

"We'll see" were the last words I heard before closing the glass panel behind me.

Chapter 12

Savannah

When I left the studio, I had five notifications on my phone screen. Two from my agent, one from an unknown number that I deleted without even looking at it, scared it could be another one of my mother's attempts to reach me, and two from Carter.

My lips stretched into a smile when I saw the last two.

We'd been seeing each other for almost four months now, and things were going great. I could tell he was starting to get attached. Every other week, he'd fly to Los Angeles to spend the weekend together.

I climbed into my car, put my sunglasses on, and ignored the wave from the security guard when I exited the parking lot. Last month, I got a small recurring role on a sitcom. My contract stated a total of six episodes, but my agent confirmed that if the producer and the public liked me enough, it could be extended, and I could be added to the regular cast next season. It wasn't a super dramatic role showcasing my full range as an actress, but it was getting my name out there.

Gridlocked on the highway during rush hour, I fixed my lipstick while I dialed Carter.

"Hey you," he greeted me, the low timber of his voice spreading goose bumps along my arms.

"Miss me?"

"How was your day? Did you get any hints they're adding episodes to your contract yet?"

I sighed. "Nah. I should know the decision by Friday. Are you still coming this weekend? We could celebrate if I get the role."

"About that. I gotta go to Atlanta for a day to check out a venue with Riley, and I'll be in Green Mountain for a day or two afterward. Instead of Friday night, I might fly in on Saturday morning."

My lips shaped into a pout. "I was looking forward to having you all to myself for two nights. You could skip Green Mountain and fly from Atlanta, no?"

Carter cleared his throat. "You know Jack and Dahlia are my family. I haven't seen them in three weeks. It's a long time apart for us. I'm sure you can understand that. Jack is a toddler. He doesn't comprehend why I'm always leaving. It's hard on both of us."

I honked at the car slipping in front of mine, trying to shake off the irritation diffusing through me. I used my most innocent voice when I added, "I don't get it. Jack has a dad now. He doesn't need you as much. After all, you're just his uncle, no? I'm not sure it's healthy for you to live in the past. Dahlia has moved on. You should give her some air. And space. Your relationship is not normal. No doubt it confuses the poor boy."

I honked again. Because it helped me relax after a long

day on set. Over time, I'd convince the studio to provide a chauffeur, letting me relax in the backseat in the mornings and after long, draining hours of work.

Carter remained silent for a beat. I knew my honesty would hit a raw nerve, but the truth had to be said, and I wouldn't pretend otherwise for his sake.

"Savannah, I thought you understood. You were the one who said it was hard growing up with divorced parents and a step-dad. All Jack has ever known is me and Dahlia. Nick is still new in the equation. No matter what everyone says, I'll always consider him mine somehow. He's my blood, my family. I'll never make him feel like a burden."

Carter's words were clipped. He was mad, and I had to ease the tension between us. And fast. Long-distance relationships were hard. If we both put in the effort, we'd both win in the end. And the truth was that I never lost. Losing wasn't even part of my vocabulary.

"The last thing I want is to upset you. I just miss you so much when you're away. It's hard for me to share you with some other woman when I only see you twice a month. Maybe you could make it up to me when you get here." I let the words hang between us.

The silence stretched for an infinite minute.

"I'll see what I can do," Carter said.

"If you play nice and surprise me, I've got a few tricks of my own that will make you very *very* happy." My lustful tone couldn't be missed. Even over the phone. I had talent, and my seduction power was one of them. "Do we have a deal?"

Carter coughed. I could imagine him getting a boner just by the unsaid promises I spoke.

"Carter, baby, do you agree to your side of the bargain? You won't regret it. I have it all planned already."

He coughed again, his voice deeper than usual when

he answered, "Yes. I'll find a way to make it up to you. As always."

I exhaled. We were back on good terms.

"About Dahlia, I'm sorry if I sounded jealous. It's just —" My lips shuddered, and I lowered my voice. "It's hard for me to compete with her. She's like the most important woman in your life, and I wanna be this woman. I wanna become the center of your universe, the one you would kill for. Maybe I don't show it and look confident, but underneath, I'm afraid I'll get hurt. It's hard for me to measure up to your childhood crush." Tear leaked from my eyes, and I sniffed while wiping them off with a finger. "I didn't mean to have a breakdown. It's just… Sometimes, I-I feel like the second best, and it makes me insecure." I sniffled again. "I…I hadn't planned to tell you all this. Even less over the phone. I'm sorry for putting pressure on you... It wasn't my goal."

Carter's voice soothed me, even from two thousand miles apart. "Hey, hey, don't be envious of Dahlia. Yes, she and Jack will always be my family. They won't go away, but they also have their own family now. I agree it can be hard for someone new to fit in, but don't worry, there's a place for both of you in my life. It will never be one or the other. And Dahlia is happily married. We're not together, and we'll never be. Right now, I'm dedicated to you. That's why I fly to see you every two weeks and fit my schedule around us. Don't worry, okay? I'm serious about this relationship, or I wouldn't come to see you next weekend."

I sighed loudly. "Okay." My voice was still quivering, but the tears had disappeared. "Thanks, Carter. I might freak out about it again someday, but I get what you're saying. I'm not sure I will ever truly understand your dynamics, but I'm willing to try."

"That's all I'm asking." A pause. "Can I call you back?

Addison is here to look over the new merch designs and my next album cover."

"Addison who?" A chill worked through me. How many girlfriends did Carter Hills actually have? I was stuck here in LA traffic, while he was inviting women over. He was lucky I trusted him because I could get really angry right now. I tightened my grip around the steering wheel and forced my wrath to stay put.

"Addison, my childhood friend. Remember? Her twin brother and I were best friends growing up."

"Why can't you meet at her workplace then if it's a business meeting?"

"She's in Nashville. I'm in Nashville. She's in a serious relationship. I am too. We both have crazy schedules. We're just gonna go over the latest designs, grab a bite, and that's it. Don't make a big deal out of it."

I said nothing, not sure how to tread the situation without sounding jealous and possessive.

"Are we good?"

I blew out a long breath, locking my uneasiness away. "Sure. Call me when you're done. I love it when you wish me good night before I go to bed."

Carter's smile could be heard in his voice. "I will. Talk later."

On Saturday morning, I woke up in rumpled clothes, dried mascara streaks down my cheeks, my hair in a messy nest at the top of my head, and my eyes swollen and red. Yeah, I just passed a mirror and scared my own self.

The doorbell rang, and I buzzed my guest in. When Carter knocked on the door, I yanked it open before jumping into his arms without a word. The flood started over, blurring my vision.

"Hey, what happened?" He hugged me against his muscular chest, his strong arms feeling like a shield around my body. "Shhh. I'm here. What's going on?"

I hiccupped, unable to form coherent sentences. "I-they… We didn't… He said that I was…not-not working —" Another hiccup.

Carter led me inside, dropped his bag on the floor, and kicked the door shut before framing my face and pulling away from me to study my features. "Talk to me. In English, this time. I heard nothing you just said."

I took a deep inhale. "I-I didn't get the part. They said…they said they were bringing in a new writer for next season and that my character didn't suit the direction the show was heading, so they let me go. Next week is my last week on set. I-I really thought I would get it. My agent said it was a done deal. They…they all lied to me."

"It sounds like a bullshit excuse to me. Do you know why they changed their minds?"

I shrugged. Then nibbled the side of my thumbnail. It was a bad idea. I would ruin my manicure. "Maybe… It's just a supposition, but the director invited me to his trailer on Thursday. It-it looked suspicious…and creepy as fuck. I pretended I had somewhere else to be. He said, 'You know how Hollywood works, Savannah, right? For your own sake, I hope you're not making a huge mistake.' Then he left and went to get Lydia. Lydia is an…huh…extra. She… she was happy to follow him. Do you think…do you think I ruined my own career?"

Carter blinked, a red flush creeping across his face. His whole demeanor steeled, and he took a step back. "Are you fucking kidding me right now?"

I shook my head, using a tissue to dab under my eyes. "Why?"

He blinked again. "This is harassment, Savannah. The guy is a sick psycho. Imagine what he would have asked of you if you had gone with him. Who knows how it would have turned out? Fuck. You don't need that motherfucker around you. He's a creep. Can you imagine how many women may have fallen for his pretenses over the years?" He drew me against him and kissed the crown of my head. "Want me to pay him a visit? Or ask Taylor to show up on his doorstep?"

I shook my head. "No. News travels fast in Hollywood. The last thing I need is to make a bad name for myself so soon. Let it go. In a week, it will all be history. No need to panic. He won't be the first man to proposition me. I better get used to this kind of behavior."

"Still, it should never happen. I'm so glad you refused to go with him. You're better off without that job. I would go crazy if you were still on that set for more than a week."

"But…I need the job…and the money. My savings won't last long if I'm jobless. I have two ad campaigns to shoot by the end of the month, but other than that, there's nothing coming up until Wesley decides whether he's giving me that part or not. I don't wanna end up waiting tables for a living. I have bigger ambitions than that. I'm worth much more than a low-wage job for the rest of my life."

"You'll find something else. Something fitting. You said yourself that playing a brainless high school girl wasn't helping you show the range of your acting skills." Carter stepped back to glue his eyes to mine. Assertive and unflinching. "Don't worry about the money, okay? We'll find a way to make it work."

I nodded. "Thanks. I'm so glad you're here. It makes everything better."

"It's Saturday morning, and it's a sunny day. Let's go to the beach. I have a surprise for you later. We'll get dressed up and hit the town. What do you say?"

With a shake of my head, I refused. "I'm a hot mess. No way am I going out like this. What if someone recognized me? I would die if they got a shot of me in this state."

"Sunglasses and a hat. Nobody will bother you. I swear. And Ed, he's my bodyguard when Taylor is unavailable, will shadow us. Nothing to worry about. Do you trust me?"

I nodded again.

"Then let's get ready. First, take a shower to wash the mess off your face, then we'll grab breakfast on our way to Laguna Beach. It's a longer drive, but I heard it's worth the detour."

I huffed and finally agreed. "Okay. Let's do this." My happiness returned. "Wait until you see that bikini I got. I bought it thinking of you. I bet you'll have a *hard* time resisting me when you see me wearing it."

Carter leaned forward and kissed my forehead. "Can't wait."

Before I could move too far, he peeled my wrinkled clothes off me and did the same with his.

I cocked one brow. "Wanna play with me while we get ready?"

That smirk. "What do you have in mind?"

"Lots of things." I knitted our fingers together.

His lips, insatiable and hungry, sampled my nape. His palms traveled all over my naked flesh, leaving addictive shivers in their wake. "Show me the way."

Before the water had even gotten hot enough, I dropped to my knees and pulled Carter's length into my mouth. By the groans and curses leaving his lips, I had him exactly where I wanted him to be. At my mercy. Having someone like Carter Hills ceding all his power to me was a sight I could never get tired of. I relished every second as I sucked him deeper and played him with my greedy tongue.

"Fuck, Savannah."

I dug my fingertips into his ass cheeks, erasing any distance between us.

"Did you miss me?" I asked as I pulled back to catch a full breath in.

"I did." He growled, and the sound reverberated through his entire being.

I increased the cadence, relishing every reaction of his body.

"Don't forget to show me later." I winked, and his eyes turned feral.

He fisted my hair and set the pace. He tensed, and before he could tell me to back away, I moved to my feet, strangling his erection with my hand. "Don't come just yet."

He watched me. His dilated pupils looked black instead of steel gray. His jaw was set in a firm line, and his lips were pinched together. All signs he was doing his best to restrain himself.

"So, what's next?" he asked through gritted teeth. By now, Carter was aware I savored control in the bedroom. Sometimes, I would let him lead, but I craved the command. Being in charge gave me a new sense of power that got me hornier than anything else.

I winked in the most devilish way I could muster. "You'll see. But I can already tell walking a straight line will be a challenge later. Are you in?"

He watched me, and something resembling fear passed through his gaze, but it only lasted a second before disappearing. The other day, I introduced him to some of my fetishisms, and let's just say he didn't enjoy the pain. Me, on the other hand? I was dripping wet upon seeing this man squirming to avoid the torture and begging me to stop when I presented him with nipple clamps after I handcuffed him to the bed. For a reason I couldn't explain, Carter wasn't enthusiastic about my proposition to add some excitement to our sex life. When he was left with no route of escape, I speared myself over his sex, so aroused that no orgasms were powerful enough to quench the thirst inside me. I was a sexual creature, and I fully embraced that role.

I splayed a hand across his chest. "Relax. No handcuffs this time. I just want you to take me on my bed, and look me in the eye when you push me over the edge. Is it too much to ask?"

"You said—"

I placed a finger over his lips to silence his protest. "Not this morning. I missed you too much. Let's just enjoy each other."

We toweled ourselves dry, and Carter didn't budge when I motioned him forward.

"What?" I asked in my most innocent voice.

His eyebrows bunched together. "You never wanna *just enjoy each other*," he said, emphasizing the words with air quotes.

I offered him a half-shrug. "It's a one-time offer. Take it or leave it."

With one last dubious look my way, he followed me without questioning my motive anymore.

Chapter 13

Carter

Savannah lay half on me, with her chin propped on her joined hands, her breasts pressing against my chest, and our faces inches apart.

White walls and furniture, her small bedroom consisted of a queen-size bed, a dresser, and a nightstand. A few crimson pillows over a white comforter, a bedside lamp, and a throw blanket added some personality to the cramped space. Over the months, Savannah's place had become our love nest every time I was in town.

"You're coming to Nashville for the party my record label is throwing next month, right?"

Savannah shook her head, flipping her hair over her shoulder, reminding me of Carla—the only woman I had grown to hate. "No."

"Come on. We've been together…what? Eight months now? And you haven't met any of my friends."

She slid forward to kiss my lips. "Carter, if I come, I'll

steal the show. It's better if I stay here. You know how I hate to leave LA anyway. The Tennessee weather isn't good for me or my skin. See? I'm doing you a favor. Making *you* my priority." She flashed me a large grin.

"What?" I pushed myself up into a sitting position and tilted my head, staring through the window, the brick wall of the building next door blocking all the sunlight, and swallowed my annoyance.

"Come on, Carter. Don't get mad. I'll make it up to you. I always do."

Everyone would be coming to my label's anniversary party with a date. Guess I'd be fine on my own. I always have been in the past. It just seemed weird that my own girlfriend wouldn't join me. I couldn't ask any other woman to accompany me without the press making up stories about my having an affair or whatever shit they could come up with—and infuriate Savannah in the process.

I sighed, forcing my ire down, not in the mood to start a fight.

I really needed to work on this dating thing. I'd never been in a serious relationship before, and I felt there was room for improvement. I wasn't in love with Savannah Prince, not yet at least, but I hoped that one day I would feel this way about her. Without questioning everything between us.

Nick was at the opening night of Dahlia's store, even though they'd just met and weren't even dating.

Back in the Carter Hills Band days, Belinda always cheered Stud on every night on tour, even when they weren't together.

Was I doing it all wrong, or did I have unrealistic expectations?

Savannah moved to her feet, her grin brightening up

her entire face, and grabbed my hand to pull me out of the bed. "Let's go out. To celebrate us."

I pushed my irritability away and forced an almost-smile to my lips.

"You know that new restaurant downtown? The one you told me you would take me to?"

I nodded.

"Well, I got us a reservation. For tonight. I'm super happy you're taking me. I love it when you indulge in our happiness."

Giving me the best view of her backside, Savannah changed into a number that left no place to the imagination. A skimpy red dress, barely long enough to cover her ass, and a pair of black stilettos. All of which, I had to admit, made her look divine.

She adjusted her boobs and fluffed her hair.

In front of the full-length mirror set in one corner of the room, she examined each angle of her outfit before touching up her makeup. "People will envy you tonight. I look like a million bucks in this."

I offered her a faint smile, still uneasy about her not coming home with me and not wanting to meet my industry peers, friends, and family, or learn where I came from.

Was I selfish to ask for it? To expect it?

Savannah always threw me off my game. Big time.

She coated her lips with thick red lipstick, slipped on the diamond earrings I got her for her birthday, and looped her arms through mine once I got dressed in slacks and a dark shirt. "Let's go, pretty boy. Show me the way."

In the most upscale eatery in town, waiting for our main courses, I watched Savannah in the dim light. High cheekbones, straight nose, full lips. Her phone went off, and she accepted the call, breaking my admiration.

Her face blanched as she replied with a series of *"Yeses"* and *"Nos,"* nodding and twisting her lips.

"You can't be serious?" she asked, her tone half-glacial, half-fearful. "And how am I supposed to relocate on such short notice?" Her lips quivered, and her eyes filled with tears. She listened to the person on the other end of the line, fidgeting with the fork on the table with the fingers of her free hand. "Can I refuse? Do I have a say in the matter?"

I covered her hand with mine and raised a brow as if to ask her what was going on.

She shook her head, chewing on her lower lip, defeat clouding her now-tense features.

"Thanks for letting me know. But no thanks for being such an asshole and ruining my night. You'll hear from my lawyers." She hung up and slammed the device on the table face down.

"Hey, tell me what it's about?"

She swallowed, somehow looking even sexier when she was angry. "It was my landlord. They've decided to reno-vate sections of the building—my apartment included—and he informed me that I was evicted and needed to move out by the end of the month." Her shoulders slumped in defeat, and she pushed her hair back, trying to look stronger than she really was.

"Can he do this?"

"Yeah. It…it seems so. He read me the section of the lease, and it appeared I had agreed to this. Anyway, he claimed it was for security purposes. Something about the structure." She hid her face in her hands.

Over the months we'd been together, I'd learned that my girlfriend wasn't good at showing her emotions—espe-cially sadness. She usually tried to change the subject or seduce me whenever she felt vulnerable in my presence.

"Listen." I rubbed my short stubble with my hand, reflecting on the words I was about to say. Sure, the thought had been nagging at me for a while, but I'd managed to keep it under wraps...until now. Perhaps this was the perfect opportunity, and my chance, to really show my commitment to an *us*. "I've been thinking..."

Savannah's eyes rested on mine.

"I could rent a place here. In LA. It could ease both our lives. I'm here more often than I'm in Tennessee these days, and you wouldn't have to find another apartment in a not-so-safe neighborhood. To be honest, I'm not really a fan of the fact you're there by yourself when I'm not around."

She blinked, her eyes widening. "You want us to move in together?" She blinked again, her lips parting, as if to speak, but no words followed.

I rubbed my neck. "Yeah, well, I know it's a bit precipitated, but since I'm gone on the road a lot, we won't be in each other's business all the time. I'll set up a little studio in one of the rooms so I can record my stuff. Remember when you said you were stressing about having to put your career on hold just to pay the bills after losing that sitcom role? If we do this, it would be one less worry for you. I can afford the lease. We'll see about splitting the other bills if you want to pay your share...or not. We can discuss it later." I expelled a shaky breath. I did it. I put myself out there. New beginning. I was taking my dating life into my hands and moving forward with my relationship. Maybe Savannah Prince was the woman for me, or perhaps she wasn't, but the only way to find out was to give it a real shot.

An adorable blush covered her cheeks. "Carter, you're serious?"

I pleaded with my heart to decrease its thundering.

This whole moving in together and trusting life thing was a big step for me. "Yes. Wanna move in with me?"

My girlfriend jumped up from her seat, rounded the table, and kissed me like we were alone in the world. A loud moan left her mouth when our tongues tangoed together.

I pushed back, gulping some oxygen and putting a stop to our public display of affection. "So, I guess it's a *Yes*."

Savannah hugged me tight. "It's a million *Yeses*. We'll be super happy together, I can already tell."

We finished dinner, and after we left the restaurant, we walked hand in hand on the sidewalk.

Savannah halted and turned until we faced each other. "Can we go apartment hunting like tomorrow?" she asked, unable to hide her excitement. Seeing her happiness made me smile too. "I'd like it if we could move in before you gotta leave so I won't have all the burden on my shoulders. Oh wow. I can't wait for us to pick up furniture and silverware together. This is the best news ever." She rose onto her tiptoes and pressed her lips to mine. "Thank you. For being the best boyfriend ever. You won't regret it. I'll rock your world later to show my gratitude properly."

I wished I could add *I love you* to the ending of a perfect night. Not now, though. I wasn't ready to say those words yet. Someday soon. Maybe.

I tucked her hair behind her ear and glued my gaze to hers. "I can't wait to do all those things with you too." I leaned forward to kiss her once more.

A small voice in my head warned me I was moving too fast, but I silenced it. Fear was whispering in my own voice, and for once, I chose not to give it any room in my mind.

———

I landed in Nashville a month later for my record label's twentieth anniversary party. Riley picked me up instead of Taylor driving me. My manager hugged me the moment I neared him. "I'm so happy you're home, man. You spend way too much time in LA these days. I miss having you around." His gaze swept around me. "Where's your pretty girlfriend?"

I mustered my fakest smile and greeted him with it.

"C'mon, Carter, I really wanted to meet her in person. Not just see you guys looking cute on tabloid covers." Yeah, even after vetoing Carla's ideas, my relationship with a Hollywood star had attracted the attention of the press more often than I would have liked. Carla had been blowing up my phone with requests for another meeting to put the ball into motion as she called her stupid PR plan. A side of me wondered if she was behind the paps following me. If she'd been calling the shots, even though she said she wouldn't.

I punched Riley's upper arm. "Don't start. She decided to stay in LA. Nothing too juicy on that front. Anyway, who's the girl who gets to tag along to Sunday night dinners with mama and papa Burns these days? Anyone I know or another flavor of the week?" I smirked, like the asshole I could be if poked. Like I would've done with my brother back in the day.

Riley raised his hands between us. "Fine. I won't meddle in your love life if you stay out of mine. I'm not looking for a serious relationship, and you're well aware. Can't a guy just have fun before committing to marriage and babies? You, my friend, are looking for love, so I'm fully entitled to mess with you."

"I'm not…"

He clapped my shoulder. "Yeah, yeah. Keep lying to yourself, lover boy."

I said nothing because we both knew he was right. One day. With a woman who would love me back this time. But for now, my heart was hidden behind a wall of ice, and it suited me. I had my fun, out-of-this-world sex, and my career fulfilled me more than it ever did.

We walked side by side to his car.

"Is Taylor coming with us?" Riley looked around while I stuffed my luggage inside the trunk.

"Nah. His wife is coming to get him. She's not really a fan of my going to California all the time either. She misses having him around. He sends Ed to watch over me now and then to appease her."

"June is so excited to have you back. She even shopped for an outfit for tonight."

"Let's pray she didn't let that kid of hers choose it."

We both burst into a fit of chuckles.

"I swear, when you're on tour, we're aware you're away, but when you're in-between engagements, we're used to having you stop over at the office unannounced just for the sake of it. Your living in Los Angeles changes things. Green Mountain is a three-hour drive. LA is not next door." He shrugged. "I'm rambling, but all I wanna say is we miss you, man." He pulled me into his arms again, and I hugged him back.

"Yeah, well, I miss you too. LA can get pretty lonely. And in my opinion, it doesn't have the same appeal as Nashville. The vibe isn't the same."

We broke apart.

"Wanna go to your penthouse now to unwind and get ready early, or are you coming home with me for an hour or two to catch up?"

I glanced at my phone for an instant, wishing Savannah had reached out. Negative. "I have nowhere to be until tonight. Let's go to your place. A jamming session with you sounds about perfect right now."

Riley lowered his golden aviator shades over his eyes as he wheeled out of the parking lot. "Works for me."

Riley Burns wasn't as musically talented as me or his famous dad, but he could find his way with a guitar. As long as he didn't have to sing—the man couldn't hold a note even if his life depended on it—we had fun playing together. However, his musical ear was irreproachable and his sense of business too, which made him not only the most talented and sought-after music manager I knew but also a true music mogul. The guy was a tiger in a ring when you mixed both of his gifts together. He had the connections and the will. He was also the most loyal and caring person I knew. Nothing could stop him, and I was the lucky bastard he'd discovered at the beginning of his career and whom he'd taken under his wing.

We arrived at the label party at six. Wearing a new pair of denims and a dark plaid shirt—my usual outfit since I was a kid and the one June got for me—I raked my fingers through my hair, probably messing it up a little as I took it all in. Over fifty people stood in a half-circle and clapped their hands at my entrance.

A banner with my name hung over the far wall. I perused the space around me, not really understanding what was going on.

"Ry?" I asked my friend still by my side. "What is this?"

His smile broke free, and with an arm draped around my shoulders, he tugged me closer. "This, Carter, is the record label celebrating your success. 'One Of Us' has been topping the charts for over four months now, which is a record. You deserve the recognition. Enjoy tonight."

I blinked. "You mean…you all knew about it?"

My friend shrugged. "I must say, having you in LA

helped a lot. June was in charge. She did an incredible job." He winked and let go of me, accepting the flute of champagne servers were passing around.

Seconds later, a mocktail was handed to me.

"Thanks." I brought the sparkly lemon concoction to my lips and smiled.

This time, I surveyed the room in slow motion, taking every detail in.

Set in an old barn, with a rustic chic accent of steel, black velvet, and dabs of gold, tonight's decor looked masculine and sober. Low profile and simple. Very much like me.

Dahlia came to join me and pulled me into her arms. "Cart, see? I knew you were the best. Congratulation. This is incredible."

I kissed her cheek and held out my hand to shake Nick's, who stood beside her.

"You guys came?"

"We wouldn't have missed it for the world," Nick said. "This is really impressive. Congrats, man."

Dahlia pushed a curl of my hair away from my forehead. "Are you okay? Did you have any clue about tonight? You looked surprised when you walked in."

"No idea. I swear."

My best friend scanned the room. "Where is she? I thought you said Savannah would be here."

"She has a work engagement and couldn't make it." I shrugged it off with as much nonchalance as I could muster.

Dahlia's eyes pierced me with an intense, laser-like focus. She could read me. She knew I was lying through my teeth right now. I was pretty sure Riley saw through me too when he picked me up earlier. My friends always said I had the worst poker face, that my face showcased every emotion I felt. I couldn't deny it. Lying wasn't something I did well.

Are you okay with that? Dahlia's eyes asked. *You don't look happy about it.*

It is what it is, mine replied. *Let's not talk about it tonight, okay?*

She nodded.

Nick spoke next. "What do I always feel like I'm missing something when I'm with you two?" He shook his head and grinned. "Riley wanted to talk to me about a construction project. I'll be right back." He kissed Dahlia's temple and left, still shaking his head in disbelief.

Dahlia tapped my forearm, and we watched each other for a few seconds. "It'll be all right, Cart. I can tell."

"Maybe."

An over-enthusiastic June interrupted us when she hugged me. "Sorry. I was on the phone with the babysitter. My munchkin was down with a fever when I left."

"Go if you need to," I said.

She flicked her wrist. "Nah. All fine now. Munchkin is sleeping, and the fever has broken. The babysitter will keep me updated if it changes." She looked around. "It turned out pretty great."

"You're kidding, right? I love it. It's very much me."

She pumped her fist before fixing her composure. "Knew it. It was so much fun working on it as a side project. It's your friend Addison who was hired to set it all up. She's talented. I focused more on the guest list. We made a great team."

"I agree," Dahlia chimed in from my left. "If you two could excuse me, I have a few people, I haven't seen in ages, whom I wanna catch up with." She motioned to leave but spun back to face me. "Oh, Cart, Stud and Belle were supposed to be here tonight, but Tristan had a stomach bug, and they canceled their flight."

"Shit. I'll call them later."

"How are you doing?" June asked once Dahlia left us.

"Good."

"You're Mr. Invisible nowadays. That relationship… Is it going like you want?"

I shoved my hands into my pockets and rocked on my heels. "Yeah. I'm determined to make it work. We—" I cleared my throat. "We moved in together last weekend."

I averted my eyes, not sure I was ready to assess the worry I knew I'd find in her gaze.

June coughed and gripped my chin, forcing me to swivel back toward her. "Are you serious?"

I swallowed. "Yep. It was easier this way. Savannah got evicted. They're renovating her old place. I needed a place to set up a studio and leave my stuff. It's the best decision for both of us."

Why was I feeling awkward when I said those words out loud? As if something was wrong but I couldn't exactly pinpoint the source.

"That's wonderful news. If you're happy, then I'm glad for you. I'm just sad you'll be spending all your free time down in LA now." She hugged me again, appearing genuinely happy for me. "Wow, you must really love her."

"I-I'm not…"

June stepped back to study me. "You're not what?"

I waved her off. "Nothing. Doesn't matter. I could—"

The vice-president of my record label came to me, and I silently thanked him for the interruption.

"We'll continue this conversation later," June said before walking away.

Love. No, I definitely didn't feel love toward Savannah Prince. Attachment maybe. Or perhaps something a bit more, but love, nah. I wasn't there yet. And at that moment, I wondered if I would ever be.

My heart had been broken in the past, stomped over, and I was being careful.

In my short existence, I had gone through too many heartbreaks. No way would I submit myself to one more if I could prevent it.

A song I had written last year played on the speaker. The music carried a wave of nostalgia with it and a whole lot of pride too with all the progress I'd made since I decided to give my career another shot. A song I wrote when I imagined, for a moment, I had found my soul mate and was taking a leap of faith and trusting love.

Even though I yearned for it, Savannah didn't fit the lyrics—not yet at least—and in that instant, I wished she would.

One day.

Eventually.

Chapter 14

"**I**'m so excited we're doing this," I exclaimed as we entered the elevator leading to our apartment. Yes, Carter had agreed to rent us a place in Los Angeles with the most magnificent view of the city skyline.

The high-vaulted white ceilings and panoramic windows made this place appear bigger than it was. The floors were white marble, the kitchen cabinets exotic wood, and the furniture high-end and straight lines. An apartment I could never afford but deserved. No actress of my caliber should live in a dump. What if magazines ran a story at home? This new place screamed wealth and fame. It defined me perfectly. Renting this place was the sensible thing to do. Clearly, Carter knew it too.

He wanted me to succeed since I was the best thing that had ever happened to him.

Every time I said that, he changed the subject or

professed many good things had happened to him in his life, but deep down, he had to know I spoke the truth.

I was everything a star like him should marry.

Gorgeous, a body to kill, and stamina to last all night.

See? I was the real deal. The perfect woman on his arm.

And his best fuck.

He didn't have to tell me, I knew how talented I was in bed.

Another thing that had come to me naturally in my life.

Carter's notoriety shone on me, which was a plus. Sure, people would think I was the lucky one in this relationship, but we all knew that behind closed doors, Carter Hills was the fortunate one.

As we stepped into the apartment, I still couldn't believe he offered and agreed to pay for the entire thing by himself. I wasn't as wealthy as him—not yet at least—so, I loved that I could spend my money to make myself more gorgeous instead of on a lease that wouldn't help to propel my career in any way.

"I'll need a new dress. I can't go to a movie premiere dressed in rags."

In the foyer, Carter stopped and turned to face me. "I bought you over ten-thousand-dollar worth of clothes not so long ago. I'm sure you can find something to wear."

I pouted and rubbed my hand over his manhood, using my most honey-dripping voice. "You wouldn't want people to think you're cheap, right? That you let me wear used dresses every time we go out. We'll be walking the red carpet together. People have eyes, you know. They sense these things. I have to look impeccable. And so do you. Imagine all the pictures of us they will be taking that night. It's the real deal."

I licked the length of his neck, and he grew harder under my palm.

"Don't try to manipulate me, Savannah. I'm not financing your shopping spree this time."

As if stung by a bee, I removed my hand and stepped back. "Fine. I'm not going then. I'll pretend I'm sick or something."

"Don't be a baby. I'm sure you can find something nice enough to wear," he said, pointing to the twenty-by-twenty-foot space we'd transformed into a dressing room to accommodate all my clothes and every designer purse and pair of shoes Carter had bought for me since we'd started dating.

Every time I admired the gorgeousness of our living situation, I still couldn't believe Carter offered for us to move in together. He had uprooted his cowboy life to be with me. We already spent so much time with each other that the moving together part seemed like the natural next step for us to take.

Just for show, I pouted a little more, using fake tears to add to the drama. I was an actress after all. I had skills. "You think I'm a baby? You're being insensitive right now."

He stuffed his hands into his pockets and sighed. "No. I said you are acting like one."

I spun on my heels, unbuttoned my shirt, my red lacy push-up bra making my breasts look like a buffet only gods could afford—yeah, I had a plastic surgeon on speed dial —and turned back to face him. While giving my doe eyes another try, I sucked on a red-manicured finger, batting my eyelashes.

"Do babies look as hot as this?" I asked, closing the gap between us.

Carter shut his eyes for a second and reopened them with a curse.

"You like these girls," I said, kneading my breasts and doing my best to tempt him so he wouldn't be able to resist. I had a whole range of well-mastered skills I had perfected over the years.

His Adam's apple bobbed, and he swallowed. Oh, oh, it looked painful.

I would have him in no time. I just needed to show him what he was missing. And what he'd lose if he didn't get me what I wanted. Because I was entitled to another dress. The white designer one I saw on the runway last month.

As if I were a magnet he couldn't resist, Carter padded my way, his pupils dilated and his tongue grazing his lips.

He moved closer, his breathing now mixing with mine.

My pulse raced. I loved the game we played.

"Sorry, pretty boy. These are not for your personal use."

As if I had all the time in the world, I shimmied out of my leather pants, swaying my hips to silent music, staring at him the entire time.

"Fuck," he groaned.

I untied my hair, letting the strands fall loosely over my shoulders, and gave him a one-sided shrug. I unclasped my bra and let it pool on the floor in a red lacy puddle. "Going to take a shower. Don't follow me."

The air tensed around us. I turned my back to him and removed my panties, sliding one leg out, then the other.

I smiled at the sound of Carter's quick intake of air.

Doing my best catwalk impression, I waltzed away, letting my man simmer in his need.

My hand connected with the shower door handle, but I didn't have time to open it before being swept off my feet and laid on our bed. Carter, already suited in a condom, had a predatory spark shining in his eyes.

"You can't tease me like that and just walk away, Savannah," he said, breathless. The guy worked out like crazy. He could run miles without breaking a sweat, but now, hovering over me, he could barely catch his breath. "Your little game is juvenile."

I arched my back to offer him a better view of my stiff nipples, skimming his bare torso with their tips. "You're not being nice, so I'm not having sex with you. I can take care of my own needs."

He lowered himself over me. "I know what you're doing. It's not working."

"You'll buy me this dress, no matter what. We both know it. You love it when I look like a shiny diamond by your side. You love the attention. You love that people are jealous because they think I'm hot. You love the high that comes with your treating me like the queen I am. Me on my knees, stealing every last thread of composure from you. Don't deny any of it. If you could just stop being a greedy jerk, we would have already ordered that dress and started having the sex we both crave." I licked my finger and brought it between my thighs, relishing the feeling as I rubbed my swollen bundle of nerves.

Getting my way was the best foreplay I could ever get.

I loved the power that came with the knowledge I dominated this game.

It turned me on like nothing else could.

"You're crazy," Carter articulated, studying me with bunched eyebrows.

"But you love how hard it gets you."

I licked my finger again, but this time, I pushed it between my legs, whimpering as it entered me, my body shuddering at the sensation of getting myself off in front of him.

"That's not fair," he pleaded.

"Oh, it *is* fair. I want something, you want something. Everything in life is a transaction."

His erection pressed against my lower belly, and his body temperature soared.

"To hell," he said, plunging forward, his starving lips connecting with mine. "I'll fucking buy you that stupid dress, but now open your legs because we're here for a long ride."

I high-fived myself in my head.

"You better get on to it right after because that dress hasn't hit the market yet. Lucky me, your charm is hard to resist. I'm sure you can pull some strings. I have faith in you."

I dug my fingernails into the flesh of his back as I deepened the kiss, ready to rock his world.

———

Carter kissed me before I hauled myself out of his SUV. This morning, he had insisted on driving me to the studios. He tended to do that often when he was in town and I had to go to work. Like he enjoyed making sure I got on set on time and in one piece. "I'll grab food from your favorite salad place and meet you at lunch."

I felt giddy at the idea of parading my boyfriend in front of the two Hollywood-fake actresses I didn't consider my friends. One was a nepo baby of a long line of Hollywood celebrities with an ego problem, and the other found fame when she uploaded a homemade sex tape on the internet a while back and it went viral. They made everyone's lives a living hell on set. Since they were cash cows that brought in millions of dollars each, nobody raised an eyebrow, and they let them act out without saying anything.

I knew for a fact one of them had a thing for Carter. She didn't even shy away from it on the day I joined the cast. Once, I'd entered the wrong dressing room and seen a picture of him stuck to her mirror. If I flaunted my hot man in her face, perhaps she would think twice before stabbing me in the back next time. Yeah, that girl was a two-faced hypocrite.

Carter didn't know about her infatuation with him, or else he would have liked to intervene and make things better. Yes, he was a fixer. But I didn't want him to fix stuff for me. The surprise effect would be better if no one knew what I had in mind.

With hurried steps, I rounded the SUV and kissed him once more through the open window. "Can't wait. See you later."

I waved at him as he drove away. Yeah, in just a few hours, Priscilla would eat out of my hand. I would own all the cards.

Once, she tried to trip me when we shared a scene together. I called her rude, and the next thing I knew, she dropped a glass of water all over my shirt, which required a wardrobe change and a new take, making us late and affecting the tight schedule. Whatever. I was counting the hours until Carter walked in here and she would just shut up.

I wasn't on this set for long—just nine episodes as a guest star. Not being part of the main cast didn't mean I had to put up with their bluntness or mean-girl behavior without pushing back. I was simply smarter about it and would make sure things went my way without coming off as rude or a bitch.

It was almost one o'clock when we took our lunch break and Carter arrived, a bag of food in hand and a grin forming on his face upon seeing me. "Hey you," he said, inching closer and kissing my lips.

I felt Priscilla's eyes on me. They burned my back. Just for show, I wrapped my arms around my boyfriend's neck and tugged him closer, the kiss turning filthy in seconds as I moaned into his mouth.

When we broke apart, I held his hand and led him forward. "Let's eat outside. It's a beautiful day."

My nemesis walked to us, a giddy fangirl's expression tracing her features. "OMG, you *are* Carter Hills. I thought everyone was lying when they said you guys were dating." She jumped on the balls of her feet. "I'm such a fan. I love you so much. I've been following your career since you released your first single with your band." She used a hand to fan herself. "It's really you. This is the craziest day of my life. Can I get a picture? And an autograph? I just can't believe it's you. Savannah, how could you hide from me that Carter would be visiting the set today."

Like we were friends and we had that kind of relationship, she and I.

Carter blinked. I knew how much he hated the recognition. Which still made no sense in my head. Before he could reply, I tugged at his hand. "Baby, I'm starving." I used my most silky voice. "Can we eat now? I wanna spend time together."

His head traveled back and forth between Priscilla and me, debating what to do. "I'm sorry," he finally told her. "I'm not staying long. If I have some free time after lunch, I'll track you down," he told her.

If I had my way, he wouldn't have a second to spare.

Her jaw slackened. Priscilla wasn't used to being turned down. Trust-fund baby and all, everybody always bent their knees to please her. When her eyes rested on me, I shrugged, twisting my lips in the most condescending smile. One that said *Payback, bitch.*

She tried to argue, "It will only take a minute. Can't you make time for your biggest fan?"

Guilt-tripping wouldn't work with Carter. I had tried it many times and failed.

"Like I said, I'll find you later if I have time," my man said, leading me away. That shut her up.

We sat at a picnic table shaded by a big tree behind the studio. The sound of Los Angeles traffic resonated in the distance. A thick smog hung low like a dense blanket, blocking our view of the flawless blue sky above.

"Want to tell me what that was all about?" Carter asked after a moment. "I sensed some tension between you two earlier."

I shrugged. "Let's just say Priscilla hasn't been nice to me since I joined the show. She's been terrorizing everyone because her grandfather was a big-shot producer and her dad is Aaron Letterman."

Carter angled himself so we faced each other, cradling my cheek with his warm palm. "Why didn't you tell me?"

I shrugged again. "Because I don't want you to offer to fix the situation. I'm a big girl, and I can do it on my own."

He sighed. "By parading me like a possession in front of her?"

"I wasn't... It's not what I was—"

He lifted one dark eyebrow.

"Fine. I kinda liked her expression when she saw I wasn't bullshitting her about being your girlfriend. She thinks she's entitled to everything. Well, she isn't. Hope she got the memo."

"Next time, don't use me. Tell me the truth. I'll always

have your back." He forked a small quinoa ball into his mouth.

I nodded before attacking my own lunch.

"She's really being mean?" he asked after we were done with our food.

"Yeah. To everyone. Even the director can't stand her."

He nodded but added nothing else.

———

That night, we went grocery shopping after Carter picked me up. He filled the cart to the brim as I sipped on a mango and kale smoothie I got at the studio before I left.

"Don't you have people to run errands for you?" I asked when we stopped in the organic product aisle. "Like grocery shopping and dry cleaning and all the boring stuff nobody wants to do, which feels like a waste of precious time."

Beside me, Carter shook his head. "Why pay people to do what I can do? Sure, sometimes, my schedule gets hectic and I'm barely home and June orders food for me. But usually, I like to do the normal boring shit myself like everyone else. I'm not special, Savannah. I'm just a guy singing on a stage for a living. I didn't find a cure for cancer or save the world. Never will I let myself feel that I am worth more than anyone else I work with or cross paths with in a day. If a single mom of three can find time to do her own laundry or go to the supermarket, then I don't see why I can't."

"Because you have the means. What else?"

Carter stared at me, confusion painting his face. "Money doesn't define me or my core values. I refuse to let it change me. I made a promise back when I was eighteen that success would never impact my ego. This is me proving the worth of my words."

I trashed away my empty cup after Carter paid, and we left the store. "Well, when I become rich and famous, no way will I run my own errands."

Carter kissed my temple before lifting the bags in his arms. "Well, as long as we're together, I'm happy to do everyday tasks."

"We'll revisit it another day," I said. "I haven't said my last word about it yet."

Carter snickered. "I'll make sure you stay grounded. When I started in the business, I had people watching out for me. Having my back. I'll always have yours."

He winked, and after stocking the groceries in the trunk, he kissed my knuckles before we hauled ourselves into his SUV and headed home.

Home.

I liked the sound of it.

Chapter 15

Carter

Flipping the slices of potatoes and tofu bacon in a pan, dressed in nothing but a dark pair of sweatpants, I hummed the song playing on the sound system. Life was good. And I felt content.

Busy pouring two glasses of orange juice and adding the finishing touches to breakfast, I didn't notice Savannah standing in the doorway until I rolled the second breakfast burrito and plated it on a porcelain dish.

"It smells delicious," she said, walking up to me. Barefaced, her hair tied at the top of her head, wearing a large T-shirt reaching up to mid-thigh, she wrapped her arms around my middle from behind and planted a kiss between my shoulder blades.

"Hey you." I spun between her arms and kissed her lips. "Sleep well?"

"Like a baby." She scrunched up her face. "Huh, babies cry. No idea why they call it that. Anyway, I'm rested. The long hours at the studio last week had drained all my energy levels."

Grabbing a glass of juice from the counter behind me, I handed it to her before sipping mine.

"Wanna spend the day at the beach?" I asked.

Savannah's gaze drifted outside. Fat clouds hung in the sky, but the sun rays were piercing the dense cover. She frowned. "Isn't it too cold and dark to spend the day outside?"

I shrugged. "If it rains, we'll do something else. The sun is trying to shine; give it a chance."

We sat side by side at the kitchen island, and I placed a plate of food in front of each of us, a cup of coffee with two creams before Savannah, and a mug of organic green tea in front of me.

I moaned as the spicy flavors of the vegan breakfast burrito coated my tongue. The leftover salsa I made from scratch last night got my tastebuds dancing in food orgasm.

"You're not eating?" I asked my girlfriend as she brought the steamy beverage to her lips.

"Nah, I think I'll have oatmeal. Or a power juice later."

I studied her. "Be honest with me."

"Fine. Trying to lower my carbs intake." She shook her head when I gave her a dubious glance.

"Come on, don't partake in this starving Hollywood game. You're better than that."

"But—"

I moved to stand, swiveled her stool, and wrapped my arms around her. She glanced down, avoiding my gaze. I tipped her head up with a finger until she stared at me. "No but. You're perfect just the way you are. Don't let anyone tell you otherwise. Never. You hear me? I'll fight anyone who plays mind games with your appearance."

She nodded.

"Is this about Priscilla and the other girl on set?"

She shook her head but didn't convince me.

My heart sank behind my ribs. "Don't let their judgments get to you, and your own insecurities fuck with your brain. I think you're beautiful."

Her eyes rounded. "You do?"

I kissed the crown of her head. "Yep. Now eat your breakfast, then we'll get ready. I wanna spend the day together. No phone, no distraction. Just us. What do you say?"

"Fine." She nibbled on her burrito. "It's good. Like really good."

I returned her smile. "It's my special ingredient." I flashed her a proud smile.

Savannah cocked a brow. "What is it?"

"Ah, you'll need to kiss me later, and maybe I'll tell you." I winked and rounded the island to attack the dirty dishes.

Much later, stretched on a blanket on the almost deserted beach, Savannah and I exchanged stories about our lives. I told her about the time my brother and I kept the garage door open one night on purpose, hoping the skunk living underneath it would find refuge in there and we could adopt it as a pet. Little did we know our trick would work, but the skunk had actually given birth to kits, and they had sprayed the entire place after my mother closed the door the next morning without checking that we had visitors. When we returned from school, thanks to the heat wave, the smell had marinated all day, and my dad had to renovate the entire place to get rid of the putrid odor.

"Oh, this is absolutely disgusting." Savannah laughed and wiped the tears that had gathered in the corners of her eyes with her fingertips. "I would have bulldozed this thing down. Oh God, the smell…" She shivered at the thought.

"Yep, it was disgusting." I joined in her laughter. "What about you? Any childhood stories worth laughing about?"

"Nah. I was pretty shy growing up. My parents got divorced when I was ten, I think. The memory is a bit blurry. I was an only child, so I had no one to team up with to drive my parents nuts."

"I'm sure Jeff's and my stories can make up for the lack of yours."

We stayed silent, watching the waves break in the distance and half a dozen surfers catching them.

I glanced up. The clouds were still heavy in the sky, but I didn't think it would rain. "Wanna be my tour guide to the Santa Monica pier? I've never been there, and when I was a kid, I always wanted to go."

Savannah's eyes grew big. "You've never been?"

I shook my head. "Nah. Guess I was waiting for the right person to go with."

We exchanged a smile.

"Let's go," my girlfriend said, moving to her feet and dusting the sand off her skirt. "We'll see if you're brave, Carter Hills. Are you gonna ride the roller coaster?"

"Only if we get candy apple afterward."

Savannah seemed to think about it for a moment. She sighed and held out her hand. "Okay. Just this time, though."

I shook her hand. "Yeah. Deal. I haven't had one in forever."

———

"I had the best day today," Savannah said, motioning me inside our apartment, her smile a permanent fixture on her face. She looked beautiful with her pink cheeks and bright eyes.

"Me too."

I was amazed she had transformed into a kid and let go for an afternoon. Due to the unpredictable weather, the pier had been mostly empty, and we had been free to roam —no one there to snap pictures or follow us around. Savannah had a tougher stomach than she let on. She rode every ride, never shying away from any of them.

I shifted her between my arms and claimed her mouth. Our tongues cavorted in a hurried dance. My entire being heated up at the whimpers escaping her luscious lips.

Our hands got desperate, tearing every piece of clothing off each other. Soon we found ourselves naked, hungry for the other, insatiable.

When I kneeled in front of her, Savannah's fingers fisted my hair, the burn on my scalp not restraining me from my mission.

She tossed her head back, crying out my name as I devoured her in long and dedicated strokes, her wet heat coating my tongue.

In no time, she shuddered against me, the climax working through her. On my feet, I held her trembling body against mine, brushing her hair away as she landed back on Earth.

"Carter, you woke up the beast in me," my girlfriend said. "Now lie on your back. If you thought the rides today were fun, you've experienced nothing."

Mischief lit up her eyes, and she watched me as if I was her next meal, and nothing else but us mattered in that instant.

When she speared herself on my sheathed cock, I held

my breath, trying to talk myself out of coming too soon. Savannah rolled her hips, and the gasps leaving her mouth were my demise. I molded my hands to the dip of her hips, setting the rhythm. She jerked her head back, the tips of her hair skimming my thigh as she rode me to oblivion. Until I barely remembered my own name. Until every disagreement we ever had in the past was erased from my memory.

Savannah came, her voice rising as she accelerated her pace. Just when I was about to follow her into bliss, she changed her position, killing my orgasm.

Moving onto all fours, she pushed her ass against my stomach, swaying her hips against my hard-on. "I wanna see stars, Carter. Don't come until I reach a new galaxy."

On my knees, I positioned myself behind her, ramming into her depth, one hand hooked to her hipbone and the other clamped around her shoulder.

Her walls clenched around my throbbing erection. My balls tingled with the eminent release.

Reality blurred, and only pleasure dictated our movements.

I didn't recall the last we had a perfect day together. Now all I wished for was one do-over.

Or perhaps many more.

Chapter 16

Carter

The night was warm and my mood festive when we entered Dylan Daughtry's birthday party at a famous hotel in downtown Hollywood. Savannah didn't generally accompany me when I had to fulfill my social obligations, or the price I paid for being a "celebrity" as I often called it. It'd been more than a month since the surprise party my record label and management team threw for me. Initially, Savannah had been a bit detached when I returned home, whining about my absence when she was the one who refused to accompany me. Soon after, we made up and found our rhythm, and surprisingly tonight, she had agreed to join me.

Dylan was a fellow country music artist, but unlike me, he loved the fame. No, he adored it. He had his face plastered on the front page of gossip rags all the time and couldn't have cared less about the rumors swirling around him. He was often seen walking the red carpet of a movie premiere with an actress or a model or sometimes both. One on each arm.

With the two of us working in the small country music industry, we'd known each other for years and got along more than fine. He wasn't my best friend, but we enjoyed each other's company.

Savannah slid her palm into mine and whispered, "Wow, this is the most over-the-top party I've ever been to, I think."

Dylan's parties were always epic. Last year, he had a giant water tank filled with synchronized swimmers, dressed as mermaids, performing the entire night. I heard two years ago, he had a Bengal tiger, whose trainer got it to do agility tricks as the crowd surrounded them.

Tonight, trapeze artists were flying in the air above our heads, hanging by their feet, champagne bottle in hand, refilling empty glasses in between their performances. Some sort of high-end cocktail poured out from the mouth-like opening of a ten-foot-tall ice sculpture which was illuminated with color-changing lights.

"Yeah, it's super Daughtry. I wouldn't have pictured anything less spectacular."

I squeezed her hand, and my lips connected with her cheek. "You'll be fine."

We exchanged a soft gaze. For a beat, I got lost in her darkening irises. Savannah had a pull on me. It was physical. My entire body couldn't resist it. Somehow, her nervousness tonight made her look vulnerable, and enticing too. A weird combination, but on her, it worked.

"I'm glad you're here with me. It means a lot." I laced our fingers.

"What are you waiting for then? Introduce me to these people."

Rita L. Sterling, a music producer I'd worked with in the past, neared us. "Mr. Hills, how are you doing?"

Before I could even shake her hand, Savannah took it between hers. "I'm so happy to meet you. I'm Savannah Prince, Hollywood's next shining star," she said with a high-pitched laughter I'd never heard before.

Why the fuck would Savannah introduce herself this way?

Rita watched her with a frown.

I shrugged over my date's enthusiasm. Was she this anxious about being here or oblivious to civilities at such parties?

I wound an arm around her waist, bringing my attention back to the music producer, who clearly wasn't impressed by the woman beside me.

People came and went, and every time, Savannah stole the conversation, only talking about herself and her projects. I hated the attention, and right now, Savannah was attracting a lot of it. I saw the gazes the other guests exchanged between themselves. Not that I usually cared what people thought about me—about us—but tonight, part of me did. This was our first official outing in my world as a couple, and I didn't want it to be awkward.

My hand returned to her waist, and I yanked her closer. "Hey, I know you're nervous, but maybe you can drop it a notch," I whispered in her ear when we finally found ourselves alone.

"What?" She stared at me with wide eyes as if I'd spoken another language.

"Steering all the conversation toward you. These people don't need you to give them the 4-1-1 about your career right now. They just want to mingle and have fun. It's not a business gathering; it's a birthday celebration."

Savannah stepped back with a pout, her eyes brimming with tears. "Oh no, you're ashamed of me?"

Wait. What? What was she talking about?

"No." I moved forward, but she took another step back.

"Then why don't you want your friends to know all about me?" She looked genuinely taken aback by my comment.

Were my words confusing? I scratched the side of my head, not sure how to broach the subject now. "That wasn't what I meant. I—"

"I'm your girlfriend. The most important person in your life, the one you can't spend your days without. And we live together. It's only natural to want these people to learn all about me, no?"

I blinked. "Huh?" Okay, this wasn't where I thought the conversation would go. I sucked in a long breath. "Listen, I want them to know about you. But can you do it with more subtlety? Like introduce yourself and slip info in the discussion when it fits or if they ask you. Don't just spread it all out in one go. Does that make sense?"

Her teeth sunk into her bottom lip. Savannah's eyes stayed locked on mine, but she said nothing. Then her demeanor changed, and sparks returned to her eyes. A devilish smirk tilted her lips. "Want me to suck you off?" Her palm closed over the crotch of my pants, and she fisted my dick, stroking it as she pressed her front to mine.

My throat bobbed. Fuck. This woman.

For a fraction of a second, I relished the sensation rising inside me. Soon, I snapped out of the enchantment when I remembered where we were and took a step back. "No. Not here and not now. Let's wait until we return home." I removed her grip on me and held her hand in mine.

Savannah watched me with a confused expression. "You don't wanna have sex with me?"

"Huh. I didn't say that. I said later."

"But——" Her lips shuddered. "I wanna make it up to you. You're upset with me, and I want you to forget about it. To make you feel better. I know you can never resist my lips." She straightened her posture and flushed away her hesitation. Her pupils dilated. Her tongue darted out to moisten her lips in an alluring manner. Under my eyes, she transformed into the sex vixen I'd gotten to know when we were alone.

"Later," I repeated, with no conviction in my words, as she glided her fingernails across my chest, sending shivers through my whole body.

She seemed to take it as an invitation because she ate the gap between us and, with skillful fingers, attacked the buckle of my belt.

I jumped back. "Stop."

She watched me with big blinking eyes, her lips pursed, a red hue covering her cheeks. As if she couldn't believe I actually turned her down.

She spoke slowly, enunciating each word. "Wait? You are refusing me? Is this a joke?"

I dragged a hand over my face and exhaled a long breath, trying to find the right words as her face twisted with unconcealed anger. This wasn't the place to get into a fight. "Some of these people are the ones I work with. Or the closest thing I have to coworkers in my line of business. It's not just some party where we can act like hormonal teenagers. It would be wrong, even though it's tempting."

Her face turned purplish. I'd never seen her so mad before.

Okay, this wasn't how I saw our night going. Our first official date amongst industry people and we were about to clash right here. Surrounded by a hundred witnesses. I inhaled a big gulp of oxygen, needing to diffuse the situation. And fast. "The guy by the ice sculpture, he works for my record label. There are two music producers I work with. They are older, and they respect me as an artist and as a person. They believe in me and invest money in me and my music. I'm aware they've seen it all over the years, but I'm not that guy. I don't let people down. I also don't give them reasons to think I'm an airhead or to bitch behind my back about how stupid I act. Not sure they'd consider our antics as cool and fun if we got caught. I'm still young in this industry, and so far, my rep is impeccable. I'm not about to change it for a quick fuck, no matter how incredible it would be." I reached for her hand, and Savannah let me, dropping her shoulders. "Can we wait until this party is over? We could escape early. What do you think?"

Her anger and minx persona died down.

I opened my arms, and she buried herself in my chest. We stood like that for a long beat.

At some point, her face lifted toward mine. "Carter, don't you think I'm attractive?" Her big eyes locked on mine, and something close to vulnerability shone through them.

I leaned in to kiss her red lips. "You know you are," I said, unable to hide the smile and affection in my voice. "Come on, there are people I want you to meet. Keep it casual."

Exchanging a gaze, I squeezed her hand as we moved toward the crowd now crooning the birthday song.

Later, I was deep into a conversation with Dylan.

"I though Stevens would be here tonight," he said. "He RSVPed and never said he wouldn't show up. Have you talked to him recently?"

I shook my head. "Nah. He's been busy. Kids and everything. Ry says they get together now and then." Sam Stevens was a friend of ours. Another country music star, nicknamed *The Legend* after he broke the record for the best-selling album when he released his debut. We usually battled for the top of the charts, he and I. Riley was a common friend to both of us, so we often ended up hanging out together when we all had some free time and I was in town.

From over Dylan's shoulder, I spotted Savannah and almost choked on the sip of water I just swallowed when I took her in. Her gaze landed on mine, and challenge illuminated her dark irises. My free hand balled at my side. "What the fucking hell." Unable to keep quiet at the scene being played a few yards from me, the words bubbled out.

Dylan's eyes crinkled as he watched me. "What?"

I slapped his shoulder. "Nothing to worry about. I gotta go, man. Happy birthday. And next year, I expect nothing less than fire dancers or a dragon spitting flames."

His head tilted back as rumbling laugher escaped him. "We'll see, Hills. I can't promise anything."

My long strides ate the distance between us in no time. Savannah was dancing with the man who had introduced himself earlier as a movie producer, her scarlet fingernails grazing his abdomen over his shirt, the same way she did with me whenever she was on the prowl for some animalistic sex, her lips a hair's breadth from his as she murmured something that had his eyes widening with surprise and lust.

Grabbing her elbow, I gave her arm a tug as casually as I could, aware of the crowd watching us. "Hey, can I talk to you for a second?" I asked through gritted teeth while still trying to keep my tone jovial.

She cocked her head in my direction, feigning a look of

surprise. Her full lips drew into a devilish smirk. "What?" she asked as if I had interrupted something important.

"We're leaving."

She returned her attention to the man, blocking me out.

I swallowed and gave it another try. "Remember, we have *plans*? You and I. Tonight. We talked about it earlier."

"Ah, yes. Sure." She let out a loud sigh, not meeting my eyes. "Can it wait? I'm kinda busy."

Could I grate on her last nerve any more than I did at this instant? I could tell she didn't want me anywhere near her.

I cleared my throat, doing my best to keep my irritation under wraps. "Fine. I'm leaving. You either come with me or you don't. But don't play stupid with me. I know what you're doing, and it's not working."

Why was Savannah trying to get a rise out of me? To make me jealous? Was she hoping I'd throw a tantrum right here? Fuck her senseless in a dark corner to stake my claim? If so, she didn't know me at all. I usually fought my battles in private. Far away from witnesses.

I turned on my feet and seconds later, I heard "Sorry, I must go," followed by the sound of heels clicking on the concrete floor.

We remained silent the entire ride back home. Twice, Savannah tried to start a conversation, but I chose to ignore her. The last thing I wanted was for us to get into a fight and speak words out of anger we'd regret later.

As soon as the door of our apartment closed behind us, Savannah dropped to her knees, fumbling with my pants. Her entire demeanor changed. Gone was the reluctant woman and back was the sex-driven side of her persona. Sometimes, it felt like two women lived in the same body. "Stop."

She ignored me and unbuckled my belt and unbuttoned my pants.

"Stop," I repeated.

Her eyes bore into mine, and her lips parted, ready to engulf the lower part of me that swelled under her palm. "You said… Carter, you said once we get home…"

I stepped back, buttoning my denims. "Not like this. Not after you flirted with another guy right in front of me, surrounded by people I work with."

Still on her knees, she edged closer. "It was innocent flirting, you know that. Don't act like a big baby. You're sounding ridiculous right now."

I pointed to my chest with my thumb. "I'm ridiculous?"

She bobbed her head. "Yeah. Acting like jealous and shit. It doesn't suit you. You had your fun; I had mine. Stop making a big deal out of it."

I blinked. A dozen times. She was fucking delusional.

"He's producing a TV show, and they're looking for lead actors. It was business. A golden ticket you stole from me with your misplaced jealousy."

Coils of tension tightened my insides. Air washed in and out of my lungs faster. My entire being overheated. My skin felt too tight around my body. I knew the signs. An episode was coming.

Closing my eyes, I breathed in. And out. In. And out.

It did nothing to quiet the uneasiness swirling in the depths of me. I had to get out of here, breathe in some fresh air. And run. For as long and as fast as I could. To relieve the tendrils of tension swirling in me at a vertiginous speed. The walls of the apartment were closing in on me. I undid the top buttons of my shirt and massaged the column of my throat.

Nothing helped.

Snatching my phone from my back pocket, I shot Ed, my security detail, a text, then hurried to the bedroom.

Savannah's high-pitched voice resonated from the entryway. "Where do you think you're going?" she asked. "Carter, come back here. We're not done. *I'm* not done."

I blocked her voice, changed into my workout gear, laced my sneakers, and dashed for the door. "I'll be back later. Don't wait for me."

Before the door slammed behind me, I heard her pleading voice. "Carter, come back. Don't go." The confident, carnal version of her was gone. Back was the sensible woman.

Too late.

The storm inside me wasn't calming. I had to exert myself physically. Until it killed all the voices in my head.

For the first time, I found myself questioning whether Savannah Prince was the woman I believed her to be or merely using me as a stepping stone to fame.

With a shake of my head, I brushed the thought away and jogged down the stairs, not in the mood to wait for the elevator. When I landed on the sidewalk, cold air filled my lungs, and some of my angst diminished. Seconds later, Ed stood beside me, wearing an outfit similar to mine, and nodded as I tried to outrun my own self. The sound of my soles hitting the pavement, the noises of traffic and sirens in the background, the smoke and aroma from take-out counters quieted my mind as I pounded away faster.

Chapter 17
Savannah

Since the night of Dylan Daughtry's party a couple of weeks ago, Carter had been more distant. He often went for a run in the middle of the day or disappeared for hours, pretending he was recording music in a studio he booked in Santa Monica. At night, he slept in one of the guest rooms and woke up early to go for another run or hit the gym.

Last night, he announced he was going to spend a few days in Green Mountain before leaving Los Angeles for four weeks next month because he had engagements. TV interviews on late-night shows and a much-coveted spot as a guest judge on the country's most-watched TV reality singing competition, all being filmed in New York City.

How much would I give to have this kind of notoriety? Be adulated. And wanted.

I was desperate to get the real Carter back, though. The one who cared about me and my opinions. The one whose face lit up when we got together. The one happy to cook dinner just so we could spend a night in and discuss our lives and our dreams, our pasts and our futures.

This morning, we were having breakfast at a small eatery in Malibu, and if it wasn't for the fact we drove here together, I would have thought we were strangers. Knots tied my stomach. I hated the distance that had grown between us. We used to have fun together. Now I felt invisible by his side. Dressed in a black T-shirt and a pair of jeans, he looked handsome even without trying. He sipped his tea, reading the news on his phone, not paying me any attention. Like I said, invisible.

I sucked in a breath and broke the tense silence. "How about we visit that music exhibition everyone in town has been talking about this afternoon?" I waited for him to look up and answer. This was me extending an olive branch to resolve whatever disagreement still lingered between us. Carter loved music—more than he ever loved anything else in his life—and there was a special exhibition in town showcasing the evolution of music in cinema. I thought it could be fun for us to go, and it might even earn me some brownie points to make up for our fight at the party.

Instead of sounding enthusiastic about the idea, he just grunted in reply.

Leaning forward, I rested my hand over his, wishing he would grant me a few seconds of his time. I plastered the most genuine smile on my face. "What do you think? We could walk on the beach first, grab lunch afterward, and get there later."

He studied me for a minute as if to assess whether I was trying to coerce him into agreeing to something he wouldn't enjoy.

"It's both our worlds coming together. I heard great

reviews. They're displaying pieces that are usually secured in museums. Even"—I snapped my fingers, trying to remember the name of one of Carter's idols—"I can't remember the name… You know the guy. Broody. Dark."

"Johnny Cash."

I jumped in my seat. "Yes. Him."

It seemed to do the trick because the walls around Carter melted at the name of the music legend.

"Do you wanna go?" I tried again.

He shrugged. "Sure. Could be fun."

"Great."

The rest of the day passed in a blur. Carter's happy mood returned as we walked through the exhibition. The entire time, fans kept stopping him for pictures and autographs. He intertwined our fingers as we left the venue. "Thanks for bringing me here," was all he said as we reached the parking lot through a back door.

We drove in silence for a while. Carter looked more relaxed than he'd been in weeks. At some point, his fingers weaved through mine again, and he rested our joined hands onto my lap. "Sushi?" he asked, tilting his head to meet my gaze. "We could get takeout and watch a movie or something."

I loved the prospect of finally letting go of the argument that had kept us apart for far too long. "I'd like that. Same order as usual?" I asked.

He nodded, and using the app on my phone, I placed our food order.

For the rest of the evening, we cuddled on the couch, sharing food and watching a comedy we both agreed on. Life was back to normal, and it gave me hope that whatever stood between us, we could mend it if we gave it a try.

Around midnight, Carter was in the bedroom, exiting the shower with only a towel around his waist when I walked in. For a second, I admired his toned abs and the golden skin that covered every inch of him. Yes, the California sun—thanks to our walk on the beach today—had done wonders for his complexion.

After the day we had, I wasn't ready to lose him all over again to his other life.

"I was thinking," I began while I slipped into a set of silk pajamas. "Instead of going to Tennessee, why don't you invite Dahlia and Jack over for a few days? You've been saying for months that you wish I'd meet them. This could be the perfect opportunity."

Carter's eyes snapped toward mine, and surprise painted his expression. Yeah, I was never the one begging for a child to enter my perfect life, but if inviting them over would help to keep the much-needed peace between us, then so damn be it. I would sacrifice my own comfort and peace for two or three days.

Anyway, a voice in my head repeated on a loop I should size up the competition. Carter admitted one night that Dahlia Ellis, his ex-bandmate and deceased-brother's widow, was the only woman he ever truly loved. I wanted to understand why. If we were to have a future together, I had to grasp every bit of the missing piece of information.

"What do you say?" I pressed, sitting on the edge of the bed and massaging rose water lotion into my hands. "We could put them up in one of the guest rooms." My tongue burned with the urge to suggest they be set up at a hotel, but knowing Carter, he'd either refuse or would spend time with them there, and I would end up here all alone. "You could buy a crib."

Carter swiveled to face me. "Jack sleeps in a bed, Savannah. He's not a baby anymore."

With a flick of my wrist, I shrugged it off. "Whatever. You get what I mean."

He studied me with an expression I couldn't decipher. Once again today, I smiled at him in the sweetest possible way so he would have no reason to refuse—or doubt my motives.

"After over a year of dating and making all kinds of excuses to never meet my family, you're suddenly feeling the urge to play hostess? What's the catch?"

I sighed and lowered my shoulders. "There's none. At first, it was because I felt threatened by Dahlia. Now that I know we're serious, she doesn't bother me as much. Also, I know you miss them. You keep going to them every chance you get. For once, I'm offering you to invite them over." I moved to my feet and looped my arms around his neck, staring deep into his eyes. "My jealousy was misplaced. I realize it now. What do you say? It would be fun to go to the beach, the four of us. Like we did today. And dine someplace trendy. When was the last time Dahlia came to LA?" I cocked a eyebrow, hoping my sincerity showed. "I'm sure she'd appreciate the escape to sunnier scenery for a quick vacation."

Carter caressed my cheek with a knuckle and combed my hair back. "You would do that? For me?"

I nodded. "I would do anything for you." I pinched my lips together, reluctant to speak the words I hadn't planned to reveal. "I love you. Isn't this what love means? Compromises? And being there for each other?"

"I suppose." He remained silent.

I didn't miss the fact he didn't return the L-word. Truth? I didn't expect him to. If I'd learned anything about Carter Hills in the last year, it was that his heart felt unreachable. Sure, he might enjoy my company—who wouldn't?—but not enough to break the thick wall of ice he hid his heart behind. Not yet. But I'd work hard to melt every layer. One day, I would get those words back. Tenfold.

"Is that a *Yes*?" I asked, using my most smooth-as-honey voice. The one he could never resist.

He rubbed his scruffy jaw. "Let me talk to her, and I'll let you know." His smile broke free. "I'd love for them to come over. Thanks for offering."

As I moved to my tiptoes to kiss him, I untied the towel around his waist. It pooled on the floor at our feet. "Oop-sy," I said against his lips. The remaining distance and tension that had been running high between us dissolved. If I'd known inviting his unrequited love over would chase his reluctance toward me, I would have done it a long time ago.

Before I could process anything, I was thrown on my back on the bed. Yeah, Carter Hills couldn't resist me—and my selfless heart. It was about time he realized it too.

———

Dahlia and Jack flew in the next Friday. Nick, Dahlia's husband, had stayed back in Green Mountain. It was a relief when Carter told me he wouldn't come. One less person to worry about. I really wanted to observe Carter and his best friend's dynamics without any distractions. In a perfect world, the kid would have stayed behind too, but hey, I couldn't lose my mind over this, or I might be the one having to live at the hotel.

Carter held my hand in his as we waited for his family, as he called them, to walk off the plane. It made no sense to me he considered them his, but I was done trying to convince him otherwise. Sporting sunglasses and a baseball cap, so that he was not recognized and bothered, Carter stood tall. He kept checking the time on his phone while wiping his other hand over his pant leg before returning it to mine.

Why was he so nervous? Was it the idea of having both women in his life living under the same roof or something else?

I turned my head toward him. "You okay?" His gaze swept over my silhouette, and I high-fived myself mentally for choosing this outfit today of all days. I was wearing a plunging red number with stilettos that showcased all my curves perfectly. My makeup was applied to perfection, and my lips were coated in ruby-red lipstick. Los Angeles was my city—and I ruled it. Dahlia had to understand she was the intruder here and therefore had to bend to my presence. In a manner of speaking anyway.

Carter shook his head. "Sure. They're late."

"Their plane landed with a fifteen-minute delay. They're not the president. No need to get sweaty over this. Sweat isn't a good scent on you anyway. Man up and stop fidgeting."

Carter's eyebrows creased, but before he could reply, a whoop followed by ear-screeching *"Carrrter"* pierced the air.

I jumped back.

The little creature with a dark tousled mane and gray irises running toward us was the spitting image of the man standing on my left. I blinked, taking every inch of this small person in.

A wave of dizziness washed through me, and I did my best to school my features and fix an upward curl to my lips as a gorgeous—see? I could be honest about it—woman with red hair, piercing green eyes, and a warm smile closed in on us. In the last year, I had convinced myself Dahlia Ellis looked great in pictures just because she was photogenic, nothing else. But I was wrong. An aura of kindness and joy radiated from her. For a second, I forgot we were sworn enemies and found myself enchanted by the woman standing in front of me.

Before I could offer her a hand, she pulled me into a warm hug. "Ohmygod, I'm so glad to meet you. It was about time." She moved to Carter next who was holding Jack and hugged him. "Cart, I've missed you so much. I can't believe we're spending three days together in Los Angeles."

Carter hugged her back for infinite seconds. Long enough that it sank my stomach. I saw how he looked at her when she appeared in our sight. I would never measure up to Dahlia Ellis unless I upped my game. This was a truth I could no longer refute.

With Jack, still in his arms, telling Carter all about the flight and Dahlia's palm snuggled in his, we exited the airport. I traipsed behind them, and for the first time in years, I didn't feel like the queen I knew I was. Instead, I felt rejected, standing on the outskirts of a world that didn't include me.

Ed, the bodyguard on duty, waited for us and piled our guests' luggage in the trunk after we neared the car.

Carter and Jack joked around, sitting in the third-row. I couldn't comprehend how my tall boyfriend could fold his legs in the tiny and uncomfortable space back there while Dahlia and I sat beside each other in the second-row seats.

"This is very generous of you two to have us over," Dahlia said, her smile unfaltering. One I tried to mimic so she couldn't tell her presence already irked me. "Jack was so excited when I announced we'll be flying here. We really miss having Carter around." It wasn't a jab at me. She was just stating a fact.

"Carter is happier here," I said, unable to resist. "I can't deny we're awesome together."

Dahlia's smile widened. "Well, I'm happy we're doing this. I'm sure you and I will become great friends."

I blinked, doing my best not to scowl. Was Dahlia for real? How on Earth could she believe she and I would ever become friends? First, except for Carter, we had nothing in common. Second, couldn't she tell we were nothing alike? She might be nice, but let's not kid ourselves—after popping out a kid, she must have had saggy tits and her stomach probably looked like dough. Third, and most importantly, she had walked away from fame. By choice. No sane person would do that. Ever. This simple fact led me to believe there was something wrong with her. I, on the other hand, was at the top of my game. Beautiful, a body flirting with perfection, and a thirst for success and recognition hard to equal.

Infusing myself with some cheer, I pumped my fist. "Yay, can't wait for us to become besties."

For the rest of the ride, she made conversation. Snooze fest. I was right all along. This woman and I had nothing—with a capital *N*—in common.

Once we got home, after Carter confirmed he had made a reservation for us in a family restaurant, I pretended to have a headache coming on and locked myself in the bedroom. Family restaurant? This was worse than our first date, when he invited me to an outdated Italian bistro that I wanted to flee seconds after stepping inside. Just the overwhelming smell of roasted garlic and the color of the carpet were enough to send me running. What happened to dinner in an upscale restaurant with sumptuous seafood or filet mignon platters I could never afford? Why was Carter letting a spoiled brat dictate our dinner options? Nausea rose in my throat. This was worse than any scenario I imagined when I voiced the invitation.

With my fingertips, I massaged my temples, the headache about to become real.

Through the door, I could hear muffled laughter, and Carter being happier than I'd ever seen him. I heard the padding of little feet and cries of joy. Followed by the groans of an adult male and more chuckles. Ugh. Children disgusted me. They were a nuisance.

Not only did they ruin a woman's body, but they were also smelly, dirty little things—useless in every way.

After a while, the apartment fell silent, and I relished the calm. It was more comforting than any noise.

A soft knock brought me out of my reverie.

"Yeah," I called out, exiting my dressing room after I changed into a white wrap dress with a plunging neckline. "It's open."

Dahlia's cheerful face appeared through the opening. "Hey, Savannah. Since I have a few hours to myself, I was about to go shopping downtown. Ed said he would drive me. Wanna join? There's this little café I like here in Los Angeles that I haven't visited in ages. We could make a stop there afterward. Get to know each other better. What do you say? Carter and Jack are taking a nap and I—"

I swung the door open, and she stumbled, bracing herself against the doorway to avoid falling face-first. "A nap?"

She shrugged. "Yes. They often do this when they are together. Carter sings to him and reads a story, and Jack falls asleep in his arms. Then he just naps with him instead of putting him down and risking waking him up. He's great with kids. Always has been."

There. Again. The mention they shared a past together. One I wasn't part of. One that I wished Carter could forget all about.

As tempting as shopping sounded, I couldn't see myself spending the rest of my day with Dahlia Ellis. *No thanks*. It was bad enough that I'd have to share my apartment with her for three whole days—no need to make it worse than it already was.

I cast a glance down and slumped my shoulders. "Thank you so much for inviting me." I grabbed her hand between mine. "There's nothing I would like more right now than us spending time together, but this headache is a bitch, and if I don't rest, I won't be able to join you tonight at that awesome place Carter booked. I've been looking forward to having you all over for a long time, and the last thing I want is to miss the little time we have together. Can I take a raincheck?"

Dahlia's face fell. "Huh, sure. I just thought it would be fun for us women to hang out together. We'll try to fit in some alone time later. Take care of yourself. I know how debilitating headaches can be. Hope you get better before tonight. If not, I have an herbal tea recipe that could help. Let me know if you wanna try it. I'll grab the ingredients on my way back."

Of course, she also possessed the remedy to cure me. Once the door closed behind her, I breathed out. Why did she have to be so nice? Couldn't Carter's best friend be a nutcase? I was better at dealing with crazy people than sane ones.

Once I heard the front door close and I made sure I was alone, I returned to my dressing room, changed into workout gear, and made my way to the gym, two blocks away from our apartment.

Pilates, it would be. And maybe a group class or two if I could squeeze them in.

I had to burn a thousand calories since I bet tonight's

menu would only consist of carbs and fat. A wave of
nausea rose at the back of my throat. This day couldn't get
any worse.

Chapter 18
Carter

Dahlia and Jack left two nights ago, and already, I missed having them around. Their contagious happiness was hard to live without. They were here. With me. They came into my world, and I introduced them to my new life. For the entire time they were in town, I felt Savannah's resistance to their presence. Even under fake confidence, I knew she wasn't at ease with my best friend around. I tried hard to reassure her, to include her in all our outings and activities, but still, she wouldn't participate in the board games hour, cartoon-movie night, or join us when we visited the theme park, always pretending some physical ailment or conflict of schedule. Savannah's work schedule was pretty loose these days—she often went weeks without working. Other than a few appearances on TV shows, a photo spread in a magazine about the trendiest diets in Hollywood, some advertising contracts, and a small role in an indie movie produced by a streaming service, her time was mostly spent at home, working out, or shopping.

Things between us had been sailing smoothly until we got into a fight last night after I refused to throw a party and invite Hollywood A-listers over. My home was a sacred place to me, and I had no intention of playing host to a bunch of people I didn't know, just to rub my success in their faces, only for the sake of it. I despised the superficial side of the show-business. No one, not even Savannah, could convince me otherwise. After the way she behaved the last time we were around a bunch of people from the music industry, I had no intention of having a do-over. *No thanks.*

This morning, I woke up feeling agitated. My sudden burst of restlessness had everything to do with the memories of what happened at Dylan's birthday party, brought forth due to the previous night's fight. Even after all these days, and despite begging my brain to erase them on numerous occasions, every time I replayed that night in my head, wrath lodged in my chest. The images of Savannah rubbing herself against another man were inked in my mind. Last night's fight woke up my desire to deal with this situation once and for all. Yeah, I had enough time to think. We needed to talk about it—her flirting with another man and our boundaries. Until we did, I wouldn't feel at ease.

The last—and only—time I tried to broach the subject with her, it ended up causing a huge rift between us that lasted for weeks. Still, it was the reasonable thing to do. We had to set some ground rules. Flirting with other people was a big no for me. We were in a committed relationship, and it had to mean something. To both of us.

After a day spent running errands on my own and replaying in my head how I should approach the subject, I came home a little after dinner. The place was awfully silent, but Savannah was home. I could tell from the energy reverberating through the walls.

"Carter, is that you?" my girlfriend called out from the bedroom, her voice sultry.

Not in a hurry to see her just yet, I emptied a bottle of cold water I fished out of the refrigerator in one gulp to tame my annoyed self. After kicking off my shoes and grabbing a snack, I followed the sound of her voice.

"I did something, and now I need your help. It was supposed to be a surprise, but you've been gone for so long, I'm dying here."

With half-hearted steps and a collected demeanor, I padded toward our bedroom down the long hall with half a dozen doors to rooms we never used. Three guest rooms —one that had become my bedroom—another full bathroom, a second home office. I already used the bigger one on the east side to store my guitars and other musical apparatus. The apartment looked like a museum. Lifeless. White. Only displaying paintings on its walls. No pictures. No kid's drawings on the refrigerator—Savannah told me to display Jack's artwork only in my office the day we moved in.

Our place bore no personal touches.

No signs that real people lived here.

I sighed. This place was way too big, too impersonal, too frigid.

Once I reached the bedroom, I steeled my back. I hoped Savannah was in a good mood because we really needed to have a conversation. One where more than one-syllable words and moans were spoken.

In the doorway, I stopped. My heart did a tumble in my chest, and I forgot how to breathe for a split second. I blinked. Blinked again. And gulped a big intake of air. Dozens of thoughts swirled in my head.

On the bed lay Savannah, wearing red lacy lingerie, with a crimson satin blindfold over her eyes, matching lipstick, black high heels, her arms raised overhead, wrists handcuffed to the headboard.

She squirmed a little, and I enjoyed the vision. A little too much.

She looked sinful. A hot temptation with her full breasts barely covered by the sheer fabric and her long brown hair curled to perfection.

My traitorous dick wanted to play.

I didn't. Savannah and I needed to talk. This couldn't wait anymore. All the unsaid was eating me alive. I hated unresolved issues.

"Carter, is that you? Please. Help me. You can't keep me like this. Set me free."

I cleared my throat. "I'm back," I said.

"I'm glad it's you. You like your gift?" A large smile took over her face.

I cleared my throat and pushed my hands into my pockets. "Sure. But I'm not in the mood to play your little games right now. Told you when you called earlier that we gotta talk. Serious stuff. We agreed we'd do it when I got home. Don't try to distract me. It's not working."

"But…" Her bottom lip quivered, but she regained her composure quickly. "I thought you'd want to play. Get rid of your exhaustion. To relax and enjoy the fun times I'd planned."

Her pout turned devilish now, fitting her look.

And it almost—yes, almost—worked. It almost softened me. Not letting her little game get to me, I exhaled and rolled my shoulders back.

"Well, that's not what *I* planned. Not interested."

Savannah moved her legs, twisting her lower self in a slow, sexy motion.

My dick twitched. The rest of my body remained impassive.

"Changed your mind yet?" she asked, breaking the war between my two very independent control centers.

"Nope. I'll see you in a bit. Going to shower."

She pursed her lips in a pleading attempt. "Oh. You wanna punish me? This could be fun. Role-play and stuff like that are powerful aphrodisiacs. Wanna try? I've been a bad, bad girl. Shower fast. I can't wait to be tortured by you."

My gaze zoned in on her plump lips, and I closed my eyes, trying to steady my jagged breathing. "You like that? Being bad?"

"I could be your sex slave. Or a hidden treasure for you to unwrap. Whatever pleases you the most. Wanna play groupie and rock star? Or teacher and student? I could wear a plaid skirt and pig tails."

Savannah crossed her legs suggestively, rubbing herself against the Egyptian cotton sheets. She was a contrasting red temptation on the black sheets.

Now that I had seen her like this, I would never be able to unsee it. To erase it from my mind. These images would be branded into my brain forever. Savannah looked like a pornographic wet dream.

Don't let her get to you. Be strong.

"Sex won't work on me. Sorry."

She stilled. "I missed you while you were gone today, Carter. I thought you'd like this. I was wrong. Let me make it up to you, okay? Name it. I'll be whatever you want me to be. Please uncuff me first, and we can figure out what will make you happy...and help you unwind. I can give you a head in the shower. Or a lap dance. I know a place where I can book a room with a pole. Would you like that? A striptease?" She paused, her words marinating between us. "My only desire is your satisfaction. Don't leave me hanging here."

With cautious steps, as if I were walking on fire, I inched closer and sat by her side.

With the tip of my finger, I drew a line from her collarbone to the apex of her thighs.

Her breathing accelerated.

She spoke in a hushed voice, each word dripping with lust. "See? You like to play too. I knew you would. Thought this could be naughty. I'm so glad you changed your mind."

"We agreed we'd talk. Seducing me won't get you out of it. I'm not that weak."

I pinched one hard nipple through the thin fabric of her bra.

"Yes," Savannah cried out. "Keep doing this, Carter. I deserve to be punished." She pushed her legs apart. "Look. I'm dripping wet for you. Wanna taste how you make me feel? I'll be your dessert."

I moved to my feet, palming my dick so it stayed put. "Sorry, I'm not in the mood. I'll shower now. Then we'll talk."

Wearing a smug smirk, I left her on the bed and shut the bathroom door behind me. Her screams dissolved once I turned the water on.

———

What the hell. Was it a dream? I pried my eyelids open. It hurt. Like really bad.

"Good. You're awake," Savannah said in a diabolical voice I'd never heard before.

I tried to move my body, only to realize my hands were cuffed to the headboard.

My sleepy brain had a hard time reading the situation. "What are you doing? Ouch, stop."

Savannah poured some scorching hot liquid over my chest. No, scratch that, she was glazing my nipples with hot lava.

"What are you doing? Uncuff me," I barked, scooting to the side, trying to break the links tying me to the bed to escape the pain.

"Don't move, Carter, or you'll burn yourself."

"I'm already burned. Let go of me."

She tsk-tsked. "We really need to up our sex game. That's what I was trying to show you earlier. Since you refused to listen to me, I've decided to surprise you with these new tricks. Relax. You'll see it's much more enjoyable when you have an open mind about it."

She lowered her mouth to my chest and licked her way up until her tongue grazed my chin. "It's cherry-flavored. Some edible wax. Next time, you'll pour it all over me and eat me up before it hardens. For now, watch and learn."

"Stop. There's nothing enjoyable about this. It fucking burns."

"Carter, you walked away earlier. I wanted to play with you, and you ignored me for a very long time. The thing is, I really wanna have fun, so now the roles are reversed. I'm the one punishing you for what you did."

In the dark, I blinked. "For what I did? I did nothing. Are you crazy?"

"No. You left this morning without saying a word. You've been ignoring me since you came home, and you took your sweet time to free me afterward. You're lucky I didn't get a whip. Or a dildo." Her eyes sparkled. "Would you have liked that? Anal play in your virgin ass? Maybe next time." She paused. "And, by the way, the only thing I'm crazy about is you." A dark laugh filled the silence. "Hot melted wax is supposed to turn you on, Carter. Stop squirming."

"Well, it's not."

She traced the length of my arm with her sharp fingernails, no doubt leaving their imprints on my flesh.

I shivered and bit the inside of my cheek to avoid saying things I would regret later.

"That's where you're wrong. A part of you loves the pain. We all do." With one firm grip, she squeezed my balls, and the cry got stuck in my throat.

"STOP. Release me. NOW. It's not funny… It-it fucking hurts. Nothing you're doing right now is pleasurable."

"What will it be then? Will you play with me?" she asked in a salacious voice. "Indulge in my game?"

"No. I'm not doing anything until we have a talk. A real one. Not the other bullshit you call communication."

"You want us to talk about real stuff?" Savannah turned on the bedside lamp, casting a soft golden glow in the guest room where I was staying, and watched me with a raised eyebrow. "Emotions? Feelings and stuff?"

I nodded.

"Are you serious or messing with me? I thought you were joking when you said it earlier."

I moved to sit up but couldn't due to my handcuffed wrists.

"Yes. Serious."

"But why? Why would you want to talk about that stuff? This is ridiculous. We get along great. We have fun together. I already said I love you. No need to add complicated and dreadful discussions to the mix."

Right now, Savannah looked like a bewildered little girl

trying to follow a conversation in another language. She fetched the keys from her side of the bed and released my hands.

With her legs folded to her chest, she sat before me.

Rubbing my wrists, I massaged them, trying to smooth the cuff marks. "Because that's what adults do. And people in relationships… It's about time we have a real one."

Savannah laughed bitterly. "Talk about killing the mood." She pointed to the lingerie she was wearing.

"No. That's where you're wrong. I don't recognize us. We used to connect and have a great time together."

"We still do."

I touched her hand. "In many ways, we do. But not in those that matter the most. We argue, then fuck, and then act as if everything is fine."

"The sex is amazing. I know I'm great at it."

A small smile peeked on my lips. "Yes, you are. You blow my mind every time. But sex isn't everything."

Savannah looked at me with a quizzical stare as if I'd spoken words she couldn't interpret.

"Whatever you say." Something passed in her eyes. "When I was fifteen and my step-dad said he wanted to talk, it was usually a code for…huh…other things…" Tears pooled in her eyes.

The caring side of me took over, and I scooted closer to wrap my arms around her. I caressed her hair and tugged her into my embrace, shielding her from future harm.

"You never mentioned what he did to you. You wanna talk about it?" I rested my lips on the top of her head.

Savannah shook her head. "He said and did horrible things to me. When I was sixteen, I ran away from home. In all the time I was living with them, he tried to blame me…my appearance…for his deviances… He belittled me. One day, I couldn't take it anymore. My mom… She never believed me. She took his side. I've been on my own since. And-and groomed to think sex is the solution to everything. Every time Jerry, my step-dad, said, 'Savannah, I need to talk to you,' I knew that he expected me on my knees or on my all fours, nothing else."

I swallowed the lump down my throat. Chills traversed my back. With what she had hinted at before, I never believed Savannah had actually been sexually assaulted by her step-dad. That the extent of his control over her ran deeper than what she had let me know. "And your…your own mother believed him instead of you?"

She shrugged. "Jerry can be pretty persuasive. And well, I looked hot at sixteen. She probably thought I was flirting with him. Who knows. She stayed faithful to the man providing for her. Carter, I was used, abused, and shamed…for everything." Sobs rocked her body, and I fastened my arms around her.

"I won't let anybody hurt you. You have my word. I'm sorry you went through this. Did you ever go to the cops? To lodge a complaint against him? He could still be arrested." Fury seared inside me.

She shook her head. "I preferred to put the past in the past and leave it there. No need to open this wound again. Please." She lifted her eyes and locked them on mine. "Don't get involved, okay? Respect my wishes. Let's move forward. All I've ever wanted was a fresh start, and I'm finally doing it. I don't wanna revisit my teen years."

How could a man hurt a young girl without her mother stepping in and putting a stop to the abuse? Nausea swirled in my stomach.

"What can I do?" I asked after Savannah's sobs decreased.

"Hug me, okay? Tonight, stay with me. Let me sleep in your bed."

I nodded.

For the first time in weeks, we found our peace and fell asleep holding on to each other.

———

Last night was a bit blurry in my head. The conversation about Savannah's step-dad had haunted my sleeping hours. I couldn't believe all she went through when she was still just a kid. Perhaps I would ask Taylor to see if he could dig up dirt on the guy. Maybe he could be charged for other things and sent to prison where he belonged. Was Savannah the only girl he abused, or were there others who had suffered as a result of his sick ways? No wonder all my discussion attempts ended up with her naked. Geez, if only I had known.

In the shower, under the hot stream of water, I removed the last pieces of wax from my chest. I still couldn't believe Savannah wanted me to play with whips and bondage last night. I experienced no satisfaction in being tortured—the molten hot wax had been more than enough—and I'd kill myself before doing the same to a woman. No matter how much she begged for it.

This morning, I woke up with something I had been missing for weeks. A real smile. Contentment in my heart. It felt great to experience some sort of connection back with her. Since Dahlia and Jack had visited, a new rift had grown between us, and it was about time we bridged our differences.

Savannah greeted me in the kitchen with a mug of tea. She wore only a shirt of mine, showcasing her long legs, looking as incredible as always, but without trying too hard this time.

"Hungry?" she asked as I stepped up to her and placed my hands on her hips, pulling her in for a kiss.

"Starving."

She pressed one hand to my chest. "Perfect. I made you breakfast."

"You did?"

In all the time we'd been together, Savannah never cooked anything. Either I did or we ordered from some restaurant in town.

"Yeah. I like surprising you."

"I love it too."

Her smile magnified. "I hope you have nothing planned for today because I want us to just *be* all day. Before we need to get ready for the premiere tonight."

"You sure?" I tipped one brow to make sure I wasn't dreaming and Savannah wasn't bullshitting me.

She wound her arms around my neck. "Yes. I'm playing housewife."

I kissed her. "You are? Am I dead, or am I imagining this?"

She leaned back and laughed. A genuine laugh this time. "Only for today, though. It's a one-time thing. For now. And then we'll see." She shrugged. "If I like it."

I tugged her closer, and her laughter increased. "Thanks." My lips claimed hers, and when she purred, I deepened the kiss.

I missed this version of her so much.

Right now, I couldn't get enough of the sweet woman she was.

We ate breakfast together, and my hopes we could move forward with our relationship skyrocketed.

I could see myself being happy. Yeah, this time, it felt real.

For the rest of the day, we cuddled on the couch,

unable to keep our hands, and every other body part, to ourselves.

———

Hours later, we were getting ready for the movie premiere. The one Savannah requested a new dress for weeks ago. She'd landed a small role in the blockbuster, and now, we were about to walk our first red carpet together. I had made a reservation at her favorite restaurant and rented a limo to make the event one to remember forever. After all, she would never get another first movie premiere ever again.

I adjusted my cufflinks and bowtie and met her at her beauty station, as she called it. It looked more like a makeup and hair station you'd find on a movie set. Another extravaganza she demanded when we moved in together. It made her happy, and that made me happy too.

"Hey," I said, leaning forward to kiss the back of her neck. "You smell great."

"I know," she said, mirroring my smile. This time, her overconfident personality didn't seem forced. It didn't even sound narcissistic. More like a fact.

I loved how Savannah wasn't afraid to believe in herself and her abilities, and how she always went after what she desired. Not a lot of people reached for their dreams.

She swivelled on the stool and moved to her feet.

Her red satin robe opened and puddled on the floor, revealing a sinful matching set of crimson bra and panties.

"Fuck—"

A victorious grin lit up her face. "I knew you wouldn't be able to resist."

She winked, and I wrapped my arms around her, filling my nose with the delicious scent of her.

Confident and strong. That's what it should be called. And it should be bottled up. We'd make a killing off it.

It took me a while to get used to it, but now it smelled like home.

My hands molded to her gorgeous breasts, kneading the soft flesh.

Savannah moaned, closing her eyes and shivering when my tongue licked a path between them. "Carter…don't. Please." Her pleas vanished when I pushed a cup down and sucked on a nipple.

With one finger, I drew a line between her thighs and leaned closer."Now go get ready. Or we'll be late," I whispered, my lips brushing her earlobe.

She panted, watching me with glossy eyes. Eyes filled with pure and uncensored lust.

Savannah's breathing evened, and her chest stopped rising and falling in quick motions. "Wait until later. I'll make you lose your mind." Her words sounded filthy, and that diabolical spark was back in her gaze. "Now close your eyes, and I'll make an entry," she said, her tone teasing.

"Please tell me you'll be dressed, or I'll lose it."

"Yes. I will. But seeing me will shatter all your restraints, and you'll regret stopping what you were doing seconds ago."

I smacked her ass. "Put that dress on. I've been dying to admire you in it for weeks. I can't believe they had to custom-tailor it for you. Who knew exclusive designers' pieces were this hard to get? You're lucky June has connections, or this would have never happened."

That gown came with a price tag I preferred to never think about again. June called me twice to make sure I wanted to move forward with the order. I rubbed my hands together. Now that I was about to see Savannah in it, excitement bubbled up inside me.

"I know. Be ready to be amazed." She kissed me one last time before disappearing into her dressing room, while I sat on the edge of the bed to wait for her.

My heart raced in my chest.

My body heated up with ill-concealed desire.

The night would be long. I could already predict it.

"You need help with that?" I asked, not even disguising the urgency in my voice, unable to wait any longer. I already knew we'd have to get the sexual tension out of the way before leaving, or we'd both be miserable all night. "I can zip you up."

Savannah's head peeked from the doorway. "No. All good."

I returned her smirk.

"Close your eyes. Don't cheat, Carter."

I raised my hands before me. "Fine."

Leaning back and propping myself on my elbows, I did as she asked.

Savannah muttered something.

"You sure I can't help you? I volunteer."

Her laughter warmed my insides.

It felt like the prom I never attended.

The sound of ruffled fabric got closer and stopped. I could feel my girlfriend standing near me, her breathing slow and steady. I straightened my back, expectations firing inside me. I swept my lips with my tongue.

"Ready?" she asked.

I popped the *P* as I said, "Yep."

"One, two, three. Okay, look."

I parted my eyelids, admiring the vision of her, twirling on herself.

Savannah took my breath away.

"Wow." My brain couldn't come up with anything else to say.

The taffeta of her scarlet dress molded to her curves like a second skin. The plunging neckline acted like a magnet to my eyes. The slit almost reaching her hip upped the sexiness factor by a thousand percent.

She looked phenomenal.

In one movement, I leaped to my feet and curled an arm around her."Wow, you look exquisite. No doubt I'll be the luckiest man tonight."

She leveled her gaze with mine. "I'm glad you recognize it."

Her lips curved into a smile that vibrated through me, making me believe we might actually be happy in the long run, and that someday I could love her. With a capital *L*. Down the road. When my heart would be ready to take a leap of faith.

I leaned in to fuse my lips with hers, loving their taste.

Something hit me, and I released her, stepping back with a frown."Wait, you're not wearing *the* dress. Why? Did something happen to it?"

Savannah sighed and shook her head, giving me a sorrowful, tight-lipped smile.

Moving forward, she knitted her fingers through mine. "No. I spent so much time admiring myself in the mirror wearing it the other night that it didn't feel brand new anymore. I really wanted a new gown for tonight. So, I picked the one you bought for me a while back. It still had the tags on." She shrugged.

What the hell. She fucking shrugged.

"I… We… Are you joking right now?"

"Nah. To be honest, I don't like it *that* much. The way it clings to my ass… I don't know… It makes it look bigger.

Come on, Carter, you can't say I don't look like royalty tonight."

She twirled on herself again, her smile blinding. As if to prove her point.

An uncomfortable chain knotted around my stomach.

In one swift movement, I backed away from her and raked my fingers through my hair.

My pulse spiked.

Was it fury or frustration running in my veins, burning everything in its tracks?

I clenched my hands.

Nah, I couldn't tell.

Were all women this complicated?

My mom wasn't the best mother to me, but she was a good wife. She didn't make my father's life hell-worthy. No, they loved each other and surprised the other with small gestures, always kissing in the kitchen when they thought my brother and I weren't looking.

Neither Dahlia with Jeff. He would have told me. Dahlia was always there for him. Even when darkness threatened to kill everything good between them. She would have never deceived him on purpose. He was the one who made her life hell. She stuck by him through thick and thin, until they rode the wave and found their way back to each other.

And there was Belinda and Stud. They loved each other. A whole lot. Their relationship had strong foundations, based on respect. Everything they did, they did together. As a team. As a family. Because that's what being in a serious and committed relationship meant, no?

Why was everything with Savannah always ending up more difficult than it had to be? Every time I thought I had her figured out, that we were moving forward together, I felt like she didn't care about me or my feelings, and I was back to square one.

Right now, my anger wasn't just motivated by the gown's exorbitant price tag, but by the hit to my pride and reputation too. We had agreed with the designer that Savannah would wear the stupid dress on the red carpet tonight. That she'd be photographed wearing it. This could have been the beginning of a lucrative long-term partnership between them. My words meant something to me. June even got her a spread in the country's top fashion magazine to talk about the movie and her look for the event. The whole nine fucking yards. Now it was all reduced to a stupid joke.

My bowtie felt too tight around my neck.

I breathed out, trying to calm the nerves catching fire inside me.

I could feel my anger rising. Soon, I'd rip at the seams if I didn't talk myself out of throwing a fit.

Savannah would drive me insane.

She was fire and water. Heaven and hell. Black and white. Right and wrong.

All. At. The. Same. Time.

Opposite personalities that lived in the same body. Same mind.

She had a way of driving me crazy.

A ball of fury bounced around in my chest.

After last night's chat, I really thought we were doing better at communicating. That we had agreed to work toward a common goal—our relationship—together.

My blood turned to lava.

The gasket of my patience would pop any second. I cleared my throat, trying to keep my composure from bursting and destroying everything in its wake.

"Savannah, you threw a tantrum to get that dress. You

monopolized my assistant's time to get your hands on it. We came to an agreement with the designer after he refused, at first, to let you wear it."

She fixed me with those doe eyes and that legendary pout—like it was her crowning glory—then grinned at me as if I'd said nothing. As if she didn't care I had to pull strings for her to get the gown and had to fork out a pretty penny so that it arrived on time.

"All that matters is that you love the way I look tonight. Don't be silly. It's just a dress. A ridiculous piece of fabric. Not a reason for you and me to fight."

She circled my waist, her scent washing through me, before kissing my cheek. "Don't get upset, Carter. I look best in this gown." She paused. "Unless you think I'm ugly." Tears shimmered in her eyes. "Do you?"

"What? No. No. You look amazing. I already told you. It's just—" How to say the words without sounding like an egotistical jerk? The one she often accused me to be.

She tapped the corners of her eyes with her fingertips. "Then I'm happy we agree."

She squeezed my hand and without another word, exited the room, leaving me to ponder the last minute on my own.

My anger broiled inside me. I breathed out and pushed some of my wrath down.

Did I really want to let a dress spoil our night?

Getting upset about a gown seemed childish. But still…

We fought over it weeks ago. Damn it.

Yeah, at this instant, my life was a joke. I laughed it out, unable to decide if I wanted to scream at the world or forfeit the entire night and take the next flight home. *Home.* Where was it? I belonged nowhere anymore. I had no family. No roots. How did I end up even more lost than I already was?

When did my life become so twisted? When did dealing with stupid shit become my new reality?

In the middle of the gigantic bedroom, I failed to reload my confused mind.

My spirits sank. And so did my heart. The narrative I'd created in my mind since last night was just that. A narrative.

Could Savannah and I be something different one day? Something more?

Or were we destined to drive each other mad for the rest of time?

Was any of what we shared real, or just part of the act? Was love a game to her?

My eyes trailed on the dressing room where the white gown lay on the floor in a wrinkled puddle. *Don't be silly, it's just a dress. A ridiculous piece of fabric.*

My ass hit the mattress, and I bent forward.

"Fuck it," I cursed as I hurled my bowtie across the room.

Chapter 19
Savannah

ction.

The camera flashed, and I got into royalty mode. I posed, smiled, and batted my eyelashes for the photographers gathered along the red carpet. Carter stood tall by my side, his smile not reaching his eyes. I could tell he was still upset with me for the change of outfit. He wasn't the type to stay mad longer than needed, though. Soon he'd get over it. When he realized we were a hit. That people loved us together and we attracted the attention of the public and the press.

I pivoted and kissed him. Instinctively, his arm looped around my waist, and he kissed me back. Yes, we'd be all right.

In the dark, we sat in the old movie theatre, side by side for the screening of *Sailor's Wife.* I played the part of a sexy bartender falling for the main character's best friend. Nervous energy surged through every cell in my body.

Carter held my hand in his and leaned over to whisper, "You'll do amazing. Relax and enjoy."

I nodded, chewing my bottom lip, as the opening credits filled the screen.

The crowd laughed on point and *"Ahhed"* on point too. From the sound of it, they were enjoying the movie. A layer of stress melted away. Could this role propel me to bigger ones? I crossed my fingers, praying the universe would hear my plea. This was ridiculous. I was super talented. Even with just a minor role, any sharp-eyed director could see how magnetic I was and how much the camera loved me.

My first scene played on the screen. Carter's squeeze on my hand tightened. Despite myself, I mouthed the lines I had learned by heart.

Air caught in my lungs. The movie kept rolling, but I couldn't register anything. Where was the scene where I got sprayed with a hose by that kid when I walked into the backyard? Or the one where I complained about my lack of love life in front of fake-drunk patrons? Or the making-out scene in that rusty old pickup truck when my onscreen lover showered me with gifts after he thought he had lost me?

Humiliation clogged my throat.

How did they dare to cut my role to an eight-minute appearance?

Why did no one inform me? Was I being played?

My nails bit into my palms, drawing pinpricks of blood as I clenched my fists.

In one swift motion, I was out of my seat and tearing through the screening room doors. I wanted to go home. To forget all about this night. I'd never accept being the butt of the joke.

"Great job, Savannah," exclaimed a man I recognized

to be a member of the crew when I passed him in my hurry to disappear.

I murdered him with my eyes before locking myself in the ladies' room. There. No one could get me here. I was safe.

Before I could sit on the floor, a soft knock startled me.

"Hey, I know you're in there." Carter's voice sounded worried—and protective. "Open the door."

"No. Go away. Leave me alone."

"Open the door, or I'll get someone to do it."

I exhaled my frustration. No doubt he would get it unlocked if I refused. *Goddamnit.*

With shaky fingers, I turned the lock. "Happy now? You're here to feast on my humiliation? Does it make you hard to see me broken?"

He closed in on me and grabbed my upper arms, forcing me to look at him. "I have no clue what went down in there. I was hoping you'll tell me more." His soft voice wrapped around my bleeding heart.

"Why? So you can rub it in my face afterward? No thanks. Hard pass."

"Hey. Stop. I'm here because I care about you. Explain it to me because I don't get it. You were incredible in that scene. Nothing to be upset about."

"Scene. Singular. I had scenes. With an *S.* Plural. Many of them. Some funny. Some dramatic. They cut them in the final edits. They're not there anymore. How am I supposed to secure main roles if no one sees me in action for more than eight insipid minutes?" I crossed my arms over my chest. "Enlighten me. Because right now, I don't see it happening."

"It's one role. And you were great. You'll get more opportunities. It's your first red carpet, and it's huge. A moment to remember. Being propelled to stardom takes time."

"Says the guy who got millions of dollars in his bank account the first year he got signed."

Carter's gaze drifted downward before returning to meet mine. "It's like winning the lottery... It's not an everyday occurrence. Most people work hard, and their success is earned. Not given. It wasn't handed to me. For years, I worked my ass off to get where I am today. I started doing concerts when I was just a little kid. Success didn't appear in my life out of the blue...no matter what people choose to believe. Use this experience to learn and grow. Don't let one movie destroy all the hard work you put in. Your turn will come. I can tell. You *are* talented. Never believe anyone else who states the opposite."

"You really believe it?"

He nodded. "Wanna go home or are you staying here, with your chin high, not letting those eight minutes faze you?"

"I don't know... How can I face all these people now? I'm reduced to being an extra in that movie. It hurts."

Carter kissed my forehead. "I'm aware, but since when do you not fight back? Where's the woman who stands tall and reaches for her dreams?"

His words made sense. I relished the fact Carter acknowledged my dedication. And my will.

With a huff, I added, "There's this party afterward. It's supposed to be epic. Lots of big names, directors, and producers will be attending. I'd like to go."

He smiled. "That's my girl."

I squinted. "Your girl?"

He offered me a one-shoulder shrug. "I'm proud of you. For standing up for yourself." He didn't comment on the slip-up. "It will be all right. Keep believing in yourself, and you'll get there."

Chapter 20

Carter

"Do you really have to go?" Savannah asked, watching me as I packed a bag a few days later. She stood in the doorway, her arms folded over her chest, her lips shaped into a sad curve. "We never spend time together anymore."

My eyes snapped in her direction. "You're kidding, right? Since I've rented this place, I practically live full-time in California. I barely see my friends anymore. All my meetings with Riley and June are done over video chat. I see Dahlia and Jack not even once a month these days. The majority of my time is dedicated to you. We're like *always* together. You haven't worked in weeks except for a few appearances in that new series. What more do you want from me? I invited you to come to Nashville with me. More than once. You always refuse. There's still time for you to pack your stuff and get on that plane. It leaves in two hours. Tomorrow night will be fun. You'll see me on a scene for the very first time. You could also come spend a week with me in New York next month. We could revisit where we first met."

"Already told you multiple times. I prefer LA. New York is fine for a day or two but not at this time of the year. Winters are too cold, summers too suffocating. And don't get me started on your home state."

I moved to stand in front of her and grabbed her upper arms. "We'll be in Tennessee for two days. How bad can it get? You will survive just fine. This event is the epitome of fancy. I swear you'll enjoy yourself."

Savannah shook her head. Just like Jack did when I presented him with food he never tasted before and he refused to give it a try.

I sighed. "Fine. But don't be mad if I go. I promised I'd be there a long time ago. Anyway, I do this every year. It's a cause dear to my heart."

She looked away, staying mute. This little act wouldn't work with me. I was immune to her childish behavior.

"Do as you wish. If you change your mind, you know where to find me."

Before I had a serious girlfriend, I could at least invite women to join me at events. Now that I was in a relationship, I always ended up going alone. How ironic.

Savannah hadn't budged from her spot in the doorway as I passed her. I leaned forward and kissed her angry pout. It brought a smile to my lips. She should let go of the angry-teen persona. She was twenty-four, not sixteen.

With one arm around her waist, I drew her close. She kept ignoring me. "I'll be back in two days. In the meantime, do something fun, okay? And call me if you miss me. I'll see you soon."

She refused to acknowledge me, so I left with a shake of my head and a heavy heart.

———

With a roll of my eyes, I studied the hand I'd been dealt before surveying the room. Bright blue walls, lime-green accents, and jazzberry-pink furniture made it an explosion of color. I gave the table a quick scan, trying to read my opponents' inscrutable faces.

Riley scratched the side of his head with a frown that I knew to be bullshit by now…or maybe not.

Dylan Daughtry sighed and placed his cards face down on the table.

Sweat formed at the base of my nape.

Should I go all in or not?

My poker confidence wasn't at the top. *The game hates me, I swear.*

Kristoff, sitting on my left, the only one at the table who wasn't related to the music industry chuckled as our eyes met. "Having a hard time, Hills?" He elbowed me, and I winced, shooting him a glare.

I had two pairs. That was good, right?

"Scared I'm gonna beat you again?" he asked.

"Yeah, yeah, you wish."

"I'm in," Sam Stevens said, pushing half of his chips to the center of the table.

"Me too," Riley chimed in.

"What about you, Hills?" Kristoff asked in a teasing tone. "Are you gonna risk it?"

"Yeah, *Hills*," Riley echoed. "Are you in or out?"

Two pairs are good enough. Huh…maybe.

"In." I hesitated for just half a second. "All in."

"You sure?" my manager asked.

"Yep." I added my chips to the pile.

"Flush," Sam announced with a smirk.

"Straight flush," Riley announced, showing his hand. Sam and he high-fived.

"What about you, Hills?"

I turned my cards over. "Two pairs."

Kristoff grinned so big it showed all his teeth. "Sorry, guys." He displayed his royal flush.

"Again? What are you? Some sort of poker guru?" I flung my arms out on either side of me. "I'm done."

"Aren't you a sore loser?" Sam teased.

"You wish, Stevens. At least my song is still number one. Sorry, but yours has been stuck at number two for weeks now."

His loud chuckle killed the tension around the table.

Kristoff pulled his booty toward him, smirking like the badass he was. "Watch and learn, guys. Y'all may be rich and famous, but you've got nothing on me."

"Ry, remind me why I'm doing this again. I always end up bankrupt." I sighed. "I'm always the first one to go."

"You have the worst poker face ever." Kristoff shook his head at me.

"Yeah, man. The kid is right. You have no game. Your face is a window to your soul or…what's the saying? Anyway, if you think you're subtle, check yourself out in a mirror. We can read everything you're hiding when we look at you."

"No."

Kristoff's laughter filled me with warmth. "Yes, we can. Sorry to burst your bubble, Hills. You are the lamest poker player I've ever met."

"Listen to the kid, man," Riley said, unable to stop laughing. "He might be onto something."

I lifted both hands above the table. "Why are we even doing this again? Why keep inviting me then?"

My manager laughed his heart out. "It's for charity. Man, you can't even fool kids. If you get invited to an all-star big-stakes game in Vegas, remind me to stop you from going. I'll highjack the plane or something. Freeze your assets. Kidnap your sorry ass."

I joined in on his humor. "We have a deal."

A nurse neared us, addressing Kristoff. "Time for your blood work." She pushed his wheelchair away from our table.

"See you, guys," the twelve-year-old said with a wave. "And Hills, if you're up for a private poker lesson, I'll be happy to teach you. Anyway, I won all your chips today. You know where to find me."

Kristoff had been battling a blood disease since birth. A few times a year, Nashville Children's Hospital invited me and my friends to spend a day where they booked the in-hospital recreation room and organized activities the children enjoyed. Kristoff always chose poker, to my greatest dismay. This morning, I played music while a chorus of seven-year-olds sang four of my songs. Then I baked cookies with a bunch of them before working on songwriting with a group of teens.

Today's poker chips turned out to be gummy worms and chocolate. Last year, they were cookies.

But no matter the stakes, I had to recognize the kid was right. I was a shitty poker player.

"Ready for tonight?" Sam asked as we entered the ballroom where the hospital held its annual casino night. It wasn't enough I'd been humiliated because of my lack of poker skills earlier today that now I was expected to participate in many Vegas-themed games through the night.

With long, white shimmery curtains hanging from the ceiling and red and silver accents in the form of table centers and tablecloths, the venue looked fabulous.

The servers wore silver jackets over crisp white shirts and black slacks. Two hostesses wore floor-length crimson dresses with long slits along their left legs, reminding me of my girlfriend.

Trevor McLachlan took the stage, steering me away from my thoughts, and adjusted the microphone. "Thank you for joining us tonight. As the main sponsor tonight, I encourage you to please have fun and be generous. Remember all the money goes to a great cause. Nashville's Children Hospital. Enjoy the night."

Trevor was a fellow country singer. He was born with a congenital heart defect and had to undergo a number of surgeries growing up. Since he'd attained fame, he had dedicated a lot of his time to give back to the hospital that had saved his life.

"Where's your woman?"

I brought my attention back to Sam. "She's in LA. Didn't feel like coming along. And, well…huh…she met Dahlia and Jack." I sipped my virgin Bloody Mary. "They came to stay with us for a couple of days not so long ago."

His eyebrows shot up. "How did it go?"

"Not sure. Dahlia was her usual warm self. Trying to engage Savannah in conversation and offering to spend time together. I could tell Savannah wasn't enjoying the idea…and the company. In the past, she told me she felt threatened by Dah. But hey, she's happily married, and I'm living in California now. No matter however much I try to reassure Savannah, she keeps complaining about our friendship." I ran a hand down my face. "Jack will always be mine to look after. I don't know… It's getting more complicated than it should. I'm not sure how to fit both parts of my life together."

Sam clapped my shoulder. "I feel you. Is that scowl on your face because you're alone tonight or because you're still sour about losing to a kid this afternoon?"

I let out a loud chuckle. "Good one, man. Keep reminding me how bad I am at poker."

He returned my laughter. "Not my fault you have the worst poker face I have ever met. Isn't your woman an actress? I'm sure she could teach you a trick or two. Help you out."

"I helped her rehearse for a part the other day, and not to brag, but I was pretty convincing. You just have no clue what you're talking about. My bad poker face might just be an act. Have you ever thought about that?"

Sam's laughter multiplied. "God, you're even a bad liar."

"Enough about me. Where's Lisa? I haven't seen her around."

"She suffered from a stomachache that hit her out of the blue, so she left." He perused the room. "She used to love coming to these events. When she's with the girls, she complains she doesn't get out enough, but when we go somewhere, she always finds excuses to leave early."

"How are things at home?"

"Marriage, kids, house, career. It's a lot. We're trying to find our pace." He fished his phone out to look at the time. "Guess I should get ready. I'm scheduled to play in half an hour. See you later, man."

All night, before and after my set, I stuck to roulette, dice, and other luck-based games that didn't require a poker face. I had learned my lesson this afternoon.

For some reason—or divine intervention—I ended up

richer than I was when I started the night. Tomorrow, I would write a big fat check to the hospital foundation if I kept winning.

Sam returned to his wife well before eleven, and Riley disappeared with his date sometime around midnight.

I lost Trevor and Dylan in the crowd, and an hour later, I called it a night.

It'd been a long time since I found myself alone at home. In the last year, I'd barely slept in my Nashville penthouse. With high ceilings, straight lines, honey-colored hardwood floors, and wall-length windows offering the best view of the city skyline, I used to love this place. Now I felt like a stranger in my own house. Even though I much preferred its rustic and inviting vibe to the sterile place I rented in LA. Unlike it, this penthouse was mine. All mine. I bought it before I embarked on the solo career path when I needed a place in town after I sold my house in White Crest. A clean slate after my brother died and my parents deserted me. I had no reason to visit my childhood hometown anymore, so I cut all ties with it, the memories bittersweet. Even the good ones.

For the longest time, except for my log cabin in Green Mountain, I couldn't envision myself living anywhere else but here. Until Savannah stormed into my life and I decided to give our relationship a try.

On my back, with one arm bent under my head, I stared at the ceiling for hours. The muffled sound of music playing outside comforted me.

Being here felt oddly soothing. For both my mind and soul.

As I let my mind wander, I enjoyed the near silence. I never realized how suffocating—and noisy—my life in Los Angeles had become until I escaped it yesterday and landed here. Where my heart and I belonged. In more ways than I was ready to acknowledge.

A thousand unanswered questions swirled in my mind. For the first time, I wondered if I might have been happier had I stayed here. In Nashville, I was alone and at peace with myself. In Los Angeles, I had company but sported a restless mind most of the time. No matter how dedicated I was to my relationship, I couldn't see myself falling in love with Savannah Prince any time soon. There was just something preventing me from letting go completely. To fall without a safety net and see where it would take me.

Savannah and I, we got along fine most of the time, and I enjoyed having her around, but her tantrums over insignificant details and mood swings were sometimes hard to deal with. She was asking to be the sole priority in my life. I had already put my career on the back burner, more than I should, to please her. And I had even postponed the release of my next album, unable to give my music the dedication it deserved. I refused to put something out I wasn't fully proud of, one that didn't scream perfection in my eyes.

I also lived far away from Dahlia and Jack, which made spending time with them kinda complicated. I couldn't sacrifice more. In fact, I had to make Savannah understand that I'd be happier if all aspects of my life fulfilled me. Family. Friends. Career. Music. Love. Or the closest thing to the latter I could muster.

Savannah was a smart woman. I was sure she'd understand once I explained to her how I felt. We still had a long way to go in terms of having deep and meaningful conversations, but I was not losing hope. Tonight, I missed having her by my side. Every time my gaze had landed on one of those two hostesses, my thoughts always swirled back to her. Yeah, she occupied a larger place in my life than I ever thought I'd be able to give a woman.

With my phone in hand and my thumb hovering over the call button, I hesitated to dial her. Maybe the sound of her voice could appease my mind. Just like Dahlia's did. Two in the morning. Savannah wouldn't appreciate being woken up in the middle of the night. Nah, it was a bad idea.

After I tossed and turned for a bit, I found a soothing position, and soon I surrendered myself to sleep.

Chapter 21
Carter

Two days later than planned, I returned to LA. The morning after the casino night, Riley came over, and I agreed to extend my stay so we could go over tour dates together and have dinner with the representatives of my label. Then June invited me to her kid's birthday party, an event I couldn't pass, and I ended up meeting with Addison over lunch at Wild and Country, the newest bar in town Riley and she had shares in, to discuss merch designs I commissioned. Savannah hadn't been happy when I announced I would return later than planned, but in some way, the little time apart did me good. I was ready to have a discussion with her about how I saw our future.

After we got into an argument over the phone, I let her buy stuff on my account because she complained I was taking too long to return home and she felt rejected.

Hell, she was the one who refused to come along.

This was part of everything I wanted us to discuss. I had a nice evening planned for the two of us. A great dinner downtown and a night at the most prestigious hotel in the city.

My heart danced in my chest at the idea of surprising her.

Savannah would understand she had nothing to worry about. That I was committed to our relationship as long as she did her part too. A newfound energy infused inside me as I approached our apartment building. Yes, we could make it all work. It didn't have to be one or the other. Every piece of my life could fit together. Savannah would realize how happy it made me and would have no other choice but to follow my lead.

With an impressive bouquet of red roses in hand, I entered our silent apartment on my tiptoes—pretty hard to do at my size—and spotted my girlfriend bent over the kitchen counter after I crossed the impressive foyer. Her brown hair acted as a silky curtain around her face while her eyes were trained on something. Probably a script, seeing the focus straining her features. She was wearing a pair of red spandex leggings and a white tank top over a sports bra. I relished the vision of her for a minute, feeling lucky I had someone to share my life with and to come home to.

The fragrance of vanilla from the candles burning on the kitchen counter saturated the air.

With its high-vaulted ceilings and giant windows, marble floors, and golden accents, our apartment looked nothing like I ever envisioned myself living in. But Savannah fell in love with it the first time we visited it, and I really hoped she'd like the place where we would build a life together. The fact this was the first decision we ever made together made it extra special in my eyes and meant a lot more to me.

The luxury apartment was way over the budget I'd agreed to pay for a third home—I preferred rustic, warmth, and cozy to chic, frigid, and soulless—but I could compromise. Hence, here we were, living in this over-the-top place I now called home.

When I crossed the living room, I halted. What the fuck. A new leather couch set that looked overly expensive took up residence in the middle of the room. A pool table occupied the far corner. Over the fireplace hung a giant, at least ten by ten feet, painting I recognized as one I'd seen in a well-known artist's exhibition we went to not so long ago. In the dining room, a new twelve-seat rosewood set replaced the imported Italian glass one we bought together. A chandelier made of—were they crystals, like genuine crystals?—hung from the ceiling, casting a soft glow on the walls, the giant windows framed by thick velvet dark teal curtains.

I swallowed. Hard. And again. For good measure.

My shoulders slouched forward, and all the excitement about the night to come vanished, seeming meaningless now.

My pulse hammered. A crippling feeling clung to my vertebrae. I froze, taking it all in. A thorny mass lodged in my throat, shredding the lining.

"Oh, you're back," Savannah said as she joined me, air-kissing my cheek. "How do you like my new decor?"

I harrumphed. My head spun. This was a prank. I articulated each word, praying my anger wouldn't burst out. "*Your* new decor?"

She was joking, right? She had to be. *Her decor.*

A cold chill passed through me. I bet—no, I had the certitude—I paid for the entire thing. Every fucking cent.

She pouted. "Told you I felt lonely. Thought the new furniture and expensive art pieces would cheer me up. It didn't, but it kept me busy."

"Are you kidding me right now? Is this some kind of prank?"

She crossed her arms over her chest. "When you left, you said to have some fun. I don't see what the problem is." She looked at me with a quizzical stare, as if I'd spoken words she couldn't decode. "Every time you leave town, you always run back to *her*. I needed something to occupy my mind."

"Savannah, they're my family. And Dah is married. You can't seriously be jealous. We've been over this dozens of times already. And Dahlia wasn't even in Nashville."

"I should be more important to you than they are."

"That's not how it works. At the end of the day, I'm here with you. Are you competing for my attention against a child?"

"Carter, I'm supposed to be your queen. The center of your world."

I took in the new decor once more.

The anger simmering in the pit of my stomach transformed into blazing flames.

Even the blood coursing through my veins ran hotter.

"What the fuck did you do while I was away?"

"Oh, stop being dramatic. You always say I can spoil myself while you're gone."

"A new dress. Or a purse. Or a visit to the hairdresser. Not an outrageous bill for a couch set we didn't need or a monstrous painting."

"But those make *me* happy, Carter."

"They don't make *me* happy. They fucking don't. I can't pay for everything you indulge in. I'm not Santa Claus."

"Don't be selfish, Carter. Being a jerk is overrated

anyway. And it doesn't suit you. Be honest here. It looks amazing, right?" She opened her arms toward the new living room set as if I'd said nothing. "Thank you. See? I'm grateful."

"Wait. We moved in like mere months ago and you furnished the entire place on my account back then." I clenched and unclenched my hands at my sides, trying to quiet the fury swirling inside me and longing to express itself. "Tell me. Why would we need to change any of it?"

My feet froze, unable to move forward. I glanced at all the extravagances I would never have bought or agreed to.

My breathing halted, and I rubbed the side of my head, an uneasy emotion turning my stomach into stone. I had no idea who the woman standing before me was.

I'd only left for a few days, and she had transformed into a person I didn't recognize.

Savannah studied her manicure, looking bored. "Well, it didn't suit me. Sometimes, I get tired of things quickly. This looks much better. You'll see, it will grow on you. Wait until you see the master bedroom, then you'll agree this makeover was overdue. Wine?"

"Savannah, you know I don't drink." What was the game plan here? Clearly, no one informed me about the new rules we were playing with.

"Oh yes, I forgot how boring you could be. You sound like an old man. Where's the adventurous and fun side of you? Let me tell you this, Carter Hills. You're self-centered. And narcissist. I shouldn't be surprised." She reached the kitchen and poured herself a glass of red, and I followed her, trying to make sense of what she had done. And everything she just said. *Me, a narcissist?* Did I hear her right? Unable to order my jumbling thoughts, I placed the bouquet on the countertop.

Savannah stared at me with a disgusted bend of her lips.

My thoughts refused to settle in my head. I blinked. Fast.

"Carter, why the hell would you buy yourself flowers? Told you that you were egocentric. Here's the proof. Gosh, I can't believe you bought yourself flowers but didn't get me anything."

I sighed. "Savannah, those flowers, they were meant for you. I had an entire night planned for us. Well, a two-day romantic getaway in the city."

She neared me and tapped my forearm, her red fingernails a contrast to my dark shirt. "Oh, you're cute. Still, I prefer diamonds or designer accessories. You should be aware by now. You gotta apologize anyway."

"Apologize? What did I do?"

"You abandoned me. I was all alone. You always leave. I hate loneliness. You should worship me and shower me with gifts right now. Show me how much you missed me."

"You serious?"

"Flowers die. They're of no use. Get rid of them," she said pointing to the forty-eight roses arrangement. "The scent is enough to make my head spin."

My heart rate shifted to a higher gear. An acidic taste swirled in my mouth. My eyes darted to her. "Since when? You used to love red roses." The body lotion she used every night was infused with rose water.

"Told you," she said with a high-pitched laugh. One that froze the blood in my veins. "I get tired of things quickly. Don't be stupid and make a big deal about it. Throw them away, and forget all about it. I already did. See? All good here. No hard feelings." She flicked her wrist. "I forgive you for not buying me anything this time. Oh, and while we're at it, cancel tonight's plans. I have a

Pilates class scheduled, and no way am I missing it. My ass has been looking bigger lately, and I can't afford to get fat, or my agent will kill me. You'll thank me when I fit into clothes a size smaller."

"Wait. No. Why? How? I don't care about the size of your ass. What's going on here?"

She chugged her wine down and kissed my cheek.

Unable to process everything that had just occurred, I blinked. What else could I do? An earthquake could shake the building at the moment, and I wouldn't notice. Dreadful weights pressed into my stomach. A cold wave tore through my lower back. My jaw hung slack as I begged my brain to react. I blinked again. This time, I side-eyed the woman sharing my life as she gathered her gym bag and grabbed a bottle of water from the refrigerator.

In which parallel universe had I landed?

Realization hit me. Fuck, I should go back to Nashville.

Savannah waved from the entryway. "See you later, Carter."

Her chirpy voice woke me up from my state of disbelief.

"Savannah, wait."

I turned to face her, but she didn't hear me or chose to ignore my plea.

"Men…" was all she said as she slammed the door behind her.

Like a gust of wind, she was gone.

———

The next day, I came home after a more-than-welcome workout. I'd gone for a fifteen-mile run and then punched a bag for an hour straight, trying to expend all my built-up anger toward the woman who puzzled me a little more every time I thought I had her figured out. I wondered where the Savannah Prince I met that first night had gone. Even though, over our time together, I realized she was some sort of sex maniac, she possessed a sweet and funny side that appealed to me. In the last twenty-four hours, she had transformed into a tyrant.

This morning, we had gone for breakfast at the little restaurant on the main floor of our building, and when the waitress had asked for my autograph, Savannah accused me of cheating on her every time I flew to Nashville.

"You can't help yourself, can you, Carter? Everywhere you go, you collect girlfriends. I can't deal with you right now."

"What?" She stood up, disgust written all over her features, and I grabbed her wrist before she could fly away. "Wait."

"Stop playing dumb," she said. "It makes me sick to see you in action."

I had followed her toward the elevator to escort her upstairs. "Stop this nonsense. You're not acting like yourself. What's going on?"

She'd thrown her arms up and wrenched herself free from my grip. "Your dishonesty is pouring out from you. Since when have you become a liar, Carter?"

I'd blinked, unsure I was hearing her right, when she added, "Consider yourself lucky I'm not kicking you out for being a cheater."

Minutes after we returned to our apartment, she'd gotten naked and handcuffed herself to the bed—again— begging me to ravish her. Calling me a coward and insulting me after I refused and walked away, scratching my head as I reflected on what could have happened while I was In Tennessee. I couldn't keep up with Savannah's sudden bursts of temper. One moment she acted nice and flirty, and the next, she shifted to evil. Even her laughter had gone from clear and light to dark and scary.

June had sent me a copy of the new furniture and decor bill. I almost fainted. That explained my punishing training session. I was still not over the insane amount that had been put on my account.

In the elevator leading to our floor, I wondered which version of her I'd get now. Deep down, I wished she had left for the studio or had gone to run errands, needing a moment to myself to assess the sudden disaster that had taken over my life.

Leaning against the back wall, I pulled at my hair, ruminating over it all. Where had the pleasant side of my girlfriend gone in the four days I was away? Soon, I'd be in New York for a full month. Once more, I asked myself how it would be then if just a few of days had turned her into this.

Did something go down during my absence? It would explain her antics. Did she lose another part? Or get bullied again on set? Was her unstable mood a result of her stressful audition process?

Maybe anxiety had fucked her mind. The same way it did with mine. Right now, this relationship felt like a vise, strangling me and depriving my brain of oxygen and messing with the rational side of my decision processing center.

Changing my mind once I reached our floor, I hurried down the stairs until I landed in the parking garage. In my SUV, I called Riley. I needed my friend right now, not the manager but the guy who was able to rationalize my thoughts when they went haywire and someone who could look at the situation with a cool head.

"Hey man. How is it going?" he greeted me. "Missing me already?" He chuckled, but it died quickly when I replied in a strangled, anxious voice.

Like he said, I wasn't good at hiding my emotions.

"Hey, Ry. Do you have a couple of minutes? I kinda need your input about a personal matter."

I heard low voices in the background. "Sure. I was just leaving the office and going home to work remotely for the rest of the day. I'm all ears."

Once I heard the door of his car shut and all the background noises melt away, I switched the call to video chat.

"Oh shit," Riley exclaimed with rounded eyes. "What's got into you? We parted ways like forty-eight hours ago, and back then, you were thriving. Did you even sleep last night?"

I rubbed my face with a sweaty palm, searching for the right words. Usually, I kept my personal life...well, personal, but right now, I was about to blow a gasket and had to get it out.

"Savannah Prince" was all I said. A long pause followed. We both remained silent until I was ready to explain myself. "I think she's a fucking psycho, man. I swear, she's the devil. Something's wrong with her."

His bunched eyebrows and serious expression told me he would listen to everything I had to say. "Since when?"

I flung an arm up in the air. "I don't know... Always. Maybe. So far, they were small things. Details that seemed insignificant, but when added together, they showcased a whole new picture. Either she's going through some mental issues and having a breakdown or she's batshit crazy. At first, I enjoyed her wilder side. The thrill it provided. Now she just doesn't care to hide that devilish persona anymore. She flaunts it like it's a virtue and then blames me when I call her out on her actions. Something's wrong." I breathed in to dissipate the tension rising inside of me. "When I was in Nashville, she redecorated the entire place. On my dime. And I'm not talking about a few thousand dollars. I'm saying almost a hundred thousand. Without consulting me. I have no idea how she planned it, but she did. She called me an egotistical jerk when I got mad, said it was due to how insecure she felt about my friendship with Dahlia, then left as if nothing happened. She was laughing. A witch's laughter. A *freeze the blood in your veins* kind of laughter. And this is just one episode. I have many more to tell. This morning, she called me a cheater after the server asked for my autograph, and then tried to seduce me with her wicked games."

"Fuck."

"Yep. Fuck. That's not all. Once, she told me about her step-dad abusing her when she was a teen. I don't have all the details, but it sounded bad. Not sure if he screwed up her mind good. Since Dylan's birthday party, the one you didn't attend, I can't seem to catch a break. It's like two women share the same body. I don't know what to believe anymore. A hunch tells me I'm being played. Big time. I need answers."

Riley cleared his throat and said nothing for a minute, probably assessing everything I just threw at him. "Have you talked to Taylor about it? He still has contacts. He could get a hold of that jerk of a step-dad. See what's the story there. Perhaps you could convince Savannah to consult with a doctor until we know more. You'll be in New York for a month. The timing couldn't be better. You don't need this shit now that you've claimed your life back."

"Yeah, well, what do I do now? Savannah can't know I'm reconsidering our relationship if I don't have solid proof she's bad news. What if it's really a mental breakdown and she requires psychological care? I can't walk away if she's sick. She'll need me. I'm not that kind of guy. I stay by the side of people I care about." I paused, massaging my temples. So many scenarios played out in my mind. "On the other hand, if she's really nuts and suspects I'm looking into her past, she'll either lay low for a while until it dies down and plan my demise or act out and threaten me."

"Be in New York. Far from the West Coast. While you're away and safe, it will give us time to dig up all the dirt we can. See if there's a reason to doubt her, or if she has a history of mental health issues. Nothing came out when we did the background check, but maybe the firm didn't look closely enough. It has never happened in the past, but hey, we'll do another one. Just to be sure. Savannah won't be able to get to you while you're gone. Act as usual. For now. Let Taylor do his thing."

"Okay." With my fingertips, I rubbed my nape until it felt raw.

"Send me everything you know about Savannah and her past. I'll make a plan. Tomorrow, let's have a conference call with Taylor, and we'll start from there."

"Okay, I'll see what I can do. Thanks." Riley didn't have to take care of my mess, but he and Taylor were the only two people I trusted to help me out. "I'll text you when I'm free to talk."

"Perfect. And Carter? Don't worry. We'll get to the bottom of this."

"I'll owe you one."

He let out a loud chuckle. "One day, you'll repay me when I need a favor. Don't worry about it."

The next day, I did my best to stay as far away from home as possible. When I woke up and padded to the kitchen to make tea, the fucking new furniture still stood there as if to nag at me. Looking at it was enough to start another tug-of-war inside me. The sane part screamed at me to run for my life, but the empathetic side begged me to wait and see if she needed help. That there could be some sort of explanation for Savannah's behavior. Not in the mood to spend another minute here, I grabbed breakfast to go and parked by the beach. After a long conversation with Taylor and Riley about our plan of action, I felt better somehow. Still, the restlessness wouldn't leave me. Agitation traveled through my bloodstream. I couldn't stay still for more than a minute without crippling thoughts messing with my mind.

I replayed every conversation Savannah and I ever had on a loop in my head like a freaking ongoing movie I couldn't escape from. All the moments we shared, all our interactions. Were any of them genuine?

Grabbing the duffle bag I kept in the trunk for situations like these, when my mind wouldn't shut off, I made my way to the gym. Some place downtown where I knew I wouldn't be disturbed.

For the next five hours, I ran eleven miles on the treadmill and pumped iron until my arms called it quits. In a calmer state, I returned home around six, only to find Savannah in discussion with a man I'd never seen before. In our kitchen.

Other than to fight, Savannah and I had barely acknowledged each other since I returned from Nashville.

"Oh Carter, you're here," she exclaimed in a small, overly cheery voice that didn't sound like her. She air-kissed my cheeks. "Oh, you smell." She pinched her nose. "Freshen up and change. We'll wait for you. Food is almost here. And please burn those clothes while you're at it."

She turned on her heel and brought her attention back to her friend without introducing me.

I shook my head, my hopes for any cease-fire tonight sinking. No, Savannah hadn't gotten out of her crazy ways. All day, I had prayed this was all in my head. That I'd dreamed the entire episode since I flew back in town and we would go back to being us. No such luck.

So far, I'd identified three distinct personalities of her. The vulnerable child-woman needing protection, the entitled diva, and the insatiable siren.

Right now, this version of her reminded me of the one I'd encountered at Dylan Daughtry's birthday celebration a while back. One I had forgotten to include in the list.

I studied her profile and demeanor for a long minute. Her gestures told me a lot. She leaned in, pressing her hand against her male friend's chest, whispering something in his ear, and laughing at everything he said.

She batted her eyelashes a few times and bit the tip of her forefinger, an unmistakable sign she was on the prowl.

Yeah, I knew all her telltale signs. In the past, it usually ended up with her lips around my cock or scorching hot sex.

At their interactions, my insides twisted.

The man cupped Savannah's cheek as she stared at him with soft eyes, and I almost lost it.

What was the game she was playing here? Because, by now, I'd realized everything with Savannah Prince was some sort of competition or a means to an end. How could I have been so blind for so long? How had she succeeded at sucking me into her diabolical vortex?

She tipped her head backward and laughed, the sound

grating on my nerves. My heart churned at the over-whelming whiff of her perfume lingering in the air.

Was she trying to make me jealous? Or to prove a point? Right now, I had no idea and didn't care. This little tactic, using another male to taunt me, had become stale. It didn't affect me like it used to.

After I showered and dressed in washed-out denims and a vintage Carter Hills Band T-shirt, I rejoined them in the kitchen.

With purpose in every step, I walked to Savannah and her friend and interrupted their fun as I held out a hand. "Hi, I'm Carter. Nice to meet you. And you are?" I glared at the man from my height, squeezing his hand more than necessary.

He swallowed hard and gave Savannah a hesitant glance.

She shrugged but said nothing, watching us with glee in her eyes.

"I'm Jean-Jacques. A producer on Savannah's newest project. Nice to meet you, Mr. Hills. I've heard about you, but I'm not a country music fan. I prefer indie music and opera."

I released his hand from my tight grip, and the man stepped back, massaging his palm with a thumb.

"Too bad your tastes in music are questionable." I winked.

Savannah slapped my chest. "Carter, don't be rude. Jean-Jacques is our guest. Not everyone enjoys your weird love songs and sad melodies. They're not even *that* good." She moved to the refrigerator and grabbed a bottle of wine and poured three glasses as if she hadn't just insulted me and my career. Those weird songs had paid for her new decor. And she knew I didn't drink, yet these days, every chance she got, she tried to encourage me to. No. Not happening. I wouldn't fall for more of her evil schemes.

I placed the glass she handed me on the counter.

Before I could say something, the doorbell rang.

"Carter, could you please answer the door? Get some money or your card. I haven't paid for the delivery beforehand."

Why wasn't this surprising me? Savannah almost never paid for anything. If she wanted a sugar daddy, she should've told me. I would have refused the role on the spot. No amount of companionship or dirty sex could ever convince me to play the part.

I massaged the skin of my nape to relieve some tension, cursed under my breath, and went to the door, my wallet in hand.

Savannah's fake laughter resonated through the entire apartment.

And it turned the blood in my veins into icicles.

What was her endgame here? Had she been wearing a mask all this time as I had told Riley, or was she really having some kind of mental breakdown?

When I returned to the kitchen with the impossible amount of Thai food she'd ordered—seriously, we could feed a baseball team with this—my girlfriend was all over the producer. The guy didn't seem to mind that I was here, his hands planted on her waist, his lips a hair's breadth from hers, grinning at something she said.

At the table, Savannah and her guest sat next to each other, angling their bodies so their faces were inches apart the entire time.

"I really like what you did with the place, Sav," Jean-Jacques said.

Sav? What the actual fuck.

She flipped her hair over her shoulders. "I worked on a limited budget, but sure, it looks okay-ish."

Jean-Jacques squeezed her forearm. "No, Sav, it looks fabulous. Just like you. Your taste is immaculate."

He kissed her knuckles, and she fawned.

A sour taste crept into my mouth.

Hell no.

"Oh, you're so sweet. Imagine what I could have done with a decent budget." She shook her head as if our place looked like a dump, and she had to suffer through it.

I coughed on a forkful of rice. Stones filled my stomach, making it impossible for me to swallow another bite. I washed the food down with a sip of water. Rage coursed through me at high speed. Even the food had lost all its appeal. Refusing to make a scene, I pushed my plate away, stood, and locked myself in the office slash music studio. The only room that fit me in this presumptuous apartment.

My eyes landed on pictures Jack drew when he was here. Our family. Stick figures of Dahlia, Nick, me, and him, all holding hands, a mountain and sunset in the background.

Sadness clung to all my cells. With my fingers, I brushed the tears forming in the corners of my eyes.

With a long exhale, I focused on my music.

Strumming my guitar, I added a melody to the lyrics that had been swirling nonstop in my head for the last week. Music always helped to calm the emotional surges inside me.

I wished it could do the same with the panic attacks. The ones that had started after my brother's death, and I couldn't seem to keep away no matter how hard I tried or whatever techniques the specialists and doctors recommended I use these days. Lately, they had come back with a vengeance.

I put my pen down and sang the chorus.

You don't know me
Don't pretend to understand where I'm coming from
You don't know me
Don't blame me for all the bad choices you've made
Lately.
Because you seem to forget who you are
Or where you've come from, oh yeah
Do you want me to tell you the story
Of how the pretty princess turned into the evil
queen

With my pen wedged between my clenched teeth, I changed a few notes and one line of the lyrics until every piece fell into place.

A smile peeked on my lips.

Music made me proud and happy, and I wished I had more time to dedicate to it. It'd been months since the last time I wrote a song. I loved the sense of accomplishment it provided me.

I missed it.

Even though I dreamed of a new beginning, in all honesty, I missed so many things from my old life. All the good parts. Even some of the bad ones because compared to what I endured during dinner or what my life with Savannah Prince had become, those seemed minuscule now.

Once my anger had dissipated, I returned to Savannah and her guest and glanced at the clock on the living room wall. *Nine twenty-one.* Whoa. I'd been in my studio for almost two hours.

Just as I walked into the dining room, Jean-Jacques stood with his empty plate.

Savannah waved her hand at him. "Oh, no need to clean up after yourself. Carter is on dishes duty tonight. Just leave it there. I have a long day tomorrow. I need my beauty sleep, so I won't be of any help." She shrugged.

I used the fact that the man was already standing to walk to him, place my hand between his shoulder blades, and lead him to the door. "Like Savannah said, she needs her beauty sleep. You should go."

He glanced at his expensive watch. "But it's not even ten o'clock."

"Sorry, man. You'll see her on one of her sets. Good night."

I yanked the door open, and Jean-Jacques walked through it before Savannah could register what I'd just done.

With a shake of my head, I closed and locked the door after him, and my eyes met her furious ones when I turned around.

"What?" I asked, pretending to have no idea why she was mad at me.

"How could you? You can't treat my guests this way, Carter. I'm so ashamed of you right now. You made me look bad in front of him. I'll never forgive you. Imagine what he'll tell the crew tomorrow. That I'm living with a caveman in a low-class apartment, who has no manners and who threw him out like a savage beast."

I closed in on her. "What the hell was this night all about? Don't tell me it's to get a role because you already have it. Is flirting with the producer a requirement of the movie? You told me when we first started dating that you would never use sex to get a role. All night, you acted like a desperate woman to get his attention. You let him touch you in front of me. If you want to blame someone for their manners, then check your reflection in the mirror. There's one that cost me a few grand, hanging on the bedroom wall."

Savannah waved both her arms around her.

Anger spewed from her eyes.

"This again? Carter, your jealousy and greediness are out of control. Why can't you ever let me have some innocent fun? We were just flirting. Grow up." She quirked a brow, and I had to stop myself from encouraging her attempt to fight. She pursed her red lips. "How do you think I felt when Dahlia came to visit you and you guys kissed and hugged all night?"

Sure, my best friend and I were affectionate toward each other, but the entire time Dahlia was here, we stood more than three feet apart because knowing Savannah's unpredictable temper, I didn't want her to assume anything.

"We didn't hug. And we didn't kiss. And my hands weren't all over her while she was here. Nor were hers all over me."

"That's not the impression I got. You guys looked at each other with starry eyes. It was repulsive." She paused and erased the distance between us. "If you want her, we're done. I'm not going to be second best here."

"Are you fucking serious right now, or have you lost your mind?"

Savannah's onyx irises threw daggers at me. "Your choice, Carter. It's either her or me. You can't have both. I thought we had already decided I was the only woman in your life. Did you forget, or are you being stupid on purpose?"

"You both play different roles in my life. And for your information, if you haven't noticed yet, I live in Los

Angeles with you. And Dahlia lives in Green Mountain, Tennessee, for fuck's sake. With Nick. I'm not there right now, am I? I'm tired of having this conversation with you. You're projecting your insecurities on me. Stop making assumptions. This is getting ridiculous." I averted my eyes, begging the wrath erupting inside me to stay put.

"Then I'm choosing for you. Until you can prove to me you're committed to our relationship, you'll avoid seeing her. No phone calls. No text messages. No contact. For everyone involved, I hope you'll follow the rules."

My eyes rounded. "The rules? What the fuck. Where is this paranoia coming from? And what does it mean 'for everyone involved'?"

Savannah smirked. "Like I said, you agreed to it already. Get your head screwed on straight. You're wasting my precious time by acting like a man-child. Grow up. You're not fifteen anymore. For the record, I'm citing you. *Dah is married, and she lives in Green Mountain.* Enough with the unrequited love, Carter. It's about time you forget about her and realize your place isn't beside her. This pathetic puppy act of following her around is over. Can't you see that's what I'm trying to give you? Love. A future. Why are you so reluctant to let her go?"

We glared at each other for a long moment.

"I'm here with *you.* Paying for all *your* extravaganza and watching *you* rub yourself on another man all night and *you* think I'm the one who's not serious about us? Whoa. I never saw this one coming."

"Well, you better get used to it because if you don't wanna share me, then you'll avoid putting yourself in situations that will lead me to think you're not being faithful."

Savannah's anger faded, and she moved closer. Her voice turned gentle. Almost protective. "Carter, you can't be mad at me for wanting to protect what's ours. I know you love Dahlia. It's written all over your face every time she calls or walks into a room. But perhaps if you give me a chance, you could love me just as much. Think about it."

She rose to her tiptoes, kissed my cheek, and left me there, in the entryway, to ponder everything she unleashed at me.

Chapter 22

Carter

In the hallway, not brave enough to enter the hell waiting for me inside my apartment after another punishing workout, I dropped my bag on the carpeted floor and fisted my hands, then unclenched them. I stared at the front door, unable to convince myself to get in.

Breathe in. Breathe out.

After last night's fiasco, I had barely slept, replaying the terrible episode in my head.

Right now, the idea of walking away from Los Angeles and Savannah Prince and never returning sent a rush of adrenaline through my veins.

Dahlia and Jack. Music. Those were the only things that mattered. The things that kept me going. And sane. Even through bad days.

And none of them held a pole position in my crazy existence nowadays.

Tears rushed to my eyes, blurring my vision.

A dead weight coiled around my stomach.

Breathe in. Breathe out.

I had no fucking idea what to do.

Did I miss the signs Savannah Prince wasn't the woman she pretended to be all this time, or was this just a bump in our road?

My life resembled a house of cards. Looking sturdy on the outside and so fragile on the inside.

With my back pressed against the wall, I slid until I landed on the floor and folded my legs before me, hanging my head between my knees.

Air had a hard time traveling to my lungs.

The fucking world was closing in on me.

Breathe in. Breathe out. Breathe in. Breathe out.

Damn, I was suffocating. Dying from asphyxiation right there on the over-expensive floor in the hallway of my apartment building.

More hot tears rushed to my eyes.

I grabbed my phone, needing to hear her voice. The only one powerful enough to calm the surge of panic swirling inside me.

With shaky fingers, I scrolled through the contacts on my phone searching for Dave McGinnis, personal trainer, and pressed the call button. My heart hammered in my ribcage as I waited for it to connect.

My entire body quivered.

Breathe in. Breathe out.

This time, nothing calmed the tremors inside me.

My shoulders heaved as I tried to keep the emotional tidal wave, emerging from the deepest parts of me, locked in.

"Hey, Cart." Dahlia's soft voice rattled me. "How are you? I was about to call you… No idea why, just a hunch."

After Savanna's ultimatum to cut communications with her, I had hidden her number in my personal trainer's contact information. Yes, I'd become the guy who had to sneak around just to speak to his own family, afraid of getting caught.

I sat there, with all the words I wished I could speak tangled inside me.

A river drenched my face.

Right now, nothing I did or said would stop the current.

"Carter?" Dahlia's voice acted like a balm around my bruised heart. "Are you okay? Talk to me."

With the phone glued to my ear, I said nothing.

"I know you're listening to me right now. You know I can feel your emotions even from this far away. So, you listen to me, Cart. Inhale. One… two… three… four… Exhale. One… two… three… four… Again." She paused for a minute. "See? It's working. Keep going. Remember what the doctor told you. When you're overwhelmed and you feel a crisis coming, stop and breathe."

I did as she said, following her lead as she counted out loud.

"Inhale. One… two… three… four… Exhale. One… two… three… four… What went down?"

Some sort of strangled hiccup—part cry, part snort— left my mouth.

"When I visited you, I could tell something was wrong. That it weighed on you."

I rested my forehead against my folded knees. How could I tell her I'd not been honest with Jack and her because I had made a pact with the devil? That sometimes I barely recognized myself nowadays.

"Cart, I wish you would talk to me. Instead of keeping everything inside. That's not like you. To bottle up your feelings. I'll just say this, okay? Don't be miserable because you think that's your only option."

How could she always dig up the truth buried inside my heart?

"You're one of my favorite people on this planet. You've been through too many adversities already, and you don't deserve to keep punishing yourself. Whatever happened in the past and whatever you choose to do from now on, stop thinking you deserve shit and hell. Because you don't. You never did. You never will." Dahlia breathed loudly, and her voice shuddered, filled with her own emotional overload. "Cart, what's going on? Please don't shut me out." The softness of her tone wrapped like a blanket around my heart. Shielding it from the agonizing pain strangling it.

We remained silent for the longest time.

"Should I worry? Are the demons from your past back to haunt you, or is it something else?"

I forced in a jagged breath, trying to clear the thick fog sticking to my mind. "It's all messed up," I whispered, my voice strained.

Dahlia stayed mute, waiting for me to continue.

"I miss you and Jack. I miss my old life. I fucking miss my—" I dragged a hand over my face. "It's just… huh… sometimes… it feels like I'm drowning. Or a steel hand is wound around my windpipe, choking me until I can't breathe."

I leaned back against the wall behind me, trying to untangle my thoughts, keeping my eyes shut.

"Are they memories or current events?" my best friend asked.

I exhaled. "A mix of everything. Right now, I miss him. A whole lot. I wish he were here, and he could spill his wisdom on me. There are days when I *do* need my big brother. Even if it's just for a headlock or talking shit about whatever I do. And he's not…he's not there… My love life is going down the drain, and I would really like his insights… Or-or just a tap on the shoulder. A sign. And his unbiased opinion."

"Cart, I'm sorry. I still miss him too, you know. Every day. Like deep down, in my heart, there's a scar that will never heal. That will stay raw forever. One thing I know for sure is that he would be proud of you. That would have never changed. I swear. I know it deep in my core." Her own tears drowned some of her words. "God, I love you, Carter. I always will. Life threw us a shitty hand, and we all had to deal with it. It wasn't supposed to go down this way. I-I'm sorry. I really am. For everything."

"Dah—"

"No. Listen to me, Carter. I said I'm sorry before, but I really am. For everything that happened between the three of us. I'm aware it fucked with your mind for a long time. You never got angry at me. For a reason I can't figure out, you still fight for me. Beside me. With me."

Dahlia paused to blow her nose. I could picture her: red-rimmed eyes, fair skin, swollen lips. My heart hurt in my chest at the thought. I would forfeit everything I cared about just to hold her right now. And feel her warmth coursing through me as we comforted each other—like we used to do. Fuck, my feelings for her had been complicated for so long. Had I ever wondered if I'd truly gotten over my love for her, right now, I had my answer. I still loved her, but for once, my love wasn't a prison around me. It was freeing. Dahlia and I, we were friends. Best friends. And I could live with that because the thought didn't shatter my heart or my soul.

"Tell me now. What's wrong? Why are you sad?"

Everything inside me screamed in blazing pain.

"My relationship… It's not what it seems." There, I said it.

"What do you mean, *it's not what it seems*?"

The weight of the world pressed down on my chest. Breathing became a challenge.

"Cart, how bad is it?" Dahlia's emotions coated her words, and the sound of her own pain rippled through me. She didn't need me to answer. She could always tell what was haunting me.

My tears rolled down my cheeks like rivulets, drenching my T-shirt. My mouth popped open, but the words stayed prisoners inside.

"I will never interfere in your love life. I never did, even when you made some pretty questionable choices in the early band days, and won't start now. I know your ways of coping with hurt and sadness can be extreme. And I wish I could be by your side to help you through this. Cart, I'm not going anywhere. I'll always be there for you. No matter where you are in this world, I'll come to get you if you ask me to. You don't have to tell me anything. But if you do, I'll listen."

A heart-wrenching sob tore out of me.

I tried to keep it inside but failed, the amount of pain too heavy to vanish on its own. Years of being deceived by people I cared about pressed down on me.

I strangled my phone.

"Shhh. It's okay. You'll figure it out."

Dahlia's words soothed me, but still, I had no idea if I should hang on to this new life I was creating here or if I should go back to my old one and hope this time around, things would be different. That my loneliness wouldn't still be an issue, but something I could embrace.

The idea of a new beginning still appealed to me. I was desperate for it. No matter the cost.

To re-invent myself. Not for anyone else's sake, but my own. To move forward. And free myself from any remaining chains the past held on me.

To let go of the pain once and for all and move ahead with my life. I thought being here, in Los Angeles, was my doing that. Now I wasn't so sure anymore.

"Carter? Are you still there?" Dahlia asked, her voice quivering.

I grunted and ran a hand down my face. "Yes." I breathed out.

"Don't rush into anything, okay? Promise me you'll think before you make a decision. Whatever it is."

A fresh batch of tears made its way down my cheeks. "I miss you, Dah. I wish things could be different. I wanna be with Jack and you and just stop feeling like I don't belong anywhere. You all moved on. Everything was so much easier before—"

Dahlia swallowed. The sound reverberated through the line. "I know. But you were still unhappy, Carter. You just closed yourself off, wrote songs, and managed to convince everyone—including yourself—that you were fine. But you weren't. Even before Jeff passed, you were a mess. You drank. You disappeared for weeks. You trashed hotel rooms. Now you don't hide from it behind your music or unhealthy behaviors, but I don't think forcing a life that doesn't suit you is the solution either. I spent time with you two. I saw how different you were around Savannah… How you went out of your way to please her and she didn't appreciate you or your efforts. She dismissed you as if only her own happiness and needs mattered. Carter, you're a pretty fantastic person already. You don't need to change who you are. Not for me or anyone else. You only need to let go and move forward, but with a clear mind. Not to patch some holes in your heart."

A sarcastic laugh bubbled out of my mouth.

"Take your time, okay? Give yourself space to figure out what *you* want. Where *you're* heading. And then you reach for *your* dreams. Not other people's dreams, but *yours*. Genuine ones. Not what you think you should want, but what your heart really desires. Don't put yourself last, Carter. For once, make yourself a priority."

I bobbed my head. "I love you, Dah."

She sucked in a breath. "I know." A long pause. "I love you too, but I wish my love for you as your friend was enough."

"It is. I see it now." I sighed. "Dah, I'm scared of losing you…and Jack."

"You won't. Never. I'll never allow that. You are our family."

"No, you have your own family now."

"Which you are a part of. Forever. One day, you'll have your own too. When the right person enters your life. A healthy relationship isn't supposed to bring you pain. It should fulfill both parties. Help you thrive instead of spreading yourself thin."

We remained quiet for a minute.

"Can I come get Jack and spend some time with him?"

"Yes. Whenever you want. Let me know. Nothing has changed between you guys. Even if I'm married now. You are still his daddy in every way that counts. And will forever be."

I blew out a cleansing breath and unfolded my tall self, stretching my legs before me. "I'm coming to Green Mountain. Before flying to New York."

"Oh yes, that TV singing competition. I can't wait to hear all about it."

"Yeah, well, I was ecstatic when I agreed to it. Now it feels like yet another dead weight on my shoulders."

"It won't. Enjoy the experience. It will be good for you to put some distance between yourself and everything else. Clear your head. Be surrounded by people from the industry. Find your mojo back."

I moved to my feet and wiped my eyes with the sleeve of my shirt.

"When are you coming?" Dahlia asked.

"Now. I'm coming now."

"You are?" She did a poor job of hiding the surprise in her tone.

"Yes. I'll come to get Jack for a few days. You're right. I need some time to think. Away from here."

"Great. I'll tell him. He'll be happy to see you. Since our visit to LA, he's been asking about you a lot. More than usual. I know he misses you too. Begging me to board a plane daily."

"Good. Because I miss him like crazy. Always do."

On reaching the lobby, and without a second thought, I boarded the first cab to the airport, not even taking the time to call Ed so he could drive me or ask June to book me a private flight.

Every mile taking me away from my apartment loosened the knots tightening my chest.

"Have a safe flight," my best friend said.

"Thanks. See you in a bit." With a curve resembling a smile on my lips, I hung up, feeling better than I had in days.

———

"I love you, Jack," I said, pulling the boy to my heart and nuzzling his neck. He giggled and twisted in my arms. "Ready to spend time with me?"

A wide smile brightened his face, and he bobbed his

head in that way he always did. With so much energy I feared it would fall off. He wrapped his tiny arms around me and pressed a moist kiss to my cheek.

"Awesome, because I'm making your favorite dish tonight. Hungry?"

"*Yesss*," he said, his smile never faltering.

"How do you feel about camping in your room? With flashlights and bedtime stories under a blanket? Wanna build a fort with me?"

"Yay," he exclaimed, clapping his hands. "I want to go camping."

"I see you boys have it all covered. Just ring me if you need anything. Or if you have no idea how to set up a tent," Dahlia said, laughing. The sound clear and addictive.

"Nah, we're good. Hills men here. We'll figure it out. Or we'll sleep under the stars. Heard the ceiling of his bedroom in there," I pointed to my cabin, "is full of them. And they even glow in the dark." I turned my attention back to the little boy in my arms. "Ready?"

He nodded with enthusiasm, and the sight brought a curve to my lips.

"Say *Bye, Mama*."

Jack echoed my words.

"Behave, you two." Dahlia kissed both our cheeks before driving away.

I fisted my hand, and Jack bumped it like I showed him to do when he wasn't even two.

"Let's set up camp, buddy."

Hand in hand, we walked inside, and before I could even say a word, Jack ran upstairs to his room and opened his toy chest. Because I kept everything he needed at my place—toys, clothes, favorite snacks—he always felt at home here.

Hours later, I lay on my back, an arm bent under my head, in the low glow of the lantern Jack and I used for his bedtime stories. With his body snuggled into mine, his little boy's snores warmed me from the inside, melting away all the tension in my upper back.

I grazed his cheek with the pad of my thumb, and he scooted closer, nestling his pajamas-clad self under my arm. Propped on an elbow, I kissed his forehead and turned off the light after pulling the cover over us. With my legs sticking out of the makeshift tent—they were too long and the mattress too short—sleep finally claimed me, and for once, I wasn't haunted by nightmares.

"Up. *Up, up, up,*" Jack chanted the next morning, shaking my arm. "Wakey, wakey."

He pried my eyes open with his prickly fingers.

"*Up, up, up,*" he repeated. "Are you awake now? I wanna play."

I played possum, then pounced, grabbing him, tickling his ribs, and lifting him over my head.

"Plane. *Vroom. Vroom.*" He extended his arms on either side. "Higher."

Jack's laugh cut through the gloom, chasing every dark cloud away.

After we ate a copious amount of pancakes—our little ritual—we drove to the park and spent the rest of the morning playing before heading home for his nap.

"Can we sleep in the tent again tonight? Please, *Carrrter,*" he begged.

"Why not? Let's talk about it after your nap, okay?"

He nodded twice. "Okay."

At his request, I lay beside him and sang him one of my songs. My eyelids grew heavy, and with our heads pressed together, as Dahlia and I did countless times while growing up, I fell asleep too.

I woke up hours later, my mind murky, using my fists to chase the remaining traces of sleep from my face.

When I checked my phone, I had six missed calls and two text messages from Savannah. With my thumbs, I typed *Sorry, I'm busy, can't talk right now*, as I often did nowadays, and shoved the device in my pocket after turning the ringer back on.

Jack woke up minutes later from his nap and sat on my lap.

"How about we play cooks for a night and invite Mama and Nick over for dinner?" I wrinkled my face. "I think the four of us need some family time. What do you think?"

Jack watched me with a sleepy grin and bobbed his head, a smile forming on his lips.

"Okay, come on. We'll call them, then prep dinner and dress to impress to welcome them. Sounds good?"

Jack nodded again. "*Yesss.*"

"Great, let's call them first." I brought my focus back to him. "Can you tie a Windsor knot?"

His eyes grew big. "A *wintersor-what?*"

"A tie."

"Oh. No. I never wear ties."

I ruffled his hair and burst into a fit of chuckles. "Me neither. Let's draw the line at dress shirt then."

"Yes. No tie."

"No tie," I repeated.

———

The four of us sat around the table—a recycled barn wood piece that could seat ten people.

When Dahlia and Nick started dating, I'd never imagined one day I would consider him family too. But here we were. After an incident that took Jack to the emergency room, we made peace and agreed to give each other a chance because neither of us could fathom the idea of our relationship being strained in front of Dahlia and Jack. Even though it took me time to admit and accept his role in their lives, I knew from the start he cared about my family too and would do just about anything for them. Make them a priority. That's all I'd ever wanted. For my family to be happy and safe.

"So, how was camping?" Nick asked from his side of the table.

"Great," Jack yelled, clapping his hands.

"Yes," I replied, ruffling his hair. "We had a pretty amazing time. We're having a do-over tonight."

"Want to go camping with *Carrrter* and me?" the boy asked Nick.

The man shook his head. "Nah. This is your boys' time. And I'm pretty sure the tent isn't big enough for Carter, so imagine the four of us."

Jack giggled.

Nick continued, speaking in a hushed voice as if telling the kid a secret. "See? I'm sure I'm right. No one wants to sleep outside the tent. What if we get cold or it starts raining? Or a bear is lurking around?"

Jack's giggles multiplied.

I stroked my chin as I pondered. Maybe my little guy was onto something. "What if you guys sleep in Dahlia's room tonight?" I shrugged. "Could be fun to have breakfast all together in the morning. Family-bunk night. Think about it."

Dahlia had a room at my place where she kept clothes in the wardrobe and other personal items in the dresser for the nights she spent here. On occasions.

"Like a vacation bunk night?" Dahlia asked Jack.

"Yes," he said, his grin reaching both ears.

"Fine, let's do this," Nick chimed in.

I bowed my head in his direction, and he mirrored the gesture.

———

How we ended up bringing mattresses to the den and lying down in sleeping bags like kids at summer camp with pillows and a bunch of blankets was a mystery.

But it happened.

I even took the time to hang the fairy lights Dahlia had always been a fan of to give the space a real cozy vibe.

Jack slept beside me, the sound of his breathing soothing, his tiny fist locked around my index finger.

"I can't remember the last I slept in a tent," I said, lying on my back, casting shadows on the ceiling with the flashlight in my hand. Nick and Dahlia did the same.

"We go camping a few times annually. Every time, it reminds me of our younger years," Dahlia said. "Those trips to the beach that both our families took when we were little… Gosh, they were always the highlight of our summer vacations."

I let out a chuckle.

"Do you remember that time we were afraid of bears?" Dahlia asked.

My face lit up in the dark. All my muscles stretched in glee. "Jeff was an idiot. He enjoyed messing with us way too much that summer."

"What did he do?" Nick asked.

"He told us he saw a bear after he went to gather firewood. I hated bears. I still do. Just for the record." Dahlia said.

"Yet you live in the mountains," I replied, unable to hide the teasing in my voice.

"Now you're getting off-topic," she said, her clear laughter vibrating through me. "That night, we had convinced our parents we were old enough to sleep in our own tent. Yes, we were super brave ten-year-olds. In the middle of the night, Jeff exited the tent while we were asleep and groaned and scratched the fabric, pretending to be *the* bear."

She whisper-laughed so loud that she had to stop to catch her breath.

"I started screaming, waking Carter up. I'm sure I left marks on his arm. Woke up half the campground. I refused to leave the safety of the car the next day. Jeff had to come clean because our parents were not buying the bear story, and everyone knew it was him."

"Yes. I can't believe we went for it." A smile peeked through as the memories played in my head. "That's when I told you about Jack-the-Bear hidden in his sleeping bag. To prove to you he wasn't as brave as he claimed to be."

"*The* Jack-the-Bear?" Nick asked.

"Yep. The one and only," I said. "This stuffed animal was always hidden somewhere. Jeff tried to keep it a secret, but we all knew."

That stuffed bear was the inspiration behind Jack's name. Since my brother passed away before the birth of his son, Dahlia gave him the name of his most precious possession as a child. When they were adding the finishing touches to the nursery, my brother found the stuffed animal in a box full of our kid stuff my mom gave him and placed it in the crib.

"Gosh, it seems like a lifetime ago," Dahlia said with a sigh.

I echoed the sound. "Yeah. Life was much easier back then."

"I kinda like our lives now, though. And none of us would have this little guy in ours if we were still young and clueless and hadn't found our way to one another," Nick said after a long moment.

"I kinda love this boy," Dahlia said, a smile in her voice.

"Yeah," I agreed. "He's quite something. I see so much of Jeff in him. But he's also his own person. You did a good job, Dah. You should be proud. Life didn't make it easy on you."

"All of us can be proud, Cart. We each bring him something he needs. He's the luckiest child in the entire world. Since before he was born, you were there for him. Even from the opposite side of the world. You didn't have to stick by us, but you did. And for that, I'll forever be grateful. You're my rock, Carter Hills."

Dahlia stretched her arm above her head, and my hand met hers halfway.

I cleared my throat. "I'm glad you guys agreed to stay tonight. Jack is happy, and that's all that matters."

"Yeah, we're creating memories. When are you going back?" Nick asked.

In the darkness, I was thankful they couldn't see the gloss filling my eyes. "Tomorrow...after breakfast. I'm flying to New York. I'll stay there for the next month for that TV gig." I swallowed the lump growing and blocking my airways.

Dahlia's breathing hitched. I knew what she wanted to ask but didn't dare to.

"Say it, Dah."

She angled her face in my direction. "Do you wanna talk about it? What happened that made you break down?"

"Not yet. I need a little more time to clear my head first."

"We're here when you're ready."

Why were just her words powerful enough to soothe the panic surging inside me? It pushed some of my queasiness down.

"Let's just say I uncovered a side of Savannah that freaks me out, and I have no clue if I should stick around and help her through this. Or if she's been playing me all along and she's nothing short of crazy."

Thinking about Savannah got me restless. Our entire relationship replayed in my head as I tried to pinpoint all the signs I missed and tried to convince myself her behavior lately was some sort of short-lived mental breakdown. A one-time occurrence.

A voice in me echoed it wasn't, though. That her true nature had been revealed fully for the very first time. Without knowing it, all along, I had been sharing my life with the human version of Lucifer.

Chapter 23

My phone went off as soon as I landed my ass in the hotel suite in New York City. *That Talent*, the show I was invited to as a guest judge for the next month, had booked me a room with a majestic view of Central Park. From here, I could see the track circling the park and already, my legs tingled at the thought that I could go for a run anytime I felt like it.

Fifteen-foot ceilings, honey-hued hardwood floors, and birch-tree-patterned, shimmery wallpaper on the wall opposite the floor-to-ceiling windows, complemented by silver and eggplant-purple furniture. The room looked utterly grandiose. Thanks to the open floor plan, the space gave the impression it was a loft instead of a hotel suite. Gigantic artworks dominated the white walls of the dining room. The bedroom, hidden from the entrance by a lush wall of exotic green foliage, featured a California king bed with a tall headboard, flanked by nightstands on either side, and an en-suite bathroom clad in white marble. The entire suite radiated elegance. A far cry from that awful over-the-top suite in Las Vegas or the country chic vibe of my penthouse in Nashville. I felt great here. And calm.

This gig was like nothing I ever had done before. During the week, I would help the contestants with songwriting and melodies, and on Sunday nights, I'd be sitting at the judges' table, helping decide who would advance to the next round. When I first got the offer, I wasn't ecstatic about the idea of booting contestants home every week. Judging people based on one performance felt wrong. Everyone was allowed to have a bad day. And it shouldn't impact their dreams and future. One night, June came over to my place and convinced me to give it a try after she forced me to watch a dozen episodes with her. "Those kids need your guidance," she had said. "Just imagine how much they could learn from you. It's not only about winning the competition. In a sense it is, but it's also about growing, refining their vocal range, and improving their technique." And so, I had agreed to be a part of this adventure. Now that my life was in complete chaos, I couldn't be happier to be as far away from Los Angeles as possible, and this time, for a longer period.

"Hey, found anything?" I asked Taylor on video chat. While he worked on Savannah's case, Ed had been assigned as the main security detail for my stay in the Big Apple. We got along just fine. We weren't close friends like Taylor and I, but the guy was dedicated and smart, and could keep people away when I was out and about.

He scratched his jaw. "Well, there's no record of Savannah Prince going back over three years ago."

"Strange," I said.

"Yeah. The firm we hired to perform a screening on her when you both first got together fucked up. They should have seen it. I can't understand how they missed that vital piece of information."

"Riley was right. What does it mean?" I asked, my mouth getting drier by the second.

"She's a ghost, man. No past. No records. No, nothing. We've got those partial fingerprints you sent over. I'll ask my friend at the district to run them. Hopefully, he'll come back with an ID. We'll keep digging, man. This screams fishy from miles away," he added. "Burns's lawyers searched California databases, school and medical records. Nothing there either. The timing of your being in New York for a whole month couldn't have been more perfect. While you're there, forget about Savannah. Let us deal with this shit while you enjoy the experience. We'll call you in a couple of days with an update. We also ensured the bank would notify us if any transactions were attempted using your name or credit cards. Hang on, Carter. I'm sorry you got mixed into this."

"Yeah, well… Thanks." We hung up, and instead of exerting myself like I would normally do, I decided to try to relax. My body was exhausted from the hours of training I'd piled up in the last few weeks. After I showered, I slipped under the covers and prayed sleep would claim me and ease my mind.

A knock on the door woke me up the next morning. Unplugging my phone from the charger, I looked at the time. *Ten twenty-two*. I didn't remember the last time I had slept in. Stretching my arms over my head and sliding my legs into a pair of sweatpants, I opened the door.

"Surprise!"

My blood iced. My tongue stuck to my palate. I rubbed

my eyes with my thumbs, desperate to clear my vision. This was a nightmare.

I regained some of my composure to let nothing show, steeled my back, and moved to the side to let my guest in.

"You're not happy to see me?" Savannah asked with a pout, rolling a huge suitcase behind her.

"Huh, I-I didn't…well… I didn't expect you."

"You invited me to join you a while back, remember?" She lifted both arms in the air. "Here I am."

"Yeah, I can see that."

"Stop with the attitude, Carter. You should hug me and kiss me senseless because you've missed me. How can you not?" She shook her head and looked around. "Not bad. I thought you would have requested a bigger suite." She shrugged. "This will do."

After slipping on a T-shirt, I clamped a hand to the nape of my neck. "How long are you staying?" Every possible answer to that question made my head spin. I crossed the fingers of my other hand behind my back. *Please say you're not staying.*

"Until tomorrow night. I have big plans for us. I'll show you what a committed relationship should look like. Hope you're ready."

I blinked. Why was I still surprised by her actions and words? "I'm busy all afternoon, and we're filming the live segment tonight, which means I won't be done until maybe ten."

She huffed, crossing her arms and pouting. "And now I'll be all alone. All my calls are sent to voicemails, you don't text me during the day, and when you do, it's short, vague messages that lack emotions. Aren't you gonna beg me to stay with you while you're stuck in New York?" She batted her lashes. "I know you miss me. Why aren't you showing me how much already?"

Act casual, man. For once, don't let your non-poker face betray you.

"I can't stay, but make yourself at home." I cringed inside as the words passed my lips. "Let's meet at ten-thirty at the bar downstairs tonight. We could grab a bite." Would she catch the bait? The last thing I wanted was for her to ask to join me backstage or on set.

"Okay. I'll go shopping. You're really selfish, Carter. I flew here to spend time with you, and you prefer to work. Do you know how much flight tickets cost?" She flicked her wrist. "Whatever."

As fast as she'd stormed into my room, Savannah was gone, slamming the door behind her. As if a tornado had hit the hotel suite, the peaceful space was left ravaged, her baggage discarded on the floor, and her perfume imprinting every molecule of air around me.

Standing there, I wondered if I had just dreamed the last five minutes of my life.

At nine forty-five that night, we were done filming the first Sunday night live episode when my phone buzzed with a text. Apprehension about the next twenty-four hours crept up my spine and settled in my shoulders. I let out a deep sigh at the name flashing on my screen.

RILEY

Look to your right.

I craned my neck until my eyes took in Riley and Sam with VIP backstage passes hanging from their necks.

"Hey, what are you guys doing here?" I neared them, and we exchanged hugs. "You should have told me you were in town."

"Last minute change of plan." Sam shrugged. "Lisa left for the week, and my kids are at their grandparents' for three days. My label asked me to scout an old warehouse as a potential location for a music video and maybe even the release party for my new album. Riley decided to tag along. We're leaving in the morning."

Riley nodded. "We were also curious about how tonight would go."

I scratched the side of my face. "I'm happy to see you guys. It's just… The timing sucks." I exhaled and lowered my voice. "Savannah is here."

Riley's eyes rounded. "Here? Like here in New York? I thought she refused to tag along. You were supposed to keep your distance."

"Well, she appeared on my doorstep this morning, stating she'll teach me how committed relationships work. It's bullshit. Anyway, she's leaving tomorrow."

"Shit. I'm sorry. What are you gonna do?" my manager asked with a scowl.

"Still trying to figure this one out. We're supposed to meet in the hotel bar later. There's an afterparty tonight, but I'm not sure I'm ready to risk setting her free amongst the people I work with. She's too unpredictable. Last time was a disaster."

Riley squeezed my shoulder. "Maybe it's not a bad thing. It's about time I meet the woman driving you crazy. This way, I'll size up who we're dealing with. There are three of us. What could go wrong, right?"

I swallowed hard. "Why does it scream disaster then? Never underestimate the games Savannah Prince—or whatever her name is—can play, man. I am warning you."

He tapped my back. "Nah, let us go to that bar first. Introduce ourselves. Join us there in an hour." Riley winked. "Around us, I bet she'll act all nice and stuff."

Sam burst into a fit of laugher. "God, I can see trouble in our future. Can't wait to see what it's all about. Is she really that much of a madwoman?"

"Yep. And it's getting worse every day."

Sam nodded, a look of understanding taking over his face. "C'mon, let's get out of here."

Ed drove us back to the hotel, and we parted ways in the lobby as I went to my suite and my friends hit the bar.

I changed into dark denims, a gray shirt, and a black jacket. Descending to the first-floor bar, I scanned the dimly lit room for my people. Riley had texted ten minutes ago to inform me that Savannah had arrived. And a second time, four minutes ago, to tell me she had been hitting on both of them after they sent a drink her way, even though they told her they were waiting for me to show up too.

I rubbed the column of my throat, trying to open up my airways. My heart hammered in my chest. Once again, I'd need to put on my best poker face tonight. Could I play the part without Savannah sensing our ulterior motives? I had to. Riley had a plan. He always did. Right now, I'd run with it without questioning the execution. With one last deep exhale, I rolled my shoulders back, trying to inject myself with a dose of fake confidence, and closed in on them.

"Carter," Savannah exclaimed as I took a seat facing her at the small table. "You should have told me your friends were joining us. I would have made a reservation in the most exquisite restaurant in town. Champagne, wine, seafood. Now I look like a cheap hostess meeting them in this dive bar."

We were in one of New York's most upscale hotels. There was nothing crappy about this place. The servers wore black uniforms with stainless steel name tags and served champagne in crystal flutes.

I forced a tilt to my lips and patted her hand over the

table. "Don't worry, they're here for me. And to meet you. Not to be impressed by expensive dishes."

Her lips transformed into a pout. *Sorry, woman, this doesn't affect me anymore.*

She moved to her feet. "Well, if you're being your boring self, I'm calling it a night." Her voice lowered to a suggestive tone when she purred, "Are you coming to our suite with me, *Carter*?"

I lifted a finger. "In a bit. I just got here, and I'm starving. I'll order food and join you later."

Savannah blinked. If smoke could've escaped her ears, people would've thought she was on fire. "Carter Hills. I traveled all this way for *you*. To show you *my* commitment." Her words were clipped. I did my best to pay her no attention. It worked because soon enough, her tone smoothened again. "Honey, I've missed you. Can we make up for the time we were apart? I brought toys because I know how much you love them too. I thought we could try one on you…like we discussed."

From the corner of my eye, I caught Sam pinching his lips together to avoid laughing. Yeah, I wouldn't hear the end of that one. If only it were true.

Standing in front of Savannah, I stared into her eyes when I repeated, "For now, all I wanna do is eat something. Either you stay here and join us when we go to a party later or you spend the night on your own. Your choice."

Her face lit up. "A party? What kind? Not a country music snooze fest, I hope. I hate that music. No offense."

"None taken, woman," Riley said from behind me.

How could Savannah be this brusque without blinking?

"A production party." I offered her a half-shrug. "You might know some people already."

Maybe it was better to keep tabs on her than leave her to her own devices alone in the city. The woman was a loose cannon. As Riley said, there were three of us to keep an eye on her. What was the saying again? Keep your friends close and your enemies closer. I couldn't agree more right now.

The offer I dangled in her face did the trick because sparks returned to Savannah's gaze. "Gimme an hour. I need to freshen up. I can't wait to get there." Spinning on her heels, she hurried away.

Raking my fingers through my hair, I sat back and propped my elbows on the table as I blew out every particle of oxygen from my lungs.

"Okay, this is worse than I thought," Riley said, breaking the tense silence that had fallen upon us. "Has it always been like that?"

I shook my head. "No. I'm telling you she's going nuts. Or is so sure of herself that she doesn't even pretend to play a role anymore."

"We'll get to the bottom of this," Riley said. "I promise." He clapped my shoulder, bringing me some much-needed comfort.

———

"Everyone is ignoring me," Savannah complained as I sipped a lemonade, and she downed her wine as if it was water. "You lied to me, Carter. I know nobody here."

"You usually don't have any problem introducing yourself. I'm sure you can find people to chat with."

"All you do is flirt with women right in front of me," she accused, waggling a red-manicured finger before my eyes.

"You can't be serious. Are you jealous of Aisha Jones? I told you she was the live act for the show tonight. We've known each other a long time."

"Don't force me to go to people so you're free to do whatever pleases you."

I snickered. Where was a mirror when I needed one? Savannah deserved a reality check. And fast.

"Are you listening to me or just pretending to be?" she whisper-screamed, poking my chest with her digit.

I shook my head and stuffed my free hand into the pocket of my denims, trying to even my breathing and not give her words too much importance. "You are delirious. I heard everything you said. Doesn't makes sense to me, nor do I agree with any of it."

Savannah glided her ruby fingernails down my chest.

My eyes traveled to the people mingling around us. We hadn't caught anybody's attention yet. I hated myself for bringing her here tonight. At least Riley and Sam were witnesses to her antics.

From further away, my manager nodded and made his way toward us. Mentally, I thanked him because every argument with Savannah always escalated from zero to one thousand in seconds. "Can I steal Carter away for a minute?"

Savannah leaned back, pouting again, but nodded, her arms folded over her chest. "Okay, fine. You'll come back to me quickly, right?"

"Yeah."

Riley led me away. "You looked like someone desperate to be rescued. I volunteered to be the man for the job."

He shrugged, and I burst out laughing.

"You gotta cut her loose, Carter. And fast."

"I know. I must make sure I cover all bases first. She's a time ticking bomb."

"I'm calling it *The mission to reclaim your freedom*. And your sanity. Why haven't you told me until now how bad it's been?"

"I'm not a quitter. I didn't wanna fail. For a long time, I made excuses for her behavior. Now I can't deal with it anymore. What we had—or I thought we had—is unsalvageable."

"By the way, you're not failing if you call it quits. I know how loyal you are…gosh, you've always been…but this needs to end before it burns you alive. You've lost some of your essence in this relationship. Savannah has been driving a wedge between you and the people who care about you. Listen to me. Never again will you settle for something less than you deserve, okay? I won't let you become the guy finding excuses for a woman who's pulling all the strings as if you were her own puppet. You're lucky she hasn't caused permanent damage to your soul yet. All night, I've witnessed her nonsense. It's not healthy…for anyone involved. This relationship has impacted your career. You don't write music anymore. You postponed the launch of your next album. You used to complain you were alone, but she has isolated you even more with her stunts."

I raked my fingers through my hair, averting my eyes for a second. I hated how all his words rang true.

"Dahlia called me a while back. Told me she was worried about you. I was like, he's a big boy, and he'll tell us if he needs an out. But now I get what you've both been saying. With what Taylor has dug up so far, we're all worried about you. The other morning, when you called me to explain what was happening, you were a shell of yourself, Carter. I'm missing the guy with the best one-liners, the one who called me at midnight because he wanted me to hear his new song and couldn't wait until the morning. You've become too quiet. I should have guessed something was wrong. We're bringing her down, man. You're not returning to LA. Not under my watch."

"Dah called you?"

My manager raised his hands. "She asked me to keep an eye on you. Said you weren't being yourself. After she visited you, she had a bad feeling about Savannah and feared for your mental health. Said you were kinda keeping her at a distance. We all know that if you're keeping Dahlia Ellis at a distance, it means you're either sick or you're acting out of character."

I sighed "Savannah and I used to have fun together… At least we were good at that. Until we weren't. I just can't figure out what's her angle. No matter what, don't worry, I'm over it… I'm over her."

He clutched my shoulder. "Glad you're back to your senses. For what it's worth, Savannah is not Dahlia. And she's not a second-place prize you have to deal with because you have no other options."

"I'm over Dah. For good."

"Great, because she wasn't *the one* either. Even I could tell the first time I met you guys. Her heart already belonged to someone else."

"I keep being reminded of that fact."

"Carter, you're losing your spark. Find it back. Don't ever let people steal it from you."

"I won't. I'm done taking shit from people who aren't worth my time and my dedication anymore."

"About time—" Riley's eyes flared as he stared at something over my shoulder, and all the words died in his mouth.

I spun my head to see what caught his attention, and my throat seized.

I blinked.

What the hell.

I discarded my glass on a small table and hurried toward the dance floor where Savannah had stripped out of her burgundy dress—down to a matching lacy bra and panties set—and a man I didn't recognize, with long, curly blond hair, was fondling her from behind.

I removed my jacket and wrapped it around her shoulders as soon as I reached her and shoved the man away with my hand on his chest. "Back off. Now."

Savannah gazed at me, her pupils dilated and her cheeks red.

"What did you give her?" I asked the man.

"Nothing," he said, raising his hands in surrender. "She was already plastered when she came on to me."

A high-pitched laugh exited Savannah's mouth.

"Whatever." I brought my attention to her. "Come with me," I said in her ear, close enough so no one could hear our conversation. "We need to get you to the hotel. What did you take?"

She smiled, showing her extra-white teeth. "A blue pill."

I blinked. For fuck's sake. "Why?" My insides tightened in a ball, the knots multiplying. The desire to punch anyone or anything standing in my way grew bigger by the second.

Lava simmered in my veins, setting my insides ablaze, consuming everything in its wake.

My heart thundered in my chest, its thrumming almost deafening.

All my muscles flexed.

I was about to explode.

Savannah raised her voice. "Because, Carter Hills, you're no fun. You ignore me all the time at home but collect girlfriends everywhere we go. I'm done being an arm candy, a prize in your life, that you show off to look good."

Bullets of fiery-hot rage fired in my stomach.

I inhaled, but it did nothing to cool the anger smoldering inside me.

If only the floor could open up and suck me in.

I pasted a calm mask over my face—or at least I hoped I had—and led her away.

We were almost at the elevator when she squirmed out of my grip.

"Don't touch me, Carter. I'm a big girl. And…and I'm sure someone here would fuck me since you won't."

I stood there, numb, about to burst into an inferno, while she lurched back toward the party.

It took a few seconds for me to react. Once I did, I stormed after her and clasped her elbow, holding her close. Leaning in, I whispered in her ear. "Don't make a scene here. You're not in the right state of mind. Now, let's go." My words sounded harsh. They gave her no place to argue.

The night was over.

Riley neared me and whispered, "Ed is waiting for you in the car. The hotel manager will meet you downstairs and show you the way through the service entrance. Your ride is parked there."

"Thanks."

"You good on your own?"

I could see the worry dancing in his eyes. "Yep. I'll be fine. I'll text you later."

I gave him a final nod and pushed Savannah into the elevator, stabbing the button, heart racing, as the doors inched shut, just fast enough to block her next escape.

On the way down, I exhaled, trying very hard to keep my fury locked in.

The drive to the hotel took less than ten minutes, but the entire time, I sat rigid as a board beside Savannah, silence permeating the car. My molars felt like they might fuse from how hard I was grinding my jaw. Gasping for air, I unfastened the top buttons of my shirt, hoping that letting more oxygen into my lungs would chase away my wrath faster.

In the bedroom of the hotel suite, I helped an intoxicated Savannah settle in bed before retreating to the bathroom. When I caught my reflection in the mirror, I winced. My relationship had taken a toll on me. I could see it now. Dark shadows under my eyes, wrinkles, and the absence of spark in my gaze confirmed that I had to walk away. No way would Savannah Prince ruin my life more than she had already done.

Within the confines of the shower, the hot stream relaxed my back muscles and washed some of my anger down the drain.

The night replayed in my head. I wasn't built for a life of drama. With my eyes closed, I tilted my head back until it pressed against the glass wall, breathing easier for the first time in hours. Soon, I snapped back to reality when a warm mouth engulfed my soft cock. All of it.

My eyes sprang open.

With both hands, I pushed a now naked Savannah back, but she tightened her clasp on my ass cheeks, her long fingernails like claws tearing through my flesh, holding me in place.

"Stop. Why aren't you asleep? Get away from me."

It had been fucking long since the last time we touched each other or shared affection.

With both hands, I pushed harder. "Let go of me."

She tumbled back and finally released me. With a firm grip on her arm, I supported her so she wouldn't crash on her ass.

"Enough. I'm going to bed. Stay away from me."

She watched me with big eyes as if I'd spoken another

language. Her pupils were still dilated, proof she was still high as fuck.

Seconds later, with a towel draped around my hips, I returned to the bedroom, and after I got dressed—no way was I sleeping in just boxer briefs tonight—I grabbed a blanket and a pillow, ready to spend the night on the L-shaped couch in the living room section of the suite, which offered a perfect view of Central Park at night through the panoramic, curtainless window.

Restless energy coursed through me. My mind wished I would run a dozen miles to clear my head. My body refused to move, exhausted by the day.

Slowly, my mind lost the battle, and I drifted into an agitated sleep. This time, it wasn't Jeff's life I saw through that glass wall, but mine. And it scared the shit out of me.

———

The next morning, I tiptoed out of the room, and after I exhausted myself with a run around the park, I showered and met Sam and Riley, who were having breakfast at the restaurant downstairs.

I took a seat opposite my manager, and a smile tugged at my lips when I noticed the cup of tea, bagel, and plant-based egg casserole he'd already ordered for me.

"Hey guys," I said, rubbing my nape to relieve the last traces of tension from my upper back.

Riley brought his coffee mug to his lips. "How is she?"

I sighed and shook my head. "Okay. I-I think. Still sleeping. I went for a run. We haven't talked since last night."

"How are you holding up?" he asked.

"I'm fine." I took a bite of my breakfast to avoid talking any longer.

"Is she still leaving later today?" Sam asked.

I nodded. My food tasted like acid now, and I took a sip of tea to wash it down.

"What time is your flight back?" I asked

Sam sipped his coffee as he replied, "Ry booked us a private jet leaving in two hours."

"Isn't your own manager or label supposed to book your VIP flights?" I teased. "After all, they're the ones who sent you here."

"Well, they are lax about every privilege these days. You would think they would make their biggest client feel special. Nope. On my own. I'm just a meal ticket to them."

I shook my head. "I know the feeling…"

"One day, you'll both be under my management, guys," Riley announced. "It's written in the stars. And we'll all travel together. You're both too great to waste your time with people who don't appreciate you fully."

"Told you already, Ry," Sam added. "Mixing our friendship and business isn't a good idea. I don't want things to become awkward if we don't agree."

I grinned. "It's working for us."

Sam shook his head. "You guys are different. You can separate your professional relationship from your personal one. I have no idea how you can do this. What if shit happens and Ry and I get into a fight? No. Not risking our decade-long friendship for money. Not happening. I much prefer watching you two banter like an old couple when you disagree, rather than being involved."

My smile grew larger. "We're not bantering. Ry knows I'm always right."

My manager threw a balled napkin at me. "Yeah, I can't wait to see that day coming. Keep dreaming, man."

"I've missed you guys," I said, breathing out. "This.

Here. Hanging out like this is what I find hard about living in another state."

Riley's smile dissolved. "The extraction mission is on. We'll save your ass." He tapped his watch. "It better not take too long. My patience is running out."

I nodded in appreciation.

He locked his eyes on mine for half a second before bringing his attention back to his plate of scrambled eggs and grits.

Sam talked for the next fifteen minutes, taking the conversation away from my disastrous love life, and I was grateful for my friends and their moral support.

"Gimme a call when you're in town, okay?" Sam pushed his chair back as we all stood.

"I will."

Riley pulled me into a hug. "You know Dr. Diaz, that therapist you saw after Jeff passed? Perhaps you could give him a call. Once it's all over. Could do you good to vent it out."

He tapped my back, and I nodded. "Sure. I'll let you know."

My friends waved as they left while I stood there, feeling more homesick than I'd been in months.

The world spun around me. My heart lurched in my throat.

Breathe in. Breathe out.

I thanked June mentally for encouraging me to take this gig and preventing me from returning to Los Angeles.

Soon, I'd get my life back on track. I would walk away from Savannah and regain full control of my existence. No more blackmail or false promises.

I exhaled my angst and sauntered toward the elevators.

With a stretch of my neck and a roll of my shoulders, I entered the suite.

Savannah greeted me with an annoyed scowl, completely dressed for a day out with me, her fists planted on her hips. "Carter, where were you? Who's the woman you were banging? Don't play stupid." Tears streamed down her cheeks. "I can't believe this is how you treat me. After I warned you last night. After everything I sacrificed for your happiness."

I blinked.

A glint I had never noticed before shone in her eyes.

The spark of the devil.

A chill moved up and down my back

"You can't treat me like this." Her shriek iced my blood.

Anger simmered inside me. I breathed out through my nose.

One more stone wall grew around my heart, suffocating the life out of it.

A dreadful prickling, one resembling shards of glass, lashed my vital organs.

With resolute steps, I padded across the living room toward the bedroom. With her suitcase open on the bed, I thrust everything she brought along on this one-day round trip inside.

Savannah followed me, babbling, still blaming me for things that never occurred, her voice high-pitched and annoying.

She parked herself next to me. "You're not even listening to me. When did you turn into a thoughtless prick? Why did you invite me here only to disappear on me in the middle of the night?"

I ignored her nonsense the best I could while she kept insulting me.

"What are you doing? You can't shove my stuff like

this. Careful with those shoes." She shot both arms up at her sides. "What's going on with you?"

"Nothing. Helping you pack. That's it."

"No. I'm spending the day with you. You said we could revisit where we first met."

"Can't. Got a phone call earlier. Team meeting. Gotta be there in half an hour. Next time, call beforehand when you decide to pay me a surprise visit."

"Well, I'll spend my day at the spa then, and you'll treat me to an expensive dinner later. It's the least you can do for canceling on me. Can you give the spa a call to ensure they make room for me?"

"No time. I changed your flight. It's leaving in an hour. You should hurry."

"Carter? Are you ditching me? What's got into you? You can't send me away like an animal. Is it about last night? Get over it." Her strident voice irritated my eardrums. "Call the production team of *That Talent*. You're not going back. I swear, Carter, you better come home with me. Right now. If you don't, I'll make your life miserable. My own brand of personal hell. All for you. When I'm a girl on a mission, nothing can stop me. Before doing anything stupid, like breaking us up or sleeping around, I would think twice if I were you."

She kept mumbling, trying to get a reaction out of me, but to no avail.

Swearing under her breath, she strode forward, her heels clicking angrily, until she stood in front of me, forcing me to stop packing. Before I could react, her palm connected with my cheek. Hard. The tingling sensation radiated down to my toes.

I blinked in slow motion.

"Carter," she hollered. "Say something. Don't act as if

I'm not here. Come on, hit me back. I know you dream of doing it."

She presented me with her left cheek.

Okay, this morning was surreal.

With my thumbnail, I scratched the middle of my forehead.

Savannah pointed to her face. "Come on. Hit me."

A weird sensation unfolded inside me.

I swallowed.

In what reality did I land?

Fury spewed from her onyx-brown eyes. "Carter," she screamed, stomping her foot like an angry toddler. "Hit. Me."

I inhaled and watched her as I shook my head. "I'll pretend the last ten minutes didn't happen. The plane leaves in an hour. You'd better get a grip on yourself, or you'll have to find your own way back home."

"You can't." Her lips shuddered. "You can't send me away."

I shrugged. "Watch me. I have engagements and have no time to deal with your drama."

I stepped aside, and she followed all my movements with wide eyes. "Oh, and by the way," I continued, "don't ever slap me again. This time, I dropped it. Next time, I won't."

She crossed her arms over her chest. "Or what?"

Poison coated every word she spoke.

Her eyes were trained on me, but I said nothing, refusing to fall for her tricks this time.

With a loud growl, she pivoted on her heels, out the suite, dragging her huge suitcases behind her. "Fine. Go to hell."

Fuck.

How many more sides of Savannah Prince actually existed?

The door slammed behind her, and for a long moment, I stood there, frozen, trying to make sense of the clusterfuck the last twenty-four hours had been.

My eyes were trained on the door, praying she wouldn't change her mind and walk back in. After ten minutes, I called Ed, asking him to get new keycards for my room and to deactivate the old ones. Then I gathered my phone and wallet once the concierge came over to hand me the new room keys and met my security detail down the elevator.

With one last glance over my shoulders, I made sure Savannah wasn't hiding somewhere, ready to follow me, then trailed Ed to the car waiting for us, my head hanging low as I spotted paparazzi standing outside the hotel lobby.

"Carter, a picture…"

"Carter, who do you think is gonna win *That Talent*?"

"One picture, for your fans…"

"Over here, over here…"

"Tell us more about your relationship with Savannah Prince…"

One grabbed my jacket, and I barely contained my anger as my bodyguard led me away, preventing me from doing something I might regret later.

Someone else got a hold of my elbow, and I yanked it free from their grip.

Another bodyguard flanked my side until I made it to the idling vehicle.

Breathe in. Breathe out. I tried to find my peace. This morning had been a disaster of epic proportions so far. I needed to get my head back in the game. *Breathe in. Breathe out.*

"Make sure she gets on that plane," I told Ed as the car pulled away.

He nodded. "On it. The guy I posted to watch over her informed me Ms. Prince boarded a cab fifteen minutes ago. I'll make the required verifications and keep you updated about her whereabouts."

I slouched back into my seat, unclenching my fists and drawing a full, cleansing breath. "Thanks." A wave of calm spread through me, and some of the tension in my back faded away.

For the rest of the drive, I kept my eyes fixed on the city passing through the window, wondering how the entire breakup would play out. And how dirty Savannah's intentions would get when she learned about my endgame.

Chapter 24
Carter

For the next three weeks, my appearance on *That Talent* kept me busy. I barely had time to think about the mess my personal life had become. When I wasn't on set, or in the studio teaching the candidates, or out and about with the fellow judges, I was in my room, working on my music. My mind was still restless, the threat of Savannah Prince hovering over me, and I could barely write a song. But still, strumming the guitar, playing old songs of mine, soothed my heart. And my soul.

Taylor called me as I was returning to my suite after the party celebrating my last night as a guest judge.

"Any news?" I asked.

"Hey, Taylor. How are you doing?" he teased.

"Sorry, man. So much going on. How is it going?"

"Great." I could hear the smile in his voice. "Ready for some good news?"

"Always."

"First, you can't go back to LA for at least three more weeks. I'm trying to secure a meeting with Savannah's parents. They're out of the country right now. Coming back by the end of the month. Until then, please lie low because from what I've dug up so far, your girlfriend isn't who she says she is."

Cold sweat pearled on my nape.

I swallowed the sawdust lining my throat.

"What do you mean?"

"As you already know, her name isn't Savannah Prince. Once we figured out that piece of the puzzle, everything else tumbled down. I'm having a chat with her high school principal on Monday. The woman in charge of the center she was sent to at sixteen refused to talk to me because of doctor-patient confidentiality, but she identified Savannah as Savannah Carpenter, a troubled teenager who ran away from the center three months after being brought in, when I showed her a picture. An old friend of hers from high school has also agreed to talk to me, and I'm meeting her next week. From what I've learned so far, Savannah takes pleasure in ruining people. With every call I make, the list keeps getting longer. Stay away from Nashville too. Don't go to Dahlia's for now. Just in case. We're closing in on her, Carter. Hold on for a little longer. Before you make your exit, we need to cover all bases so nothing comes back to hurt your personal or professional life."

I blew out every particle of air lodged in my lungs. Tears pooled in my eyes. My shoulders relaxed under the weight my friend had just removed from them. Sitting on the edge of the bed, I leaned forward, my elbows resting on my knees and my head hanging low, letting all the conflicted emotions spiraling through me settle.

"You okay?"

I nodded, clamping my device with my fingers harder

than I needed to. "I will be. Fuck. We opened a can of worms. I am dating a sociopath. Is Savannah Prince her stage name?"

"Nah. She got her name officially changed a little over three years ago. Everything screams sketchy from where I stand."

I stayed mute, processing the info.

"The good news is, now we know who you're dealing with. Why don't you go on a vacation? No work, just leisure. Someplace Savannah doesn't know about. When the shitshow hits, you gotta be prepared. Level-headed, rested, and calm."

I ran my fingers through my hair. "Yeah, well, I might just know the perfect place to unwind. I'll keep you updated. Do you think she could hurt Dahlia or Jack?" My heart cracked at the mere thought that I might have put my family in danger because of the choices I made.

"Is Savannah still sending you angry messages every day since she left?"

"Yep." Since the day she had been forced to leave this place, I had been going to bed every night listening to passive-aggressive voicemails in between crying jags. Her messages oscillated between threats to destroy me or fake vulnerability about missing me. I was glad I was on the other side of the country.

"I'll send one of my guys to Green Mountain. I already have two of them following Savannah's every move down in Los Angeles. She's been checkmated, Carter, she's just not aware of it yet. Keep calling her every few days. Pretend you care and want to fix your relationship. Tell her you got into a nasty fight with Dahlia over Jack or something. Nothing that gives Savannah the upper hand— nothing worth really talking about. She'll think she succeeded in breaking you two up. Sociopaths love feeling like they have won. It might deter her from interfering with them if she believes they serve no further purpose in her little evil master plan."

"Can she really go as far as harming them?" Just the thought of it sent my heart into a frenzy and made me want to throw up.

"We don't know for sure. All we know is that she's tenacious."

"Whoa. This is a lot to take in." I clenched and unclenched my hands, forcing my breaths to even out. I coughed to relieve the tightness in my throat. "You're the best, man."

"Well, I'm just doing my job."

"You know you're doing much more than this. And I'm thankful."

Silence stretched between us.

Taylor spoke first. "The plane is picking you up tomorrow morning at nine. Get some rest while you can. Ed has been briefed already."

"Hey," I said, my voice still strangled from the emotions stuck in my throat. "Thank you. For proving I'm not the one losing my mind. For a while, I started doubting I was going nuts. That *I* was to blame." I sighed. "Thanks for being my friend, Taylor."

"Anytime, man. Call me if you need anything. Good night."

"Night."

In the comfort and peace of my hotel suite, I lay on my back. Unable to stop the flow running down my cheeks, I let the tears stream down freely. I got played. Big time. I let my guard down and tangled with the devil. How could I have been so clueless? How did I not see the signs?

Would I ever be able to forgive myself?

I lost almost two years of my life to this dead-end relationship, and I almost ruined myself—mentally and financially—in the process.

Sad laugher filled the silence of the night. If I wasn't so tired, I would go for a run.

Breathe in. Breathe out. Breathe in. Breathe out.

A last thought invaded my mind before I fell into an agitated slumber. *Was any of the moments we shared real, or was it all a lie?*

———

After a short stop in Nashville to meet with Riley and Taylor in person, I landed in Portland around eleven the next night.

Stud Burgess, my friend and ex-bandmate, came to pick me up from the airport.

"How is it going, man?" he asked, pulling me into a hug.

"Fine. Hopefully. How's the family?"

"They're great. And can't wait to see you. It's been a long time, man."

"I'm sorry. Let's just say things got really heated. There's so much you don't know." I exhaled. "Bella and you are lucky to have each other."

In light of the recent discoveries about the woman I used to call my girlfriend, my own words spoke to me more right now than they ever did before.

Stud turned to face me after climbing into his pickup truck. "Quick question while it's just the two of us." We slid into the car, and once we closed both doors, he continued, "And no lies. You know I have a bullshit radar and can smell yours miles away. What's going on? I'm worried about you, man. You're usually pretty vocal about everything. You used to fly out here for a weekend just to surprise me, or call because you wanted my opinion on a new song or whatever idea popped into your head. Now you're mostly silent, and it takes you days to return my calls—when you deign to. Your face is plastered everywhere when I go grocery shopping, and we both know it's very unlike you to indulge in a relationship the press will dissect just for entertainment. We've been friends for years. You hate those gossip rags." He scratched his bearded jaw with his fingers. "Man, you're not being yourself. Talk to me. I've been waiting over a year for you to say something, but you've been mute about your relationship…and I have a bad feeling about it."

I ran my hand over the column of my throat. These days, just the mention of Savannah or my relationship felt like I was eating shards of glass. "It's…huh…it's complicated."

"Last time we talked, you were living full-time in LA with that girlfriend of yours. Why do I sense there's a shit-show going on?"

How could all my friends be so astute when it came to my love life?

Oh yeah, because they all knew I'd been nursing a broken heart since I was fifteen. And they had all been witnesses to the clusterfuck my life had turned into before I cleaned up my act and found my way back.

No way could I pretend with him because he'd call me on it. Like he'd just said, he could smell my bullshit from miles away.

Not ready to admit aloud that I'd gotten myself into another dead-end love story, I stared out the window. Stud and I had always been honest with each other. We often proclaimed ourselves brothers from different mothers back in the Carter Hills Band days. Yeah, he and I had that chemistry thing going on strong. We were opposites in many ways, yet so much alike at the same time.

"Carter Hills. Talk. Now."

Geez, he was *Carter Hillsing* me.

"Technically, I'm still living down there. In the last couple of months, I've been suspecting Savannah Prince is batshit crazy. Taylor confirmed my suspicions a few days ago. She's…I can't find the words to describe her. All I know is that I'm the guy who fell for her charades."

He cocked his head and studied me. "How bad?"

I shrugged. "On a scale from one to ten… Huh, I would say a hundred."

"Fuck."

"Yep. Now I gotta spend some time in the middle of nowhere, preferably at that fishing cabin you own and stay away from LA until Taylor has gathered enough ammunition to expose her and make sure the threat is contained."

"Wow." He shook his head. "I'm speechless."

I breathed in, focusing on the scenery passing through the window, not registering anything.

Stud said nothing, waiting for me to continue. Yes, he was that kind of friend. A listener.

"Savannah Prince isn't her name…or even…or even a stage name. She changed it to escape her past. She's gone from sweet and fun to a freak show. Since I took a step back, I have gained some perspective. It's a mess. One moment she's cute and harmless, and the next, she tugs at my balls and thinks it's funny that I'm hurting. Only to strip naked and beg me to fuck her afterward. She doesn't even hide her dark side anymore. Her laughter…it's creepy."

Stud clapped my shoulder the same way my brother used to do. "What's next?"

"Been busy with *That Talent*. It was actually a fun experience, and a much-needed change of scenery. Now I gotta keep away from my own home and the people I care about. How did it get this far? All I was looking for was a steady, long-term relationship. Now I'm the lead in a psycho movie." At that instant, blood dripped from an old scar around my heart.

"I know you can't see it now…you're too emotional, man…but it's gonna work out. In the end, it will all be worth it. The pain, the struggles, the tears. It'll make you stronger. Everything happens for a reason. It's part of a bigger plan. When I was sixteen and left everything and everyone behind, I never could have dreamed of this life. If they had told me I would be free one day…nah, I would've called them liars. And now? I'm happier than I've ever been."

"Dahlia's words echoed yours."

"What you have right here," he pivoted and poked a finger into my chest, "nobody can steal it from you. Hold on to it. It's a great asset. Don't sell yourself short. Don't lose faith." He paused, his wisdom marinating between us. "Carter, you're not alone. You know Belle and I, we're here if you need our help and support. Or a shoulder to cry on. My family is yours too. My wife is worried about you."

I bowed my head. "I'm fine. Or I'll be. Don't worry."

Stud studied me but chose not to call my bluff.

"Promise me you'll visit whenever you need to blow off some steam, okay? While you're in town, we could play lumberjacks for a day. Chop wood and get all that angst out of you. A wooden bookshelf would be perfect in the kids' room. Just sayin'."

Stud and Belinda owned a huge piece of land over an hour outside Portland city limits.

"Thanks, man. Murdering logs would do me good."

We said nothing else for the rest of the drive.

Once Stud pulled into his driveway, it was well over midnight. Every time I traveled to Oregon, I stayed at my friends' house. It felt like home, and I missed them—a lot. I wished I could spend more time with them in my everyday life, like we used to back in the Carter Hills Band days.

"Carter." Belinda, or Belle as we all called her, greeted me once we made our way inside. She framed my face with her tiny hands and studied me like a mother checking if her kid looked fine. "How are you? Gosh, I'm so worried about you. I was about to fly to LA to check on you myself if you hadn't come here first."

Stud shrugged as if to say *Told ya*, and I couldn't contain my smile.

"I love you too, Belle," I said. "Did we wake you up?" I asked, pushing the conversation away from my life and my dodgy choices.

"No. I put the kids to bed a long time ago and was just enjoying the quiet of the night. I also wanted to see you before calling it a day."

I drew her into a hug and kissed the top of her head.

"What did I tell you?" my ex-bandmate said, burying it behind a cough.

I shook my head.

A sense of peace ran through me, filling every corner of the void within my being.

"I've missed you guys. Stop worrying about me. With Tristan and Kimmie, you have enough to keep you busy as it is. I'm a grown man."

We broke apart.

Belinda shook her head. "It doesn't matter. You and I will talk in the morning, okay? We need to catch up. And don't think for a second I didn't notice you trying to avoid the subject. Tomorrow, you'll tell me everything, Carter

Hills. The ugly truth and all that's going through your mind."

I nodded. If Belinda wanted to chat, nothing I could do would get me out of it. I loved her for caring so fucking much. "Sure."

I moved into the guest room, and before I could replay the last few months in my head, I fell asleep in the household that hosted four of my favorite people in the world, knowing I was safe from any harm here, even the one I induced on myself.

———

Stud's fishing cabin was a small shack in the Oregon wilderness. Sitting on a piece of land bordered by thick lines of mature trees and crossed by a stream, it had all the basic necessities—water, electricity—and was everything I needed. Located a few miles outside a small town, I could easily get groceries and run errands when required. With dark brown log walls, plank floors, and ceilings of the same shade, it wasn't chic or modern, but it was exactly what I yearned for to reclaim my soul and find peace. The closest neighbor was a ten-minute walk down the narrow country road, leaving me free to be as I pleased, without interruption. During the day, I kept myself busy—reading from the shelves, cooking, and taking long runs across the property.

At night, I sat with my guitar by the fireplace and played for hours until the pads of my fingers hurt and I couldn't evade sleep any longer.

Riley and June kept me updated almost daily. We had started talking about releasing my new album within the next year—the one I'd been putting off for the longest time —and about getting back out there. Tour. Travel. The whole nine freaking yards.

Every few days, I texted or called Savannah and pretended the connection was static or I was busy with a secret project to keep our conversations short. All I was left with was listening to her complaints, her threats to make me pay for abandoning her, and her constant whining about missing me. Nothing new. Nothing exciting.

When Taylor's name flashed on my screen three weeks later, I braced myself for the news he was about to deliver. Cold sweat beaded on my neck. This was the moment of truth.

I fortified myself, my eyes perusing the space around me before I walked outside to get a better connection. The smell of pine and humidity clung to my nose.

I circled the cabin, fresh air filling my lungs as I took a big inhale, tilting my head back to stare at the sky. In a few strides, I reached the barbecue and bonfire area, a small clearing free of trees, where I knew the connection would be the best. With one roll of my shoulders, I paced the ground covered with fallen leaves and pine needles and accepted the call.

"Hey man," I greeted Taylor after the video chat connected.

"Carter, I think you should sit down."

Chapter 25

In four-inch stilettos, I paced across the living room. Soon, the tips would leave permanent imprints in the wooden floor. On the coffee table, incense sticks burned, filling the air with a patchouli scent strong enough to singe my brain cells. The lady at the voodoo-thing store told me they could help with the apartment energy and soothe the atmosphere. Right now, I was desperate and ready to try about anything to bring back my good fortune. To bring back my man into my life. And go back to the time when we were happy together.

The call went through, but no one picked up on the other end.

Balancing the phone in the crook of my neck, I tugged at the hem of the leather mini-skirt I was wearing. So much for looking like a thousand bucks. With no one around to get slack-jawed over me, it served no purpose. In front of the full-length mirror, I fluffed my hair which fell into soft curls over my back and used my fingertip to fix my eyeliner.

"Come on, pick up," I repeated for the umpteenth time with a sigh.

Why was Carter not answering his phone? It'd been six days since we had a conversation that lasted more than thirty seconds. Each time I got a hold of him, the line was either filled with static or he said he had a busy schedule and had no time to talk. Whatever his problem, I wouldn't let him ignore me once he came back home. I deserved better than a boyfriend who made me feel like a second-string.

Our fight in New York replayed in my head. If I had to —and only as a last resort—I would say *I'm sorry* to him. Something I usually refrained from. Apologizing displayed your weakness, and I refused to be weak. No, I was strong and confident and wouldn't reduce myself to low standards unless mandatory and left with no other resources to fix our miscommunication.

Anger simmered inside me, and I tightened my fists, careful not to mess up my manicure. With determined steps, I approached the coffee table and crushed the incense sticks in the porcelain plate holding them, trying to dissipate the overwhelming scent with my hand. It didn't work. I wasn't calm—or in control—anymore. I was losing the advantage.

The voicemail kicked in.

"Stop avoiding my calls. What's wrong with you? You should be ashamed of yourself, Carter Hills. I'm here missing you, while you're doing God knows what with God knows who. Probably some skank. That's not the way to treat your queen. And. I. Am. Your. Queen. No one else. Better get your ass back here. And quick."

I killed the call with my finger, shaking with so much wrath, even my breathing hastened.

I sighed and plopped onto the couch.

Then it hit me. Carter wouldn't return my calls if I wasn't gentler. The guy had a weak personality and far too many emotions. Didn't his father ever tell him to suck it up as a kid? Guess not. Oh yes, he was the black sheep. The unloved offspring. Yeah, I had to tread carefully.

My back was ramrod straight and my chin high when I dialed him again. This time, I used my most innocent voice. The one he had trouble resisting in the past. "Hey, baby. It's me. I didn't mean to go all angry on you before. It's just"—time for some Oscar-worthy acting—"I miss you so much. I'm going crazy here. The last time we were together, we fought, and it's been keeping me up most nights since then. I really miss you. This place is so empty when you're not around. I can't wait to feel your arms around me again. It's been too long. Maybe I could come visit you. And we could make up. I'm pretty good at rocking your world. Please call me back. I long to hear the sound of your voice. It makes my days better. I bet you've brought me some designer items from New York, and I can't wait to see them. You know how much I love it when you gift me things like that. They put sunshine into my life. It's like my birthday all over again. Please be quick. I'm wet just at the idea of having you back home—*our* home. Our little love nest. Call me when you have a minute. Better yet, surprise me in bed. Naked. I love you."

There. No way could Carter resist me now. If this didn't make him come running back to me, then I had no idea what would. Saying *I'm sorry* would be my last attempt before I had to fake an accident or something to compel him. Yes, it was about time Carter Hills returned home.

Two days later, Carter still hadn't returned my call, so I

decided to take the matter into my own hands. Sitting on the guest chair in a prime-time celebrity talk show, I wiped the forced tears with my fingertips. After I leaked information to the press about Carter vanishing into thin air after his appearance on *That Talent*, I received multiple offers to voice my side of the story.

Putting my most distressed face on, I blinked back the fake sheen in my eyes and answered the interviewer's questions. "Yes, Carter Hills has gone to a…ohmygod, this is so shameful… he's gone to…gone to a sex rehab center for treatment. He's a…he's a sex addict." Crocodile tears. A little breakdown. A tissue to tap underneath my eyes. "I-I'm sorry. The last few weeks have been hard on us… on me."

Inside, I high-fived myself. If this wasn't enough to bring my man back, then I would be at my wit's end. After all, I had learned to do what it took years ago.

———

My parents had always told me I knew what I wanted, even as a baby. If I saw something I liked, I'd do anything to get it. No matter the price or what I might have to do to get it. Or the consequences.

And today, at sixteen, what I wanted was Jerry, my mom's boyfriend. Over six feet tall, with broad shoulders and a dark five o'clock shadow.

He wasn't one of those creepy trailer park boyfriends. No, Jerry was hot, successful, and funny. For a forty-six-year-old man. Even his laughter woke up an army of butterflies in my belly.

Tonight, with Mom working late, I finally had a chance to make my move.

Operation Seduction—or OS as I called it—was on.

I'd been waiting for over six months for this moment, planning everything in my head.

*My fingers itched to dial Meghan, my ex-best friend, but after I made out with her boyfriend under the bleachers last year and she caught us—*oopsy*—she refused to talk to me ever again.*

I shrugged. Her loss.

I didn't unzip his pants. He did it. And I didn't push his dick into my mouth. He did. Of his own will. Well, after I begged him to. Stupid men and their sex drives.

Meghan shouldn't blame me; I did her a favor. I exposed her cheating boyfriend. Instead of pushing me away, she should've thrown me a party. A thank-you bash. Whatever. It didn't matter. Dimitri asked me out once Meghan dropped his sorry ass. He meant nothing to me. I got what I wanted. And he got what he deserved for being an easy prey. Humiliation.

Now I had my sights on another male specimen. A real man this time. Not a stupid high school kid who came in under two minutes. This time I was aiming for the real deal.

*I'd heard Mom and Jerry going at it, more times than I could remember. And I might even have spied on them once or twice—*oopsy *again—to see what he liked. He wouldn't push me away if I fulfilled all his fantasies and blew his mind…amongst other things. The idea of seducing him made me smile.*

Sure, Jerry would play hard to get, but I never backed off.

Goal-oriented, remember?

"Hey, Savannah, dinner is ready," Jerry announced from the kitchen down the hall. The whiff of chicken parmigiana filled my nose. My step-dad had many talents, and cooking was one of them. I fixed my makeup, refreshed the red killer on my lips, fluffed my straightened brown hair, and stared at my reflection once more. Everything had to be perfect.

Showtime.

I swayed my hips as I made my way to the kitchen, dressed in a cheerleading skirt so short that it left nothing to the imagination and a cropped white tank top over a red push-up bra.

I used my most sultry voice, and licking a bright pink lollipop, I sat on the countertop, my legs spread and my back straight. "I'm starving, Jerry. Are you hungry too?"

He discarded the oven mitts and pivoted on his heels.

His eyes flared.

In a slow sweep, his gaze took me in. Every inch of me.

He threw his apron over me. "Cover up, Savannah. The game you're playing isn't funny. For fuck's sake, get dressed. Dinner will be served in a minute."

With his hands lifted between us, Jerry stepped back.

Without breaking eye contact, I sucked on the lollipop faster, twirling my lips around it—just like I'd seen girls do in X-rated movies.

"I'm hungry, Jay-Jay, but not for food." I dropped to my feet, the apron billowing on the floor, and prowled toward him.

He took another step back. "Stop, Savannah. Whatever game you're playing, it's not funny. Why would you try to seduce me?"

"Because I can and I want to."

"You speak nonsense." He shook his head with too much velocity, a disapproving look straining his face.

I sucked on the lollipop and used a finger to trace my lips, before moving forward to push my sugar-coated digit into his mouth.

He jerked his head to the side and took one more step back. "Enough with this little act. Savannah. I love your mom."

"Doesn't mean we can't have our fun on the side." I high-fived myself in my head for the languorous tone of my voice. "I'm all wet for you, Jay-Jay. Wanna see? Or lick it off my finger?"

"Stop. Jesus, you're a kid. A daughter to me. And you are just being ridiculous right now. Your little plan isn't working. I won't fall for it. Not interested in being your new experiment." He waved a hand in front of me. His voice was icy when he added, "Go to your room and change, and we'll forget this ever happened."

Tears prickled my eyes.

I wasn't used to being turned down.

I always got what I set my eyes on. No exception. A-L-W-A-Y-S.

Jerry should know better.

I wanted him. Simple as that.

And I wouldn't take no for an answer. In fact, I relished his hard-to-get persona. It turned me on even more.

"Jay-Jay, don't call me a kid again." I pushed my boobs up with my hands. "Do kids have these?" I cocked an eyebrow.

A loud chuckle left his mouth. "Jesus, Savannah. Are you done yet? It's enough. Go. Change. And come back to eat when you're decent."

"But I don't wanna be decent." A moan passed my lips. "Not with you." I twirled my tongue around the tip of the lollipop and rubbed my thighs together. "Do kids do this to a big, hard dick?" I stepped forward, and Jerry sidestepped to his right. Oh, I loved the challenge. I was addicted to it, even.

"Savannah, for the last time, stop. This isn't funny."

I pushed my hand under the waistband of my skirt and panties and hummed, closing my eyes. "And do kids do this?" A warmth crept up my face as my finger dived inside me, and a cocktail of sensations filled me. I brought my wet digit out and wiped it off onto his chest. "I'm sure you'd like to taste it. It's sweet. Just like me." I dropped to my knees and opened my mouth. "Fill me, Jay-Jay. Make me gag on that big dick of yours. I saw you in your swim trunks. I'm aware how huge a package you own down there. Now feed it to me."

"Jesus, you're making a fool of yourself." Rage poured out from his eyes. Disgust took over his face. With one hand, he helped me up to my feet. "Go to your room. This…whatever this is…is over. I won't play any games with you, kiddo. You can eat later when your mom is back. Until then, you're grounded."

"You can't do this. It's unfair. You're not my dad. Who do you think you are? You have no rights over me." I clenched my hands at my sides. "You'll regret it, Jay-Jay. Nobody tells me no. And I'm not a kid." My voice turned high-pitched as I yelled, "I'm a grown woman,

and I don't have to listen to anything you say." Who was he to tell me all those things? Anger. Rage. No, fury—yeah, fury—boiled inside me. Jerry had no grounds to reject me. I let out a glass-shattering shriek, digging my fingernails into my palms. One day, he would be sorry. He'd pay for this. Big time. I'd make sure to humiliate him when the time was right. I'd give him a taste of his own medicine.

Screw you, Jerry, I never lose.

The front door opened, and both my parents appeared in the doorway.

I cleared my throat and blinked my tears of humiliation away.

"Mom? Dad?" I asked in a small voice. "Ohmygod, you're here. I'm so scared right now." Fat tears pooled in my eyes. "I was about to be abused... If you hadn't arrived, I...I... You saved my life."

Neither of them reacted like I anticipated they would. They just stared at me, something resembling sorrow flashing in their somber gazes. My mom's lips twisted. My dad's jaw flexed. Their eyes found Jerry's, and they all looked so pained.

My eyes traveled between all of them, my step-dad standing as far away from me as possible.

"Hey baby," my mother said as she closed the gap between us.

"What's going on?" My attention drifted to my dad. "Daddy, why are you here?"

My father walked forward, his hands stuffed into his pockets, face worried. Wrinkles around his eyes and hair disheveled, his shoulders slouched forward in defeat.

"Baby, we gotta talk," he said. "The little stunt you just pulled, it's not okay. Jerry is a good man. He loves both you and your mother. Why would you do this to him? Why would you try to trap him in a scandal? What's going on with you?"

Wait... How did my parents know what happened? Had I been set up? Were they standing outside the house the entire time? It was Jerry. He did it. He wanted to humiliate me further. He wouldn't get away with this. The stakes just got higher. I hated him. Why did I ever think he was hot? He was a dead man. I'd make sure of it.

With a forced smile pasted to my lips, I pushed back as my dad moved closer.

"Daddy, Jerry tried to seduce me. It all went down so fast. He tried to kiss me and forced himself on me. He made me promises. And said I couldn't tell anyone about our little secret. You're lucky I'm smart enough and didn't go through with it. Who knew what could have happened? I'm so happy you're here. Both of you," I said, my eyes traveling from my dad to my mom, tears shining in the corners for a greater dramatic effect. "As I said, you might have saved my life."

My mom caressed my hair. "Baby, you're sick. You need help. We've been trying to manage it on our own for years, but it's getting too much. You need professional help before you get yourself into a situation you can't get out of."

I shook my head. "I'm not sick. Jerry seduced me. He tried to kiss me. I pushed him back. Mom, your boyfriend is a child molester. Don't you see it? He's the one who's sick."

My words—a mix of shrieks and sobs—exited my mouth as a new surge of anger rose inside me, leaving a trail of destruction behind.

"Baby," my mom said, her voice low and comforting. "We installed cameras all over the house months ago. With all the stealing, lying, and manipulation, we had a feeling you might try something like this."

I sucked in a shaky breath.

"Your dad will pack your stuff. You're coming with us. There's this center for young ladies just like you. They can help you. You'll have access to the best mental health professionals."

Tears rolled down my cheeks, and my mother wiped them off with a tissue. My parents were turning their backs on me. They were pushing me out of their perfect lives.

"Daddy, please say something. I'm not sick. I'm smart and driven. Also, I do well in school. It was a mistake—"

"You did the same thing to your math teacher last semester," he interrupted, not affected by my tears this time. Since when had my dad

stopped falling for one of my acts? In the past, they had always worked. Every single time. "And your gym teacher last semester said you stripped off your clothes in front of him once and propositioned him in his office a week later."

Daddy was my rock. He wouldn't turn his back on me. I wouldn't allow it. He used to call me his princess when I was a little girl.

"Please, Daddy. I want to come live with you full-time. Far away from creeps like Jerry."

"Savannah, you need help." The resignation on my dad's face messed up my heart—and I hated the feeling.

"No, I don't. And I hate you. All of you," I screamed, now feeling ridiculous in my miniskirt. I rushed to my room and slammed the door behind me. My parents might have won this round, but never again would I get caught. I was good. I was bright. A whole lot smarter than most people my age.

After I brushed my tears off, I rolled my shoulders back, packed my own bag, and returned downstairs. They wouldn't win. I was better. And wiser. Time to show them I could master this game.

My parents and Jerry stood around the kitchen island, talking in hushed voices.

They were now dead to me. I didn't need them in my life. One day, they'd pay for what they had done to me.

As I neared them, I pasted a beatific smile on my face, and using my most charming voice, I said, "Listen, I'm sorry for what I did. You're right. I need help. I'll get better, you'll see."

I changed my mind. I wouldn't be a banker like my dad one day.

I'd be an actress.

And I'd be the best one.

———

I sipped my wine, years later, my eyes trained on the crowd. Contrary to my belief, New York City weather was not that bad at this time of the year. Warm enough I could wear a tight dress, showcasing my perfect curves without having to hide under a jacket. Someone earlier had mentioned influential people would be here tonight. So, I refused to get drunk and make a fool of myself. I had big dreams. Ambitions to fulfill. And one of them included getting a handsome, wealthy, and famous hunk to propel me toward the stardom I'd yearned for so long.

"Ohmygod, it's Carter Hills," a woman exclaimed behind me. "He looks hotter in person. And much taller."

"I wouldn't mind him taking me to his hotel tonight," another replied.

"Do you think he's into threesomes?" the first one asked. "We could share him. Oh, he glanced my way. Do you think I have a chance?"

"Nah. I heard he's pretty hard to impress," a third voice chimed in. "He always goes back home alone. He's a loner or something. Maybe he's gay. There are so many rumors surrounding him. I once heard a story about him struggling with depression after his brother was shot in the Middle East and returned home in a casket. Carter went ballistic and had to do a stint in jail. When he got out, he had to raise a child as his own after his ex-bandmate got knocked up by a roadie. If I were you, I'd stay away from him. He may be hot and loaded, but he's not worth the risk. Too much drama going on with him."

Their conversation piqued my interest.

I had heard all kinds of rumors about the man, but the last time I checked, none of them were true. Except for the one where he was raising another man's baby.

If he were really here, perhaps I could get him to notice me.

Turning my back to the mingling crowd, I adjusted my breasts in my dress and applied another coat of lipstick.

I was well aware of my assets, and I wished they were enough to catch Mr. Bachelor's attention.

All night, I studied him. Talking and laughing with strangers.

He didn't look at ease here.

Once the mandatory socializing portion of the night was over, I retreated to a solitary high table at the edge of the room.

I perfected my damsel-in-distress face and waited.

Soon, Carter Hills turned my way, and I offered him a timid smile.

Those women earlier were right. The man looked hotter in real life. Even his uneasiness made him more attractive.

On his arm, I would shine like the princess I was, and it would turn me into the queen I deserved to be.

With careful steps, he walked toward me, holding a glass of red wine in one hand and water in the other.

Showtime, I told myself.

"Are you here by yourself?" he asked as an introduction. Okay, from up close, he looked insanely sexy. His eyes sparkled in the low light.

Maybe it would be easier to catfish him than I thought. Would he go for the bait, or would I have to up my game?

He placed the wineglass on the table before me, and I flashed him a smile I knew not a lot of people could resist.

He held out his hand, and I met it for a handshake. "Hey, I'm Carter. You looked lonely just now, and I thought you might enjoy some company." Ohmygod, he looked adorable. Clearly, he wasn't the flirting type. I could use it to my advantage.

I raised my glass in his direction. "Thanks for this. I'm Savannah. Savannah Prince."

"Are you here on business? Or are you here with the crew?"

I wasn't a household name in Hollywood. Not yet. So, I could still use it to act all innocent.

I cleared my throat, trying to look impressed by the crowd surrounding us. "I might star in Wesley's next movie. I'm here because he asked me to come and mingle with people. I'm not an A-list actress, so it requires more work to get my name out there. I want the role so bad I'd do just about anything. But I've socialized all night, and now I'm done. It's quite intimidating."

"I can empathize. I'm here because I need to be. This isn't my scene either. I'd prefer being home right now than having to smile at all these people and pretend I'm interested in this Hollywood circus."

"Right? I can totally relate." I sipped on my wine. "I've never seen you around. Are you an actor?"

This performance alone should earn me an award.

"No."

"Oh, are you someone else's date?"

He ran his fingers through his hair.

"I'm Carter Hills. It's nice to meet you."

I lowered my voice. "Like *the* Carter Hills? The music superstar Carter Hills?"

"That would be me."

"It's nice to meet you. I know nothing about the music industry, but I've heard your name a lot. I know you're a big shot on the country music scene."

He offered me a shy smile.

He wore his emotions in his eyes. The man had been hurt, and guilt was eating him alive. I could work with that. First, weakness assessment: *check*.

"So why are you here, Mr. Hills? Why did you agree to suffer through this night?"

"Carter, please. No Mr. Hills. I'm not old enough for that."

I watched him and pushed a timid smile to my lips, hoping my cheeks would flush just a little to add some credibility to my act.

"One of my songs is featured on the soundtrack, so this is a requirement of the job."

His eyes traveled to my cleavage, and I noticed, so I folded my arms to bring his attention to my expensive set of breasts.

His throat worked.

Yeah, I could have him if I played my cards right.

He was on the lookout for something, and I'd find whatever it was and provide it to him.

Second step, nailing the damsel-in-distress act: *check*.

Carter Hills eyed me with a gaze I had trouble deciphering.

I pouted a little because I was aware of the way men zoomed in on my lips when I did. "I'm out of here. Do you want to grab a bite or something? I ate nothing since I got here. And now I'm starving." My stomach grumbled as if I'd rehearsed this scene a thousand times.

Inside, I congratulated myself for being such a great actress. Soon, Hollywood would be my playground, and I would make everybody eat from my hand.

The man facing me downed the rest of his water, and the bobbing of his throat pulled me into a trance. "A midnight snack sounds awesome."

I breathed out.

Part one of my *Seduce-Carter-Hills* plan was complete.

Time to put part two into action.

God, I loved the chase. And I was the best at this game.

His hand drifted to my lower back, and I walked two steps ahead of him. Swaying my hips just a little, to give him the perfect view of my backside, I gave the audition of my life.

———

And here I was, having obtained everything I dreamed of, but now standing on the precipice of losing it all. Carter should have landed by now. Los Angeles was his home. His vanishing act had lasted long enough. These two months, since he kicked me out of his hotel, seemed like forever. When I called him yesterday, two days after my interview on the celebrity talk show, he said he was on his way. This little stunt he pulled would have consequences. The deal was one month in New York City. Not two months away with a cryptic agenda. I surfed the web, trying to find out where in the world his stupid manager had sent him, but I could find no trace of my man anywhere. Ever since our fight in New York City, things had been tense between us, and I couldn't seem to find a way to bridge our differences.

Poor Carter. He didn't get that everything I did was for his own good. With him about to return, I had to flaunt every charm I had to bring back the peace between us.

Often, I congratulated myself for finding the perfect man to date. His broken heart over his stupid childhood friend was all it took for me to swoop right in and make him forget about her not reciprocating his feelings. And his poor mommy who ditched him without a look back after his brother died. Those two women gave me all the ammunition I needed to make him believe I was here to salvage his heart—and his trust in women. To save him from a life of loneliness.

Carter Hills couldn't resist me, and I intended to use it to my advantage.

Always.

When he'd be home, I would bring my A-game. I was done being kept at arm's length.

Sex usually helped me get what I desired. It'd been too long since I used my most precious talent with Carter. Now that I was set on earning back his trust, I would use every skill I possessed. And I possessed many to lure him back.

Lately, a part of me started believing he had figured out I had tricked him into this relationship. Like the good student I was, over the length of our time together, I had learned all about his weaknesses. Carter Hills was sweet, caring, and loyal to a fault. I took advantage of his vulnerabilities to fulfill my own ambitions, but perhaps I overdid it a little because now I could sense him drifting away. I would have to dial down my needs for luxury for a while. Until things between us were back to normal. Yeah, I could be sweet, nice, and even fragile if the situation called for it.

Humming a song, I used my key and opened the door to our apartment, my gym bag hanging from my fingers.

The sight before me froze me on the spot and made me drop the bag at my feet.

What was going on?

Not breaking character, I fixed the widest smile to my lips and stepped inside.

Chapter 26
Carter

"This is it. I'm done."

Savannah walked through the front door as I dropped two suitcases in the entryway. Surprise flashed in her eyes as she stood there, blinking. For once, I was the one shocking her with events she hadn't anticipated.

I breathed out. The ball was in my court right now, and I relished the feeling I was the one in control of the situation. Today, this nightmare would end once and for all. After everything I learned from Taylor last week, I was ready to put the plan we came up with into action. All the time I was away, I told Savannah I had engagements overseas and that I'd be back soon. The days spent at Stud's fishing cabin in the wilderness had been the perfect refuge to think. With no distractions, I had all the time to assess my past, present, and future.

Goose bumps bloomed on my arms as I recalled the

nauseating truths about the woman I'd been sharing my life with for the past two years. Like a movie in slow motion, I replayed all the scenes we lived through, analyzing our interactions.

Savannah squinted, standing tall before me, clearly unaware of my intentions. She schooled her features, erasing the shock that had marred her face seconds ago, and sent a blinding smile my way. "I'm so excited to have you home. You were gone much longer than you said you would be." She started toward me, arms outstretched, but halted halfway. Her full lips transformed into a grimace. "Why aren't you happy to see me?"

Our upcoming face-off would close this chapter of my life. Finally. I sucked in some air, summoning my courage. I hated confrontations. Always had. Yeah, I much preferred peace to war, but this had lasted long enough, and I was here to take my power back. Every single piece of it.

The woman I used to consider my girlfriend glared at me. "Carter, what is happening?"

"What I should have done a long time ago. In fact, I should've never offered for us to move in together. I don't know what your deal is, and at this point, I don't care. I tried. Fuck, I've tried—again and again. More than I should have. But something's wrong with you."

Tears filled her eyes. She blinked them away with her dark mascara-coated eyelashes. Her hand reached for my chest, but I stepped back. "But-but…you don't mean it." A look of hurt flashed in her eyes.

I wouldn't fall for her lies and acting skills this time. I knew better. "Don't try to seduce me, Savannah. Or should I call you, Savannah Carpenter?"

Her eyes widened, and all traces of moisture vanished. Her lips firmed into a thin line.

"That's right. I know all about your little lies, and the

sick attempts you used to ruin people's lives over the years. That poor Jerry. All along, I believed you when you said he abused you. That you were a victim. Fun fact. He's the one who suffered from your wicked ways. The man is smart. He kept the footage of that night. The one where *you* tried to seduce him, dressed in a skimpy outfit, in the kitchen."

Savannah's mouth opened and closed like a fish. For once, she had nothing to say.

"I saw the video. All seventeen minutes and eleven seconds of it. How pathetic. You tried to frame a man who loved you like a daughter. You destroyed him. He's been waiting for years to see if you'd try to ruin his life again."

She fisted her hands on her hips and glared at me, the coldness of her gaze rivaling an iceberg. "Stop spreading the lies of a child molester."

I lifted a finger to shut her up. "Please, stop talking. I don't feel sorry for you, and I hate myself for ever caring."

She took a step toward me. "Carter, I love you. You don't mean any of this. Listen to me, I'll explain everything." She cast a glance down as if it hurt to say the words. "The name thing, it…it was for my safety. The police put me under the witness—"

"Stop. Enough with the stories you make up in your mind. The all-girls school you went to was a mental health facility. You are a pathological liar. And a manipulator. Nothing you ever say is true. For fuck's sake, you never even rode a horse in your life."

More fake tears shone in her eyes. "Don't bring up Savane. You have no right. We were best friends."

"Your mother told us you were allergic to horses. Stop. Lying. It's. Not. Working. Anymore. I couldn't care less." I shook my head, my lips parted in disdain. "Back in high school, you ruined the lives of your best friend and your teachers, and everyone who's been around you has been tainted by your actions. Does it bring you pleasure to hurt people? Does it get you wet? Or high?"

Her lips parted, but I continued before she could add another lie.

"Don't say anything. We dug up all your dirty little secrets. Being evicted? A lie. Probably to get me to rent you a fucking palace you don't deserve and that we never needed. Who called you that night? Who did you pay to fake being your landlord over the phone?" I shook my head. "Getting fired from that TV show because you wouldn't sleep with the director? All a lie. You're the one who harassed him and showed up at his house one night, naked. His husband walked in on your making a fool of yourself. Yeah, he's gay. Bet you didn't see that one coming, right? You threatened to spread rumors about him to save face, but guess what, he's better connected in Hollywood than you are, and you were the one who got fired."

Venom spewed from her eyes. "You have no right to spread rumors, Carter. Who's lying now? Every word you speak is bullshit." She let out a shrill laugh. "Who would believe you anyway? You're a loser. A pathetic individual who has been loving a woman, who never reciprocated his feelings, for so many years that now your heart is screwed. Who's sick, tell me? I'm not the one pining for my dead brother's widow like a lame puppy. Or the one having paralyzing panic attacks like a four-year-old afraid to sleep at night. Stop insinuating you know me or my past. All you've heard are angry people thirsty for vengeance because I turned out better than they did, and their existence is useless."

She inched closer.

"The way I see it, you have two choices. One, you become one of them. Or two, you get your sanity back and realize I'm the best thing that has ever happened to you and you thank me for being so awesome and dealing with your stupid self."

"Okay, you really are delusional. Your parents warned us." A wave of nausea hit me. Again, how could I have been so blind?

"I am the woman of your dreams. Stop pretending otherwise."

I scoffed. "From now on, you're not allowed to reach out to me ever again. You'll be served a restraining order later. If you haven't computed anything I've said so far, we are done. D.O.N.E. Forget my name, my number, and that we ever crossed paths."

"No. You can't do that." Her eyes threw poisonous daggers my way. "I won't let you."

"Savannah, don't bother. I already did."

"What about us? Our love? Our future?"

"There was never an *us*. I thought there might have been one, way back at the beginning of this thing you call a relationship, but that was all pretense. I'm seeing the entire picture now, and I'm telling you. There. Is. No. Us. I want nothing to do with you anymore. I'm ashamed to say I ever did. Congratulations. You ruined another relationship."

"Carter, you're such a hypocrite. You can't live without me. I'm the best girlfriend you'll ever get. Scratch that. I'm the best. That's it. You'll never find someone else like me."

I ran a hand down my face.

Her eyes locked on mine, and chills moved along my spine.

Savannah neared me and reached for the lapel of my jacket, but I dodged her and took a step back for good measure, my hands in front of me, to avoid her getting too close. Her gaze darkened.

"I wish you could hear yourself right now. You're not

my girlfriend. Believe whatever you want. I'm done being your provider. If you're the best I can get, then there's no hope for me. I'll be single for the rest of my life if it means I'll stop being unhappy, starting today. You're like a poison that has made its way slowly through my bloodstream, Savannah. I won't let you kill everything good inside me. I'm out of here. For good."

I strode toward the bedroom to grab more of my stuff.

"Hey, Carter?"

I turned around to look at Savannah. The diabolic glint in her eye shone brighter than usual. I cocked my brow, waiting.

What venom would she spew out next? What false promises would she shove down my throat? With a straight back, I braced myself for another one of her rants.

"You'll regret this. I'm telling you. If you think your life was hell, you've seen nothing."

"Enough. Nothing you say affects me anymore. If I were you, I'd save my breath. You'll need it later. Trust me." She had no idea what was coming her way. I smirked at her furious expression.

Like I predicted, another high-pitch screech escaped her lips.

"You keep proving you're a nutcase, Savannah. Come on. Feel free to make a fool of yourself."

"Oh, you've seen nothing. You have no idea what I can do. I'm not ready to let you go, Carter. I want you. All of you. Nobody walks out on me. You hear me? NO-BO-DY."

"You're rotten from the core. I'm sorry I ever thought you were a nice person inside."

"You can't live without me. Sex with me is incredible. I know you're aware. Soon, you'll come running and beg me on your knees to take you back."

My eyes widened. "Are you kidding me right now? We haven't slept together in almost a year. We haven't even shared the same bedroom in a long time." I shut my eyes, trying to keep my calm. But when words left my mouth, they were laced with wrath. "How can you be so conceited? Any lay in the future will be better than what you can provide. Stop putting yourself on a pedestal. Don't be selfish, Savannah," I added, using her own words. "Being a jerk is *so* overrated anyway."

She clamped her mouth shut before saying, "I love you."

A sarcastic chuckle bubbled out. "You wish."

"Don't go, Carter. Stay with me. We're good together. We'll work out our differences. I'll make it up to you. I always do."

She inched closer and raked her long ruby fingernails down the length of my chest. Iciness ran up and down my spine.

I circled her wrist, took another step back, and moved out of her reach. "We're done. We were never good together. Not interested in your toxic behavior. You have another boy toy, anyway. You don't need me."

All color drained from her plastic face.

"You know about Jean-Jacques?"

A guttural grunt escaped my lips. "You're not even subtle about him. I know you've been having an affair for what, six, eight months? How stupid do you think I am?" Her red-painted lips parted. Who wore scarlet lipstick this early in the morning anyway? "Stop. Don't. Not a word. I don't want to hear anything else from you."

Savannah used her sultriest voice. "Stay. Jean-Jacques means nothing. I want to be with you. He was merely a means to land a role, nothing more." She batted her long dark eyelashes.

As if I was dumb enough to fall for her sham after almost two years of hell. The sound of her voice alone made my stomach churn and the hair stand on end on my arms.

"I don't owe you anything. Go, dig your claws into someone else's heart and bank account, and leave me alone." I exhaled hard, nostrils flaring. "By the way, I broke the lease. You have to get out of this apartment by the weekend." No way would I let her surf on my money any longer. Screw that. It cost a pretty penny to forfeit the lease, but it was worth every cent from the look on Miss Lucifer's face.

A dark red hue crawled over her neck and painted her entire face.

Her eyes bulged, and for a second, I believed her eyeballs would pop out of their sockets.

Her lips twisted with derision. Mine curled up into the biggest smirk my face could contain.

Then she lost it. Her bone-chilling scream resonated throughout the apartment.

My grin broadened. This sight alone was worth millions of dollars.

I dodged the vase she hurled at me that crashed on the wall two inches from my head.

Next, she threw a pillow.

And a TV clicker.

One black high heel.

I moved to the side to avoid being stabbed in the chest by the stiletto.

One step to the right and she missed me when she tossed a glass my way.

Then another black heel.

Fury had taken over her features.

Her face, already red hot, now looked almost purplish.

I blinked as a plate flew my way.

It crashed on the side of my skull.

"Stop. For fuck's sake, stop. Enough."

I lifted my finger to rub the sore spot where the plate had collided with my head.

It fucking hurt.

Blood. Damn it.

"You and I, we belong together." Her satanic laughter turned into a flood of tears, leaving trails of mascara down her cheeks. "Carter, stay." It reminded me of the morning where she pretended to have lost a role, playing the victim and calling to the protective side of my personality after I flew in to spend the weekend with her.

"Sorry, Savannah. That little number doesn't work on me anymore. I'm done. Oh, the moving company will be here in twenty minutes." I motioned to the apartment with my hand. "I gave all of this to charity."

"B-but what about the painting? You can't give that painting away."

"Already did. It's fucking hideous anyway. The art gallery is coming to pick it up later. It was all in my name. And your precious dresses are gone too. Donated them to a woman's shelter earlier."

My smirk returned as someone knocked on the door. I checked my phone. Just in time.

"Honey," I said, using the same syrupy voice she always used around me, while yanking the door open. "We have guests."

Chapter 27

Carter went to answer the door as I remained rooted to the spot, unable to process the scene playing in front of me. How could he have the audacity to leave me behind? With nothing? He would take it all. Everything I worked so hard to own, he was throwing it away. Shelters and charities. Carter was sick. There was something wrong with his head. Who would give away designer dresses and purses to people not deserving of such luxuries?

The mere thought of that hurt me more than knowing he was leaving me.

He would change his mind. In which world would a man be able to walk away from exquisite perfection like me? I snorted. I gave him my all, and this was how he was thanking me. Nonsense. Not sure if I would take him back once he realized his mistake. With a wedding proposal and many carats, I might consider it. Maybe.

I was everything he should aim for in his life, the finest partner he could ask for. All this time, I always offered him the best of me. And what did he do? He rejected me. Tossed me away like an outdated pair of heels.

Sobs strangled me as I surveyed the apartment. Sure, it was modest compared to what I was entitled to, but I was starting to enjoy it. To feel at home between these walls.

If Carter thought I would let him steal everything I deserved from me, he had another thing coming. I'd fight back. Maybe he ignored this about me, but I was never bluffing. Now that he chose to ruin me, I would tear his world apart. I would take everything from him, starting with his stupid best friend and her son.

Over the two years we spent together, I had accumulated all the dirt I could find about him. In case, one day, he walked out on me. Carter Hills was a straightforward guy. Loyal to a fault—yeah, this one played in my favor— generous, polite, honest. People genuinely loved him. This was about to change. His flaws and faults weren't worth the front pages of a tabloid. Except for one. The dirty little secret Dahlia and he shared and that nobody knew about. I had my suspicions from day one. I had heard the stories, had seen the pictures on his phone, and I could tell with almost complete certitude, I was right about this one.

Tomorrow, I'd hit the gossip rags with the story and watch the fallout begin, which should bring me a pretty penny and position me as the leader in this war we were about to enter.

Carter Hills's good name and reputation would be stained forever. His fans would reject him. Call him a fraud. A liar.

The world would see him as he truly was. An untrustworthy man who wasn't the good guy he pretended to be, but a backstabber and a hypocrite.

Once he hit rock bottom, I would come up with more stories to bury him alive. Until there was nothing left but a shadow of himself.

Nobody messed with Savannah Prince.

I was a queen, not a peasant. And once again, I'd play the act of my life.

I thought the photographer I'd been tipping off to follow us around and snap juicy pictures of us together since the first time Carter came to Los Angeles would also fulfill the other part of our deal: taking incriminating shots of Carter that hinted he put himself in compromising situations. The goal was to humiliate him and teach him a lesson—while making him come running back to me, on his knees, promising that nothing was going on whenever I acted insecure and hurt. Each time a new picture surfaced on the internet over the last month, it came with a statement from *a source close to the couple*—aka me—confirming just how heartbroken I was over Carter's cheating allegations.

Nobody needed to know that those too were released by me. To provoke Carter and coax him out of his hidey-hole.

Instead of helping my cause, the ploy backfired.

I looked like an idiot because his team was always one step ahead of me, turning the narrative around. No matter what the photographs hinted at, they continually portrayed Carter as the nice, selfless guy, who was there for his loved ones, even for the women friends who were going through a tough time. His disappearance was excused as time spent on a mysterious new project. As for me, I ended up being depicted as the jealous, over-the-top girlfriend, especially after the interview I had given.

I was done being played for a fool. It was about time I

regained control of my story and the narrative. And this time, I'd hit him with everything I had.

I had gathered text messages Dahlia and he exchanged. I even recorded their conversation the one time she stayed over. She didn't reveal their secret out loud, but by taking them out of context, her words would incriminate them.

I even shot videos of Carter slamming doors while cursing and screaming profanities at me. The world didn't need to know all these videos were filmed when I was pretending to need his help to rehearse for an audition. Then there was one where he was sitting in the living room, while I was off-screen, pleading with him to never hurt me again. That idea had genius written all over it. He had memorized the few lines because I said it would make the scene look more genuine if we didn't use paper scripts. He bought the lie without question. Stupid men.

My backup plan didn't end there. Three bad-angled pictures I took of myself on different occasions that shadowed my face to make it look like I had a shiner. A shot of the split lip I got after I bumped into a wall one night when I had too much to drink. All of those, when added together, would spiral his life downward and make Carter Hills wish he'd never met me.

———

I sighed at all I was about to lose when Riley Burns, Carter's manager, and his rude, cutthroat bodyguard Taylor walked in as if they owned the place, following the man I was starting to despise.

Chills lined my back at the sight of Taylor. The guy freaked me out. Always had.

"Savannah, please sit down," he ordered.

"Why? I'm not a dog, and you're not allowed to boss me around."

He cocked one eyebrow, not looking impressed by my rebuttal. Cornering me, he repeated, "Sit. Down." His chilling voice silenced all objections.

Carter inched so close that I could feel his breath on my cheek and pointed to the kitchen table. "Just fucking listen."

Facing an impossible situation and with no option to escape the confrontation, I decided to use my most special assets. Up until now, in my life, they had saved me more than once from unfortunate circumstances.

I tipped my chin up, rolled my shoulders back, enough to push my breasts forward, and using my most sultry tone, I said, "Gentlemen, I'm sure whatever it is you want, you don't need me here." I batted my eyelashes, pursed my lips —because I knew men easily fell for this shit—and offered them a timid smile. "Now, if you'll excuse me, I have a hair appointment I can't miss."

I had nowhere to go, but I wouldn't stick around these three morons for another minute.

When I tried to leave, Taylor stopped me with a muscular hand on my shoulder. I shook underneath the weight of his palm. Broad shoulders, short hair, somber expression, if he didn't appear so lethal, he could be my type. Since day one, I'd been keeping him at a distance, believing he could tell what I was up to. Call it instinct, but I couldn't trust him. A girl didn't need more complications in her life. No, thank you.

"Remove your dirty paw off me," I screamed.

"Don't try to run" was all he said. How rude. We'd never interacted before, and this was how he addressed me.

"Come, sit at the table with us, Savannah," Riley chimed in. In his tailored suit and business attitude, he watched me as if my humiliation amused him. Another waste of a man.

I folded my arms under my boobs, trying to showcase them and distract their attention.

Another failed attempt. Were these idiots even real? No hot-blooded male had ever ignored my physical charms before.

Carter snickered. The temptation to strangle him right now grew in me, but I wouldn't break a nail over his stupid self.

Squeezed between all of them, I walked to the dining room and rolled my eyes on purpose. My hair stood on end on my arms. As if I was going to face an unknown executioner. I had no witnesses. Would someone believe me if I pretended all three had assaulted me? There must have been some footage of Carter's friends entering the building when they did, no?

Riley made a stack of papers appear from his jacket pocket and placed it before me. His expression cut through the room like a blade, sharp and unforgiving.

"What is it?" Trying to look bored as hell, I sighed while examining my manicure.

"Paperwork our legal team penned for your attention," he said.

I cocked my head, ignoring them. "I'm not signing a thing. You can walk yourselves out of here. You're wasting your time. Like I said, you can't order me around."

Carter sighed. "Stop wasting everyone's time. You've been unmasked, cornered, and checkmated. Drop the act, and sign the damn papers already."

"I said no. Ever heard of women's rights? Freedom of speech? *No* means *No*."

Riley snorted. "God, you're even more difficult than I thought. Listen, let's be real. We know you're about to turn this breakup into a full-blown media circus. Unless you babble out about anything worthy of a lawsuit, we'll let it slide, but whatever you know, or you think you know, about Dahlia and Carter's history, you won't tell a soul about it. Do I make myself clear? You'll keep your collagen-filled mouth shut. There's a child involved, and his business is no one else's business."

It did the trick because my focus snapped back to him. "And why would I do that?" The fake tears, the well-practiced kind I'd mastered after years of pretending filled my eyes right on cue. My lips quivered. I wouldn't let these men intimidate me in my own house. "Carter is aiming to ruin me. I've been nothing but a perfect girlfriend, and he's decided to destroy my life. And my career. You can't ask me to lie for him. Not anymore. Do you know how he has treated me all this time? I'm a victim of abuse here, and I'm allowed to use my voice to defend myself. And clear my name. I've sacrificed enough to protect him. He's a sex addict. And a liar. A manipulator, and you can't trust him. No matter what he told you, it's false. All of it."

"*Ohmyfuckinggod*," Carter said under his breath. "Are you done already?"

He leaned over me until his breath mingled with mine and hit the papers with an open palm. "Savannah, your reign of terror is over. Sign the damn papers. Every dotted line."

Riley jumped in. "You may not know it yet, but we had a lengthy discussion with your parents not so long ago. They had a lot to say about your antics. Want me to write you a summary?"

I flinched but forced a neutral expression upon my face, determined not to let them see how much it affected me. "They're craving attention. Nothing they say is legitimate." I shook my head and exhaled my annoyance.

"Did Carter tell you we met with your classmates? Teachers? Principals? Are you telling me all those people are spreading lies?"

I blinked a dozen times, too shocked to reply. They had no right to dig into my past. I thoughts I had covered my tracks well enough. The guy, whom I paid with some filthy sex, promised me no one would ever find out about it.

Riley continued, "Two can play this little game. You're done pulling all the strings. See? We're a team, and you're not equipped to play dirty anymore. Speak a single word against us—especially Carter—and we'll make every piece of evidence we've collected public. You'll be done. Hollywood will spit you out, and no one will come near you when we're finished."

I steeled my posture, trying to inject myself with confidence. "Are you blackmailing me? Because it's a serious offense and you could get arrested for it."

"Do you want me to bring you a mirror? The one in the bedroom that cost me a fortune?" Carter taunted. "One last look at yourself before it's gone? My treat."

I remained mute. I was outnumbered.

"That's what I thought." His tone turned glacial when he pointed to the bottom of the first page with his finger. "Sign here."

"What does this even say? You didn't give me enough time to read it."

"A contract," Riley said. "If you speak about our visit today or our little chat, then you're in breach of contract. And in this case, along with our exposé to the media, it will cost you a lot of money."

Swallowing the taste of rage lingering in my mouth, I executed myself. I felt attacked. Pressured to comply. Like thieves were holding me hostage at gunpoint.

Riley flipped the page. "Here. To attest that if you

spread rumors or lies about anyone in Carter's entourage, you'll get sued."

"Don't threaten me."

"Stop talking."

"I'm not the bad guy here." My pleas weren't heard. They had all decided to break me. How couldn't they see *I* was the victim? Did they believe Carter because he was a man? Because he had more contacts than I did? Because he was wealthier? My rights as a woman were trampled. Any judge would recognize it. These men were stealing my voice. I steeled my back and met their gazes. "I see what you're doing. Muzzling a woman for your own benefit."

Riley turned a blind eye to my objections.

"Sign. Here." Taylor's voice reverberated through me, and I couldn't breathe. "Do what he said." He resembled a fucking giant on steroids and could probably crush me with just his thumb if he put his mind to it. Not a theory I was willing to test.

With a trembling hand, I signed on the line.

"And finally, here." Riley pointed to another page. "If you ever try to get any money from Carter for any reason, you'll get sued. This states that you're a lying sociopath and nothing you say is true."

"What? You can't? I am not."

"Sure, I can. And yes, you are. You picked the wrong target, missy. You should have done your homework first before digging your claws into Carter Hills. And please stop spreading rumors, you sound pathetic."

I signed the last page.

"Can I get a copy?" I asked, barely able to contain the tremors in my voice as Riley slid the document back into the inner pocket of his jacket.

He shook his head. "No, because you'd be violating the first term of this contract, which states you can't disclose our visit today to anyone. Have a great day." He winked and left the apartment.

Carter leaned in close, hands spread wide on the table, his breath hot near my ear, making me shiver. "Have a good life. And stay the fuck away from mine. Keep your psycho ways far from me and the ones I love, or we'll have a problem."

When he moved back, I jumped to my feet and tried to bury myself in his chest in one last attempt to get him to realize he was making a huge mistake.

Taylor positioned himself between us. "Step back from my client."

"Carter," I pleaded.

"Goodbye, Savannah." Like his manager did minutes ago, he spun on his heels, grabbed one of the suitcases, a duffel bag, and his guitar case, and slipped through the door.

Taylor didn't budge from his stand on my right.

"What?" I asked. "Why are you not leaving?"

He opened his hand. "Gimme your phone."

"No. I won't. You have no right."

He lifted his brow, waiting. Geez, that brow of his was like a weapon all on its own.

I placed my device in his waiting palm. He plugged it into his own phone with what resembled a charger and tapped a few keys before handing it back.

He had scrapped everything. It was back to its default settings. I tried to access the cloud, but it was empty too. All the proof I had accumulated, gone.

A surge of rage built up inside me. "Carter put you up to this, didn't he? Stealing everything from me wasn't enough? He had to humiliate me even more. It's all part of his master plan. He's dangerous. You shouldn't trust anything he says." I had nothing else to lose. "Can't you see you're being played? Help me, Taylor. I'm scared of him. I need protection."

"The movers will be here in a few minutes. Get out of my way, Savannah."

The beast turned his back on me, ignoring all my pleas and cries.

"You can't do this. You'll all pay for it. It's wrong."

———

"No, you can't touch that. It's mine." With a sharp tug, I wrenched the blue crystal vase from the man in charge of removing every single item from our apartment. *My* apartment. The one I was entitled to. Just because I deserved it.

A small, chubby man climbed a stepladder, reaching for the chandelier. My breath stalled. No. This couldn't be happening.

"Stop," I screamed. "Get your filthy hands away from those crystals. Do you know how much they're worth? No, you do not. Because if you did, you wouldn't manhandle them this way."

The man acted as if I'd said nothing. My heart bled at the sound of the expensive pieces of ice clinking together.

The moment the man's feet touched the floor, I maneuvered to snatch the overpriced lighting fixture from his hands. I stood a few inches taller than him, but his shoulders were wider than mine, and his hands bigger. Could I match his strength if I ever needed to?

"Lady, this does not belong to you. Please step away," he said in a strained voice.

"This…This…" I motioned to the room around us. "All of this belongs to *me*. You have no right to barge in here and take it away. I'll sue you. Every one of you. And you'll lose your jobs and everything you own. Do you hear me? You'll lose everything."

A man in his late forties joined us with a pad in his hands. He flipped the pages. "According to the copy of the receipts I have here, everything in this apartment belongs to a certain Mr. Hills. They have all been put in his name, so technically, you own none of it." He shrugged and turned around.

I cupped my trembling heart with both hands.

My head became light from the lack of oxygen due to my hasty breathing.

I wouldn't go down without a fight.

Those were *mine*. I chose every decor element *myself*. I owned all of this. I didn't care what those stupid receipts said.

"All of you, get the hell out of here. Now. Or you'll have to deal with my lawyers," I yelled at the top of my lungs, my fingernails cutting into my palms.

I stomped my feet.

I let out a murderous shriek, but no one looked my way, too busy destroying my dream.

I was about to strangle the chandelier-man—he was the only one smaller than me—when a strong hand clutched my elbow and pulled me back.

"What?"

He harrumphed. My skin crawled. I closed my eyes. In the commotion, I had forgotten he was still here.

"Savannah, please step away from these men. Let them work."

Tears rolled down my cheeks as I watched two men wrapping the giant painting in the living room and carrying it away. I loved that painting.

Taylor led me to my bedroom. "Now pack your stuff. And if you cause another scene out here, you'll have to evacuate the property with nothing. Trespassing is a serious offense."

I shivered down to my toes.

Carter would pay for this. I'd make sure to give him a taste of his own medicine. If he thought he could get away by humiliating me, he had more coming his way.

Since his bodyguard had erased the data from my phone, I would formulate a new plan to ruin him. I was a resourceful woman and wouldn't scare easily.

My pulse spiked, and adrenaline coursed through me. I would find a way to destroy him. He just had no idea the storm he'd just unleashed or the devastation I could cause when pushed to my breaking point.

Chapter 28
Carter

I yanked the door open and slammed it behind me, storming to my truck, using the staircase instead of the elevator, to sweat off the remaining fragments of angst stirring inside me.

I did it. I left. With a shake of my head, I failed at reeling my smile in. Wow. I had taken control of my life back.

Sitting behind the wheel, I shot June a text.

ME

> Leaving LA now. All set. I'll keep you updated.

JUNE

> Drive safe. Riley will fly the rest of your belongings with him.

A little over three hours later, I crossed the Arizona state line, and my body relaxed. The more distance I put between Savannah Prince and me, the more tension left my upper back and shoulders.

I breathed in and out, relishing the freedom seeping through me. My grip around the steering wheel loosened. A new sense of peace invaded me. I reached for the dial and turned the rock music down a notch and drove for twenty more minutes.

Adrenaline soon deserted me, and emotions were now raging a war inside me. Pride. Frustration. Anxiety. The cocktail was making me agitated.

Jittery, I called my best friend, the need to hear her voice strong.

"Hey, Dah." Exhaustion sliced through my words.

"Ohmygod, Carter, are you okay? How did it go? Did the plan work? I was thinking of you, pacing the kitchen for the last hour. Tell me everything."

Moisture filled my eyes. The sound of Dahlia's voice had never sounded so good as it did at the moment. The weight on my back dissolved bit by bit.

"I'm coming home. Alone. It's over. I'm a free man. I thought I could be happy with her, that it could maybe be genuine. Instead, it turned out to be a fucking nightmare. Dah, I tried everything to make it work. I gave it my all, and it burst in my face." My voice quivered on the last word.

"Cart, you're an amazing man, an amazing person. Savannah Prince has no idea how big she lost today, and I'm not talking about the money or the designer stuff. You are the most devoted and trustworthy person I know. You've been my rock all my life. You are a great man, Carter Hills. Never believe anyone who tells you the opposite."

I used the sleeve of my shirt to wipe my teary eyes, dissipating the fog blurring my vision.

"All those people who wronged you and left you, they have no idea how unlucky they are. You are precious. To me. To Jack. To Riley and June. And all your friends. To everyone who has had the chance to know the real you. I'm sorry it took your going through hell for you to realize your worth. Never settle for less."

I remained silent, my emotions clogging my throat. Today had been one crazy-ass ride.

Dahlia's voice calmed the tsunami forming in the depths of me. "Where are you? Do you want us to come get you?"

"On my way. In Arizona."

"Is Taylor or Riley with you?"

"Nope. They're both flying back. I requested some time alone."

A beat passed.

"Should I worry?"

"Nah, I'll be fine. I've missed you guys so much…"

"We've missed you too. I'm so proud of you right now."

"Dah, I was taken advantage of. How did this happen? How did I let my guard down? How could I have been so blind to her manipulative schemes?"

"Carter, stop. Abuse is everywhere, and there are people whose specialty is to lie and fool others. They don't discriminate by sex or age or profession. They play mind games, and they are the best at them. Savannah Prince is a sociopath. She saw an opportunity, smelled your weaknesses, and attacked. It's not about you. It is, but she would have got another prey if you hadn't taken the bait. What you went through is called psychological violence, and it can happen to anyone. People often realize this once they're both feet in. It takes a lot of courage to leave because these manipulators, they see no wrong in their doing, and they are pretty convincing at making you believe *you* are the problem and that they are the victims. It's not personal. It's not your fault. Don't ever blame yourself for others' insecurities and fraud. You are strong. Otherwise, you would still be trapped in her drama."

"And yet, I lost two years of my life. For a moment, I became someone I barely recognized. My team had to get involved to help me sever the ties linking me to Savannah once and for all. I made a fool of myself."

"See this as an experience. You learn from it. You grow up. And next time, you won't trust people too easily, but at the same time, you can't spend your life thinking everyone is fake. There are good souls in this world, and your person is out there too. I believe it. Now that you recognize the signs, you'll just be more careful. But don't lose faith in people. In women. Not everyone is Savannah Prince. You just got unlucky." She paused. "But you know what? Luck turns. Like the wind. Are you gonna reach out to that therapist?"

"Yeah. As soon as I'm home. We talked on the phone three times already. The day has been exhausting. This morning, I felt confident. Now that the adrenaline is waning, I'm crashing. I think I'll get a hotel room and sleep it off. Even though it's just"—I looked at the time on the dashboard—"mid-afternoon where I am. Can we talk later?"

"Sure. Call or text me when you get back on the road, okay?"

"I will. Thanks, Dah. For listening to me. And having my back. Always."

"Cart, I'm sorry I didn't pull you out of there myself." Her voice cracked. "You had to do this on your own. It had to be your decision. I'm just glad you came back to your senses. I'm relieved this chapter of your life is over.

Are you driving to Green Mountain, or are you staying at your penthouse in Nashville?"

I sighed and rubbed the back of my neck. "I'll be in Nashville for now. I need to fix my life. Get it back on track. Figure out my next move. Shit, I don't know. I need to talk to Riley and June and get rid of anything linking me to Savannah Prince forever. I am craving a moment on my own. To just be. And regain my strength. And focus on the good in my life. Record some music if I can get my mojo back. I never realized how isolated I'd become until Riley mentioned it. I went to visit Stud, and he pointed it out too. It's like I've been brainwashed…hard to explain. Anyway, gimme some time to get back on my feet."

"It's okay. Let us know when you're ready. If you need anything in the meantime, we're here for you. All of us."

"I know. Thanks for being in my corner."

"Always."

"Dah, I'll come to you soon. Never again will I stay away from you guys. It broke my heart when Taylor advised me to keep my distance. You're my family…and where my heart belongs."

"Quick reminder. If you want me to go to LA and kick Miss Evil's ass myself, just say the word. It will be my pleasure. She has no idea how we Southern girls can defend ourselves and those we love."

A chuckle left my mouth. It felt good to laugh again.

"I'd pay good money to see you teach her a lesson the Tennessee way. Tell Jack I love him, okay? I'll try to video chat with him tomorrow."

"I will. Be careful, Cart. We'll wait for you. Heal. Take as long as you need."

We hung up, and my heart floated in my chest, lighter than it'd been in a long time.

Now I could breathe. Like really breathe.

Savannah Prince was a bad decision. A bump in my road. Yeah, I wouldn't waste my life thinking about her. She didn't deserve a single moment of it.

I exited the interstate, in search of a hotel to nap for a few hours.

When I got off my truck, I stretched my arms over my head and inhaled the floral scent that permeated the air. A small smile peeked out. Being alone had never felt so good.

Yeah, I could be happy again. I'd make it happen. Love. One day. I wouldn't lose hope.

Perhaps being on my own wouldn't be so scary this time. The days where I belonged to someone who didn't deserve me were over. For good.

I breathed in the essence of my newfound freedom, enjoying every tingle lining my spine.

The knots strangling my stomach loosened.

The giant rock sitting on my chest fractured a little.

My heartbeat evened out.

Yeah, I could do this.

Carter Hills against the world. This could work. I could reinvent myself. I'd done it once before. Maybe the second time would come easier. I'd also bring back music into my life. It was the thing I missed the most these days. Writing songs. Coming up with melodies. Creating musical pieces I'd be proud of.

With a pep in my step, something I hadn't felt in what appeared like ages, I entered the lobby and paid for a night. The room looked nothing like the ones I usually stayed in with its drab green-stained maple wood floors, cheap wallpaper fraying at the corners, and worn uphol-stered chairs. For once, it felt oddly satisfying to do some-thing Savannah would never have agreed to. The scent of stale humidity and years-old cigarette smoke was imprinted on each particle of air here. With a finger, I rubbed my nose, trying to adjust to the dust covering every surface and avoid sneezing. Once in the modest ten-by-ten room that had seen better days, I dropped face-first on the ragged queen-size mattress and fell asleep before I even had time to undress. The day's events were catching up with me.

For the first time in months, my brain conjured new possibilities. And I felt safe. And happy.

The curve on my lips followed me into my dreams.

Chapter 29

Carter

"Tell me, Carter. Why do you believe you tried so hard to make this relationship work and ignored the warning signs?"

Sitting in an opal-green leather chair, I bent forward, resting my elbows on my knees and burying my face in my palms.

Once I left Los Angeles, I had agreed to meet with Dr. Diaz in person after my manager suggested it. To clear my head and help me let go of the fact I had shared a bed with the devil. Riley didn't like the fact I sometimes blamed myself for how things turned out.

Dr. Diaz was the psychologist I consulted after my brother's death. The one who helped with my episodes. Breathing techniques to quiet my mind and kill the voices of guilt in my head. All his doing.

He was a man who took no bullshit and encouraged you to face your fears and your doubts head-on. He wasn't renowned for his gentle ways. In this industry, he had seen everything. No doubt that my life's struggles were mild compared to what he dealt with on a regular basis.

"Carter?"

I sucked in a shaky gulp of air. Every cell in me trembled.

I balled my hands to avoid the tremors.

The thing was, I didn't feel like opening up today. My emotional state was a mess, and I feared I would lose control if words traversed my lips.

"I heard you," I whispered, still avoiding his eyes.

"In the last two weeks, we've made progress. We've talked about the psychological violence you went through and concluded together there is no shame in admitting your ex-girlfriend abused you. In many different ways. Mentally, financially, emotionally, physically. Today, I wanna know why you endured it for so long. On Monday, you enumerated a list of occurrences where you believed you should have reacted. Where you could have understood the game she was playing. We went over the stories her childhood friend and family told your team. The false accusations she made against her step-father. So, you know you weren't her first victim."

"I'm not a victim."

"Well, I'm glad we agree. Being a victim is a passive role. It puts you in a corner with no defense. I prefer the term survivor. Or fighter. You got out of there, Carter. It's an important part of the story."

"I endured it. And I let her use me. For far too long. I should have seen through her. I should have——"

"It's easy to say afterward. When you're in the middle of it, you don't have all the clues." Dr. Diaz's words simmered between us. "Now I'll repeat my question. Why do you believe you tried so hard to make this relationship work and ignored the warning signs?"

I remained silent.

Breathe in. Breathe out. Breathe in. Breathe out.

It felt like the temperature of the room soared, and I leaned to the side to grab the bottle of water on the table, fidgeting with the cap after I gulped half of it in one go.

I ran my other hand through my hair before clamping it around my throat. I was suffocating. The room spun around me.

"Carter, breathe. You're safe." Dr. Diaz lowered his voice. "Tell me why you punished yourself in a relationship that made you miserable?"

I exploded. The wires in my head touched and things I kept locked inside burst out. "My brother is dead. And it's all my fault. I-I should have been the one dying that night. He had his whole future ahead of him. He had just got married…with…with a baby on the way."

Dr. Diaz cleared his throat. "Carter, we already assessed that guilt a few years ago. Please be honest with me now. And with yourself. Don't deviate from the question. No more hiding. That's the key to clearing your head and moving forward."

I hid my face in the crook of my elbow, fighting through my emotional overload.

It took me a while to recoup my thoughts.

"I-I didn't… I didn't think I deserved better. For the longest time, I believed myself to be unworthy of love. Happy now? This time, I didn't wanna be failed by another woman. I had hoped this was it. That it would break the curse. That a woman would love me back. Me. The man. Not the fucking music star or the best friend or the child, but me. Carter Hills, the guy from White Crest, Tennessee. The guy who misses his mother more than she deserves and the one who would have given his life so that his best friend loved him back…and returned his feelings one day…and not move on with another guy and fucking marry him. That they would raise Jack together and be a real family, the three of them. Like he pictured it so many times in his dreams."

Dr. Diaz said nothing.

"I thought if I put all my energy into this relationship and ignore the voices in my head that told me to run away, I would succeed. I know better now and understand what you mean when you say I had to go through this…huh… that it was part of my journey. Doesn't mean I'm grateful I did. Yeah, I learned a lesson or whatever life tried to teach me. I get it. And I left. I put an end to the misery. Still, it's another failed relationship with a woman. Happy you got it out of me?"

I flexed my jaw and wiped my palms on my denims.

I hiccupped, the air coming in and out of my lungs hurting its lining. I was suffocating. This morning, I felt stronger, ready to take the world by storm, but the intrusive session wasn't going as planned. It kept me on the edge of my seat.

"That was before you jumped into the relationship. Does the man sitting in front of me today still believe he's not worthy of love? Or can you categorize this period of your life as a bad experience? You faced your aggressor. You put an end to your hell. You showed strength."

I shrugged. "I guess."

"The way I see it, you have two choices here. One, you accept this and use it to move forward. It will always be a part of you, but it doesn't have to define you. You can acknowledge it happened and keep going."

I offered him a pointed look.

"See it as a toolbox. All your life experiences, good or

bad, can become tools in the future if you know how to use them. Your second option is to let this relationship eat you from the inside and ruin the rest of your life. To let it define you. Which one are you choosing?"

My eyes connected with him.

He suspended his hands as a balance on either side of him, moving them up and down. "Being miserable and living a passionless life? Or growing from it? Dusting yourself off and not stopping until you get where you wanna be? Like in your career. You persevered even when it felt like the world was crumbling around you. Show the same determination in your love life, and don't lose hope."

I snorted.

"I knew it," Dr. Diaz said, what resembled a smile forming on his thin lips.

I raised both hands between us. "You're right. I won't let my failed relationship get to me. Throw yourself flowers, Doc." My lips tilted up of their own volition.

Dr. Diaz nodded and continued. "Now, let's talk about your mother. Because a mom is a child's first love."

The topic of my parents abandoning me five years ago still hurt like hell. Over the years, I had made multiple efforts to reconnect with them. In vain. They didn't just push me away the day they flew out of the country, they also turned their backs on their only grandchild— and on Dahlia, who had always been like a daughter to them— when we all needed them the most.

Under the shrink's heavy gaze, I averted my eyes.

"Carter." He had lost his confrontational tone. "In order to move on, we gotta address your mother's actions. I believe it's the root of your complicated relationship with love. And why your feelings for Dahlia took a long time to settle into friendship."

"I don't wanna talk about my mother. She has always

preferred my brother to me. I've known all my life. He was her favorite child. She wasn't even subtle about it. She would always prioritize him and his well-being. In every-thing. When Jeff asked Dahlia out, she was so proud. She radiated with glee. She knew how I felt. She must have known because the entire fucking world was aware. Everyone says I have the worst poker face. She was my mother, and she did nothing to comfort me. She didn't hug me that night. Or tell me I would meet someone else one day. She stood there and smiled at him as if he had gifted her the world. And my dad, well, he stood by her, no matter what."

I ran the back of my hand under my runny nose.

Reliving those moments hurt like a fresh wound. They shook me to my core.

"Every music festival I played at, every award I won, every platinum album I sold, she never once congratulated me. She never said a word about it. She could have said she was proud, that she knew I would make it and I had what it took to succeed. Talent. Drive. Whatever. She. Never. Did. She didn't even come to see me play when I was touring, before being signed and after being signed."

Another hiccup.

"Jeff was the one driving me from festival to festival. He was the one cheering me on. My greatest fan, as he used to say." Tears choked me. "He was my *only* fan. My biggest supporter. My only blood relative who believed in me…and he…he fucking died, leaving me to do this on my own."

The fog clouding my vision thickened.

"I send them plane tickets. Every Christmas, on Jack's birthday, sometimes just because I miss them…"

With the heels of my hands, I pressed my eyes to relieve them from the sting.

"Carter, listen to me. None of this is your fault. Those are your parents' choices. Their decisions. Even though you're the one paying for their mistakes, you're not responsible for their actions. Just like you are not responsible for Savannah's actions."

"How do I heal from this? Once and for all. How do I cut the cord making me feel obliged toward them for good? I'm done suffering."

"That's what I'm here for if you're ready to deal with it and put it behind you once and for all."

I rubbed my hands together and leaned back in the chair. "I am."

"Let's do this then."

Epilogue
Carter

Breathless, I bent in two to catch some fresh air, before stretching. Running helped me to clear my head. This time, I was trying to be smarter about it. Every time I had my anxiety-induced episodes, I would run for hours until they passed. Today, I chose to run for the fun of it. Five miles. Not to exhaust myself, but to feel better.

Taylor stopped beside me. "Feels good to be back in town?"

I nodded as we crossed Centennial Park side by side. "I've missed Nashville. It feels great."

"How are you doing?" my chief of security asked.

"Better. I'm glad it's all behind me. Savannah has only given a handful of interviews so far, and it's been three weeks now. She's cooking something up. I can tell."

Taylor clapped my shoulder. "I wouldn't worry too much about it. Whatever rumors she comes up with, we'll intervene if she goes too far. Up until now, she's been claiming you've cheated on her and that you need to enter a rehabilitation center. All those statements have been denied. If she had something important to share, she wouldn't make claims without having anything to back them up. She signed those papers. She's trying to surf the breakup wave. Her five minutes of glory. Let it slide for now."

I cocked my head to stare at him. "Maybe."

He walked me to my building and turned away to leave.

"Taylor," I called out before he climbed into his car. "I'm going to spend some time in Green Mountain. It's overdue since I missed the holidays with Dahlia and Jack. It has never happened before, even when I was touring the other side of the globe. I know it was for their safety but still…" Tightness clamped my heart at the thought I'd sacrificed too much for a woman who should have never earned any minute of my time. "Anyway, you deserve a vacation too. Stay here, enjoy life, be with your wife. I'll call you if I need you to come over. I'll spend time with Jack and Dahlia anyway. Nothing to worry about."

"You sure?"

I bobbed my head. "Yes. Thanks for always having my back."

"I checked your security the last time I went up there. All safe and sound. Enjoy the time off."

"I will. See you soon."

My phone went off before I reached my floor. "Hey, June. What's up?"

"Cart, can we talk?"

"Huh, sure. Gimme thirty minutes? I'll shower and eat something. I just came back from a run with Taylor."

"Listen, I just got off the phone with someone from

your record label. They heard from Savannah Prince's people. Some things we need to discuss."

"The fuck."

"Call me when you have a minute. I'll see what I can do in the meantime, okay?"

I huffed my frustration. "Yeah, I'll do that."

With my fists clenched at my sides, I tilted my head back and exhaled.

———

When I arrived at Green Mountain, most of the lingering anger from my phone call with June had melted away. On my way here, I tried to forget what I'd just learned about another one of Savannah's evil deceptions. She had not only been feeding information about my whereabouts to the press, but she actually found an ally in a person close to me. Teaming up to play me behind my back all this time.

The news of their association shouldn't surprise me, yet I couldn't believe how low people were willing to go for a taste of power, fame, or money. A recipe for disaster. These people didn't deserve a moment of my thought anymore. I was done with opportunists trying to control my actions and using me for their own twisted games.

The sight of Dahlia and Jack waiting for me eradicated every remnant of fury in me.

"*Carrrter*," Jack said running my way.

Here. Them. They healed all the pieces of my broken heart.

How could I have limited my time with them for so long when I needed them the most?

I raked my hand through my messy locks. The ones I hadn't cut in months. Savannah had fucked with more than just my sanity over the years we were together.

The idea of spending time with my family had brought my hopes up. For a better life. A better future. A better everything.

After I pulled my beanie back down on my head, I exited my truck and lifted the boy into my arms and held on to him.

My lips curled up.

Peace invaded me.

And all the demons dissolved.

Dahlia announced they would stay with me for a couple of days, and just like that, I turned back into the Carter Hills version of me I loved and respected. The one I recognized. The one I was proud of.

Surrounded by the people I loved, I found my groove back. My momentum. My life.

In the last few weeks, I'd even started writing songs again. I had many things to say. Many emotions to express. Two years of struggle to share.

I was ready to conquer the world again.

Later, outside my cabin, fishing something out of the trunk of my SUV and filling my lungs with the distinctive and addictive mountain air, I spotted Dahlia and Jack sauntering my way after they returned from a walk. They joined me, large grins stretching their lips, mirroring mine. In one swift movement, I picked Jack up to twirl him around, his laughter shooting doses of happiness into my heart.

With one arm draped over Dahlia's shoulders, I pulled her to me, kissing her temple.

That's when I felt eyes on me.

Was I being paranoid? Nah, I could feel the warmth on my skin even from a distance.

I knew someone had moved next door for a month but had yet to spot the woman staying there.

A sudden surge of heat ran through me.

My pulse kicked up.

Trying my best to be subtle, I cocked my head to catch sight of whoever was watching me.

Had a stupid fame-chaser found me? No. How could they? I had a gate installed. And people renting the two cabins on my property had to go through thorough background checks.

Right now, one was being rented by that woman and the other by a group of businessmen having their annual retreat. They came here every year, and I never had trouble with them in the past. Anyway, they barely ventured out of their cabin, busy with workshops.

My breathing halted halfway to my lungs when I spotted her. Her pink hair glowed around her pretty face. Her vibrant eyes appeared like blue diamonds through the second-floor window.

We stared at each other for a long moment, neither of us breaking eye contact.

My Adam's apple worked.

A zing traveled the length of my body.

Her lips parted, and when she blinked, it broke the spell we were both under.

The woman moved to the side, but the towel wrapped around her caught onto something and fell to the floor, exposing her bare chest in all its glory.

I blinked, not sure whether it was all a dream or not.

The flustered woman looked mortified and dropped down until all I could see was the top of her head. I stifled a laugh.

"Everything all right?" Dahlia asked.

"Yes. Everything is perfectly fine. I think my stay here will be good for me. Yes, I feel it in my bones."

I tilted my head once more, but the woman was still

squatting down, pink strands visible through the window from my point of view.

Did she recognize me, or did she feel embarrassed for flashing me?

I had a newfound mission because I intended to find out what her deal was.

And I had nothing more important to do than to spy on her too.

————

Thank you for reading the prequel of Carter's story.
Continue his story in **Blindsided**

emmanuellesnow.com/products/blindsided

————

FREE bonus chapter
Want even more? Your deleted scenes await here
emmanuellesnow.com

————

Dahlia and Nick's story: Read **Cruel Destiny**
Riley Burns's story: Read **Last Hope**
Sam Stevens's story: Read **Fallen Legend**

WANT MORE EMOTIONAL LOVE STORIES?

WHICH COUPLE WILL YOU PICK NEXT?

False Promises

★★★★★ "The angst, the utter heartbreak, and protectiveness I felt for Carter during this book is unreal!"

★★★★★ "Emmanuelle Snow really knows how to tug at all of your emotions and does such a great job of bringing her characters to life!"

A gripping story of sizzling passion, lust, and the price of fame.
Start Carter Hills's story now

―――――

Sweet Agony

★★★★★ "If I could give more than 5 stars, I would."

★★★★★ "This is not a romance, it is a story about first love, first heartbreak and growing up."

A compelling tale of love, friendship, and self-discovery that will tug at your heartstrings.

Start Dahlia's story now

———

Cruel Destiny

★★★★★ "Wow. Just wow. If that could be my review, that is all I would write."

★★★★★ "Emmanuelle has done it yet again. She found a way to slip into my mind and heart with her words and the creation of characters you can't help but fall in love with."

★★★★★ "This book broke my heart in the first twenty five percent and sewed it back together."

A story of healing, second chances, and the risks of opening your heart to someone new. Can they trust each other with their hearts, or will their pasts keep them apart?

Read Nick and Dahlia's love story now

———

Wild Encounter

★★★★★ "This is by far one of the most well-written book I've read this month. It is dynamic, intriguing, interesting, unafraid to go there and most of all touching."

★★★★★ "I personally wouldn't call this book JUST a romance novel because it's so much more. I 100% recommend it no doubt in mind."

A tale of passion and perseverance that will leave your heart racing and your spirit soaring.

Read Tucker and Addison's love story now

———

Last Hope

★★★★★ "This book was not only about the darkness but it was about pure love, hope, spice, family, and friendships on point with just the right amount without overpowering the storyline at all."

★★★★★ "Devon and Riley's story is a beautiful one with a lot of emotions. The subject matter is intense but it is handled very gently."

A tale of resilience and second chances in a world where love and danger intertwine.

Read Riley and Devon's love story now

———

Midnight Sparks

★★★★★ "The characters, the love, the humor, the steaminess, the emotions… it's everything I hoped and more."

★★★★★ "I think that is one Emmanuelle Snow's sexiest novels yet."

Welcome to the island where Holiday magic meets unexpected romance and a chance at a fresh start.

Read Gavin and Aisha's love story now

————

Fallen Legend

★★★★★ ""The love that grows, not only through tough angst but through unconditional moments had my heart. This is a spicy and riveting book"

★★★★★ "Emmanuelle Snow doesn't just tell a story, she creates an entire world."

A poignant and uplifting journey of hope, love, and the power of second chances.

Read Sam and Madison's love story now

————

Snowbound

★★★★★ "5 big stars from me for this amazing story. Absolutely loved it!"

★★★★★ "Emmanuelle Snow's stories are always full of angst, and Snowbound is no exception."

The intertwined lives of two strangers bound by fate in the midst of a snowstorm.

Read Anderson and Abigail's love story now

———

All available at emmanuellesnow.com

ACKNOWLEDGMENTS

Wow, this book was a long project in the making. It started back in May 2021 when I released my first novella titled *Men and Country – Carter*. Back then it was just an eleven-thousand-word story to get my toes wet in the publishing world. But that story kept haunting me since I felt it wasn't as complete as it should be. It needed more.

And here we are, almost two years later to the day, as it's now a full-length novel.

So much happened since I published my first novel back in June 2021, and some days, it feels like forever. *False Promises* isn't your typical love story. It's messy, beautiful, and heart-breaking all at once. It speaks to your heart and your soul equally. It's a tale about two people, who, I believe, had to meet to move forward in their lives, even though it wasn't an easy journey for them and hearts were broken and tears were shed.

For everyone who's been in a toxic relationship, this book is for you. And to every man who chooses to remain silent after facing psychological abuse, my heart is with you as I release this new more thorough and detailed chapter of Carter Hills's life. Abuse affects all of us, and no none is immune to it.

Carter Hills. You own a part of my heart (please don't tell my husband!) and you are the muse behind the entire Carter Hills Band universe. You are my book boyfriend, and I couldn't be prouder of every story I've published since our very first collaboration. I hope this book has portrayed you as the amazing and selfless man you are. I can't wait for your trademark smirks and the best one-liners in future books that will come in your universe.

To my real-life husband, thank you for your love and support. Nothing means as much to me. Thanks for joining me on signing events and being my biggest supporter.

To my four children. I love you with everything I am. I am so grateful to be your mom, and no matter what you aim for in life, I'll always help you reach for your dreams.

Shalini, my books' fairy godmother. Thank you for your insights and talents. Even when you tell me I must rework parts of a book and I feel like it's impossible, you always have my back and push me to be a better writer. And a better author. I know how much you've enjoyed Savannah's antics. She was such a fun villain to work with. Yep, she was her evil self from the first to the last page.

My readers. Thank you so much. I'm always happy to hear from you and chat with you. And to those of you I met at signing events, thank you for making them super special. I can't wait to meet you again.

Bookstagrammers. Booktokers. Bloggers. Booktubers. You guys rock. I can never say this enough. Thank you for reviewing my books early, for spreading the word about them, and for being overjoyed when I announce a new release. Your enthusiasm is really precious to me.

With much gratitude and a lot of pride, *False Promises* is now a wrap.

Cheers!

Emmanuelle

ABOUT THE AUTHOR

Soulfully Beautiful Love Stories

USA Today Bestselling Author Emmanuelle Snow is an author of contemporary YA and women's fiction love stories, who gives life to strong characters who'll fight with all they have to reach their life goals and find their own happiness. She loves her characters to be relatable and realistic.

Emmanuelle is in love with love. Especially complicated, deep, and passionate feelings that make a relationship extraordinary and complex all at the same time.

In her spare time, when she's not writing or reading, she likes to go on road trips—with her four kids and her own soulmate—watch movies, paint, or do some DIY, always with a cup of green tea in her hand and listening to country music.

She splits her time between beautiful Canada and the small US towns she adores.

Find all of Emmanuelle's books here:
emmanuellesnow.com

———

Want to connect with Emmanuelle online?
You can find her here:

Website
emmanuellesnow.com

Author's bookstore and merch store
emmanuellesnow.com

Snow's VIP newsletter
emmanuellesnow.com

Readers' VIP group Snow's Soulmates
facebook.com/groups/snowvip

amazon.com/author/emmanuellesnow

goodreads.com/emmanuellesnow

bookbub.com/authors/emmanuelle-snow

facebook.com/esnowauthor

instagram.com/snowemmanuelle

x.com/snowemmanuelle

pinterest.com/snowemmanuelle

tiktok.com/@snowemmanuelle

ALSO BY THE AUTHOR

CARTER HILLS BAND UNIVERSE

(suggested reading order)

Carter Hills Band series

False Promises

HEART SONG DUET

Blindsided

Forevermore

Whiskey Melody series

Sweet Agony

SECOND TEAR DUET

Cruel Destiny

Beautiful Salvation

BREATHLESS DUET

Wild Encounter

Brittle Scars

Upon A Star Series

Last Hope

Midnight Sparks

Love Song For Two Series

EMMANUELLE SNOW

USA TODAY BESTSELLING AUTHOR

CRUEL DESTINY

a love story

Whiskey Melody series - book two

CRUEL DESTINY

NICK

I rapped on the ajar door with my knuckles, pushing it open when the words "Come on in" resonated from inside the room. Murielle, Derek's mom, gestured for me to join them.

"Nick," the boy exclaimed, a permanent smile etched on his face, as if his life was fucking fantastic.

"How are you doing, big guy?" I asked, quirking an eyebrow at him, pulling my lips into a warm smile when we fist-bumped.

"Amazing. Look at this," my little friend said, pulling a red jersey from the side, pride gushing out from every pore of his being. "Barry Hamilton came over this morning."

"The hockey player?" I asked.

"Yeah. He's so huge. Cory Black and Rory Dupont came too."

I smoothed the polyester fabric of the shirt between my fingers, taking in all the signatures written in black ink.

"Man, this is awesome. The entire team signed this?"

Derek bobbed his head, stars twinkling in his eyes, his

grin stretching to both ears. "And we took pictures too. Show Nick, Mom. Show him."

Murielle handed me her phone, and I swept through the dozens of pictures with the pad of my thumb. My heart frizzled in my chest. I blinked, pushing my emotions down. Derek didn't deserve my being an emotional mess beside him. He needed my strength. And my unconditional optimism.

"Man, this is pretty cool." I lifted the paper bag I'd dropped on the edge of the bed when I walked in. "Thought you and I could have lunch together, you know, just us guys. I've had a shitty week—oops, sorry," I said, wrinkling my face and offering Murielle an apologetic smile.

Derek let out a heartfelt laugh. "I'm not six anymore, Nick. It's okay, I won't repeat it."

His mother rose to her feet. "Since Nick is here, I'll take an hour or two to run some errands. You boys be good, okay?" She turned to face her twelve-year-old. "You all right, baby?"

Derek nodded, the smile still anchored to his face as if every day was the most amazing one in his short life.

"Make sure you keep Nick out of trouble."

The boy's laughter reverberated through the small room and multiplied when I shrugged. Murielle gave a head shake and spun to face me. "Can you stay until I'm back?"

"Sure. My entire Sunday afternoon is dedicated to my friend here. I'm not going anywhere."

She squeezed my upper arm and bowed her head before walking out of the room, her lips pressed together in a thin line. I knew the look. Something was going on. It was in the air. Thick and barbed. With a grin plastered across my face, I tried my best to avoid bringing the subject up while Derek could hear us. It could wait. *Later*, I reiterated to myself.

With a soft thud, I landed my ass on the chair Murielle vacated seconds ago and fished the food out of the bag. Greasy cheeseburgers, seasoned fries, extra-large sodas— root beer with no ice for my young friend, just the way he liked it. I knew Derek wasn't supposed to eat junk food, but I'd asked his doctors a few months ago, and they agreed he could use some fun in his life. And if it meant eating burgers or tacos with me once a week, then so be it. Even Murielle concurred.

Derek lifted his cup and clinked it to mine. "Thanks for the burger, bro."

I coughed, almost choking on the pieces of fries in my mouth. "Bro?" I repeated, taking a sip to alleviate the itchy feeling in my throat.

Derek shrugged and ended up giggling. Like a kid should always do. "Saw it in a movie last night. Sounded nice. Since we're best friends, I thought it was fitting."

I swallowed hard. Sometimes I forgot I was the closest thing Derek had to a friend. His peers from school had stopped visiting him a year ago. Kids his age ought to be running around on a soccer field or riding bikes, chasing frogs or going to camp, not stuck in a hospital bed, bald, skinny, alone all year round. It wasn't fair. None of this was how childhood should be.

My eyes found a picture of us by his bed, back when I coached his Little League team, before cancer, smiling on the field with matching golden jerseys and unruly blond hair. A mixture of emotions swirled inside me. I remembered that day as if it were yesterday. When we used to be carefree.

I swiveled my gaze to my friend and mirrored his smile.

"I'm fine with bro if that's what you want. What do I call you from now on then?"

Derek sighed. Like the pre-teen he was. "Bro. C'mon. If I call you bro, you call me bro. That's how it works, no?"

I nodded. "I guess." Bro wasn't a word I used with Tucker and Jace. We usually called each other *man*. "Bro's fine, bro."

After a game of chess, which Derek won, as always—this kid was smart beyond words—he asked in a small voice, needing the reassurance of my presence, "If I take a nap, will you be there when I wake up?"

I nodded.

There was no other place I'd rather be. Since we'd known each other, this kid had touched my heart in countless ways. I didn't have it in me to refuse him anything. Minutes later, the sound of his steady breathing filled the air, and my heartbeat kicked up. A nagging feeling clawed at my spine, crushing each vertebra. Derek could bring much-required sunshine to this world in the way he beamed and left a permanent mark on those he blessed with his presence rather than being stuck in this room, glued to a bed, too weak to get up. A dark cloud hovered over me each time the thoughts ran freely in my head. With a deep inhale, I scanned the room, pushing all my gloomy reflections as far as I could. Over the last year, Murielle had decorated the walls with her paintings and framed family pictures. The hospital allowed it. Since cancer hit Derek five years ago, this room had become a second home to him. Between surgeries, radiation, chemo, and an endless list of infections, he now lived here full time.

My gaze lingered on his taut face as he slept. Pain dodged his footsteps and won most days. Purple rings shadowed his eyes. In the last year, they had lost their vibrant blue color and were now more a dull shade of gray after everything his body had been through. A baseball cap covered his bald head. My eyes drifted to a picture on the wall. A six-year-old Derek blowing candles on his birthday cake, the same smile he bore earlier today, lighting up his healthy little boy's face. A weight grew in my chest, pressing against my lungs, suffocating me. Nowadays Derek's skin looked pasty white—almost translucent—having lost its rosy tone.

The boy was dying. I could feel it. My soul recognized the signs as my body ached at the realization. Chills ran through me, involuntary tremors shaking me. The sight of him brought back the memories of watching my father fight cancer when I was fifteen. But my father survived. Derek wouldn't.

I put the remnants of our lunch back in the paper bag and took everything to the trash can next to the bed.

My gaze lingered on the boy I'd got attached to over the years. Each time I had time off, I swung by the hospital to spend a few hours with him. It felt important. Filling my lungs with quivering inhales, I pinched the bridge of my nose, fighting the emotional storm spiraling inside me that threatened to shatter the facade I usually wore in his presence.

Memories of my time spent with him resurfaced. A tiny smile tugged at my lips.

I was barely seventeen when I met him on the field before one of our Little League games for the first time. From that day on, I'd stuck by his side. His spirit of the game, his cheerfulness, the glow in him drew me in. He was always eager to learn more, always giving his best. We connected big time during those games. Soon Derek felt like a little brother to me. Murielle, being a single mom, often ran late to pick him up after practice. He and I started hanging out together while we waited for her, eating ice cream from the truck parked next to the baseball field, chatting about school and his friends. In more ways than one, from that moment, Murielle and Derek became my second family.

I watched him the nights Murielle had to work double shifts at the restaurant.

Sometimes I'd invite him to throw the ball with Tucker, Jace, and me.

Once a week, Murielle would have me over for dinner after my parents left town so I wouldn't feel left out. Because four months after I turned eighteen, my folks moved to Italy. A dream they both cherished. One they had been caressing for years. But also, one I didn't share. They asked me to come with them. My younger sister, Jessica, did. I refused. My life was in Chicago. My friends were here. And as much as living in Europe sounded awesome, just the idea of going away would knot my stomach in a tight bundle back then.

This was my home. I loved it here. Instead of chasing other people's dreams, I chose to cherish mine. Because I only had one shot at this life, I wanted to make mine count. On my own terms. I got a job, worked my ass off to get experience, showed my commitment and integrity, and secured my own money. So far, my plan had worked great.

Two years after we met, Derek began chemotherapy. All his hair—including his eyebrows—fell off, and he kept fighting. Thinner and frailer through the battle, he never lost that mischievous spark shining in him.

Still on that bed, his breathing shallow and his frame delicate, I could picture the healthy boy he had been. Because no matter how the illness had changed his appearance, it never altered his essence. It shone bright like the scintillating gem he was.

A long huff escaped my tight lips as my eyes stayed anchored to Derek's figure.

Murielle came back at the exact moment. She touched my side, her tiny hand feather-light against my muscles. "Thank you for spending time with him," she whispered, her loving eyes resting on her son's recumbent form, so small under the covers I'd adjusted around him.

I shoved my hands in my pockets, my shoulders sagging forward. "What's the prognosis?" A lump grew in my throat, and I pushed it down to even up my breathing. I could do this. I had to know. I deserved to know. No matter how bad the truth would hurt.

Murielle cast a glance down and took a wheezing breath before meeting my eyes. "Not good. A few weeks at, huh, the most… If at all… His body can't… His body can't take it anymore. His white blood cell count is too low… He's tired. The last infection drained all the energy reserves in him. He doesn't want to fight anymore. We talked about it… He-he says he's ready to go."

I wiped the tears building in my eyes with my thumb.

"It's unfair. I'm so sorry…" I shifted around to wrap a defeated Murielle in my arms, rocking her back and forth. I'd do anything to stop the heartbreaking, silent sobs coming out of her. Her shoulders heaved in my embrace. Nothing I could say would make this moment less painful, so I kept my mouth shut, my throat constricting painfully with unshed tears.

———

Hours later, after I promised Derek to visit the next day, I slouched my ass on a bar stool, my fingers knitted together on my nape, my elbows anchored to the worn ebony counter as I tried to wrap my brain around all the jumbled-up emotions in my head. And my heart.

Tucker, my best friend since we were five, lightly punched my arm and slid onto the stool next to mine.

"I knew I'd find you here. Bad day?"

I huffed before turning my head to stare at him. "Derek. He's dying. For real this time. Nothing the doctors can do. It's over. He's done fighting."

"How long?" he asked, motioning the bartender over with a flick of his hand. "We'll have two more of those," he said to the man, pointing to the empty tumbler before me.

"Weeks. A month or two at the most."

"Sorry, man. I know how much you love that kid. Life is fucking unfair. In which world do children have to fight for their lives? It's a freaking joke." Tucker shook his head and guzzled half the drink the bartender brought over.

"He asked me if I would look after his mom." Moisture welled behind my eyeballs, stinging the already raw emotions lingering there.

Tucker glided his finger into his shirt collar and cracked his neck before loosening the navy tie.

"Fuck," was all he said. Yeah, no other powerful word could translate the feeling we all shared.

In silence, we sipped our drinks while my best friend gestured to the bartender for another round.

"Make them double this time."

The bartender nodded and turned to grab the whiskey bottle we'd surely empty tonight.

After another minute of silence, where we each ruminated over the unsaid words floating between us, Tucker cleared his throat as his somber eyes fixated on mine. "How's Murielle?"

The lining of my throat hurt as if a million needles

prickled the flesh. It wasn't from the liquor we'd been drinking. I blinked fast, pleading my emotions to settle and prevent the tears from blinding me. If Derek could be strong facing a death sentence, then I had to be too. Only then could I support his mother when she'd need me the most. My gaze drifted to a table where a group of women was celebrating one of their milestone birthdays. Big silver balloons, a two and a five, were attached to the back of a chair, and a dozen cherry-red shot glasses were spread on the table. The birthday girl rocked a white top and a teal crown, her smile huge and expectant for the years to come. As if nothing could shadow this moment. I used to be that guy. Years ago. Before I understood life was a flimsy line that could fray any moment and shatter everything in its wake. With a shake of my head, I swigged down half my drink in one go and focused my attention back on my friend.

"A wreck. The worst part is I couldn't say anything to lessen the pain. For once, I couldn't find the words." I sank my face into my hands and dropped my shoulders with a loud sigh. "What are you supposed to tell a mother who's about to lose her only child?"

"Nothing, I guess."

I brought the whiskey to my lips, enjoying the trail of fire down my throat, reminding me I was still alive.

And about to get wasted.

———

Read Nick and Dahlia's story,
Cruel Destiny, now

emmanuellesnow.com/products/cruel-destiny

Author's bookstore at emmanuellesnow.com

"This is a novel with so much depth, so much heart and so much love. There is steam, there is loss and there are moments of shock." (Book.ish Julie)

"Emmanuelle has done it yet again. She found a way to slip into my mind and heart with her words and the creation of characters you can't help but fall in love with." (The Cozy Pages blog)

"A book that made me smile through my tears...
Read the book with your heart as only Ms. Snow can break it as well as glue it back together. Emotions are her forte. And she get me every single time." (Book reviews by Shalini)

Cruel Destiny is book one in the
Second Tear duet.

Read the first part or the complete duet now
emmanuellesnow.com/products/cruel-destiny

CARTER HILLS BAND
CARTER HILLS BAND
FOREVER WORLD TOUR
NOVEMBER 22, 2022
TUESDAY
6:00pm - 10:00pm
NASHVILLE, TENNESSEE